On the Winds of *Destiny*

On the Winds of *Destiny*

Betty Godfrey

Foreword
Betty Godfrey

VANTAGE PRESS
New York

Although this is a work of nonfiction, some names have been changed to protect the identities of those depicted.

FIRST EDITION

Published by Vantage Press, Inc.
516 West 34th Street, New York, New York 10001

Manufactured in the United States of America
ISBN: 0-533-13877-9

Library of Congress Catalog Card No.: 01-126122

0 9 8 7 6 5 4 3 2 1

To my husband—without his love and confidence, I would never have finished this trip.

and

To my family, who worried about me but still encouraged me to go on the adventure.

also

To my dear friends Bob and Leslie Blum, who loved the story so much they constantly encouraged me to continue writing my adventure story.

One

It had been a crystal clear morning with the sun sending out its warm rays. There wasn't a gray cloud in the sky. By noon, dark clouds had overshadowed the sun and lightning flashed across the sky like a laser show. The booming noise of thunder echoed through the air like bowling balls rolling down an alley, as hard pellets of rain beat against the living room window. It was a typical June day in Ft. Lauderdale with heavy rains lasting only an hour or so.

Quietly Betty Rennie sat on the living room floor cross-legged in Yoga style, listening to the thunder. She was not meditating, although she often took refuge in the calmness. Ignoring the thunder that vibrated through her body, she looked around at the monstrous mound of groceries scattered across the floor waiting to be sorted.

For the past month, Betty had been shopping for groceries and supplies, preparing for a sailing trip around the world with Bob Godfrey, the handsome hunk in her life. A sixty-five-foot ketch had been built specially for the trip. For the last few months she had been clipping coupons. Then she proceeded to buy everything in sight. Seven people were going on the trip—six who wanted to go, and Betty, the frightened first mate who had been talked into going.

Purchasing food and supplies for that large of a group was not an easy chore, but that was Betty's job. She crammed Bob's red Cadillac convertible so full it was hard to close the trunk. With the top down, the car looked like a grocery store on wheels, boxes piled to full capacity, and anything remaining in the cart ended up on her lap. She looked rather silly with mops and brooms sticking out of the car, with popcorn and potato chips piled all around her. The only part of her that was visible when she drove away was her head. Now she had to organize everything, and get ready to store it on the boat.

Betty was a stickler for everything being neat, orderly, and in its proper place. Each pile had to be lined up perfectly with labels facing forward. Her ex-husband had been a Marine officer before they were married and he insisted on running the home in military tradition. Everything had to be "inspection ready," as he called it. When the pressure of being under a commanding lieutenant grew more than she could take, she had messed up all the cupboards and closets and left him. She could still hear him screaming on the phone, "Did you have to mess up the place when you left? It took me hours to get everything cleaned up."

Now, even though she had been away from her ex for fifteen years, his meticulous orders were ingrained in her mind. For two hours she separated the provisions into neat piles, building the toilet paper and towels into a towering high-rise. Cans of vegetables, fruits and soups were in alphabetical order, while the Raisin Bran®, Cheerios® and Instant Quaker Oats® sat in square piles. An assortment of rice, packaged potatoes, and pasta stood beside the soap powder, bleach, and face soap. Just about anything one could think of was scattered somewhere on the floor. She managed not to forget the candy and cookies needed to help soothe the volatile moods the sea might create.

Leaning back against the white couch she stretched out her legs and surveyed the supermarket in her living room. Betty let out a deep sigh and picked up a cookbook lying nearby and flipped through the pages. She'd have to read the books eventually if she planned to make a month's supply of dinners and freeze them, but she didn't feel like it now. Betty closed the cookbook and threw it aside. Overwhelmed and frustrated by the whole project, she started to talk out loud to herself, as if she was her own psychiatrist.

"I must be crazy! I'm getting ready to sail around the world even though I've never been out of sight of land. I've got to be some kind of nut to think I can handle long weeks at sea. Oh God, I hate getting seasick. It reminds me of morning sickness when I was pregnant."

Betty had never planned to go on this trip with Bob. He had talked about it but she never included herself in his plans. Betty picked up the Betty Crocker® cookbook and thumbed through it, but the pages went blank as her mind drifted.

2

Was it really a year and a half since I met Bob? It was the first of December. The weather in Cherry Hill, New Jersey had been cold and windy. She'd been working harder than usual and needed a break. With her friend Marion, she took off for Ft. Lauderdale, Florida looking forward to the warm weather. Betty owned an apartment in Ft. Lauderdale that looked over the white sandy beach. Two weeks soaking up the sun was going to make a new woman out of her.

They arrived late in the afternoon and after unpacking, they went out for dinner at Stan's, Betty's favorite restaurant. The upstairs dining room had an ambiance that soothed her and she always felt relaxed there. Music from the downstairs piano bar drifted into the dining room. As they finished dinner, Marion cocked her head. "Listen to that music. Wow! That's my kind of sound. Let's have a drink downstairs at the piano bar."

Betty grabbed her purse from the table. "That sounds good to me. I'm going to the ladies room. I'll meet you there."

After using the restroom, Betty washed her hands and glanced in the mirror. She was an attractive woman. Most people said she was pretty. She was tall, five-foot-seven, and a stunning mauve Oleg Cassini dress showed off her willowy figure. She liked the dress because when she walked the slit in the front of the dress parted. It emphasized her long slender legs.

Betty had worked hard through the years to support her three children. Now that they were finished with college and two of them married, she felt free. It was her turn at last to enjoy life. A few romances had entered her life and one had lasted seven years. Breaking up with him had been rough. He'd been a great companion but the chemistry just wasn't there. Besides, Betty wasn't ready to give up her independence. She had no demands on her time now except for her car-rental business. She loved her life, and she had become somewhat of a social butterfly, hobnobbing with the elite in New Jersey, New York, and Washington.

"Done pretty well for yourself, haven't you?" she murmured as she fixed the loose strands of her auburn hair. "I might be fifty but I'm far from over the hill. It's my turn to enjoy all the world has to offer."

Betty walked toward the piano bar, confidently aware of the

approving glances. Men offered drinks in the hope of striking up a conversation, but she kept walking. *I'm not in the mood to talk to anyone tonight,* she thought.

Every seat was taken when Betty arrived, so she stood behind Marion as the combo played, "Sweet Caroline." Mel, the lead singer, belted out the words.

"Close your eyes, you'll swear it's Neil Diamond singing," she whispered to Marion.

Mesmerized by the music, Betty barely heard the pleasant voice behind her.

"Hello! Would you like a drink?"

Turning, she said, "Yes, I'd like a Chivas, and water. Oh, I'm sorry, I thought you were the waiter."

What a good-looking man, she thought. *Hmmmm, must be in his early fifties.* His golden tan made his curly white hair stand out in contrast. Her eyes swept over his broad shoulders. *Oh my, the clothes don't fit the man,* she thought. An outdated striped sport shirt with a frayed collar covered his well-developed biceps and flat stomach. He stood out like a sore thumb among the other men in their stylish designer jackets and ties. His scuffed tan boat shoes were run over at the heels and in dire need of a shoemaker.

Good lord! Maybe I should buy him a drink, Betty thought. Yet there was something warm and friendly about him that over shadowed his frayed clothes. His face lit up with a smile like an unpolished gem, "The offer still stands. I'd like to buy you a drink."

"Ah well" . . . Betty hesitated then said, "sure, why not?"

When he returned from the bar, his worn shoe caught the edge of the rug and he fell forward, splashing the drink down the front of Betty's dress.

Bob's face turned red. "I'm so sorry. Just call me clumsy Bob." He handed her the remaining scotch and water and reached for his handkerchief.

Betty let out a squeal as the cold drink soaked her dress. Quickly she wiped the droplets off with her hand. "Well, clumsy Bob, you sure know how to make an impression."

"I'm really sorry. Here, let me help you," he said, as he dabbed at her dress with his handkerchief.

4

She grabbed his hand as he swept down the front of her bosom. "It will be all right."

Bob dabbed awkwardly at her hem line. "I'll pay to have your dress dry cleaned. I really feel bad about it."

Betty stepped back out of his reach. "Look, I'm fine. It will dry," she said as she started to walk away.

His voice broke as he called out, "Don't leave."

Betty stopped and gave him an irritated look. In a nervous gesture he ran his hand through his curly white hair, a pleading look in his blue eyes.

Betty gave in. "All right . . . let's start over." She moved back toward him. "Do you live in Ft. Lauderdale?"

"No. I sailed my boat down here. I'm planning on staying a few months. I'm retired and live on my boat most of the time. Are you into sailing?"

"I don't know the first thing about boats. I don't mind going out for a day sail, but that's it."

Betty no longer felt annoyed. Bob had a gentle way about him and was certainly different from the men she knew.

He rattled the ice in his empty glass. "Would you like another drink?"

"No, I'm fine. Are you nervous or do you always drink that fast?"

"Maybe a little of both. Excuse me I'm going to get a refill."

Bob was easy to talk to and told Betty about his sailing trip from Massachusetts. She felt increasingly comfortable with him, and was aware of an intense physical attraction.

Marion strutted over from the piano bar. "I'm tired, and ready to go. I'll get the car and meet you outside."

"I'll be right out." Betty smiled at Bob. "Thanks for the drink. I enjoyed talking to you," and she turned to walk away.

"Hey, wait a minute. Give me your phone number. I'd like to have dinner with you."

Betty didn't want to give him her phone number. Despite the pleasant interlude she wasn't sure she wanted to see him again. "You'll find it in the telephone book. Betty Rennie on Galt Ocean Drive."

Marion was sitting in the car waiting impatiently. With a sarcastic tone she snarled, "You finally tore yourself away. Who

5

was that clothes horse you were talking to."

Betty glanced over at Marion. "Why the attitude? He's a nice guy with some interesting stories."

Marion snickered. "He looks like he buys his clothes at the Salvation Army."

"Maybe he wasn't the best dressed man in the place," answered Betty defensively, "but he's good-looking."

Marion waved her hand in the air. "Forget him, he's not your type. Take my word, I know the type you're attracted to."

Betty's eyes were on the road as she drove, but she stole a quick glance at her friend. "What do you mean he's not my type? You hardly looked at him."

"You go for the sophisticated, well-dressed man and he's far from that." Marion laughed.

Betty said, almost sadly, "Don't worry, I didn't give him my phone number, so we'll never know."

By four o'clock the next afternoon the shadows of the condominium buildings overtook the beach area where Betty and Marion were sunbathing.

Betty shook Marion awake. "I'm chilly. Let's go upstairs."

As they walked into the apartment the telephone was ringing. Marion answered it and frowned. "Bob's on the phone. Should I tell him you're not home?"

"No," Betty said as she grabbed the phone. "I'll take it. Hi, I'm surprised to hear from you."

Bob's voice was deep and sounded a little sexy. "You thought I wouldn't call?"

"Well," Betty said shyly, "I didn't give you my phone number and I thought you might think I was giving you the brush off."

There was silence for a second, then in an unsure voice he said, "I never thought of that. Were you?"

"No, of course not. I, eh . . . I never thought you'd go to the trouble of looking it up."

"You looked like you're worth the trouble." Bob's voice was deep and sexy again. "Do you want to go out to dinner?"

She really didn't feel like meeting him. Marion had convinced her that he couldn't possibly be her type. "I'm busy for the next few days."

"Come on, give a guy a break. You can't be busy every night." He paused as if he were checking his calendar. "How about Thursday night?"

Betty liked the sound of his deep voice. It sort of vibrated through her and for some reason she didn't want to hurt his feelings. "Okay. I can make it Thursday." She tried to think of a place close by so she could cut out quickly if the evening didn't go right. "I love Frankie's Italian restaurant on the Intracoastal. Want to go there?"

Cheerfully Bob said, "Fine with me. I'll pick you up at seven. If your address is the same as the phone book, I know where you live."

"Yes, it is. I'll see you then." She felt a ripple of excitement as she hung up the phone.

Marion jumped up from the couch, her face in a scowl. "Don't tell me you're going out with that loser."

"I didn't want to hurt his feelings. It won't hurt to go out with him once. Maybe he doesn't dress like that all the time."

"Yeah, sure. You're just wasting your time. He's—"

Betty stamped her foot. "Never mind, I don't want to hear it. What do you have against him? You don't even know him." Betty walked out of the room, saying, "I'm going to take a shower."

Thursday night, Bob arrived wearing a tweed sport jacket that was two sizes too large for him. His khaki trousers were loose and had seen better days. The collar on his blue-striped shirt was limp and frayed. It looked weary, hanging down on the oversized jacket. His navy blue tie with bright-colored flags lay crooked across the front of his shirt.

Betty tried not to show her disappointment in the way he was dressed. She greeted him with a smile but her expression changed when she saw his shoes. *I don't believe it*, she thought. *He's wearing the same old run-down boat shoes. I suggested Frankie's for dinner. I wonder if he can afford it?*

Bob stroked his damp hair, patting it flat. "I'm sorry I'm a little late. I guess you can tell by my wet hair I just got out of the shower."

There was no enthusiasm in Betty's voice. "That's okay. I was running a little late myself."

7

When they got to the restaurant, they were seated at a table overlooking the water. Red roses and flickering candles sat on the table, creating a romantic setting. Bob ordered a bottle of Chablis Silvigon, and after the waiter poured the wine, Bob lifted his glass and said, "Let's drink a toast to our first dinner together and our new friendship."

Betty tried to make light conversation but her voice sounded a little awkward, "What did you do before you retired?"

Bob took a sip of wine, then said in a voice that was calm and impressive, "I was in the publishing business, but I sold it a few years ago. Now I have enough money to relax and enjoy myself."

Is he putting me on? thought Betty. *If he's that well off, why does he dress like he shops at Goodwill?*

She now soothed her voice and probed further. "Are you married?"

His gaze came to rest on her questioning eyes. "I'm in the middle of a very unpleasant divorce. We separated several times during our short marriage, but this time it's over. What about you?"

She pushed back a wave of hair that had fallen upon her face. "I've been single for fifteen years and just ended a seven-year relationship."

Bob had just sipped his wine, and choked as he said, "Seven years! That's longer than some marriages."

The waiter served their lobsters and the conversation came to a standstill. The sound of the slow mellow music from the band filled the air.

"Let's dance," said Betty, in a low silvery tone.

"I'm not good at shuffling my feet but we'll give it a try," Bob said, leading her onto the dance floor.

"They're playing 'Lady.' That's my favorite song," Betty said, as Bob took her in his arms. His rhythm was faster than the beat of the music. His arm kept rising up and down with the beat like he was pumping water. Betty tried to keep up with him and not step on his toes. Finally out of desperation she asked, "Have you ever tried body dancing?"

"No—but I'm willing to learn."

Betty stepped closer to him and put her arms around his neck. "Now put both arms around my waist. That's right." Bob eagerly moved his muscular arms up as she said, "Now just move your body to the rhythm of the music. Now move your feet slowly, like this," she said. Her feet barely moved as her body swayed to the rhythm.

"Hmm—this is nice, and I'm much closer to you," he said, gently swaying to the music.

"Come on, concentrate," she laughed. "See, it's easier to keep in time with the rhythm."

"Yeah, I see what you mean. I don't have to move my feet that much, I like this."

As they danced, Betty felt a warm glow encircle them. Bob kissed her cheek as they snuggled closer. She had been embarrassed about Bob's clothes, but suddenly that didn't matter. All that mattered was how she felt in his arms. They danced until the band paused for a break, then holding hands they returned to the table.

Softly he asked, "Would you like cognac and coffee?"

Betty nodded her head as their eyes met. He searched her face, reaching into her thoughts. They held the gaze for a moment before Betty glanced away. *What in the world is happening here? Am I flipping over this guy?* There was an undeniable chemistry that was like lightning between them, and she loved it.

Bob started to say something and then stopped. She was sure he was going to say something romantic; the mood was ripe for it.

Her fingers stroked his hand as she asked, "What were you going to say?"

His eyes brightened. "I was going to ask you if you liked to cook?"

A blank look came over Betty's face. She hadn't expected a question like that. "Do I like to cook? That's what you wanted to ask me? Do I like to cook? Why?"

Bob was no longer relaxed in his chair but was stiff and leaning forward. "Well—I was wondering if you are a good cook?"

Feeling curious about where the conversation was heading and disappointed in the change of mood, she said, "I haven't had any complaints. Why?"

Still leaning forward as if anxious, he asked, "Do you like to sail?"

9

Betty forced a laugh to lighten her mood. "What are we playing, twenty questions? Is there a joke behind this?"

Bob looked confused, "No. No joke. I just wondered if you like boating."

"I told you before I'm not into sailing," she said, curtly. "I get seasick if the water is the least bit rough."

Now Bob seemed nervous. "The reason I'm asking all these questions is . . . I have this desire, maybe you'd call it a dream, that I've had most of my life."

Betty sat back in her chair and in a deeper voice said, "Oh, this is some deep dark secret you're about to reveal to me."

Bob seemed embarrassed. "No, don't kid around. I'm serious. I've always wanted to sail around the world in my own boat."

Betty studied him for awhile and she could see how serious he was. "Think you'll ever do it?"

He was still for a moment as if in deep thought. "Yes. It's something I have to do before I'm too old. I was hoping you would go with me. It would be the trip of a lifetime."

"Whoa, are you kidding? No, no—I couldn't handle that. Why on earth would you want to take me? We hardly know each other."

He reached for her hand. "I'm planning on seeing you as often as possible, and I could teach you to sail in no time."

Betty listened in bewilderment. *Who knows, maybe he'll do it, but not with me. I'm a butterfly, not a sailor.*

She felt uneasy and she didn't want to talk about boats. She picked up her evening bag and stood up. "I think it's time to go."

Bob was dismayed. "Did I say something to upset you?"

"No. I just think it's time to go." Feeling stupid just standing there, she said, "I'm going to the ladies room. I'll meet you out front."

Walking to the car, Betty felt confused. She didn't know why she was upset. That's all she needed, to sail out to sea with some guy she didn't know. *What was he, out of his mind?* After all, she hardly knew him. She shook her head to clear her mind. *This relationship wasn't going to go far.*

It was a warm pleasant night, and Bob had the top down on

his red convertible. As they drove along the beach road, he put his arm around her shoulder. Betty rested her head against him, trying to bring back the feelings she had on the dance floor.

When he parked at her condominium, he said, "I'll walk you to the elevator."

They waited in silence until the elevator reached the first floor. Betty thought about their conversation back at the restaurant. The part about sailing left her feeling odd and she was sorry because she really liked him.

When the elevator door opened, Bob took her hands. "Are you sure you have to go up? It's too early to end an evening."

She saw the heartrending tenderness in his eyes and the chemistry between them vibrated.

He leaned forward and kissed her lightly on the lips. "It's only ten-thirty."

Betty melted. "I didn't know it was that early. Let's take a walk on the beach."

She led the way until they reached the beach. "Let's take our shoes off and walk along the water."

The full moon reflected on the rippling water that washed up on the beach, leaving white bubbly patterns. The beat of the cresting waves and the sound of the sea gulls in the distance blended into soft music. He pulled her close to his side as they walked along the moonlit beach, the gentle waves washing over their feet. There was not a soul in sight.

"Ouch," Betty cried, as she hobbled on one foot. "I stepped on something."

Standing on one leg, she leaned forward to inspect her big toe and lost her balance. Bob's strong hands caught her around the waist and held her firmly.

"Thanks! You saved me from falling into the water," said Betty.

He brushed a strand of hair from her face and his lips moved closer to hers. When she didn't pull away, Bob kissed her. First a short tender touch that sent a shock wave through her entire body. Then, their lips locked in a long lingering kiss that left them breathless.

"You feel so wonderful in my arms," he said, as his hands slowly caressed her back. Then he kissed her again.

Betty pulled away, trying to throttle the dizzying currents racing through her. Things were moving too fast. "I think I better have a look at my toe," she said, hobbling over to lean against the sea wall. A small stream of blood trickled from the jagged cut, and a piece of shell was lodged in the plump part of her big toe. Bob knelt down and held her foot tenderly in his hand and removed the chunk of shell. He wiped off the blood with his handkerchief and wrapped it around her toe, tying the ends into a small knot.

Betty smiled warmly, "Thanks, you're very gentle."

"My pleasure," said Bob, standing up. "I can't have you getting sand in the cut."

Betty felt giddy and laughed. "Do I call you Dr. Godfrey from now on?"

"Oh yes, and wait till you hear what my fee is," he said with a laugh.

He put his arm around her to support her as she started to walk. As their bodies touched, his eyes clung to hers, analyzing her reaction. A wave of desire swept over them and their lips met. Their emotions responded as they slowly eased down onto the sand. They were lost in the ecstasy of their love on the lonely beach.

Walking back they entered the elevator and when the door closed, they embraced again. "I'll call you tomorrow," he said as he left her at the apartment door.

It was well past midnight and Betty was surprised to see Marion lying on the couch, a bored look on her face. Betty sat on the edge of the couch beside her and asked, "What are you doing up? I thought you were going to bed early?"

Marion swung her legs off the couch, "I wanted to find out how you made out. Well, was I right?"

"You were so wrong," Betty said with a dreamy look. "He's like a diamond in the rough. There's much more to him than the shabby clothes." Marion started to interrupt, but Betty stopped her. "Hey, I can always change the way he dresses."

Marion got up and faced Betty. "You're certainly not going to see him again, are you?"

Betty stuck her chin out at Marion, "Yes, I am going to see him again. He's warm and sincere and we get along wonderfully.

There's a lot of chemistry between us, more than I've felt with anyone."

Marion stomped into the bedroom, and climbed in bed. "I don't believe it. You're making a mistake. He's not your type."

Betty climbed in and pulled the covers over her head. "Good-night Marion."

*   *   *

In the morning the phone rang as they were heading down to the beach. "How would you like to go sailing? It's a perfect day for it," asked Bob.

Betty hesitated, "I'm not good on boats, remember? I get seasick."

"Not on a day like this. I promise it will be smooth as glass. If you start feeling sick I'll bring you right in."

"Boy, you're a smooth talker. What time do you want to go?"

"Is ten too early?"

"No. I'm already in my bathing suit."

Bob gave her directions and added, "*Icarus* is my boat's name. I'll be on deck watching for you."

After packing a small duffel bag she drove to his dock. Bob was standing on the deck of *Icarus* waving. He helped Betty onboard then said proudly, "Let me show you around before we get under way."

Bob lead her down into the boat. It was dark and dreary and Betty felt uncomfortable on it. She could see it needed cleaning and refurbishing.

"It has two staterooms—this is the master stateroom," he said as he slid back a curtain that covered a doorway. "Over here is the head, it's a little small but does the trick. There's a shower on the wall for navy showers."

Twisting her mouth in a scowl Betty asked, "What is a navy shower?"

"You wet yourself all over then turn the water off. Then you soap and wash yourself, then turn the water on and rinse off. You use less water that way."

"Ugh—that's no shower. Do you always shower like that?"

"No, only when I'm out at sea. When the boat's at dock I have a hose that I connect to shore water."

Bob walked into the galley. When he switched on a light, a scatter of roaches ran for hiding.

Betty let out a scream and jumped back. "I hate roaches, they make my skin crawl. Why don't you get rid of them?"

Bob stuttered defensively, "I try, but there's so many of them. They won't hurt you."

Betty was completely turned off by the roaches and the condition of the boat.

"I'm getting out of here," she said climbing up the stairs. "I don't want to be down here with those things."

Bob tried to calm her down, "Let's not spoil the day over a few bugs. Come on, let's go sailing." He handed her a line, "Here, cast this off when I tell you." Starting the motor, he called out, "Okay, throw it now."

When she threw the rope it hit the dock and bounced in the water. "I'm sorry . . . I didn't do a very good job throwing it."

"Don't worry about it," said Bob. His attention was on steering the boat away from the dock. Betty settled down on the seat next to the helm and Bob reached over and brushed her hair from her face. "I'm going to make a sailor out of you, and you're going to love it."

"Not with all those roaches onboard, you won't."

It was a clear day and a light wind billowed the sails to a half-moon as Bob slowly released each sail.

"This is the genoa," he said, pointing to a small sail on the bow of the ship. "The one next to it is the mainsail. The mizzen is behind us. The lines attached to the sails are called *sheets*."

Betty scratched her head in bewilderment. "Why do you call it a sheet? It would be easier to call it what it looks like, a rope."

Bob laughed. "That's sailor lingo. You'll get used to it."

It wasn't long before all the sails were up and they were sailing along the intra-coastal waters. After they went through the inlet to the ocean, Bob took her hand. "Come over here by the helm. I want you to steer for a while."

"No way," Betty said pulling away. "I don't know how to steer a boat."

Bob pulled her back, "Come on, give it a try. I'll be right here to help you."

Betty took the wheel; her knuckles going white from gripping it tightly. Bob laughed at her, "Loosen up, don't try to strangle it. Hold the wheel lightly. Look behind you and see the wake you're making with the boat. It looks like a snake following us." Hugging her around the waist he said, "I'll just call you Snake-Wake Rennie."

Betty was frustrated, "I can't make it go straight. Here, take the wheel. I feel stupid."

"No." Bob said putting her hands back on the wheel. "Try it one more time. Make small corrections on the wheel when you turn. Just make little movements at a time. See? You're getting it now."

Betty felt proud of herself, *Icarus* was now sailing in a straight line. The elated feeling didn't last long. Again the boat was zig-zagging back and forth, leaving a curving trail behind them.

Feeling stupid she said, "Here, take it. I've had enough."

Bob put *Icarus* on auto-pilot and sat next to her. He placed his arm around her shoulder and she leaned against him, resting her head on his chest. The sea danced with small waves as the boat cut a path through the calm water. They sailed in silence for a while, enjoying the tranquil surroundings. A rosy haze across the sky blended with the blue speckled clouds drifting here and there.

Betty closed her eyes, enjoying the cool breeze. She could smell the freshness in the salty air, and the cool mist sprinkled her face. "You're right. This is a perfect day for a sail."

"How about some lunch? I stopped by Wolfe's deli for sandwiches and a bottle of Merlot® wine," asked Bob.

"Wow, you thought of everything. I'm glad you did . . . I'm famished," said Betty.

Bob kissed her tenderly on the cheek. "Are you glad you came?"

"Yes, very, I feel so relaxed and peaceful."

They went up on the bow where the breeze was cool and light. When they finished the pastrami sandwiches, Betty lay back against the mast sipping her wine. Bob reached over to kiss her and the wine in his glass dripped down the front of her bathing suit.

"Oh," she cried as the cool wine touched her warm skin. "Bob, you're being clumsy . . . again."

"Here, let me wipe it off," he said as he dabbed the wine at the top of her bathing suit with his napkin.

Betty felt his hand on the swell of her breast making circles with the napkin. As his hand gently lingered there, her nipples went taut under the thin material.

"You have a little wine right here," he said, as his tongue flickered, licking a spot of wine from her neck. His lips gently seared a path down her neck, then her shoulders, as his hand gently outlined the circles of her breast. A pleasant jolt of pleasure surged through her body.

Bob eased the straps of her bathing suit off her shoulders as her body melted against his. Together they found a tempo that bound their bodies, oblivious to the world around them. Only the birds flying overhead witnessed their love making as *Icarus* sailed on the open sea. Their bodies were still entwined as they relaxed and savored the feeling of satisfaction in the sun light. Suddenly, a seabird landed on the railing and stared down at them, moving his head back and forth in a darting motion.

"Think he came down to get a closer look?" asked Betty.

"Too late buddy, the show's over," said Bob as he glanced at his watch. "I hate to ruin a great mood but it's time we headed back. It's four o'clock."

Betty adjusted her straps and said, "Four o'clock already; this day sure went fast."

"Yep. You know what they say—time goes fast when you're having fun."

Betty threw her towel at him, "Oh no, that's an old cliché."

When they were nearing the dock, Bob pointed at three men standing on the pier. "See those friendly faces? They'll give us a hand docking. Go out on the bow and catch the lines when they throw them." He steered the boat toward the side of the pier.

A heavy line was thrown from the dock and Betty caught it. The forward motion of *Icarus* started to pull the rope through her hands. Hysterically, she called out, "What do I do with it?"

Pointing to a stainless object on the bow he yelled, "Put it on the cleats on the deck."

She looked around frantically. *What the heck are cleats?*

16

Betty spotted a long stainless steel thing, and did her best to secure the line around it.

"Get back to the stern quick and catch the other line," yelled Bob. Betty was still fooling with the rope on the cleat and didn't go right away. Bob yelled in a commanding voice, "Betty, do it now. Hurry, the wind's blowing us away from the dock."

Frustrated by the yelling and not sure of what she was doing she hollered back. "Don't yell at me! I'm doing the best I can."

Then, she ran to the rear of the boat. The men on the dock were laughing and a line came flying across the water, almost hitting her in the face. She ducked and grabbed at the line, almost missing it. "Darn it, I just broke two nails."

"Forget the nails, tie up the line," yelled Bob. "Quick, before you lose it."

Once the boat was secured Bob came to the stern where Betty was wrapping the line on the cleat. "No, not that way, here let me show you. See? It's easy."

"Yeah, sure. Easy for you, but it's not for me." Feeling stupid and awkward, she grabbed her duffel bag and jumped off the boat.

"Where are you going?" asked Bob in a calm voice. "Don't you want to stay and have a drink?"

"What, and have you yell at me again?" she lashed out. "I've had enough, thank you. Maybe you were planning on having your pet roaches join us for a drink? No thanks, I'm going home to take a nice leisurely bath."

"I'll pick you up for dinner then? Say about eight?"

"I don't feel like going out tonight, I'm tired." Betty walked off in a huff .

Betty was fuming about the situation. She especially didn't like Bob hollering at her and was sure all the men were laughing at her clumsiness. "A beautiful day was ruined in twenty minutes," she muttered as she climbed into her car.

As soon as she reached her apartment, she sank down into the hot perfumed water in her tub. She was glad Marion wasn't home. She could talk loudly to herself.

"I like Bob, he was so gentle most of the day. Except for the docking, the day was terrific. Boy, then I definitely saw another side of his personality. Maybe I need to cool things, it's going a little too fast."

Betty was lying on her bed resting when Bob called. "Hi! Feeling relaxed and ready for dinner?"

"I told you I don't feel like going out tonight. I'm tired and a little uptight."

"I've got an idea. I'll stop by the Golden Pavilion and pick up some Chinese food. You have to eat. Besides, I want to talk to you about today."

Betty sighed, "All right, but let's make it an early night."

Betty was quiet during dinner. She refused the plum wine he brought and started to clear away the dishes before he had finished. She sat at the other end of the couch and flicked on the television.

She heard Bob clear his throat. "I'm sorry I yelled at you this afternoon. It's just that docking a boat, especially a sail boat with one engine, can get pretty hairy. You have to grab the lines quickly. The boat has to be tied down as fast as possible or it can get away from me. If I lose control, I could bash the other boats in the marina, or crash into the dock. I wasn't *really* yelling at you. I just get excited when I'm not sure of the conditions. I'm sorry, really sorry. I didn't mean to hurt your feelings."

Betty watched his expressions as he talked. He seemed so genuine. "I felt stupid with all those men laughing at me. I've never helped dock a boat before. I don't know anything about boats and after today I don't think I want to," she said as she flipped the channels.

They sat watching a movie neither knew the name or was interested. Bob moved closer and put his arm around her. He pulled her back against his chest and kissed the back of her head but Betty pulled away and sat up.

"Please don't be mad," he whispered in her ear.

Betty looked at him and with disappointment in her voice said "We had such a great day, why did you have to spoil it?"

They sat watching the movie and before the end of the show, Betty had drifted off to sleep.

The unpleasant moments had been forgotten and her two week vacation went swiftly by. It was filled with the excitement and happiness of two new lovers. Bob had an exterminator clear some of the bugs away and they went out on the sail boat again.

He was patient with her mistakes and let her get used to sailing. They went shopping and bought clothes for Bob in the same style he liked, but new and more stylish. They sat quietly as he drove her to the airport. They both hated to part. Marion jabbered on in the back seat, oblivious that no one was listening.

"I'm going to miss you," he said as he placed her bags by the porter.

Betty held his arm, "I'll miss you too, but we'll see each other. You said you were coming to New Jersey."

"You bet I will, " he said, staring into her eyes, then he kissed her goodbye. "I love you."

On the plane Betty said, "I've only known Bob for two weeks but it seems much longer. I hope this is not just a vacation romance."

*   *   *

Two weeks later, Bob flew to Cherry Hill, New Jersey. He wondered how the weekend would go. They were no longer in the glow of a vacation affair. When he got off the plane, Betty was waiting for him. Bob took one look at her and knew he loved her. Once he met her family he was more relaxed. Their time alone held the same excitement as when they were in Florida. Bob came up every weekend and as the months flew by, sailing around the world seemed to be forgotten.

The Fourth of July was celebrated with a barbeque at Betty's house. Friends and family were there, including Bob's son Scott. He had flown in from California.

Bob was sitting by the pool enjoying a glass of iced tea when Scott asked, "Hey Dad, have you been sailing lately?"

"Not since December when I was in Florida." Bob turned to Betty's son, Clint. "Scott's a sailor, too. I taught him to sail when he was just a little kid. Look at this strapping guy now. He's taller than me and still a bachelor at twenty-eight. Speaking of sailing, Scott, what do you think about sailing around the world with Betty and me?"

Scott scratched his beard, "Well, I don't know, Dad. Give me a minute to think about it . . . okay, I'll go."

Bob looked over at Betty, his eyes were bright with happiness. "You know the more I think about making the trip with you, the more excited I get. There are so many places in this world that you can't get to any other way."

Betty was talking with her daughter Loretta when she caught his conversation, and she couldn't believe what she was hearing.

Her daughter Loretta showed surprise, "Mom, you didn't tell me you were planning on sailing around the world."

Betty stood there speechless as she realized he hadn't given it up. He was serious about going. *This will probably end our relationship*, she thought.

"I—I never mentioned it because it's just something Bob talked about doing. I didn't realize he was serious. I never planned to go."

Loretta called to her brother and sister. "Clint, Debbie, do you hear what Mom's going to do?" Then she said, almost in tears, "Mom, I don't think you should do it. We'd miss you."

Clint came over and put his arm around her, "You should go, then I could join you somewhere."

Debbie was squealing, her brown eyes lit up with excitement. "That would be *sooo* exciting. Imagine sailing all around the world in a yacht."

Betty felt annoyed. "Yes, it does sound exciting until you *think* about it. He's talking a five-year trip. I'm not retired, and I have a business to run. I couldn't give that up."

"Come on, honey, don't get excited, things can always be worked out," said Bob, taking her hand.

Betty pulled away. "No, they can't always be worked out. I couldn't handle a trip like that. I'd be out on the rough seas for days and days. What about storms and pirates? Bob, how do I know how much experience you really had sailing."

Bob's face got red. "My God, Betty, I've been sailing for twenty-five years." Bob was irritated as he continued, "I've been in races from Duxbury to Bermuda and back. I've been in knockdowns where the boat heeled over so far the mast was in the water. I know how to handle a boat."

"All right, but you're not me. I've never been under conditions like that and I don't want to be. Besides, how can I leave these precious grandchildren?" she said, pointing toward the six children of various ages swimming in the pool.

Debbie was excited. "Mom, don't worry about the children. Think about the adventure you'd have."

"Once you get used to sailing, you'll love the open seas. I'll teach you all you need to know," said Bob, putting his arm around her.

"I couldn't stand to live on that boat of yours. It's dark, dreary, and full of roaches."

"Hey, don't talk about my friends. I know them all by name," joked Bob.

"Yeah, well, I can't stand roaches, and they're the biggest ones I've ever seen."

Scott was taking the whole scene in. He gave Betty a wink and stood beside her.

Betty reached up affectionately and tugged his black wavy hair. "Talk some sense into your father."

"I would, but it sounds pretty intriguing to me. Dad's a good sailor, he really knows how to handle a boat," Scott said.

"It's exciting to think about making a trip like that," Bob said, as he stood and stretched. "Give it some thought and we'll talk about it later." He grabbed her hand, "Come on, let's go for a swim."

Still upset, she pulled away from him and in an angry voice said, "Why can't you understand how I feel?" As she went into the kitchen, she screamed, "He doesn't listen to me!"

On Monday, Bob flew to Ft. Lauderdale to check on his boat, and Betty promised to fly down on that weekend. When she arrived at the airport, his face was beaming with excitement. "Wait till you see the boat I found. You'll love it. I know you don't like *Icarus* so I sold it."

Betty was surprised. "You sold the roach boat?"

When he parked the car at the end of the pier, he pointed to a line of boats. "See the boats over there? Which one do you like the best?"

Betty stared at the line of huge sailing boats, each one more magnificent than the next. "Let's see . . . I like that sail boat with the wide blue stripe on the side."

"You picked the right boat! I knew you'd love it. Come on,

we'll go aboard and you can really see her."

The owner was onboard but at first, all you could see was his bulbous stomach as he sat in the cockpit. He tried to get up when he saw them coming, but his bulk weighed him down.

"Hello Bob, good to see you. Come aboard."

"Betty, I'd like you to meet Doug Fonrath. He's the distributor for the company that builds these boats." Doug still struggled to get off the chair, but his bare feet kept slipping under him. Bob pulled him to his feet.

Doug laughed and his belly shook like Jell-O®. Rubbing his watermelon stomach he said, "Got to cut back on my food and lose this gut. Trouble is my wife's such a good cook and I love to eat." Turning to Betty, he said, "Nice to meet you young lady, you're just as pretty as Bob said you were."

Betty smiled, "Thank you. Wow, this is a magnificent boat. How big is it?"

Bob was so excited, he answered for Doug. "It's a sixty-five foot ketch. Just what I was looking for."

Doug waddled to the companionway and said, "Show Betty around the yacht and holler if you need me."

There were four steps that led down into the salon. Betty called it the living room. It was tastefully decorated in beige, mauve and blues. The room was brightened by large windows that curved all across the front of the cabin. The walls throughout were smooth, well-rubbed teak wood. The workmanship was incredible. Betty had never been on a boat this size. The salon held a washer, dryer and ice maker. When she walked into the galley, Bob pointed out the freezer, microwave, refrigerator and stove.

"See this?" Bob said, releasing a catch on the stove. "It's *gimbaled*. See how it swings back and forth. The pans stay level when the boat's heeled over."

She was impressed and couldn't get over the amount of closet and counter space the galley had. It was as big as her apartment.

Entering the master stateroom, Betty let out a squeal. "Look at the king-size bed! I don't believe this."

There were three other staterooms, roomy and tastefully decorated in the same mauve and beige colors as the salon. They worked their way back on deck where Doug was sitting in the double cockpit sipping a bourbon-on-ice. Struggling to his feet again he demonstrated how each sail furled in and out when you pushed a special button on the helm. "The heavy duty hardware on the boat makes it perfect for hard sailing," said Doug.

"Well, what do you think, Betty? Great ship, isn't it," asked Doug.

Betty had become as excited about the boat as Bob. "I've never seen a boat this superb, but then I've not been on many yachts."

Bob was thrilled. "I'd like to place an order to have one built. I'll be over tomorrow about eleven to go over things with you and I'll bring Frank along."

"Who's Frank?" asked Betty.

"Oh, he's the broker that's sold *Icarus* for me. He introduced me to Doug. You'll meet him this afternoon."

As they drove home they decided the boat had to be named. They made a list and came up with a lot of crazy names. They finally narrowed it down to three names, *Goodie Two Screws, Let Me Be Free,* and *Destiny*

"Forget the other two names. I like *Destiny*. It was our *Destiny* to meet," said Betty.

"I'll go along with that. It was our *Destiny* to meet and our *Destiny* to sail the open seas together," Bob said, giving her a bear hug. "It will take months to purchase the rigging and electronic equipment. I'll have to schedule workmen to complete *Destiny* as soon as it gets here. Bob grinned ear to ear as he said "...*Destiny*, doesn't that name sound great? I'm so itchy to get started, I can hardly wait."

Frank came over to Betty's apartment just as they were ready to leave for the airport. He had a smile that took up most of his face, and his pearly whites were as perfect as a dentist-ad. When she opened the door, he took one look at her and said, "Well, I must have the wrong place. No way Godfrey could get a girl like you."

As he walked through the door, his clear deep voice filled the room. He was short in stature but his shoulders and biceps would be the envy of any man.

"Have you seen the boat yet?" His black eyes sparkled

with mischief. "Lover boy here," he said pointing to Bob, "is always giving me a hard time. You should see the list of things he gave me to look into. He wants everything on the new boat built to his exact specifications. Someone might think he knew boats or something." He caressed his graying mustache and goatee while looking Betty up and down. "So this is the gal that's got you boat shopping?"

"Don't mind him Betty, he's just a loud mouth Greek. Frank, get over here and check out the changes I've made on the plans."

Betty picked up her suitcase. "You two have a lot to discuss—I'll take a cab to the airport."

"Hey, Bob, if you don't drive this good looking wench to the airport, I will."

Bob guided Betty to the door. "No way, you leech. You stay and work on the plans."

As they drove down the expressway, Bob said, "I'm so excited about the boat, it's the ship of my dreams. It will take me at least a week to make the changes I want. By the way, thanks for letting me stay at your apartment while you're gone."

"You're welcome. Just don't bring another woman there." Betty laughed. "You know I'm really happy that you found your dream boat."

"Not *my* dream boat, *our* dream boat," said Bob as he kissed her goodbye.

*   *   *

A bolt of lightning flashed through the air, and the thunder roared so close it sounded like a jet passing overhead. The lights flickered throughout the house, jolting Betty out of her reminiscing mood.

Whoa, that was a close one. God, I've been goofing off for an hour! I better get back to work.

Two

Betty finished organizing the groceries then looked over her list of things left to do. She tried to keep her mind off of the inevitable decision by going through cookbooks and copying easy meals to make and freeze. She made menus for three meals a day for a month. Then Betty remembered she still hadn't bought any meat to fill the large freezer. She drove to the butcher shop and ordered steaks, roasting chickens, pork, veal and lamb, even two turkeys. The butcher wrapped and labeled the meat. He would store it in his freezer until *Destiny* was ready to leave.

Medical supplies would be needed and Betty asked a local doctor to give her prescriptions for different types of antibiotics. Bandages, ointments, and splints had to be purchased, and in case of really serious problems, scalpels, needles and morphine were also included. Then, she was off to the bookstore for a few 'how-to' medical books. She needed the kind that tell you how to operate or set a bone in an emergency. Also how to take care of burns and what to do if poisoned. She wondered if anyone would have the guts to operate if it was necessary.

When she returned home, Bob was there with an assortment of fishing gear, tools and spare parts for the boat. "What did you buy this time?" he asked.

"Mostly medical supplies but I also picked up some roach motels, boric acid and bug sprays. I'm determined not to have roaches on this boat. You know I have this thing about bugs. They make my skin crawl. I'll never forget your old boat; it sure was loaded with them."

Bob put on a sad face as he said, "Yeah, I'll never forget the day you killed my buddy, Jake."

Laughing, Betty replied, "How can you call them your buddies? You're sick. I heard it's hard to get rid of roaches once they're on a boat."

"If you don't allow cardboard boxes onboard, you can keep

25

the boat roach-free, said Bob as he unpacked the fishing gear. "They get in between the flaps of the box and eat the glue and lay eggs."

Betty was very serious when she said, "OK, we'll make it a rule to keep cardboard boxes off the boat."

Bob gathered his fishing gear. "I'm going over to *Destiny* want to come?"

"Sure," said Betty, "I'll take this roach stuff with me."

Betty sprayed every closet, storage area and bilge with bug spray. Then she sprinkled boric acid in the same places. To complete the job she placed the motels in each of the areas for any unwelcome guest that might arrive. The following day was spent bringing all the food and supplies over to *Destiny*. They were stacked alongside the boat waiting for her to find places for them. Betty climbed aboard and started to store the many rolls of toilet paper and towels. She thought she had found the perfect spot. She was leaning over an opening stuffing the paper goods into the spot when Bob came down. Sweat was rolling down her face from the exertion and Betty looked up proudly and said, "Well, I've got two boxes of paper towels and all the toilet paper tucked in here."

Bob roared laughing, "You can't store paper down there!"

Betty got indignant, "Why not, it's a perfect place. Look, there's plenty of room and it's easy to get at."

"That 'perfect place,' as you call it, is the bilge. Any water that comes into the boat flows down there," he said, laughing at her inexperience. "See the little pumps? They pump the water out when it hits a certain level. It gets pretty wet down there and everything will be soaked."

Betty felt so dumb as she unloaded the paper products. "Trying to find places for everything is going to be impossible," she grumbled.

She used one closet to hold a week's supply of groceries and made lists of where everything was going, so she could find it later. The trick was to know where she put the supplies without having to lift every cushion and floorboard to find them. All the floorboards as well as backs and bottoms of the couches were pulled out. Any board that would lift up was opened and things were crammed into the space. It seemed never-ending, yet she was amazed at the number of objects she had already stored on the boat.

Betty knew *Destiny* was a big boat, but the pile of supplies was huge and they continued to add to it.

"Every time I think we have all we need, someone brings another pile," Betty said in exasperation. "Look at this mess stacked waiting for me to put away."

The next morning when she arrived to finish the job, she noticed the pile was smaller than when she had left it. She took her inventory list and started to look for different items.

Bob was working on deck and she called him. "There are things missing. The sewing kit and two cases of coke are gone, so are the fishing supplies you bought the other day."

"Damn," said Bob in a burst of anger. "I thought the security was good. We're the only boat here and the boatyard locks the gate at night. It's got to be an inside job."

Betty started to pick things up. "Ask some of the workers if they'll help bring the pile in, we'll stack everything in the salon."

Boxes were piled on top of one another, on the couch, chairs and the navigation desk. The floor held the rest, barely leaving enough room to step through. When she started to unpack, there was no room to move. She crawled over the boxes trying to get to the items she needed.

Frustrated, she yelled, "I'll go out of my mind with this mess."

In the midst of all the chaos, workers were coming down into the salon, and climbing over things to install the electronic equipment. For the next four days, Betty worked at a steady pace and made some progress, the pile diminishing. Days later, all the supplies were stored, floorboards were back in place, and the salon was neat again. The sails and equipment were installed and the last thing to be done was to have the compass calibrated. Betty wasn't sure what that entailed or when it was going to happen, but that was Bob's job.

The small stateroom in the bow of the boat was for storing tools and parts. Betty went in to put a screwdriver away, and found the room in shambles. Extra parts, a large assortment of small items and an array of tools were lying all over the counter and floor.

Betty threw her hands up. "What a mess," she said. "Now I have this clutter to put away."

An hour, later she had the screws, nuts, and bolts separated and arranged in neat piles ready to be stored in the cabinets and drawers. Betty heard the engine roar, and *Destiny* was moving away from the dock. She knew they were taking the boat out to calibrate the compass, but she hadn't realized it was today. It was too late to get off of the boat, so she continued to work. The air conditioning was cut off when the shore power was disconnected. Betty could feel the sweat building on her body as the tool room started to get stuffy and hot. She reached up to open the hatch above her head, but it was latched too tight. She opened one of the cabinet doors to put the screws away just as *Destiny* made a sharp turn. The unexpected movement threw Betty off her feet and onto the floor. The tools flew in all directions as the boat turned first to the right then another turn quickly to the left. The screws, nuts, and bolts that she had sorted, were now lying under her. Betty tried to get up but the boat made another quick turn. Her sweaty body slid back and forth on the floor among the screws and tools.

She felt so helpless and yelled, "Someone, please help, get me out of here." But no one heard her.

With great effort she managed to get on her knees and reached the edge of the counter. Betty got to her feet and stood against the counter trying to keep her balance, as she was tossed back and forth. The room was like a stifling oven, and sweat ran down her face and body. Her clothes damp from perspiration, stuck to her body and nails and screws protruded through her blouse. Blood trickled down her arms and legs that were scratched from the tools. Now *Destiny* was making twisting turns from west to east and north to south, as the electronics man continued to calibrate the compass. It was a windy day, and *Destiny* was rocking back and forth like a pendulum as it spun around in the different directions. Betty's head started to spin and her stomach churned, sending a bitter gull taste to her mouth. She knew she had to get on deck and towards the fresh air fast. She forced herself to move and staggered through the other staterooms into the salon. Then finally on deck she laid down on the long bench in the cockpit. Her stomach convulsed ready to vomit as the bile surged up in her throat.

Bob's mouth dropped open, "My God, where did you come from? I didn't know you were onboard. Are you all right?"

Too seasick to answer him, she took deep breaths to keep from throwing up. Betty lay there with her eyes closed rocking back and fourth with the boat. Before she fell off to sleep, she wondered, *how did I get myself in this mess? Is this what it's going to be like at sea? Oh, I feel so sick . . . .* Her mind reflected back and she remembered how Bob almost died. That's how she got herself into this mess.

*   *   *

She remembered Bob was in Ft. Lauderdale working on the plans for his boat. He had called Betty, but she hardly recognized his voice. It was hoarse and strained, "Bob you sound terrible."

"My asthma's acting up. I'm going to fly home to Massachusetts to see my doctor, I'll call you when I get there."

Bob got off the plane and went directly to the National Car Rental office. While he waited outside for his car, he noticed a phone booth and called Betty.

"I've been so worried about you. Are you feeling any better?" asked Betty.

"No, I feel dizzy and nauseated. My damn plane was two hours late and now I'm waiting for a car. Shit, get the fuck out of here," he yelled.

"What happened?" Betty shouted. She had never heard him use that language before.

Bob continued to cuss and holler. "A goddamn dog just pissed on my leg."

"What?" Betty tried not to laugh, but the image was funny. She pictured him standing there feeling down and out, and then a dog comes over and uses his leg as a fire hydrant. It was just too much. Stifling a laugh she said, "How can you joke when you feel so bad?"

His voice trembled as he said, "I'm not joking. The goddamn dog pissed on me. I mean things are really bad when even a dog picks on you."

"Promise me you'll call your doctor as soon as you get home."

"Okay, Okay. My car's pulling up, I'll call you later."

When Bob arrived at his motor home in Duxbury, he crawled wearily into bed and fell into an exhausted sleep. About two in the morning, he suddenly sat up gasping for breath. His chest tightened as he gasped for breath. He grabbed his chest as a deep pressure loomed through his upper body and cold sweat covered his body.

"Oh my God," he gasped. "I'm having an asthma attack! I've got to get to the hospital."

Staggering to the car he fell on the front seat. His heart was beating so hard it echoed in his ears. He felt so weak he could hardly press the brake pedal. A lonely desperate feeling came over him as he drove the thirty miles to the hospital. He wiped the tears from his eyes and prayed he would make it. "I hope this is just a bad dream," he murmured.

Bob pulled up in front of the emergency entrance and staggered toward the door. The security guard called out in a gruff voice. "Hey, you can't park there."

"Go to hell," said Bob, his voice barely a whisper. As he reached the admission desk, circles flew before his eyes; and a echoing sound flooded his ears, and he fainted.

"Get a stretcher, *stat*," yelled an intern standing at the desk as he grabbed Bob before he hit the floor.

*   *   *

Betty's day had been hectic. She just finished going over the last stack of contracts. Leaning back in her office chair, she sipped her coffee. She was worried since she hadn't heard from Bob. The phone startled her when it rang.

When she answered the phone, it was Dr. Ramsey from Mass General Hospital. "Bob Godfrey asked me to call you. He came to the hospital early this morning and we have him in intensive care."

"Oh no!" Betty gasped. "What's wrong with him? Did he have an accident?"

"He's had heart failure," said the doctor. "We have him stabilized now."

Betty felt numb and was not able to speak for a moment.

"Hello? Hello? Are you still there?" asked the doctor.

"Yes. Please tell Bob I'll get there as soon as possible," answered Betty trying not to cry. When she hung up the phone, she let the tears flow, sobbing silently. Then, she called the airlines and caught the first flight available.

When Betty reached the hospital, the nurse took her to his room. She was shocked by his appearance. Tubes and wires were connected to his ashen skin. She wasn't sure if he was asleep or dead.

"He's in serious condition," whispered the nurse.

Hearing their whispers, Bob opened his eyes. A slight smile flickered in his eyes when he saw Betty. "You're here, I—don't know if I'm going to make it."

Betty kissed his forehead and gently took his hand. "You're going to get better. You're not getting away from me *that* easily."

Betty stayed with him, leaving only to catch a few winks of sleep at a nearby hotel. A week later, he was moved from intensive care to a private room. His spirits were brighter and he seemed to be improving a little each day. Then one morning when Betty arrived Bob was curled up in a fetal position, the sheet pulled over his face as if he was hiding.

She was confused when she came into the room, and touched him lightly. "Bob, are you all right?" She pulled the sheet down and his face was stark white.

His lips quivered as he said, "The doctors were in to see me this morning."

A puzzled look came on her face as she asked, "So . . . what did they say?"

"They don't think I'll completely recover," his voice shook with emotion. "I don't want you stuck with an invalid. I want you to find someone else."

Betty was shocked. "What are you talking about? I don't want to find somebody else."

Tears rolled down his cheeks as he said, "I'm going to cancel the boat."

Betty was furious with the doctors. How could they be so insensitive and take away all his hope? "Don't listen to them, you're a fighter and you will get better, I promise. Please don't

31

cancel the boat. Remember you have a dream to fulfill."

They held each other close, trying to fight the fear in their hearts. They didn't know what their future held but they were determined to fight for it.

Bob sat up in bed with his eyes closed." I'm not going to get better, I know it. I'm going to cancel the boat."

They sat there in silence until the nurse came in with his lunch. "I'm not hungry," he said, pushing the tray away.

"Come on, you have to eat. Don't you *want* to get better?" Betty said as she started to feed him. "Come on, open your mouth. You've got to eat to get your strength back."

Bob took the spoon from Betty, and with his eyes glued to her, he said, "If I get better will you go with me?"

Betty looked at him puzzled by what he had asked. "Go with you where? What are you talking about?"

His voice quivered and in a rasping voice, he asked, "Sail around the world on our new boat. It's been my dream for so many years. Help me make it come true."

Betty was caught by surprise. She didn't know how to answer. He didn't need another negative blow, but how could she say yes? She didn't want to sail across the ocean. Bob kept staring at her waiting for her answer.

He reached for her hand and with a pleading look asked, "Please say you'll go."

Betty stuttered, "Eh -let's get you better first then we'll talk about it."

Tightening his grip on her hand he said, "That's not an answer."

Betty fussed with his covers and poured some water in his glass. "Here, have some water, your mouth's dry."

Bob just stared at her with a desolate look on his face, waiting for her answer.

She sat thinking for a while before she answered. *If what the doctor said was true he wouldn't be well enough to go on such a vigorous trip. Maybe I'd be safe in making the promise.*

Finally, to comfort him, she said, "I'll go with you, but only if the doctors say you're well enough to go." She had just made a commitment she didn't want to keep.

After two weeks of hospital care, the doctor felt he had

improved enough to go home. They started to drive to his mother's house in Marshfield, where Bob would stay and recuperate. At first, the trip went smoothly until the traffic slowed to bumper-to-bumper. The forty-mile trip had turned into a slow process. Bob was sitting in the passenger seat, his head back, his eyes closed. Betty tried to make idle conversation about the snow that was falling, but he made no reply. It was a bitter gray New England day and there was no sign of a break in the heavy traffic.

In a shaken voice Bob whispered, "I can't go any further. I need to lie down."

Betty slowed the car and started to pull off the highway. "Do you want me to stop and let you lie down in the back seat?"

His voice cracked as he said, "No. See if you can find a motel."

Way ahead, sticking high up in the air was a hotel sign. "I think I see a Marriott sign up the road. We'll pull in there," said Betty, picking up speed and entering into the flow of traffic.

After arranging for a room on the first floor, she helped Bob out of the car. Leaning on her, he shuffled like a weak old man down the hall. Betty felt so sorry for him, how could this be the same vigorous guy she'd met ten months ago. Bob's arm was around her shoulder as he leaned his full weight against her. "Just hang on Bob, we're almost there," she said, struggling to open the door.

Bob collapsed on the bed, his face covered with sweat. "I want to get undressed and get in bed," he said as he fumbled with the shirt buttons.

Betty reached over and started to unbutton his shirt. "Here, let me help you. If you weren't so sick, I'd think you had something else in mind. "

Half-sobbing, Bob complained, "Stop joking, Betty, I feel terrible. I'm never going to get better. I know it."

Betty covered him up and reached for the phone. "Boy, you are in a bad mood. I'll order you some hot soup and tea it will make you feel better."

He ate a small amount of the soup, drank a half a cup of tea and fell off to sleep. Betty listened to the rhythm of his breathing. *Will he ever be the man I used to know, or will he be sickly and housebound? I didn't want to promise him I'd sail with around the world. I really don't want to go, but I had to say yes,* she thought as she drifted off.

Betty was dressed and had ordered room service when Bob woke in the morning. After breakfast they continued on to his mother's house. Edythe, Bob's mom, welcomed them with a warm smile, but concern lay heavy on her face. Eighty years young, she had the white hair and ivory skin of her English ancestors. Her husband had died ten years ago and Bob was her only son. The thought of losing him haunted her. She wanted to know all the details of his illness.

Surprisingly, Bob knew very little, "I feel like I'm in the dark about what caused my heart failure and infection. Before I left I tried to get answers, but the doctor said to call for an appointment in two weeks and he would explain everything then."

"I know, I tried to get some answers too. Now that I have some time I'd like to go to the library and find a few books on heart problems. Maybe we can find cases like yours and get a little more insight," said Betty.

While Bob took a nap, Betty went to the library and found four books on the heart. After dinner, they started checking his symptoms against what they read in the books.

Betty said, "Listen to this. It says that large doses of the asthma medicine *Theodore* given over a long period of time will jolt the heart. It can cause the heart to fibrilate and enlarge." Bob gasped. "Oh my God. My asthma doctor put me on a large dose of *Theodore* a year ago and never changed the dosage. No wonder the lab man was surprised at the amount of *Theodore* in my system."

Betty put the book down, "I see why they didn't want to discuss your problem. You ought to change doctors."

Edythe had a worried look on her face, "You need someone you feel confident with."

Bob reached for the phone and dialed an insurance friend. His voice was weak and slurred as he talked. "Hello, Roger. Bob Godfrey here. How are you?"

"Hi, buddy. Sorry to hear about your illness."

"That's why I'm calling. Who's the best heart specialist in the area?"

"Dr. Ryan, he's the top heart man in the Boston area. Also call Dr. Brown. He's the best internist around and they work together."

"Thanks, Roger, I need a good one. I'll stay in touch and let you know how I make out."

The appointment with Dr. Ryan went well. He requested the files and x-rays from the hospital. After a complete examination, he felt that with proper care Bob would improve a great deal.

Dr. Ryan sat back in his chair looking over Bob's charts. "The best thing you can do right now is to rest and let your body recuperate for a few weeks. Let Betty baby you."

Bob looked over and smiled at Betty. "That sounds good to me."

Things were less hectic now that Bob was at his mother's. Betty was able to go back to her office in Cherry Hill and catch up on her work. She stayed there during the week, and on weekends would fly to Marshfield. The following week was Thanksgiving and she was torn between spending it with her family or Bob. It was a hard decision, but she discussed the situation with her family and they felt since he was so sick she should have Thanksgiving with him. When she arrived in Marshfield, she could see the improvement in him.

"Well, don't you look great! Look at the color in your cheeks," Betty said as she gave Bob a big hug.

"Are you staying for Thanksgiving?" Bob asked hopefully.

"Yes, and if you're good, I might even cook a turkey with all the trimmings."

"You don't have to go to all that trouble. We'll go out to eat," said Edythe.

"No, I really want to cook. It always smells so good when it's roasting."

Bob looked up at Betty with concern in his eyes. "I saw the doctor yesterday. He wants to put me back in the hospital Monday for a cardioversion. They'll shock the heart to a dead stop then shock it back in normal rhythm."

"Wow. What's the chances of it working?" asked Betty.

"Thirty percent, but if it goes back in rhythm, my chances of recovery are much better."

Monday morning, Betty sat praying in the waiting room;

35

waiting for the procedure to be over. The doctor came out smiling, and she let out a sigh of relief.

"He came through with flying colors. His heart's in sync again," said Dr. Ryan proudly. "We'll watch him for a couple of days and if all goes well, he can go home."

Three days later, Dr. Ryan came in the room. "Your report looks good so we're going to let you go home. The day after tomorrow, I want you to start walking every day. Start with ten minutes and then each week increase it by ten minutes until you're walking two hours a day."

"Walk two hours a day? Doctor, you're crazy. I'll never be able to do that. I can hardly walk now," Bob said weakly.

"Listen to me. Walk everyday," he said sternly. "Also, I don't want you to drive a car or lift anything, and I'll see you in my office in three weeks."

After they finished lunch Betty said, "It's the end of November and look how warm it is. It's a perfect day to start your walking. Are you ready?"

"I'm too tired, we'll start tomorrow," said Bob.

"Come on, it's a beautiful balmy day, and you know what the doctor said. If you want to get better, you have to walk."

Bob squirmed in his chair, "Are you going to walk with me?"

Betty stood up and grabbed his arm, pulling him to his feet she said, "I have a feeling if I want you to walk I'll have to go with you."

Every day they walked, and every day Bob would grumble. "Goddamnit! I feel like I am an eighty-year-old man," as he shuffled along.

Betty poked him in the ribs chiding him, "Come on, lift up those legs, don't shuffle. You think I want an old man walking with me?"

It was an effort, but each day renewed his strength and after a few weeks, he was walking with a steady stride. After three weeks, his doctor gave him the good news.

"Happy days are here, I can drive the car," Bob said, reveling over his excellent doctor's report. "I'm going to make it, baby. We're going to sail around the world."

Remembering her promise, Betty cringed. *What am I going*

to do now? Ignoring his remark she said, "Come on, I'll buy you lunch."

*   *   *

They were sitting in the living room watching television, Betty kept fiddling with her hair then her hands. She couldn't sit still.

"You're really jittery, is something bothering you?" asked Bob.

Betty moved closer to him, holding his hand she said, "It's two weeks before Christmas and car rentals are busy during the holidays. I'm going to have to stay in Cherry Hill and work at my office for the next three weeks. I also want to spend Christmas with my family. Do you feel up to going with me or would you rather stay here?"

"Are you kidding? There's no way I'd stay here without you."

Betty stood up and went over to Bob's mom. She put her arm around her and said, "Why don't you come with us. I don't want you to spend Christmas alone."

Edythe smiled, "No, dear. I'm leaving for Florida in another week. You know I have friends that I spend the holidays with every year. Don't worry about me. Just take good care of Bob."

The weather turned colder as a high from Canada rushed down from the north. The streets were paved with ice from a rain storm the day before. Betty left for the office each morning and Bob took her dog for a walk. Inhaling the frigid cold air was causing his asthma to act up so he was not able to walk very long. He'd go to the malls picking out presents for everyone and looked for small chores to do around the house. Betty was back to a routine that she loved, swept up in the hustle of the office and the pleasures of her grandchildren. She was humming away as she prepared dinner one night and Bob was sitting in the family room.

"Bob come talk to me," she called out. When he didn't answer Betty walked to the family room. The television was blaring, but Bob wasn't watching it. He was sitting on the couch with his head turned to the glass doors, looking out at the falling snow.

She went over to him and stroked his head gently, "Bob, are

37

you all right? Is something wrong?"

He looked up at her, his blue eyes showed a sadness that she didn't expect. "Now I'm the one that's restless. There's nothing I can do here. I can't walk in this weather because of my asthma, and if I don't I won't get better."

Betty sighed and sat down beside him. "I know there's not much for you to do, but it would be the same back in Marshfield. At least here we have family and friends to socialize with."

Bob threw up his hands in exasperation. "I need to get out of this weather. I want to go to Florida."

Betty was stunned. "Florida! Well, if that's what you want. When will you leave?"

Bob's face brightened, "I was hoping you could go with me."

Betty looked confused, "I can't leave New Jersey so soon. I've been away a lot and I just can't leave the business." Then, she became irritated, "I want to stay here for Christmas."

He started coughing and couldn't stop. Betty became alarmed and ran for some water.

With a rasping voice, he asked, "When can you go? I need to get out of this cold—my asthma's acting up."

Betty was torn between staying at her business she loved and going to Florida with the man she loved. She wanted to blurt out *why am I always in the middle*, or, *you go and I'll come visit*. She couldn't because she loved him and he was sick and needed her help.

Calmly, she said, "Right after New Year's, I should have things worked out by then. I'll have to fly home every couple of weeks to check on things. You know we can't stay at my apartment, it's rented for the season."

"Oh yes, forgot. Do you know anyone in Ft. Lauderdale who could find a place for us to rent?"

Betty thought for a moment, "Let me call a friend I know in the real estate business. She'll find something for us."

Christmas was full of laughter and happiness as everyone opened their presents. Dinner was enjoyed by family and friends and Bob's spirits seemed to lift. The phone rang and it was Betty's real estate friend from Ft. Lauderdale. She found the perfect house for them.

Two days after New Year's, they filled Bob's car with luggage and headed for warmer climate. They arrived at a white stucco ranch house with a red tile roof. It was surrounded by gracious palm trees and furnished with modern furniture in tones of white, beige and turquoise. As soon as they settled in, they started walking every day, rain or shine. They clocked over eight miles per day and by April, had walked over seven hundred miles.

Bob flew back several times during the winter for check-ups while Betty went to her office. She had discussions with her family, explaining that she might sail around the world. She wanted to prepare them to run the business for her if she definitely decided to go. Betty didn't want to burn her bridges and sell anything. If she didn't go, or if she went and couldn't handle it, Betty wanted to still have her life here. Debra and Clint were already living in her house so that would not be a worry.

In April, Bob had tests and x-rays taken, and the doctors were astounded at his improvement.

"You've done remarkably well," said Dr. Ryan. "There are still some irregularities but medication will control that. I'm amazed, your heart's almost back to normal size and the infection is completely gone."

Bob was elated, "What do you think? Can I sail around the world in my boat?"

"Sail around the world?" . . . The doctor was shocked and stood silently for a while.

"When do you plan on doing this?"

Bob was so excited he could hardly sit still, he was like a small boy being told how good he was in school. "If all goes well, no later than June," said Bob.

Dr. Ryan's eyes widened, "June! How long will you be gone?"

All smiles, Bob answered, "We plan on five years, but who knows."

"I don't know . . . Five years is a long time. You'll need regular check-ups, and medication. What happens if there's an emergency?" asked Dr. Ryan.

Bob looked bewildered. "Look, doctor, this is something I really want to do. It is my life's dream. I'll be careful and I'll take a stock of medicines with me. I'll even fly back every six months for a check-up."

Betty was listening to the whole conversation but kept quiet. She was glad he was healthy, but she was hoping the doctor would say no.

Dr. Ryan studied Bob's chart, "Reluctantly I'm saying okay, but I'm not real happy about you going."

When they were out of the office, Bob jumped up and down like a small child. He grabbed Betty, hugging and kissing her. "We're going to sail around the world. You know if it wasn't for you, I don't think I would have made it. You're the one who made me walk, stayed with me, and encouraged me. I couldn't have done it without you. Now my dream is going to come true."

Betty felt trapped and didn't know what to say, "I'm glad the doctor gave you such a good report."

Bob studied her for a moment, "Is that all you can say? Man, this is wonderful. I feel wonderful, we are wonderful."

Betty was quiet as they drove home. She knew he expected her to keep her promise and go with him. What was she going to do now? How could she get out of going?

Bob reached over and put his arm around her. "You seem so deep in thought. Is there something the matter?"

"I was just thinking. It's a miracle that you recovered so completely and I'm really happy for you."

Bob slowed the car and looked at her. "And—you're not telling me everything."

She looked down at her hands as she half-whispered, "It looks like you're really planning on making this trip."

Bob grabbed her chin with one hand, pulling her face toward him. "We're planning on making this trip. We're going together, remember."

Betty pulled her face away, "I know I promised to go with you, but the whole idea is just so frightening. I have no idea what it's like out there or how I'd handle it."

Bob smiled and patted her back, "Betty, you'll make out fine. You'll love it. Trust me, you'll love it."

Once Betty made a promise she never went back on her word. "Let's keep getting the boat ready and take one step at a time."

While Betty was still reminiscing about Bob's illness, *Destiny* had arrived back at the dock. Bob nudged her, "Wake up Betty. Are you feeling better?"

"I wasn't sleeping I was just thinking about you," she said as she sat up.

Three

The new boat was supposed to be delivered to the Miami Port by freighter on March 1st. It was now April 4th and the boat had not arrived.

Bob was getting concerned. "I haven't heard a word from the shipyard in Taiwan, neither has Gary, the agent."

"When was the last time you talked to the shipyard?" asked Betty.

"Not for a while. I'll call them today and see what the status is."

Betty checked their list of things to do. "All the rigging and electronics are going to be installed here in Ft. Lauderdale, aren't they?"

Bob gave an unsure laugh. "Oh yes, everything on the boat is scheduled to be completed by the end of May."

Betty laughed too, "Seems to me we're running a little behind schedule."

Bob's tone turned serious, "We shouldn't be laughing, we're *way* behind schedule. I'm going to call them right now and see what's going on."

Betty walked to the phone booth with him and sat on a bench nearby. She was furious with herself. "Well, you got yourself into a pickle jar and can't get out," she said outloud. "I'll just have to go along with it and help him get the boat ready, and see how I feel when *Destiny*'s ready to go."

Bob came back with a big smile on his face, "It's all set. They promise it will be here in two weeks, no later than the end of the month. By June, we should be sailing off into the sunset. Destination—around the world."

Destiny finally arrived on May 7th in Miami, Florida. Since Douglas Fronrath was the representative for the Taiwan shipyard, he was there to meet the boat. In anticipation they watched as the dock workers prepared to lift *Destiny* from the deck of the freighter. They placed three heavy duty canvas slings around the hull, then the head man gave a signal to lower *Destiny*. Just as the boat was lifted over the rail of the freighter, one of the slings slipped at an angle. *Destiny* slammed against the freighter, sliding sideways. Part of the toe rail split off and fell into the water, and the boat tilted downward in an awkward angle, rocking back and forth. It looked ready to slide out of the slings. Instead of trying to correct the problem, the dock men started to holler at each other in Spanish, blaming one another for the mishap.

Bob was fuming, his fists clenched as he ran up to them, ready to punch them. "For God's sake, don't stand there arguing, *do* something. My boat is about to crash on the dock."

Betty pulled Bob away from the dock men and stomped over to Gary and said, "For God's sake Gary, do something."

Gary went over to calm the men down. He had them put an additional sling around the hull, he thought the boat was too heavy for just three slings.

At long last *Destiny* was lowered in the water, her perfection damaged by the large section of wood missing from the toe rail.

Bob was a nervous wreck. "Suppose the hull fittings aren't closed and it sinks."

"Don't even think those thoughts," said Betty, mesmerized by the whole show.

"The boat's in the water and floating, do you feel better now?" asked Gary. "*Destiny*'s decks look flat and empty, but once you install her masts and sails she'll be a magnificent sailing vessel."

"Our dream boat is finally here," Bob sighed. "I'm going below to check to make sure everything's closed and latched. Then we'll motor her back to Ft. Lauderdale."

Betty walked along the deck, touching everything. "It looks so much larger than I remembered it."

Going below she looked around and was pleased with what she saw. Everything was decorated in the light beige, coral, and blues she had chosen. The couch in the salon was beige, speckled with coral, and the barrel chair was covered with a coordinating blue. Beige drapes were at all the windows, including the state rooms. The two guest bedspreads were done in the light pastel plaids. The king size bed was covered with a quilted spread of abstract design, mingling all the pastel shades together.

Bob climbed down into the salon and asked, "How do you like it so far?"

Betty stood there hugging herself, staring at the beautiful decorations. "I love it. Lets go look at the bathroom, I want to see the tub."

"Hey, if you're going to be a sailor you have to use nautical terms. It's called the head."

"The head! That sounds so crude, so mannish," said Betty, wrinkling her nose.

Bob laughed as they entered the head, "No. It's just what you call a bathroom on a boat. You'll get used to it."

"Let's walk back to the kitchen, it's so nice," said Betty.

"There you go again. You have to call it a galley," said Bob making fun of her.

Betty gave him a sarcastic look, "Okay captain, from now on it's the galley."

"Look at the freezer, it's giant. You can put plenty of meat in here," Bob said as he lifted the top of the freezer. "This should hold enough frozen food for a month."

"The refrigerator is rather small," Betty said, then she latched the gimbaled stove and oven that was swaying back and forth. Proudly, she smiled and said, "This is my galley."

It was a thrill being aboard *Destiny* after all the months of waiting and planning. Excitement was building inside Betty, she really loved the boat and for the first time a spark of, *Maybe I might be able to make the trip*, came into her mind.

She watched Bob behind the helm, and she sensed the pride he felt as he turned the key. The engine turned over on the first try and they headed for Ft. Lauderdale. They stood close together behind the helm, each with their own thoughts.

"This is one of the happiest days of my life. I'm so lucky," said Bob, kissing Betty's forehead. "Get behind the helm. I'll teach you to steer."

Betty held the wheel firmly and started to turn it back and forth.

"Keep it steady," Bob said, cupping her hands. "That's it, you don't need to move the wheel that much. You're doing great. That's it steer just like you're driving a car."

Betty was able to steer straight for a while, but soon she was over-steering again.

"Look at the wake you're making behind us," laughed Bob. "You're Snake-Wake Rennie again."

Late that afternoon, they arrived at Norseman Marina. Friends were waiting for their arrival, ready to help with the lines. An odd look came on Bob's face as reality hit him.

His voice was filled with anxiety as he said, "Holy shit, I have to dock this big sucker. Betty go up on the bow and throw the dock lines to one of the men."

"Wow, they're heavy," she said as she struggled with the inch thick rope.

"Make sure they're secured around the cleats before you heave it. For god's sake, Betty, throw it. Throw it now."

"I told you before, don't yell at me," she screamed back while she threw the line.

"I'm not yelling. Just get back to the stern and throw the other line. Hurry, the wind's in our favor and it should help push us in."

Betty missed the first toss and Bob yelled, "Oh no. Pull it in quick. Throw it now."

Frustrated, she tried again and someone leaned out and caught it, quickly securing it to the piling.

"Good docking Bob," the men said. "You did a good job too Betty."

"Thanks," Betty said feeling frustrated. "I'm kind of new at this."

"Betty, come over here. These lines will never hold the way you have them wrapped. I'll have to teach you the right way," said Bob redoing them.

"Sure, but show me another time, I'm too tired to listen. Next time don't yell at me. Just talk normal."

"I wasn't yelling."

"Yeah, yeah, yeah," Betty said, walking away in a huff.

Beer was passed through the crowd in celebration of the arrival of *Destiny*. The grill was filled with hot dogs and hamburgers and by midnight everyone had left for home.

45

At the crack of dawn, Bob was up and raring to go. "Get up Betty, let's go see *Destiny*. There's so much to do."

Betty yawned and stretched. "Can't you wait another hour or two? It's only five-thirty."

Bob pulled the covers off the bed. "No. Come on get up, I'll buy you breakfast."

Reluctantly, she got dressed and by the time they finished breakfast at Denny's, Betty was awake. Later they sat on the deck of *Destiny* with a stack of papers on their laps.

Bob pulled out his red pencil, "Let's check over the list of things to be completed."

Betty looked over his shoulder at his notes. "According to this schedule the boat should be ready to go in a month. Let's see . . . that should be the beginning of June."

Bob put down his list, "I'm going to walk over to the marina office. I want to make sure everything we ordered came in."

Twenty minutes later, Bob was back, his face bright red with anger. "I can tell by your expression you have bad news." said Betty.

Bob's hands waved in the air as he answered. "Remember the parts for the rigging that we ordered months ago? Well, they haven't arrived yet. Even the damn mast isn't here."

Betty shook her head in disgust, "I know. You paid for them way back in January."

Bob climbed back on *Destiny* and sat down. "I did. Charlie told us everything would be ready when we needed it. Now we have to wait for delivery."

Two weeks later, the electronics were delivered and the electricians arrived to install the different systems. "Pardon me, Mr. Godfrey," said one of the electricians, "we've never seen a boat wired like this. Are there special instructions on what these different colored wires mean? They are coded completely different from the U. S. Coding."

Bob looked puzzled. "The boat's electrical system was installed in Taiwan, we should have a diagram somewhere." He looked through his papers. "Aha. I found it. Oh no! It's written in Chinese!"

The electrician looked behind the circuit breaker panel. "Sometimes the layout is put here. Yep, here it is. Oops, it's in

Chinese too. We'll work on it for a while and see if we can figure out their coding."

A week later, the masts and rigging arrived, Bob was elated and asked the dock foreman, "How soon can you install those babies? Tomorrow?"

The installer laughed, "Sorry, we can't get a crane over here until next month."

"Next month?" Bob screamed at the installer. "I want it done this week."

The man shook his head, "Can't do it man. The cranes are all tied up. Not one available."

Disgusted, Bob gave up and walked away, and got busy on other jobs.

A month later the cranes arrived and the mast was installed Bob stood and stared at it. "Look at that mast, Betty, isn't it a beaut? It's seventy-five feet high. Impressive, huh? I put a silver dollar at the base before it was installed. It's an old sailor's superstition, supposed to bring good luck. Now all we need are the sails. I've called them everyday and—hey that looks like their truck now . . . .Are you delivering sails to *Destiny*?" he yelled.

"Yeah, we are," answered the driver. "Is that *Destiny*?"

Bob walked over to their truck. "Yes it is. Boy am I glad to see you. I thought you'd never get here."

As the men unloaded the sails Bob said, with relief in his voice, "This is it the final dressing."

Working diligently along with the installers Bob helped hoist the main sail. Then he let out a bellow. "Goddamn, it's too large. They did it to us again, Betty. They got us again."

Betty climbed aboard. "Calm down. You're going to have a heart attack. They'll just have to take it back and make it smaller."

"They got us again," he kept saying, shaking his head in desperation.

Betty looked confused, "Who's they, anyway?"

Bob threw his hands out in front of him, "The forces that keep knocking us off schedule. You know like the black cloud that hangs over your head. They call Mr. Fits."

"Oh, the imaginary gremlin," Betty said, laughing. "Do you feel all right? Come on, you need a break. I'll treat you to lunch."

Their problems seemed endless. Not only was the main sail too big but so were the other five. The wrong navigation equipment was sent, the power steering they installed wouldn't work, and the bow thrusters weren't powerful enough. Bob was angry and his temper showed it. Their departure date was only thirty days away.

Four

The trip across the Atlantic would be *Destiny*'s maiden voyage. There would be seven people onboard, including Betty and Bob. Four would be family and friends and one, a paid crewman. They were scheduled to leave in June, which was just a few weeks away. Betty had to make her final decision soon. Was she going on the trip or not? There was no denying she was caught up in the excitement of preparing the boat for the trip. The fever of all that was happening was making her want to go. When she thought about actually going out in the vast sea and sailing so far away, she'd shiver and had second thoughts.

*   *   *

They had met Mitch Hollaran, their paid crewman, in Hawaii last March. They had flown to Taiwan to check on *Destiny*'s progress, stopping over in Maui on their way back. They sailed on a catamaran for a day cruise to Lanai, a small island, a short distance from Maui. Mitch was the second mate on the catamaran, and Bob took notice of how well he was handling the sailing Cat. He was slender, but had well-developed arms, and was quick at winching in the sails. Bob talked with him, and told him of his plans to sail around the world.

Mitch got excited and his blue eyes widened as he said, "Wow! That sounds like a fantastic trip. Is there any chance of my signing on as a mate?"

"Yeah, sure. Everyone we talk to says that," Bob said jokingly.

Mitch sat down next to Bob at lunch. "Maybe you don't think I'm serious about going, but I am. It's something I've always wanted to do." He swept his hand through his blonde hair nervously and continued on. "My girlfriend and I just broke up and I

49

have nothing to keep me here."

Bob smiled, "Here's my address, send me a letter listing work and personal references. If they check out I'll think about it."

When the trip was over, they said goodbye, not knowing if they would hear from him again, or if they really wanted him along.

The resumé arrived two weeks later and after reading it, they decided it would be a benefit to have a paid crewman along on the trip. When they contacted the references, they were told Mitch was a good worker, honest, reliable and very easy going.

Bob called him and said. "We couldn't find anyone who would say anything bad about you. How much did you pay them to brag you up that way?"

Mitch laughed, "Sure glad to hear that."

Bob's voice turned on his business personality. "Okay! Here's what we decided to do. We'll pay your way to Florida, and you can live at our house. You can help get *Destiny* ready, and we'll pay you for your time. If we get along together you can go on the trip."

Mitch was delighted, "Great, when do you want me? I could leave tomorrow."

"Wait a minute," answered Bob. "Not so fast. How about three weeks from now? I'll arrange for the ticket and you can pick it up at the airport next Sunday."

Mitch arrived from Hawaii, jet lagged from the long trip but excited. The days that followed proved he was a willing worker and among his many talents, he also was an excellent carpenter.

One night at the dinner table he was unusually buoyant. Bob took a sip of wine and asked, "What are you so happy about?"

Mitch was so excited he could hardly sit still. "I just talked to my girlfriend Diane. We made up. Would you and Betty mind if I invited her out for a visit?"

Betty put down her fork, "You mean the girl you just broke off with?"

Bobbing his head up and down with enthusiasm he answered, "Yes, I'd like to see her again before we leave."

Bob studied Mitch for a moment then said, "We'll sleep on it and let you know."

Mitch was sitting at the breakfast table the next morning eager to hear the answer. As Bob walked in the room, he asked, "Can she come?"

"It's okay with us, but she can only stay a week. I know you'll want some time off, but it's important that we keep on schedule. While Diane's here you'll work the mornings on *Destiny* and then you can take the rest of the day off."

Mitch was all smiles. "That's more than fair."

Diane arrived from California a week later; they were two love-sick puppies. Completely wrapped up in each other and nowhere to be found. This upset Bob, as this was not what had been agreed on.

As the week ended Mitch tried to talk Diane into coming along on the trip. "Let me talk to Bob, maybe you could sail with us."

Diane was not interested, "Look, Mitch, I love you very much, but I can't go with you."

Mitch's face saddened. "How can we be together if you won't come with me?" Holding her tight he said, "I want you with me."

Diane pushed away. "I love my job in California and I've got a chance for a big promotion. If you feel this trip is something you have to do, then get it out of your system and go. I'll wait for you."

Mitch was a very emotional guy. He pleaded but Diane stood her ground and the next day left for California.

After she left, Mitch was a changed man. He hardly talked and at night he'd sit and stare into space.

Bob gave him a friendly slap on the back. "Hey, you have to snap out of it. Life still goes on you know. Come join us for dinner."

Tears rolled down Mitch's face, "I love her and miss her so much. I don't want to go anywhere without her."

Changing the subject, Bob said, "*Destiny* has most of the electronics on her now, and I'm a little worried. I don't want anythin stolen off her. We had trouble at the shipyard before. Mitch, I'll need you to sleep on *Destiny* from now on."

His face still had that lovesick look as he answered, "That's fine with me."

Betty and Bob were surprised at his immature actions and wondered if they were doing the right thing, by taking him along on the trip.

Five

It was a lovely summer night. Betty and Bob sat out on the terrace by the pool discussing their progress. Bob checked his calendar and said in an elated voice, "It's the end of July, we're two months behind schedule, but we're finally ready."

Betty was half-listening as she contemplated how she could get out of going and wondered if it was too late to back out. "What's the departure date now?"

"I figure we will be able to leave by August third. That's just two weeks away. The only thing left is to have her commissioned. We'll officially name her *Destiny* and break a bottle of champagne over her bow."

"Oh, lets have a big party and invite all our friends and relatives. We could have it at the Waterfront restaurant here in Ft. Lauderdale."

The party was held a week later, on the terrace of the Waterfront restaurant. Tables were decorated with flowers and candles and forty people were invited. The terrace overlooked the canal and *Destiny* was docked in front of the terrace. It was a fantasy night, with a bright full moon that glistened down on their dreamboat. Guests were invited aboard to see the results of all their hard labor. Everyone marveled over the size of the ship and went from stateroom to stateroom admiring the soft pastel colors that decorated each room. The gimbaled ice maker got everyone's attention as well as the size of the master stateroom.

After dinner, everyone gathered around *Destiny*, while Frank gave a speech. "I was with Bob and Betty when they first saw the sister ship of *Destiny*. Now they have their dream boat and have done a hell of a job getting her in shape. It's equipped with the best of everything and a real seaworthy craft. I was there when they bought her, there helping to get her ready and I hope to sail on her someday. Good luck Betty and Bob on your trip around the world. How about a few words from the captain of *Destiny?*"

Bob walked over to where Frank stood. He smiled as he spoke.

"I want to thank everyone for joining us in this celebration. Preparing *Destiny* for this trip has been frustrating and exciting." Bob let out a sigh of relief as he added, "I'm glad she's finished. Now if my firstmate will come over here we'll christen her properly."

Betty walked over holding a well-aged bottle of Dom Perignon champagne wrapped in netting with a gold bow at the top. Betty reached out and swung the bottle. She missed the bowsprit and lost her balance, almost falling over the embankment. Bob reached out and grabbed her before she fell in the water.

"I almost christened myself," Betty laughed. Then she swung the bottle again, this time successfully hitting the bowsprit.

'The ship is officially named *Destiny*," said Bob as he put his arms around Betty "Give me a big hug. This is it, baby, we're ready to go around the world."

Later that night as they were getting ready for bed, Bob said, "That was nice of Frank to give a speech. He sure is a great guy. He loves sailing. Do you know he sailed his small thirty-eight foot boat around Cape Horn twice, and against the wind too."

Betty climbed into bed as she said, "Frank tells such great stories about his sea adventures. I like him. He's sort of a character." As Betty tried to fall asleep, she remembered the stories Frank told her. Now she shuddered as she pictured the huge waves washing over his small craft in the rough weather. "He loves sailing the horn and swears he'll do it again," she said half-asleep.

Bright and early, Frank was on *Destiny*, checking the equipment before anyone else was up. He really enjoyed being part of the whole adventure. When Betty and Bob arrived, he put his arms around their shoulders. "How would you like some company on your trip across the Atlantic?"

Bob's face lit up. "Are you kidding?"

"I've been feeling the call of the sea, and I'd like to get out on the quiet ocean."

Bob slapped Frank on the back and said, "If you're really serious, we'd love to have you along."

Betty was pleased, she wanted people onboard that knew how to sail. "Now we have four people scheduled to go!"

"Oh, by the way, Scott called. He's bringing a buddy and flying out tomorrow. They're definitely going with us," said Bob.

"Who's Scott? I hope he knows how to sail!?" asked Frank

"He's my son. He's twenty-eight and loves to sail just like his old man. He's bringing a friend. The guys have three weeks vacation coming and they're sailing with us as far as Spain."

"Well, that only leaves my grandson Gregory to confirm that he's coming. He talked me into letting him come," said Betty. Then she whispered, "That is if I go."

Bob picked up on her last remark. "*If* you go?" He looked straight into her the eyes. In a stern voice he said, "You promised me you'd go. If you think you're going to chicken out on me, you have another thought coming. I had no idea you had second thoughts on this."

Frank flapped his arms, "Cluck, cluck, cluck, *Chicken*."

Betty hesitated for a moment, then said just as sternly, "I told you before how I felt. Or weren't you listening? I'm not thrilled about going. You're both experienced sailors you know how you'll react, I don't. I'm also worried about your health, suppose you have a problem while we're out at sea? Then what? *You could die*."

"Nothing's going to happen to me! I'm fine," said Bob.

"Yes, but what if you run out of your heart medicine, or have a heart attack?"

"I'll take a years supply of medicine with me. Believe me, Betty I feel terrific. Now what other reason do you have."

Betty didn't answer for a while then in a frustrated voice said, "I gave you my word that I'd sail around the world with you if you got better, and you did. So I'll go."

Bob breathed a sigh of relief as he said, "Well, I'm glad to hear that."

"I'll call Loretta and tell her to bring Greg down. I'm as nervous about him going as I am about myself."

Scott and Dave arrived two days later, red-eyed and tired. Scott seemed taller than Betty remembered. He was over six feet tall, lean and lanky but his body had good muscle tone. He looked like a sailor. His full beard framed his ever present smile, and his face had the soft look of an artist.

Bob put his arm around him. "Scott, good to see you. When are you going to shave that beard off?"

Scott gave Betty a hug. "You're really going to do this?"

Betty smiled. "Looks like it. If I don't go on this trip willingly, your father's going to hog-tie me to the mast."

Scott yawned, "Boy, are we dog-tired. It was a long trip. I want you to meet Dave Kroger. Dave, this is my Dad and his first-mate Betty; and you must be Frank."

Dave gave each one a firm handshake; the muscles bulging in his biceps, "I've been looking forward to this for weeks."

Frank stood with his hands in his pockets, squared his shoulders and said, "Glad to have you with us, hope you don't get seasick."

Dave laughed, as he swept back his long blonde hair, "don't usually, but then I've never sailed out of sight of land."

Greg arrived with his mother, Loretta. He was a thirteen year old skinny, feisty kid. His dark brown hair was badly in need of a trim.

He ran up to Betty and kissed her, "Hi grandma!" Then he saw *Destiny*. Greg's lips curled into a devilish grin. "Wow, that's some ship. This is going to be such an awesome trip. I can't wait to go."

"Sounds like he wants to be as daring as his grandma," said Loretta.

Mitch was working on deck and he called out. "Hey, you must be Greg. Hear you're going with us. Is that a skateboard under your arm?"

Greg hugged the skateboard. "Yep, I'm taking it with me,"

"Hi Greg. Did I hear you say you're taking a skateboard on the boat? Did you ask Bob if it was okay?" asked Scott.

Hearing the conversation, Bob said, "Sure, you can bring it, just keep it in your cabin."

Frank slapped him on the back, "Hey pip-squeak, I hear you're sailing with us for six weeks."

"If he lasts that long. Or should I say if we both last that long," added Betty. Then she whispered in Frank's ear, "I'm not sure I can handle this adventure, in fact I'm scared."

Frank gave her a hug. "With Bob and I along, you have nothing to worry about."

"Loretta, I'm surprised you're letting Greg go," said Scott.

"It was a hard decision. I even feel funny about my mom going, but I want them to have the adventure."

Bob walked over to Loretta and put his hands on her shoulders, "Don't worry, your Mom's going to be all right, and so is Greg. Well, we have a full crew now and I'm sure we're all eager to get started," said Bob. "Tomorrow we'll move our things out of the house and on to the boat. I'd like to leave around one o'clock in the afternoon."

It was the afternoon of August the third, and they were finally ready for the one o'clock departure time. Betty looked at her daughter standing by the boat dressed in white shorts and a lace top. She reached over and hugged her daughter. "I love you and I'm going to miss you," she said as she stroked Loretta's blonde hair.

Her daughter's huge brown eyes brimmed with tears as she said, "I love you too mom. Please take care of yourself and watch Greg. Don't let anything happen to him."

Betty hugged her daughter hard as she said, "I can't believe I'm really doing this, but I've made up my mind to at least try it." She tried hard to fight back the tears. Betty was leaving her family and didn't know when she would see them again. She climbed onboard with tears sliding down her cheeks, then brushed them away with her hand, fighting hard not to bawl like a baby.

Bob called out in a loud voice, "All right everyone, we've prolonged this enough. It's two-thirty, time to climb onboard. Scott, you stay on the dock and take off the lines."

"Wait," said Betty. "I have to put the Scopolamine® patches on Greg and me. We don't want to be sick. Anyone else want one?" Dave grabbed one before he jumped aboard.

Scott threw off the last line and jumped onboard just as they pulled away from the dock.

Loretta stayed on the dock until they were out of sight, waving until she could no longer could see them.

Greg looked over at Betty, his face beaming with excitement. "This is an awesome feeling. I'm going to love it."

Betty was filled with mixed emotions, as *Destiny* took them on their way. Bob had planned to sail for five years, but Betty was taking it one leg at a time. She'd see how she felt when she reached Bermuda, one thousand miles away. "If I can't take it, I'll get off in Bermuda and fly home," she said, to reassure herself.

They were about two miles out at sea, just passed the Ft. Lauderdale buoy, when Bob called out, "We have ten knots of wind, lets get the sails up. Put the main up first, then the genoa and mizzen."

The winches and lines were in the cockpit so that the boat could be sailed singlehanded if necessary. Scott and Frank started unfurling the main sail with the hydraulic winches.

"Wait a minute," Bob yelled out as he slowed the engine down. "Hold it! There's black fluid pouring out of the mast."

Mitch was sitting on the bow, so he went over to check the mast. "The hydraulic gear is jammed and it's leaking fluid."

"Try pulling the mainsail out by hand," yelled Bob.

Mitch tugged with all his strength then called out, "It won't move. Frank, give me a hand."

Frank ran out to the mast and they worked diligently, pulling and tugging. As they slowly eased the sail out, it flapped in the wind slapping at their faces. After an hour and a half of hard work it was fully out and filled with wind.

"Okay, lets try and get the genoa and mizzen up," Bob called out.

Scott looked concerned. "Dad, do you think we should go back to shore and get the hydraulics fixed?"

Bob shook his head in disgust. "No. We can furl the sails by hand, and as long as they don't jam again we can handle it. We've wasted enough time in Florida."

They were doing five knots of speed with a ten knot wind. The day was clear and the seas were calm, and everyone was ready for the journey.

"Hey Betty, when do we eat around here?" asked Dave.

"Oh, I completely forgot about lunch. Is everyone else hungry?" asked Betty.

They all moaned and groaned in response. Laughing, she went below to fix their first meal onboard. She was so proud of herself for not being sick. Betty made tuna sandwiches for everyone, with potato salad and sliced tomatoes on the side.

"Hey Bob," she hollered from below. "This isn't going to be so bad, what was I worried about?"

They ate their sandwiches around the table in the cockpit, watching Ft. Lauderdale get smaller and smaller as they sailed farther out to sea.

"When the land disappears, it will be a long time before we see it again," said Bob. "We should pick up a couple of knots of speed once we get in the gulf stream."

"Bob, what's the difference between knots and miles?" asked Greg.

Frank said teasingly, "Boy, you really are a landlubber. Don't you know that a knot is fifteen percent longer than a land mile, so if you're going one knot you're really going faster than a land mile."

"Cool," said Greg . . . . "What time's dinner?"

"Dinner? What's that got to do with knots? You just finished lunch," said Scott. "What are you—an eating machine?"

Betty still felt in good spirits, "I'll fix dinner around six o'clock, then someone else can be the chef tomorrow."

"Hey, wait a minute, I want to know what's on the menu," said Frank.

Laughing, Betty said, "Don't you want to be surprised? Maybe I'll feed you some of that canned gook you ate on your boat when you sailed around the horn."

"Oh, I told you that story, huh," said Frank. "Tasted just like dog food, but so bad even a dog wouldn't eat it."

Proudly, Betty said, "We're eating good on this boat. We're having meatloaf, brown potatoes, buttered carrots, and coleslaw."

As she started down the stairway to the galley she felt a slight heel to the boat, on the port-side, along with a short, quick motion from side to side.

"Hold on," said Bob, "the wind's picking up."

"Nothing to worry about, I can handle this," Betty said, trying to act salty as she made her way down to the galley.

Bracing her hip between the corner of the counter and stove she tried to start the oven, but the pilot light was out. She struck a match to light the pilot, but the gimbaled stove kept swinging back and forth, making it hard to reach. Betty was in a crazy position, half-stooping and twisted to the side. She tried to adjust her body to the swing of the boat and the oven. The knob of the oven had to be turned and held down while she applied the match. *It's usually so simple, but not at a time like this.* After falling on her knees, bumping her head on the stove, and burning her fingers, she finally got the oven lit.

Setting the thermostat to three hundred and seventy-five degrees, Betty continued preparing the meal. When she put the meatloaf in the oven, she noticed the temperature had gone up to four hundred and fifty. Quickly, she adjusted the knob. The temperature lowered to two hundred and fifty. With each adjustment, the temperature would rise and fall but never to the temperature she needed. After many attempts and a lot of screaming, Betty was able to outwit the stupid thing and continued on with her cooking.

The galley was stifling hot, so she opened the porthole over the stove. A wonderful cool breeze blew in and cooled down the galley. As long as the seas were calm, she felt she could keep it open. Suddenly a large wave splashed up the side of *Destiny*, sending water through the porthole. It flooded the pot of potatoes on the stove. and put out the burner. The water ran down the stove and all over the galley floor.

"So much for that clever idea," Betty yelled in frustration as she closed the porthole. The heat in the galley soon became unbearably hot, and there was very little air coming down the companion way. "Bob, can you turn the air-conditioning on? It's stifling down here."

"Can't do it, I can only turn it on when the generator's running."

Betty was frustrated, "Well, turn on the generator."

Bob came down to the galley. "It *is* hot down here. I'll turn on the generator, and put the air conditioning on. I'll charge the batteries and run the water-maker at the same time. It's important that we conserve our fuel, we might have to run the motor more than I planned."

The generator kicked over and Betty stood in front of the vent, letting the cool air blow on her sweaty body. It helped cool the galley down, but it was still hot.

She had dinner almost finished when she began to feel ill, and broke out in a cold sweat. Betty went up to the cockpit for air whenever she could, trying desperately to forget the gnawing feeling in her stomach. When she came back down, she put on the small fan in the galley. Betty stirred cornstarch and water together in a cup. She was going to use it to thicken the gravy. Just as she set the cup on the counter she heard Bob shout, "Frank, Mitch, let's jibe the sails."

The boat shifted and heeled way over to the starboard side and everything went flying. Carrots rolled across the counter. The cup of liquid cornstarch bounced into the air, splashing all over her and the galley floor. She stood there horrified.

Then stamping up to the cockpit, she hollered loud enough to be heard back in Ft. Lauderdale. "Why can't you warn me before you change the direction of the sails? How am I suppose to cook a meal with that motion?"

Betty was angry, hot, sweaty and sick. Covered with cornstarch, she was not a happy sailor.

Bob looked at her and almost laughed, her face was covered with white cornstarch. "I'm sorry, I didn't think to warn you," he said as he tried to calm her down.

She stood in the cockpit facing the wind, trying to cool off both inside and out. Frustration was eating at her. She knew this was going to happen again. Finally in control again, she reluctantly went to clean up the galley.

Mitch came down and said, "Are you feeling any better. Do you need some help?"

Betty was on her knees and in a pleading look, said, "You could help me clean this mess up."

Mitch took the rag from her, "You cook, I'll clean."

It was eight o'clock, dinner was much later than planned. She rang the loud brass bell, and called out, "Dinner is ready." There was a stampede as everyone raced down to the galley and filled their plates.

Eating dinner under the stars in the cool night air helped Betty to relax. She glanced over at Greg. His plate was empty,

61

but there was a funny expression on his face. Suddenly he got up and ran to the railing. His stomach convulsed and he gagged as his dinner gushed out, most of it landing on the deck. Betty started to get up and go to him. Bob pulled her down and said, "Don't baby him." Then he called out, "Anybody that throws up has to wash it off the decks. Sailors' rule."

Greg leaned on the rail moaning, then when he felt better, he got the bucket. Scott tied a rope to the handle and Greg lowered it into the water, then washed the mess off the deck. Betty saw him slowly climbed down the companion way. She was sure he was heading for his bunk. Instead he returned with his plate piled high. This time he lay down on his side and slid the food from the plate into his mouth, never raising his head. Everyone laughed at him but it worked. He kept the food down.

Bob watched Greg and felt sorry for him. "Do you think he'll be sick the whole time?"

Betty looked worried, "I hope not. So far, he's a good sport about it."

Talking to the whole group, Bob gave orders. "Someone has to be on watch at all times, as we'll be sailing twenty-four hours a day. We'll do two man shifts, four hours on and eight hours off. I need to be on call and also be up first thing in the morning. Betty and I will take the seven-to-eleven shift."

"Mitch and I will take the eleven-to-three shift," said Frank.

"That leaves Dave and I for the three-to-seven shift," said Scott. "That's what I wanted. Watching the sunrise is always special to me."

"What about galley duty for the dishes?" asked Betty.

"Two people will take turns each night, one to wash and one to dry. The captain—that's me—and the one who cooks never have to do dishes," said Bob.

"I don't mind taking a turn at cooking," said Frank. "You know I'm quite a gourmet."

Betty liked to tease Frank, "Yeah, you are pretty good, but you're not going to make that horrible cornmeal dish are you?"

"What's the matter with my cornmeal dish? I plan to make it every third day for lunch," said Frank, laughing.

"I don't mind cooking," said Dave.

Scott poked Dave on the arm, "I didn't know you could cook.

If I had known that I would have married you."

"Get away from me," laughed Dave. "You haven't been out to sea long enough to like men."

"Come on, be serious. Let's make a rule that everyone at the end of the day takes their belongings down to their stateroom," said Betty. "That way we won't have a constant mess in the cockpit and deck. With seven people onboard, it's important that we pick up after ourselves."

Frank added, "Not only that, but if things are left on deck they could blow overboard, or someone could trip on it."

"I'll clean Bob's and my stateroom, the salon and galley. You men can clean your staterooms and heads. Is that a deal?" asked Betty. Everyone agreed.

Scott stood up and stretched, then walked to the companion way. "Guess I'll turn in. I want to catch some shut eye before my watch."

Betty threw his shirt at him, "Whoa, wait a minute, don't forget your clothes."

"We're off to a good start," laughed Scott as he picked up his shoes and shirt.

Soon the rest of the crew drifted down to their bunks, clearing the area of their belongings.

Betty and Bob still had two hours to go before their watch was over. The boat was on automatic pilot and Betty was reading a book while Bob checked the charts. It was quiet and peaceful now that the crew had gone to bed.

Betty put her book down and looked up at the sky. "Look how clear it is, the stars seem so close I can almost touch them."

Bob looked up. "God, I love sailing. I feel so free. This is something I've always wanted to do—burn all my bridges and just go. Let's walk out to the stern, we'll see how many celestial groups we can name. Look . . . there's the big dipper," Bob said, as they sat down on the deck.

Betty pointed to a group of stars, "And there's Orion's Belt."

"That's not Orion's Belt. Orion's Belt is over here," said Bob.

"I'll bet I'm right," Betty said in a teasing voice.

The full moon stood out in the dark sky like glistening armor, lighting the deck with a bluish, silvery glow.

She snuggled close to him. "Is it going to be this romantic

and peaceful all the time?"

"Well—hopefully most of the time. The August winds should be moderate going across the Atlantic, all the way to Spain."

They strolled out to the bow, and Bob put his arms around her, holding her close. The night air was cool as the gentle breeze fanned their face. He kissed her forehead, then her lips, and stroking her hair softly, he said, "Are you glad you came along?"

"If you had asked me that question while I was fixing dinner, I don't know what my answer would have been. But now—yes. I am glad I came along."

They sat close together on the bow, staring over the horizon it was like being in another world. Betty leaned her head on his shoulder as she said, "Everyone's asleep."

"Yes, and we are out here on the bow where no one can hear us," he said as he kissed her passionately. Gently, he reached under her blouse and released her bra and his hand cupped her soft breast as their lips met again. The boat was on autopilot, sailing smoothly through the water. Nothing else seemed to matter except their few private moments. Betty reached down to unzip Bob's pants when they heard a voice from the cockpit.

"Grandma, where are you? It's too hot to sleep downstairs and I'm not feeling good." Betty started to giggle and couldn't stop, "What timing!"

They went back to the cockpit where Greg had dragged his pillow and sheet. He was lying on the bench half-asleep. Betty sat beside him and brushed the hair off his sweaty forehead, and gently kissed him. He seemed so small lying there in the dark.

"What were you laughing at, Grandma?" yawned Greg.

"Hush," whispered Betty. "Go to sleep. I love you so much."

Bob was standing on the side deck watching her. Greg had fallen asleep. He whispered, "Let's walk out to the stern." He took her hand to help her, and they sat on the deck box.

"Oh well," Betty sighed. "So much for a little time alone, I have a feeling there will be very little privacy on this trip."

One by one, the rest of the crew came up complaining about the heat in their cabins. They searched to find a flat surface in the breeze, even sleeping on sail bags and piles of lines, as they settled down .

Frank relieved Betty and Bob from their watch at eleven

and they retired to their stateroom.

"It's hot in here, but it's bearable," said Bob.

He watched Betty while she adjusted her pillow, as he said, "I'm sorry you had such a tough time in the galley."

"It was a tough introduction to cooking. Goodnight, honey," she said as she leaned over to kiss him.

Bob pulled her on top of him. "Let's finish what we started earlier."

"The hatch is open." Betty said, pointing up over their bed. "It's right next to the cockpit. Frank and Mitch might hear us."

"Well, stop talking and be quiet," he said as he pressed his lips to hers. Their lovemaking was enhanced by the gentle rock of *Destiny*.

They slept peacefully until two A.M. when they were jarred awake by strong winds. *Destiny* had shifted into the rough motion of a wild bronco. Bob could hear Frank taking in the sails.

"Reef the genoa and mizzen, Mitch. Okay now, reef the mainsail," Frank said, keeping *Destiny* under control.

The winds rose to forty knots, blowing against the bow, and the seas picked up forming ten-foot white caps. The boat slammed down hard each time it rose up on the waves.

Betty shut her eyes. Gripping the sheet, in fright she prayed for morning to come.

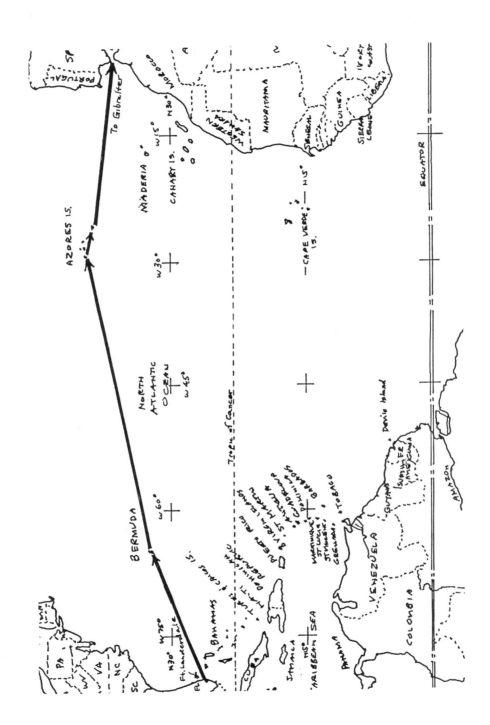

Six

By six the next morning, there was not a breeze to be felt, the sails lay limp in the still air, and *Destiny* had calmed to a gentle rock. Bob came up for his morning watch, letting Betty sleep in.

When he checked the wind and speed gauges, they were only going two knots, and he turned the engine on . Then he winched in the genoa and mizzen, leaving the mainsail up to help stabilize the boat. The next two days were uneventful, the wind was still and *Destiny* was motoring along at a leisurely six knots, as the days dragged on, the sweltering, hot August sun drained the energy from everyone. The only thing that saved them from burning was the bimini top that was over the cockpit.

Soon, it was five o'clock, cocktail time. Dave sipped his cool orange juice and vodka, and with disappointment in his voice said, "Do you realize we have only traveled two hundred and sixty miles in two days. We still have seven hundred and forty-two miles to go."

"This is a damn long trip," said Mitch sighing. "If this weather keeps up we won't be there in a week. It will take two weeks."

"Don't say that. I'll be bonkers if I have to take this rocking for two weeks," said Scott.

"Never mind the bitching and complaining," said Frank. "What are you, a bunch of sissies? Pay attention to the magnificent sunset. Hey, Greg, get me another drink."

Greg didn't answer; he laid there almost in a stupor.

Betty went over to him. "You look like you're drugged. Must be from the seasick patch, let me take it off of you," she said pulling it from behind his ear. I think a whole patch is too strong for you." Greg just grunted.

In a couple of hours, Greg became more alert, but every time he sat up, he was sick. Since laying down was the only thing that helped, he spent most of his time on his back. He continued to throw up the first helping of his dinner, but managed to keep down the second.

Each time Greg got sick, Scott and Dave would tease him, "There goes Technicolor Yawn again."

Two more days passed and there was still no change in the windless days. *Destiny* was barely moving, and even with their odd jobs to do, the crew was restless. Bob became worried about the amount of fuel they were using, and turned the motor off. *Destiny*'s gentle cradle rock now became an exaggerated rock, without the motor propelling her through the water. The motion was getting on Betty's nerves, along with the boredom. She missed the intimacy of her family and the mental activity of her job.

There was very little to do except clean up after the men and she was tired of doing that. She always paid someone to clean her house. Now here she was cleaning up after slobs. *She wouldn't mind so much if they helped,* she thought, *but they always said they were too busy. Yeah, too busy doing nothing.*

Scott was sitting on the railing of the cockpit looking out at the ocean. "Look at all that water and we can't go in and cool off."

Greg sat up from his bench, "Let's go for a swim. Come on you guys, let's do it." He was so excited he almost jumped over board.

"Calm down," Betty said, grabbing him by the pants. "You're not going anywhere unless Bob says so."

Bob looked out at the sea, and with a chuckle he said. "I don't know—right now we're in the Bermuda Triangle. I'm sure you've heard the horrible stories about boats and crew vanishing, never to be heard of again."

Dave pulled his shirt off revealing his muscular, tanned body. He looked over at Bob and said, "Who believes stories like that? Come on Bob, let's go for a swim."

Bob looked at the inviting water and said, "Okay. I'll heave to and let you go in. There's no wind so we won't drift far. Frank, you get the rifle out and take shark watch."

Frank came strutting out with a semi-automatic Ruger cocked and ready.

"Jesus Christ, look at that weapon. What else do you have aboard?" asked Dave.

"A shotgun and a pistol. We need them for uninvited guests," answered Bob.

Dave was surprised. "You have a regular arsenal, do you know how to handle them?"

"Bet your ass we do. Betty and I went to a rifle range for training." Bob answered as he went out on the bow where Scott and Greg were stripping off their shirts. Dave was balancing on the railing, ready to dive in. "Now, listen to me. No one, and I mean no one swims far from the boat."

Before Bob finished his sentence, everyone was diving off the boat into the refreshing deep blue water. It was a tonic to their bodies and spirits, and it felt good to be active again. The group splashed around, enjoying the cool water. When they dove deep, the blue color became almost black and the depth of the water seemed endless. They floated on top of the water, laughing and magnifying the stories of the Bermuda Triangle. Each visualizing boats found with no one aboard, drifting silently through the fog. Everyone was being so brave outwardly, but no one was going very far from the ladder.

Dave climbed to the top of the mast and edged himself out to the end of the spreaders that stiffen the mast. He dove off, letting out a loud Tarzan yell.

"Please don't do that again. Suppose you hit the boat, you'd kill yourself," Betty pleaded as he climbed back onboard.

Climbing back up the mast, he said, "I'll be all right, I've dove from fifty feet before."

There was a sound of material ripping and Greg looked up and started to laugh, "Dave, you ripped your shorts, your jewels are showing."

Dave's shorts were flying in the air and his "jewels" as Greg called them, were fully exposed. Everyone was laughing, but it didn't seem to bother Dave and he dove back into the water. Greg ran to the mast and started to climb up. "I'm going to do that."

"Not while I'm around," Betty said grabbing him by the arm and pulling him down.

He pulled away and as he jumped back into the water, he yelled, "You're treating me like a baby."

"There's something over port side," yelled Frank. "It's something big floating or swimming toward us."

In two seconds flat, everyone was out of the water. Afraid it might be a shark or worse yet, a ghost-boat from the Bermuda Triangle.

"Let me take a look," said Scott taking the binoculars. "It's large enough to be a shark. It looks like two sharks swimming towards us. Can't see them now, they disappeared."

Suddenly three dark long forms were swimming along side *Destiny*. Three gray stiff fins stuck out of the water.

Mitch looked over the side, "Damn, look at that! They must be at least eight feet long. Good thing we got out of the water when we did. We'd of been shark bait."

"Are you sure they're not dolphins?" questioned Frank.

Mitch got annoyed. "Hey, look for yourself. I never saw dolphins that big."

Surprisingly enough, the sharks provided entertainment for everyone onboard. Greg got the worst of it, as Scott and Dave teased him and said they were going to throw the Technicolor Yawn overboard. The sharks trailed alongside *Destiny* for three hours before swimming off. "Good thing I took the shark watch," said Frank sitting on the stern. "Think what might of happened if I didn't spot the sharks with my eagle eye."

"All right hero, stop bragging," said Scott laughing.

Dave came up from the salon and stood in front of the lounging crew, "Okay, everybody quiet, I have the mileage we made since we left Ft. Lauderdale. So far, we've sailed four hundred and eighty miles in three days and we still have five hundred and twenty miles to go."

Groans were heard from the group. "I can't believe it's only been three days. Are you sure you counted right?" asked Scott.

"Count it yourself. We left Ft. Lauderdale on Monday and this is Wednesday."

Betty walked out on deck, towels, shoes and shirts were strewn all over. "Hey, nobody's picking up their things, look at this mess."

"You don't see anything of mine lying around out there," said Frank.

"No, because you weren't swimming. Look at all the shirts and shoes lying around. Who does this belong to?" she said, picking up shorts and shirt and throwing them into the cockpit. "Who left the empty beer and soda cans? Were you all born in a pig sty?"

"Here, take your dirty shirt and put it away," said Scott throwing it at Greg.

"That's not mine," said Greg throwing it at Mitch.

They tossed things around until one fell overboard. "I don't think you're taking this seriously, you have to put your things away," said Betty.

The men snickered and laughed. Disgusted, she walked away, leaving their clothes on the deck They were still lying there when Betty went on watch that night. She could see the wind blowing them closer to the edge of the deck, so Betty went out on the bow and picked them up.

She dropped the pile on the bench in the cockpit and sighed, "Darn it, Bob, I wish they would pick their clothes up. I hate seeing this beautiful boat looking like a pig sty. In three days they managed to get oil, food and soda all over the cushions. Their clothes, cans and candy wrappers are left both in the cockpit and in the salon."

"Do you think the spots will come off?" Bob asked, rubbing his hand along the cushions.

Betty sat there fuming for awhile, then she continued, "They need to be told that I am not their maid. I can make Greg do it, but not the others. Can't you talk to them?"

"I have to say they're not the neatest group," answered Bob. "I'll talk to them in the morning." Betty folded the clothes, then picked up the crew's sneakers and went downstairs, putting them outside their staterooms.

When she went back on deck, she walked out and sat on the stern deck. The sky was clear and bright with stars. Betty called out, "Bob, come back here and sit by me. I need some tenderness."

Bob sat next to her with his arms around her, and together they kept watch for ships that might be passing in the night.

Dave woke up at midday. He showered and dressed in clean shorts and shirt. He was meticulous about his clothes and cleaned his boat-shoes everyday. He hated to wear anything that had a stain on it. Walking out to the stern with his coffee, he reached for his fishing rod. The coffee splashed on his shorts. "Look what I've done, why am I always so clumsy? Now I'll have to change my pants."

"Stop worrying about your pants and start catching some fish. You and Scott put those fishing lines out two days ago and you haven't caught our dinner yet," teased Bob.

Defending himself, Dave said, "We've had bites, and two fish broke loose just as we were pulling them in."

Frank loved to tease and he said, "How big were those little fish?"

"Little fish!" Scott jumped up and held his arms way out. "The fish were at least fifty pounds."

"The fish get bigger every time you talk about them," laughed Mitch. "The one I saw was only twelve inches."

Dave had a wet rag, and was trying to rub out the stain on his shorts, "No way," he added, "one was almost five feet long."

"I'm tired of these fish stories," said Frank. "It's my night to cook and I'm going to fix the best meal you ever had with or without fish."

Betty watched Frank as he stood up and stretched his short stocky body. His neck was thick and his broad shoulders were built for a taller man. He worked out at the gym when he wasn't sailing and it showed in his muscular arms. Betty thought he looked like a Greek warrior, especially with that grayish-black beard and mustache.

"Glad it's not my night to cook," said Betty. "What are you cooking tonight, Frank?"

"You think I'm going to tell you? You wouldn't tell me."

She laughed and stretched out on the bench, "As long as it's not that gummy cornmeal."

Tired of sitting around, Betty cleaned their stateroom, galley and salon. She had no intention of cleaning the men's staterooms.

Bob was reading when he felt a whisper of a breeze. He sat up and called, "Scott, put the genoa and stay-sail up. I'll get the mizzen. The sails might catch the wind and maybe we can pick up a knot or two."

"Aye aye, sir," shouted Scott in jest as he gave Bob a salute. Then he set the sails.

The smell of the food from the galley lingered through the cockpit, they didn't know what Frank was fixing but it smelled delicious. He rang the dinner bell and called out, "Food's on, come and get it."

The men rushed down the steps and filled their plates like starving creatures. When they finished their food, they returned for more.

Mitch went down below and when he returned Scott was in his seat and his book was on the floor.

"For Christ's sake! Did you throw my book on the deck?" roared Mitch, "you lost my fucking page."

"Then don't put the damn book on the seat when you leave," Scott fired back.

Mitch stood with his hands on his hips, legs spread apart, "Shit man, I only went down to the head to take a piss."

"Yeah, well you're pissing me off right now," said Scott getting to his feet.

Mitch lifted his shoulders and stared straight at Scott. "Well, big mouth, do you want to do something about it?"

Scott was in ready stance, his arms out from his side. "Yeah, I do. You've been pissing me off ever since we came on board."

Bob looked up from his book, "Hey, cut out the arguing. I have enough on my mind without listening to you two bicker. Mitch, there's a water pump that needs changing. Hop to it."

Mitch went down below mumbling to himself. Later, he went out on the bow and sat staring at the sea. Betty watched him for awhile. There was a sad expression on his face. She knew something was bothering him. He had never acted so hostile before.

She went out and sat beside him and gave him a friendly hug. "What's the matter, don't you feel well? You seem grouchy today."

He turned his head away and said, "I miss Diane. I'm so lonely for her."

Betty didn't know how to help him, she had that lonely feeling herself. "Why don't you call her on the ship to shore radio? That might help you feel better."

"I tried last night but I couldn't get through. Those damn cruise ships hog the air waves. I hate it out here. It's too lonely."

Betty's voice went soft. "I thought this was what you

wanted, to sail around the world?"

Tears ran down his cheeks, and he let out a big sigh, "I know what I said, but I hate it. It's not for me."

"Well, try calling her again you might be successful." Betty stood up and took his hand. "Come below, Greg's watching a movie and it's pretty good."

Mitch shook his head no. "I'm going to bed."

Late the next day, Frank was sitting at the helm talking to Betty, it was cocktail hour.

"What are you in such deep thought about?" asked Betty.

Frank stared out at the horizon. "I'm just reminiscing about my trip around the horn."

"Why didn't you go the easy way—west to east? The winds would have been behind you and it would have been much safer," asked Betty.

"Anyone can do it the easy way. I wanted to fight that wind, head right into it, and I did it all by myself. Only stopped for water, food and fuel when I needed it."

Bob joined them in the cockpit. "Your thirty-eight foot boat must have seemed awful small out here, especially with only eighteen inches of freeboard."

"Yep, and all I could think of was getting back to my wife. Only thing is when I got back she had a boy friend, and that's another story."

Bob jumped up, "Hot diggity, the wind's changing. You can tell us that story tonight. Right now, lets get the sails trimmed."

Destiny glided effortlessly on the following wind as the wind increased to twenty knots. They moved at a rapid pace, making up for lost time. They felt their luck had changed when the high winds continued through the next day and into the night. Tiny cells of phosphorescence lit up the wake as they sailed peacefully through the night, getting closer to Bermuda.

By morning, the winds were calm again. All sails were down except for the main sail. *Destiny* was rocking like the rolly polly clown Betty use to have as a child. It was a sad fat clown that had an exaggerated rock from side to side. *Destiny* made her feel just like the sad clown as she rocked with the boat. Her stomach was upset, but she tried to clean the boat anyway. It was an endless task. The crew left their things everywhere along with crumbs and spills to clean up. Frank and Bob were the only ones that put anything away.

"I've had six days of bitching and nagging and I'm tired of picking up after you men," Betty said as she kicked their clothes into a pile. "From now on I'm going to throw them overboard." When no one answered, she shouted louder, "Did you hear me?"

"Yes we heard you," said Scott. "Just leave them there we'll pick them up later. We're playing cards."

She walked away disgusted and sat out on the stern, talking to herself, trying the therapy she used at home. "The waves are driving me nuts, pounding endlessly against the boat. I can't stand this rocking anymore," she half-screamed. Betty laid down on the deck, using a sail bag for a pillow, and tried to relax but she felt like she was in a washing machine. Her body swayed back and forth, back and forth. She searched for a flat, still place to lie down, but it was impossible to find. "Everything moves and shifts, nothing's ever still," she moaned.

The smallest movement took so much effort, and each time she got up she had to think of what she could grab to keep her balance. Nervous tension built inside her and she felt she was about to explode.

Rushing to her stateroom, she fell across the bed sobbing. Out of frustration she beat the mattress with her fist and cried, "What am I doing here anyhow? Why did I come on this damn trip? I can't take it anymore. I don't know if I love Bob enough to go on. If I leave, I know it will be the end of our relationship. I just want off this fucking boat." Saying that word shocked her, "Oh my God, I'm cussing like the men now."

"Betty, who are you talking to?" called Bob. "Are you all right?"

"Yes, I'm all right. I just came down to take a shower," she lied. She didn't want him to know how upset she was. Bob had enough to handle just getting them all safely to Bermuda. She'd work out her own problems. She laid there until the nervous tension subsided. "I'll feel better after I shower."

Betty stepped into the tub and quickly sat down, afraid of getting thrown against the bathroom wall. The cool water soothed her. Then she applied a litle makeup and perfume. *It's funny how a good cry soothes the soul*, she thought as she hung on to the rail, making her way up to the deck.

As she stepped on deck, Greg said, "Phew, you smell awful. You're wearing too much perfume."

Betty's feelings were hurt. "Don't be so fresh! I only put a drop on."

"You always put too much on," said Greg.

Betty looked at Scott. "Is that true?"

Scott's face turned pink, "Well—you kind of overtake the boat."

Indignant, she asked, "Why didn't someone say something before?"

At first, nobody answered, then Frank said, "Odors are much stronger at sea. The air is pure and fresh, and any scent is magnified threefold. You notice how great my cooking smells, don't you?"

"Yeah, even though it tastes terrible, it smells good," she said laughing. "Now that I know I smell like a floozy, I'll go wash it off."

When she went down to her stateroom, water was flooding the floor. "Bob," she yelled. "Come down here, water's pouring out from under the bed."

Bob rushed down and pulled up the mattress and bed-board. He looked down at the water running out from a tangle of pipes. "One of the pipes is leaking," he said. "It will be a bitch to find the right one."

They lugged the mattress and bed-board into the galley and Frank crawled into the limited space. They searched as the water continued to leak in.

"Mitch, check the bilge pumps. Make sure they are still working and can handle all this water," called Bob.

A half-hour later they found a loose valve and were able to take care of the problem.

"After that tough job, I deserve a drink," said Frank, helping himself to the bourbon. "Who's cooking tonight?"

"It's my turn," said Dave. "I have a big meal planned."

It didn't take long for the galley to become unbearably hot. With the motion of the boat, Dave felt sick and headed for the rail.

"Stay up here in the air," said Frank. "I'll take care of dinner."

"No," said Dave looking peaked, "I'm all right. I'll cook."

Finally, the food was ready and after Dave rang the dinner bell, he ran up the stairs. Hanging over the railing, he retched again and again until there was nothing left to come up. Holding his stomach, he let the cool wind blow in his yellowish-green face. The crew ignored him and rushed below in a starving frenzy. Ham, mashed potatoes, and cabbage were waiting below. They quickly filled their plates.

Dave lay on deck sucking in the fresh air until he felt well enough to go down for his dinner. When he came up the stairs, he was balancing a full plate in one hand and a glass of iced tea in the other. At that moment *Destiny* heeled over to the port side and Dave lost his balance and fell forward on his knees. His tea splashed all over the cockpit and his face went on to his plate. When he lifted his head the mashed potatoes had covered his nose and mouth.

"Shit, shit, shit," he screamed

The sight of Dave's face covered with mashed potatoes sent the crew into hysterics.

Still laughing, Frank went to help him. "You really put yourself into your dinner don't you?"

That cracked Betty up as she said, "Can you breathe with potatoes stuffed in your nose? I'll get a cloth to wipe your face."

"No, Goddamnit, I'll clean it myself. I made the mess and I'll clean it," he said stamping back down to the galley.

When he came back up the stairs, Betty went over to help. "We're sorry, we didn't mean to laugh. It's just—you looked so funny."

A ten knot breeze rose, and Bob stepped over the spilled food and let the sails out.

It was time for Bob and Betty's watch. The skies had darkened. Soon, one by one, the crew headed down the companion way to get some sleep before their watch.

"Whoa, wait a minute. Don't forget your things," said Bob.

Mitch kicked Scott's shirt aside, and grabbed his shirt and shoes.

Scott's face hardened, "You didn't have to do that! My shirt almost went overboard."

"They were in my way," snarled Mitch.

"What do you have a bug up your ass or something? Look, I don't need this bullshit. You got a problem,man?" asked Scott.

"Yeah the captain's son gets away with everything," sulked Mitch.

Hearing the commotion, Bob called out, "What's going on?"

Mitch looked defiant at Scott, waiting to see what he'd say. "Nothing's going on," said Scott, as he grabbed his clothes and headed for the stairs.

Greg followed close behind and whispered, "Why didn't you bop him one? He's been itching for a fight. I'd help you."

Dave walked out on the bow with Mitch. "What's eating you? How come you're always such a grouch?"

"I want to get the hell off this boat. I miss Diane so much. I don't want to be without her."

"A word of advice, buddy, don't take it out on Scott. If you do, you'll be in big trouble with everyone," said Dave as they went down to their staterooms.

Betty woke to the sound of the sails being jibed. She heard Bob saying they were changing to a starboard tack and to bring the boom over carefully. She lay there until *Destiny*'s sails were shifted from port to starboard. Once the task was accomplished, she felt it was safe to get out of bed.

Dave was still up from his four-to-seven A.M. shift and as Betty came up ondeck, he had a big smile on his face. "What are you grinning about?" asked Betty.

"We're two days away from Bermuda," he said with a big grin on his face. The mood of the crew changed dramatically.

Even Mitch was smiling as he said, "I was able to get a call through to Diane last night on my watch. She still loves me and she might meet me in Spain when we get there."

"Well, let's hope that puts you in a better mood," said Betty.

"Yeah, the days are long enough without seeing you constantly moping. You know Mitch, you're not the only one with a girlfriend waiting for them," said Scott.

"Hey guys, get busy with your hands instead of your mouths," said Bob sensing the hostility. "Scott, you go polish the bright work and Mitch you can turn the water-maker on and fill the tanks." The wind had died down again and Bob turned on the engine and winched in the sails.

The daily ritual at five o'clock was to watch the sunset and that day the sky was slashed with shades of pink. It seemed to cast a spell of tranquillity over everyone as they sat anticipating the first sight of land.

As the night darkened and everyone was asleep, it was Bob and Betty's watch and Betty sat in the cockpit peering up at the starlit sky. There seemed to be thousands of stars washed across the heavens, like diamonds on a black velvet cloth. All the lights were off on the ship except for the mast and running lights; creating a dark fantasy world. The thought of making love under the stars flared her sexual desires and she moved closer to Bob and hugged him. They sat close together, neither speaking for awhile, then Betty kissed his neck softly. Nibbling on his ear, she ran her hands under his shirt and teasingly stroked his stomach, then slowly her fingers inched under his waistband.

"Whoa, wait a minute, let me put the autopilot on," he said as he pushed the switch.

Betty pulled him down on the bench-seat and kissed him passionately as she undressed him.

"Are you sure everyone's asleep?" murmured Bob as his hand unbuttoned her blouse.

"Yes, I'm sure," her lips brushed against his as they spoke, and she felt his eager response. She drew herself closer to him as his hands rubbed the bare skin of her back and shoulders. Their bodies locked together, then moved in a wild frenzy. Their sighs and squeals of passion were covered by the sound of the engine. The cool breeze softly dried the perspiration on their naked bodies. They were in a world of stirring vibrations and the sound of the waves rushing by, created tantalizing background music. Their romantic interludes happen occasionally when the boat wasn't swaying roughly, and when they were sure everyone was asleep.

Seven

Sleepy-eyed, she climbed the steps for her morning watch. She looked up at the dismal, heavy laden cloudy sky.

"Morning, hope you slept better than I did," said Bob. "Looks like a squall is heading our way."

"Those clouds really look horrendous. Is this just a rainstorm or is it something I should be afraid of?" she asked apprehensively.

Bob smiled, "No, it's just a squall, nothing that we can't handle. Relax."

"How come that doesn't makes me feel better? I don't like the looks of those black clouds."

Bob put on a sneaky grin and said, "Trust me, baby, we can handle it. You have nothing to fear with me around."

"Yeah, sure. The mighty Captain Godfrey will protect me from all harm," she said laughing. Then, she looked out at the bow. "Look at all the fish on deck. How did they get onboard?"

"They're flying fish. They get caught up in the waves and end up getting washed on deck," said Bob. "It happens during the night."

Betty was astonished, "I'll count them as I throw them overboard, then I'll take the helm and give you a break."

When she walked out on the bow, she tripped over Mitch's shoes, and almost fell. *Darn it, the deck's a mess and so is the cockpit. They even leave things lying around when they're on watch. I'm leaving everything here. If they get washed overboard, it's not my problem.* "Look," she said holding a shirt up. "It's soaking wet." She walked along the deck throwing the fish overboard as she counted. "There's twelve fish, and they smell terrible, the sun's doing a real job on them."

Bob laughed, "Scott said he got hit with one while he was sitting at the helm last night."

"You're kidding? That must have surprised him. Hey, here's

another one. My final count is thirteen," she said, as she threw the last fish overboard.

A strong wind swirled across the bow and through the open windshield of the cockpit. Heavy sheets of rain covered *Destiny* as she picked up incredible speed from the force of the wind. Betty hurried back to the safety of the cockpit. Mitch crawled out of bed as soon as he felt the wind change and was busy reefing the sails down.

"Trim the genoa and pull the main in half-way," Bob said to Mitch. "Okay, now trim the mizzen. That's enough, that's great."

Bob kept the boat under control as they sailed along at ten knots, with a thirty knot wind blowing fiercely around them. Their first real squall gave Betty an adrenaline rush. She was frightened at first and ran below. Her first thoughts were to get life jackets and grab Gregory. Then she peeked out the companionway and watched how Bob was reacting to the situation.

He showed no fear and when he saw her, he laughed, "Come on up, you big sissy. You'll be all right. Just sit down and hold on."

A wave of excitement and fear went through her as she heard the wind howling across the boat. The ride was wild and she kept her feet braced to keep from being thrown off the seat. Then she said, "*Destiny* is so little in this immense ocean. She's like a floating log easy for the waves to toss around."

Greg came running up. "What's happening, is the boat going to sink?"

Betty grabbed him and held him next to her. Their combined weight helped hold them steady on the seat. "It's just a rainstorm, we'll be fine," she said, not really convinced herself.

After an hour of drenching, the gods above changed the weather channel. The sun came out, quickly drying the decks and cushions. They were once again back to light winds.

Feeling sure the winds would stay calm now, Betty went down to the galley to do some baking. What little bread they had left was moldy. The ingredients were organized on the counter and she started to prepare the dough. Without warning, the waves and wind began to build again and *Destiny* became a thrashing machine. Desperately, she tried to keep everything on the counter, but the flour container slid off and spilled on the floor. The flour rose up like a white cloud and covered her. While she was still holding on to things, two of the upper cabinet doors flew open. Five pounds of sugar came hurling across the room, narrowly missing Betty's head. She ducked and swerved to keep from getting hit and in frustration she let out a scream, "Someone come help me."

Mitch came running down, took one look at her and laughed. "You look like a ghost."

Working together, they grabbed the things off the counter and placed them in the sink. Shaken from the experience, and feeling sick from the motion she said, "I'm getting out of here," and ran up to the cockpit.

The storm thrashed for another hour, and again the wind shifted, and was calm again. A multicolor rainbow arched across the sky, coloring the raindrops glistening on *Destiny*—a welcoming sign that all was clear.

"Bob, do you think it's safe to go down in the galley?" asked Betty. "I want to bake bread, but I don't want to go through that again."

Bob looked at the radar screen, "It looks all clear. I think the storm has passed now."

She went down to the galley and before long, the scent of fresh baked bread and cinnamon buns sent out a tantalizing aroma that weaved its way up to the cockpit. Moans and groans of anticipation came from above.

"The buns are done," called Betty. "The bread's still in the oven."

Suddenly there was hands all around her as the crew grabbed the cinnamon buns and devoured them. She couldn't believe they disappeared so fast. "All that work and they're gone already. Thanks guys, for leaving me one," said Betty sarcastically.

At five P.M., during happy hour, they sat around watching for the elusive green flash that could sometime occurs when the sun goes down. Bob had been telling stories about the green flash since the trip started but they hadn't seen it yet.

"The sun's over the yardarm so I've fixed myself a drink," Bob said, as he came up the steps with an Absolut® and orange juice in his hand. "Ah, I'm ready for a little nectar to soothe the soul."

He tripped on the top step, and his drink fell out of his hand. Grumbling, he made a second drink. As he sat down he lost his balance. Half of it splashed on his lap. "Goddamnit," he said in anger.

"Sit down," Betty said, laughing so hard it was hard to talk. "I'll fix one for you."

She brought up his third drink. Carefully, she placed it in his hands and he sat back and put his feet up, ready for a cool sip.

"Ah, this is more like it. This is what I call sailing," he said, raising his arm to take the first cold sip. His arm hit the companionway door, splashing the drink all over his shirt.

"Damnit, I don't believe I've done it again," he yelled in frustration.

"What's the matter, Captain, can't hold your liquor?" asked Frank.

Bob stood up and brushed his dripping shirt with his hand. "I don't know what you're all laughing about, look at my clothes. They're all wet."

"Dad, I didn't know you were providing the entertainment tonight," said Scott.

"I'm sorry you're upset. Should I get you a bib?" asked Frank.

Bob was furious, "No Goddammit, I need a drink."

"Let me try my luck," said Dave as he went below.

They all watched in anticipation as Bob took his first sip.

"Well, looks like that drink's a winner. The old man looks like he finally learned how to bend the elbow right," said Frank propping his feet up on the bench across from Bob. "Did I ever tell you about my trip around the horn?"

"Time and time again, we don't want to hear it again," they all said in unison.

Frank stood up, as if teaching a class, his hands in motion. "No, I mean the first time I went around. Like I said . . ."

"We know," mimicked Scott. "You had to do it the hard way. Anyone can do it the easy way."

Frank continued, "Anyhow, the second time I went around

83

the horn, it was with two other people, Tom and his girlfriend Liz. We were both in love with her, and she kept us both happy. Rough as hell out there but she knew how to keep us happy. We took turns at the helm and then we took turns with her. That girl could steer a course as well as I could. Man, when we sailed into that wind, we thought we were going to be blown out of the water. The waves came up higher than the mast and would bury us in water."

"If it was that wild, how did you ever make it back?" Betty asked in jest.

"By the skin of my teeth, I'm a tough old salt," said Frank. "Nothing overtakes me. Well, if we're going to eat tonight, I better get below and finish the Irish stew I'm making." He headed below with his drink in his hand.

Dinner was interrupted by another squall that was heading straight for them. It started with light rains, increasing to a ferocious whipping deluge. Grabbing their slickers to keep dry, they gathered around the colored radar screen to look at the storm.

"Look at the size of that storm. It's yellow with a lot of red in the middle, looks like Pac-Man," said Betty, trying not to show how frightened she felt.

Bob turned the wheel hard to starboard, "I'm going to try to steer away from the squall. The red in the middle is the center of the storm and the redder it is the meaner. I don't want to take any chances, so you men get ready to help handle the sails. We might have to take them all down in a hurry."

Dave was looking over Betty's shoulder, "It looks like its heading right for us. Can we get away from it in time?"

Bob tugged at the wheel. "It all depends on whether I can steer around it. We 'll need a bit of luck."

The winds were whipping the sails, threatening to tear them loose. Mitch and Frank reefed in the mizzen, stay sail and genoa, leaving the main half-way up. Bob kept steering to starboard, changing their course away from the red monster. Betty and Greg were frightened but fascinated, as they watched the mark of the boat on radar.

"Look! Look. There's another one way over on the right side of the screen," said Betty with panic in her voice. "What are we going to do?"

"Damn, let me take a look," said Bob. "I'm going to try and steer between the two squalls. Mitch—Frank, jibe the main sail to port."

The wind had reached forty knots and the waves were bigger than Betty had ever seen before. The rain pelted down in a flooding stream. Everyone's eyes were glued to the action on radar. It seemed as if Bob was playing a video game of true life. They were absorbed in the storms as they watched their captain maneuver *Destiny*. They could see the squalls speeding towards them.

"Are the storms going to get us?" Greg asked, as he cuddled closer to Betty.

"If they get us, we're in for one hell of a rough time," answered Frank. "If we're able to keep away from them, the worst we'll get is strong winds and rain from the tail."

"We can handle that situation," said Bob. "But the other— Well, I hope we don't have to find out."

The rain beat into the cockpit flooding the floor, and the sucking noise of the drain pulling the water out, added to the eerie sounds. Battling the wind for two hours, *Destiny* was heeled twenty degrees on the starboard-side, washing her deck deep into the water. Bracing themselves, they held on as the boat rode the rough sea. A maverick wave splashed high in the air and washed over Bob, knocking him sideways and drenching everyone.

"Goddammit, when is this thing letting up?" Bob yelled, getting back behind the helm.

Keeping the boat oncourse was difficult at times and the force of the wind tried hard to suck the boat into the center of the storm. *Destiny* quivered with each lunge of the waves.

"Look, it's clearing ahead. Yahoo, go for it Bob," called Scott.

"By God, I think we're finally getting out of this mess," said Frank giving a sigh of relief.

Greg beat his fists on the seat. "We sure beat up on those two stormy monsters."

When they were close to the clearing, the winds seemed to calm down to a whisper and the rain eased to a sprinkle, giving them false security. Suddenly a cloud shaped like a tiger's tail, thrust across the sky in front of *Destiny*.

"I think we spoke too soon. I wonder why that didn't show up on the radar?" Bob asked, as he started to change course again.

He was too late. *Destiny* was under the end of the tail and clouds burst all around them, in what seemed like never ending rain. The wind lashed at the boat; the last thrust of the defeated monsters. *Destiny*'s bow rose high on the immense waves, then slapped down in a hard thrust. Their life game had become frightening, yet exhilarating. Bob had a firm hold on the wheel, forcing the boat to stay on course. He sailed straight for the clear sky ahead, hoping it was closer than it looked. Another half-hour passed until they were in the clearing and all that was left was a mild breeze and drizzling rain.

Betty was fascinated by Bob's confidence and the way he handled *Destiny*. "I'm so proud of you," she said as she kissed him. "You got us through the storms."

"Don't I get a hug too?" asked Frank. "I did the directing."

"Greg, give Frank a hug," said Scott.

Making a face, Greg said, "Yuck, no way."

Frank went down to finish dinner and came right back up. "We have a quite a few leaks in the salon. The books are all wet and the stereo and VCR are sitting in puddles."

Bob scratched his head in contemplation. "Wonder where the water's getting in? Mitch, see if the water's getting in through the scuppers on deck."

Mitch checked the six scuppers that let air down into the cabins. "They're closed. Everything looks okay. As soon as things dry up a bit, I'll caulk around the bases."

The salon was a watery mess, counters and tables were covered with pools of water and most of the books were soaked. Betty and Frank disconnected the VCR and stereo, wiping them dry.

"I hope they still work," said Frank. "Looks like the TV's dry."

When they finished, Betty went out on the bow, needing some space alone. The serene ocean that had been so untamed a while ago was like a sheet of glass, only a ripple now and then from a jumping fish. The sky was mosaic with pink, orange, and blue streaks across the fluffy cumulus clouds. The sea was so unpredictable and she was afraid of it, yet it, mystified her. She loved to feel the cool sea breeze on her face and blow through her hair. She leaned over the deck, letting the fine salt spray splash against her arm. Then she sat back in a lotus position ready to meditate in the silence. Taking deep breaths she could smell the briny salt air, as her mind began to float away in deep relaxation.

When she was finished, she went below and saw Frank looking all around the electronic equipment. "What are you looking for? Is something wrong?"

"I keep hearing a small alarm. It keeps going on and off. I'm trying to find out where the damn thing's coming from."

"Did you say you hear an alarm?" asked Bob and he joined in the search.

"I've been looking for the fucking thing for an hour," said Frank.

Betty went up to the helm seat. It was Frank's watch and the autopilot was on. She could hear the beeping sound and it seemed close. Betty thought it sounded like the bilge alarms, but it was a quicker sound. Mitch always drank coffee from a musical cup that Diane had given him, and it was sitting on the side of the helm next to her. She watched the cup for awhile, noticing that each time the boat swayed from side to side, the cup would lift just enough to release a musical note.

Laughing, Betty called out, "Hey Frank. I found your trouble."

"Where is it? What's it connected to?" Frank asked as he came rushing up on deck.

Betty pointed to the cup that was moving ever so slightly.

He roared with laughter, "Damn! I spent an hour looking for trouble."

Greg came scurrying past Frank to reach the railing. "Oh no, not again," said Frank.

He had just finished eating a sandwich but it didn't stay down. He missed the railing and threw up all over the deck.

"Are you still getting sick? You've been sitting up more often. I thought you were getting your sea legs," asked Frank.

"I'm going home when we get to Bermuda. I've had enough of the sea. I want to see my mom."

"Listen to the sissy, wants to go home. Greg want to see

his mamma," teased Frank.

"Yo, Technicolor, can't take it anymore?" asked Scott.

They were teasing him, but they all understood his feelings. They knew it was quite an adjustment for them—let alone a thirteen-year-old.

Another day had begun, hopefully their last, and Betty was still groggy from lack of sleep as she staggered up for morning watch. She looked at the scowl on Bob's face. "Boy, you sure don't look like you're in a good mood. What's the matter?"

"Goddamn engine's leaking oil and it can't be run, and there's a leak in the fresh water tanks. Something's always going wrong with this fucking boat."

"All of the water tanks?" asked Betty.

"I'm not sure which of the five tanks are leaking, but the bilge keeps filling with fresh water. Take the helm while Frank and I work on the engine. Scott and Dave are hunting for the leak in the water tanks."

Betty sat down at the helm. "It's not on autopilot?"

"There's not enough wind for the autopilot to handle it. You'll have to steer by hand."

The winds were non-existent and *Destiny* waddled back and forth, slowly drifting towards Bermuda. Only the mainsail was up. Betty was more experienced at steering and they no longer called her Snake-Wake-Rennie.

Greg lay down near her and she scratched his head. "We're so close we only have about a hundred or so miles to go before we get to Bermuda."

"I'm home-sick. I want to go home," cried Greg. "I want to get off the boat so bad."

"I do too Greg, but we won't be able to make much time today under these conditions."

Betty sat in the heat of the August day feeling the heaviness of the hot sun. She looked around and saw nothing but ocean. It seemed like they were lost from the whole world and there was no one else alive. They were the only survivors. Betty knew better but she couldn't always control her imagination.

Putting the autopilot back on, she waited to see if it would hold, and when it did, she picked up a book to read. Her mind felt too numb to think and she felt stifled and confined and ready to blow a fuse.

"Greg, hand me that notebook on the bench. I'm going to write a letter to your mom."

She wrote for a while, then stopped. It was too much of a mental effort. "I don't believe this. I can't remember how to spell the simplest words. I really need land bad."

Betty heard the sound of the generator coming on then, Bob cussed, "Goddammit, what else can go wrong?"

"Stop cussing so much." yelled Betty. "You never cussed like this when I first met you. What's the matter now?"

"I tried to turn the air conditioners on to cool the boat down while we fix the engine. I can't though because they're rusted from salt water. You can see where it leaked in. The only one working is the one in the master stateroom."

A half-hour later he returned. "Well, the engine's finally repaired, and only one water tank was leaking. Scott used some caulk on it, I hope it holds until we reach Bermuda."

Destiny still rocked in her own wake. For the last four nights, the motion had been terrible; tonight wouldn't be any better.

Betty swayed back and forth on her bed trying to sleep, "I feel like my guts are being twisted and turned, I can't take this motion much longer."

Bob looked over at her, they were both rocking, knowing there was nothing they could do. "We should be in Bermuda tomorrow and things will be better then."

"We'll be on land—land...land.... I can't wait," she said giving Bob a hug.

As soon as daylight came, Betty rushed up on deck. "Can you see land yet?"

"We're on our last forty-five miles," said Bob.

She started to clean the boat, getting ready for their docking. She looked at the crew relaxed on deck while watching the horizon. Betty called out to them, "Hey, I need some help cleaning the boat. We'll be at the dock soon, and you won't want to do it then."

"Nay, we'll do it later. We're waiting for the first sight of Bermuda," said Scott.

"I can't do it all myself," Betty said. "Talking to you men is like talking to a wall. Greg, get down here and help me."

Greg came shuffling down, "Why do I have to help if no one else is?"

"Because I said so, now put your things away. Pile all the rest of the clothes in front of Scott and Dave's stateroom, and I hope they trip on them. After you've finished that, you can wipe off the tables."

When they were finished cleaning they went up on deck for the first glimpse of land they'd seen in eight days.

"Look over there, is that Bermuda?" asked Greg.

"I see it, over there to port side," said Frank.

Dave was drooling, "Where are the girls? I'm dying for girls."

"Look out gals, we're heading your way," sang Scott.

Land never looked so appealing. Betty had flown to Bermuda before but she couldn't remember thinking it was the most beautiful place in the world. *Destiny* motored into the town of St. George. They were flying the Bermuda courtesy and quarantine flags, and they pulled alongside the customs docks. Scott and Dave jumped on the dock and secured the boat.

Betty was so happy to be off the boat that she knelt down and kissed the ground, "It feels so good to be on land again and I've survived the first leg of the journey."

No one could leave *Destiny* until the custom's officers arrived. Their passports and documents had to be checked before they could go ashore. They waited an hour and a half before they came.

"Maybe we'll meet some girls and get lucky," said Scott. "It's been weeks since I had my arms around a female. I miss the feel and smell of a woman."

"What's get lucky mean?" asked Greg.

"Shut up twerp, this is man-talk," said Dave. "Wow, I can just see those beautiful legs, those soft delicious breasts just waiting for us. WHOA-WEE."

"You pip squeaks don't have any idea what you're talking about. They want a real man. A man that knows how to handle a woman," said Frank. "I'll sweep them right into bed before they even know it."

Betty couldn't believe what she was hearing, "You'd think

you've been out to sea for six months instead of eight days. You sound like wild animals in heat."

"What's get lucky mean, Grandma," asked Greg again.

"I'll tell you later," said Betty as she walked over toward Bob who was talking to the customs officer. "What's the matter?"

"Customs wants to take our guns off the boat. They said they would give them back when we left, but we need them onboard for protection. Officer, what good will the guns do us, locked up in your office?"

"There's a lot of people here who would love to steal the guns off your boat, and they wouldn't think twice about killing you for them, " said the customs officer. "Now, please write down the serial numbers and count your bullets, and I'll take them to my office."

Once they cleared customs and immigrations, they motored over to the Royal Bermuda Yacht Club, in Hamilton, planning to stay a week.

Betty and Greg scurried to a phone booth and called home; she was able to reach her daughter, Loretta, at her office. "We made it, honey. We're here in Bermuda. It took us eight long days."

Greg kept pulling the phone while she talked until finally she handed the receiver to him.

"Yep, mom, I made it. It was awesome, but I'm ready to come home. I miss you."

Betty felt better after talking to her daughter, and Loretta promised to tell the rest of the family they were well.

"I'm so glad we made it here safe," Betty said, hugging Bob. "The trip seemed to take forever. I can't wait to stretch my legs and walk around town, see other people."

"Tonight, I'm taking you to dinner, just the two of us," he said as he kissed her. "We'll go to the Venice. It's a five-star restaurant that the Yacht Club recommended."

Betty was excited. "Wow, we're getting dressed up in something besides shorts! It's going to be a real treat."

Dining alone for the first time in a month was peaceful and tranquil. There were no interruptions or squabbling to contend with. Sipping Chardonnay, they enjoyed the warm cozy atmosphere and savory food. They weren't used to sitting still and eating without worrying about their food falling in their lap.

"It feels terrific to be by ourselves," said Bob as he took Betty's hand. "You're a good sport. You hung in there."

"Where was I going to go?" she laughed, "I'm glad it's over."

"Over? This is just the beginning," he said as Betty groaned. "We have a long trip ahead of us."

Betty wondered if she should say something now about not finishing the trip, but instead she said, "Where did the rest of the group go tonight?"

"Mitch went for a walk. He's still feeling melancholy and misses Diane," said Bob. Frank, Scott and Dave walked into town to find a bar. Greg tailed behind them on his skate board."

After dinner, they walked down the bustling street enjoying the music that seemed to be everywhere.

"I think that's our group sitting on the verandah at the Rum-Runner bar," said Bob.

Greg's arms were leaning on the table. He was trying to act like one of the big boys.

"Did you men have dinner?" asked Bob.

"Yeah! We ate here. The food was better than my cooking. How about a rum-runner? They're fantastic," said Dave.

"Gladly, I feel like getting smashed. After spending eight days with you slobs, I need to celebrate," Betty said, taking one of the empty chairs. "God, but it feels good to be off the boat. It's rejuvenating."

"Hey, you have a lot more days ahead to put up with us. Get use to it," said Scott. "Here have a rum-runner on me, my treat. We do give you a hard time."

"The music's driving me wild," said Betty as she stood up and let her body flow with the calypso tune. "Come on, Scott, join me." They danced around the verandah until Scott bumped into the chairs and almost fell.

"Whoops," said Scott. "I must have had one rum-runner too many."

Bob gave a big yawn. "I'm tired, Betty. Want to head back to the boat?"

"Sure, I'm exhausted. It's going to feel good to sleep in a bed that's not rocking. Come on, Greg, let's go back."

"Ah Grandma, don't make me go back. I want to stay here with the guys. I'm old enough to stay out and get lucky."

"What?" laughed Scott. "Take him back. I've had enough of him. Go home twerp."

When they reached *Destiny*, Mitch was hunched over, sitting on the back deck in the dark.

His eyes were tearing, "I've just talked to Diane. God, I love that girl."

Betty was getting tired of his whining, but she put her arm around his shoulder, giving him a motherly squeeze. "Come on, cheer up. There's so much to see and do here."

Mitch sighed, "I don't want to be here without Diane."

Consoling him didn't seem to help and Betty was weary from so many sleepless nights. "I'm going to bed. I hope you feel better in the morning."

Eight

Betty had a good night's sleep, the first in eight days, but she woke up feeling melancholy and homesick. She laid in bed fighting back the tears. *I'll go home with Greg*, she thought, *I've had enough sailing. It makes me feel up tight and jumpy and I hate the long days at sea.*

Then outloud, she said. "Oh no you don't, you're not giving up that easy. You love Bob and promised to make this trip with him, now get up and get dressed. You'll feel better after you eat."

When she was dressed, she walked out to the galley, Bob was sitting at the table writing on a yellow pad.

Betty asked, "Did you eat yet?"

"No, I was checking over the boat. *Destiny*'s shake down trip has really shown up a lot of weak points. The hydraulics are completely out, the motor needs work and we have some hoses that need changing."

Betty sat listening; her mind was numb. She really didn't want to hear about the boat.

Bob continued on, "Plus we've got to get an air conditioner man in here to repair the units. The water-maker's acting up and I also want to find out where the water's leaking in. It's ruined our stereo and VCR." Throwing his hands up in the air in frustration, he continued, "I've got to take the main and stay sails down and take them to a sail maker. There's rips and holes in both sails. It looks like a couple of tough days ahead of us." He took a good look at Betty and said, "How are you feeling? You don't look so good."

"I'm all right," she answered not wanting him to know how she really felt.

"What, do you have planned today?" Bob asked.

"I have a lot to do. The galley needs a through cleaning, in fact the whole boat's a mess. I need to reorganize the closets so I can get at things easier. Also I'm going to ask Mitch to fix the cabinet

94

door latches so the food doesn't come flying out in rough weather." She kept her head down not wanting to look him in the eyes.

"Well, I've got to get moving. Call me if you need help. I'll be on deck getting the sails down."

Starting in the galley, she cleaned everything in sight. As she worked she kept thinking of how much she missed her family and house. Her hands started to shake, and she felt uptight. She started to cry, and the harder she worked, the more she cried. When someone came in the room she'd stick her head in the closets, pretending to wipe the inside shelves, so they couldn't see she was crying.

Scott and Dave came down and looked at the spotless sink. "Can we wash our hands here?"

Betty pretended to blow her nose to hide her red eyes. She quickly looked at the black grease on their hands and said, "No way, go use your own sink, it's still filthy."

"That's what we thought you'd say," they grumbled as they walked back to their rooms.

When the galley was finished, Betty put a load of wash in, then took out her frustrations washing and waxing the teak walls.

Mitch came in and stood beside her, a notebook in his hand. "I'm thinking of writing a book on the psychology of sailing...what people think and feel while they're out at sea. How did you feel out at sea for eight days?"

"I don't feel like talking right now," said Betty through clenched teeth.

"Well, can't you just tell me the thoughts that were in your mind while we were sailing?"

"No, I can't—I don't feel like talking." Betty tried hard but she couldn't hold back the tears.

"I'm sorry, I didn't mean to upset you," he said as he walked away.

Bob was on deck pulling down the sails. "Hey Mitch, give me a hand will you. What are you looking so gloomy about."

"Betty's crying. I didn't mean to upset her, I just wanted to talk to her."

Bob raised his eyebrows in wonder, "What is she crying about?"

"I don't know. I was just talking to her and she burst out in tears."

Bob went down to the salon. "What's the matter, why are you crying?"

"Who told you I was crying?" She said wiping the tears away.

Bob stared at her, "What's the matter, are you sick?"

Too emotionally upset to answer she ran into the stateroom and fell on the bed. She sobbed uncontrollably for fifteen minutes while she beat the mattress.

"I hate this boat. I hate the ocean, and I want to go home. I can't stand it anymore."

Bob sat in the galley dumbfounded. He had not seen Betty cry on the boat before. She seemed like such a trooper. He had no idea she felt this way.

After a good cry a calming feeling crept over her. Sitting up, she looked at her reflection in the mirror. *Oh . . . my eyes are swollen. I really look awful, I look like a wild sea witch.* She washed her face and walked out to the galley.

Bob sat there with a worried look on his face. "What was that all about?"

"I feel nervous and cranky, I guess it was the rough trip over. I'm also homesick. I really miss my kids."

He put his arms around her and held her for awhile. "Betty if you feel that bad, why don't you fly home for a week."

"I've been thinking about doing that, but if I go home, I won't come back."

"Wow! Then maybe you better not go. Let's talk about it first."

She started to cry again, "But I miss them so."

"Honey, why don't you stop working and call them again? Then go for a walk and do some shopping. Buy something pretty for yourself. It'll help you feel better. You need to get off the boat for a while. We'll talk about you going home later."

Betty twisted her handkerchief, "I don't know if it will help, but I'll try."

"Do you want me to come with you?"

"No," said Betty going into her stateroom, "I need some time to myself to think things out."

Bermuda was full of happy tourists, and walking through

town hearing the people laugh helped calm her. She strolled first in one direction then the other. She loved the enchanting pink stucco houses, that were tucked under palm trees. The island was so clean. There was no graffiti or trash to be seen. She bought a few things at the duty-free shops, and watched the women at the straw market weaving hats and baskets out of dried palm leaves. She had lunch at a quaint little hut whose specialty was flying fish.

"I've thrown enough flying fish overboard, now I think it's time to taste one," she said to the waitress.

"Honey, you shouldn't throw them overboard—they're mighty good eating." Betty sat thinking about her relationship with Bob. *Did she love him enough to continue on? Would she ever adjust to life at sea?*

The waitress interrupted her thoughts when she brought the flying fish order. Hesitantly Betty took her first bite and was surprised at how good it tasted. After lunch she sat drinking coffee and thinking. She had made the promise to sail around the world, but did she have what it took to keep her promise? She knew she was deeply in love with Bob, and if she left she knew their relationship would be over. Being off the boat and around people seemed to make her mood brighter. Three hours later, she felt ready to go back to *Destiny*. She had made her decision.

As Betty walked down the pier, a lady approached her. "Have you heard there's a hurricane heading our way?"

"No I haven't," answered Betty. "How soon is it due to hit here?"

"They say if it continues on the same course it will get here in two days."

Betty thanked her and hurried down the dock. Bob was on deck and she called to him. "Did you hear about the hurricane?"

"Sure did. I just heard it on the ship to shore radio. It could change course. If it does we have nothing to worry about. We'll wait and see what happens. Well, did you have a good time?"

"I just love Bermuda. It's charming and the people are so friendly. I really enjoyed myself."

Bob held her and said, "Hope you're in a good mood and feeling better."

"Yes, I think I was going boat-crazy. I'm not used to all that bumping around. I'm just a delicate butterfly."

"Yep, you're my butterfly and I'm your gypsy—always wandering. I got a lot of work done while you were gone, but I still have a lot to do. Hey, why worry about the work or hurricanes when we're in paradise. Let's go out to dinner alone again."

They went to Louie's, a native favorite. It was sort of a shanty with a thatched roof and rough wooden tables and chairs.

"You've got to try the flying fish, they're delicious," said Betty.

Bob laughed and said, "How do you know I'll like flying fish?"

"Trust me, they're delicious. I tried them this afternoon."

"Hey, you're using my line. Okay, I'll trust you."

When the waiter came to their table, Bob said, "We heard you have the best flying fish and corn bread on the island."

"Sure do. You gonna try some?" the waiter asked.

"Yep, two orders of flying fish and make sure you bring us plenty of that hot corn bread," said Bob. Oh, and bring us two rum punches."

The calypso band was playing the steel drums, and they danced to the tantalizing rhythm before and after dinner. Everything seemed funny to them as they laughed the night away. Neither one brought up the subject of going home.

The morning sun shone through the port holes in their stateroom. Betty stirred then sat up quickly. "Look how sunny it is out, the storm must have changed course."

Bob stretched and sat up in bed. "Want to go up to the yacht club for breakfast? Maybe we'll hear some news on the weather from the yacht men that came in last night."

There was very little activity at eight in the morning, but the Bermuda yacht club was busy. The huge white stucco building faced the bay, and the dinning room looked over the water. The sun reflected on the docked boats, transforming their shadows onto the water. The marina was crowded but the shadows made it seem like there were twice as many boats in the harbor. All Betty's blues had vanished and life seemed wonderful again.

"The sky's so clear, you'd never guess a storm is brewing," Betty said as they ate their bacon and eggs.

Bob dipped his toast in his eggs. "You never can tell what a hurricane will do. We just have to stay on guard and be ready to move if it changes."

Betty thought for a moment and said, "I think we ought to find a travel agent after breakfast."

Bob gave her a questioning look. "Are you just getting Greg's ticket, or are you getting one for yourself too?"

"The biggest part of me wants to go home. I feel so uncoordinated and out of place on the boat. I keep thinking a wild storm will come and sink *Destiny* and we'll all drown. I really miss my family, and I miss being active and busy at the office."

"The first leg is always the hardest to get used to. You'll adjust to the sea in a short while. I know you miss your family, but if you leave and go home, then you'll miss me—I think? Would it help if you called them a few more times?"

"I've talked to them four times. It's helped a lot. They miss me too but they think I should stick it out a little longer. I guess I've calmed down enough to try another leg."

"Boy, am I glad of that." Bob said, hugging her. "I love you and I didn't want you to go. But if you are really that unhappy, I would understand. You had me really worried, if you left I don't know what would have happened, we might never have seen each other again—okay, let's find the travel office."

After they purchased Greg's ticket, they continued to stroll along enjoying the freedom away from *Destiny*. They walked past the grand Governor's palace. The guards were dressed in red and black uniforms. School children dressed in navy blue marched in line with their teacher to see the massive building.

"That looks like two familiar figures ahead," Betty said, surprised to see Scott and Dave.

"Yo, wait up for us," called Bob. "Where were you guys last night? You didn't come home."

"Well Dad—it's like this. We met these women, had a few drinks and were having a good time. Then they invited us back to their boat."

"Wait a minute—the girls have their own boat?" asked Bob.

Scott put his hands out, "Wait, let me tell the story. It belongs to one of the girl's fathers. He went home and they're staying on the boat. One thing led to another and things got pretty cozy."

"Next thing we knew it was morning," said Dave.

"What about Mitch, did he stay all night too?" asked Betty.

"I think he got over his loneliness. He's in much better spirits now," chuckled Dave.

"All the crying about how much he loved Diane," Betty said. "And all he really meant was he was horny."

"Last night, we invited them to go snorkeling with us. After we woke up and got a good look at them, we made excuses," laughed Scott.

"I think you are animals," said Betty. "Where's Mitch now?"

Dave's eyes were bloodshot. "Back at the boat, he wanted to finish a few jobs. Mitch has a pretty bad hangover, we all do."

Bob saw Mitch sitting in the cockpit, with an ice bag on his head. "How are you feeling?"

"Good in some ways, not so good in others, but I had a great time."

"Are you feeling in shape to finish washing down the bilges?" asked Bob. "As soon as you're finished we'll take the dinghies and go snorkeling."

"Sure," said Mitch balancing the ice pack. "I just had some breakfast, I'm ready to start."

Betty wanted so much to ask Mitch why he stayed all night with another girl if he loved Diane so much, but he looked happy for a change so she let it go.

At four o'clock when they returned from snorkeling, Harvey, the dockmaster approached them. "The hurricane is on its way. It should hit Bermuda by nine tonight."

They felt the winds strengthening, and the sky was swirling with gray, angry clouds.

"You better get your boat over to the small cove called White Lake, in Hamilton bay. Do you know where it is?" asked Harvey.

"I know where it is, thanks," answered Bob. "Okay guys, get with it. We've got to get our things together and move. I want to get to the cove as soon as we can. Scott, Dave, clear the tools and things from the cockpit. Mitch, secure all the portholes and hatches and Betty you check out the galley and make sure our food supply is okay."

100

Everyone mumbled "Okay," as they dug into their work.

Waves were peaking high with white caps and the wind was beginning to reach gale force when they anchored. Looking at the sky was like peering into an angry, gray, eerie mist. You could tell a powerful storm was brewing. The look and sounds reminded Betty of the storms coming across the Atlantic. By eight o'clock, they were anchored down. The wind was gusting over thirty knots in the secluded shelter, and the water was dark and choppy. Fine misty rain fell on their slickers, as they waited for the impact of the storm.

Dave was restless. "Let's take a swim."

"All right," yelled Scott. "Last one in is a red-assed monkey."

Betty couldn't believe her ears. "What are you, crazy? You can't go swimming. There's a hurricane coming."

Scott jumped in with his clothes on, but Dave and Mitch leapt in wearing only their underwear. They swam around in the choppy water, the wind howling wildly around them.

"I don't believe they're doing this! There's got to be a strong current out there." Betty stood on the deck and screamed to be heard above the howling wind. "Get back on the boat. You're all going to drown."

Mitch came back onboard, "Relax, Betty, there's no current, but it's rough as hell."

"I'm going in too," said Greg as he climbed on the rail, ready to dive in.

Betty pulled him back, "No way, Greg, sorry, but no way."

"You never let me do anything. You take my fun away," he said as he ran into his room.

Frank was sipping a straight bourbon and taking it all in. He shook his head and said, "Crazy kids. They have no brains at all."

Betty gave up and stood under the protection of the bimini canvas with Bob and Frank, discussing the possible storm problems.

"I wonder how long we'll be anchored out here?" asked Betty.

Frank turned the radio louder, "It says it will hit about two hours from now—nine o'clock. We should be well protected here."

They listened intently to the radio, nine o'clock came and went but the winds stayed at thirty knots with ten-foot waves.

101

The three men came back onboard and went dripping down to their staterooms.

"Guess they got smart and gave up," said Frank, slurring his words. He was on his third straight bourbon.

The cove was protecting them from the worst of the storm and Betty cooked dinner and was setting the galley table. "What's that noise? Is that someone coming aboard?"

Bob went up on deck, "Scott, what are you guys doing in the dingy? Where the hell are you going in this weather?"

"We met some women this afternoon from the cruise ship. We promised to have dinner with them," said Scott. "We're already late."

"Are you crazy? What happens if the hurricane hits?" asked Bob.

They shoved off as they said, "We'll stay on the cruise ship."

Bob shook his head. "I don't believe they're willing to battle thirty-knot winds and ten-foot waves for a couple of women."

Frank made a salute with his drink, "They're just hard-headed horny youths."

Destiny was held down with four anchors. Two on each stern and bow. The wind died down and the boat was almost motionless. For an hour nothing stirred. It was like a dead period where you feel in limbo, but you know something's going to happen. Then the blustering winds began blowing severely against *Destiny*, making her rock and sway, as she pulled against the four anchors. They stayed at anchor all night, as sixty-knot winds thrust against the ship and hail stones bombarded her.

When the winds picked up, Gregory came out of his room in a flash. He sat next to his grandma. Betty could feel the fear rising in her and she fought back the feeling. *I'll be all right. Nothing bad is going to happen*, she repeated mentally. "Come on, Greg. Let's play some cards. How about you, Frank?"

"Yeah, five hundred rummy," Greg said, his mood changing completely.

"Let me fix another drink and I'll play," slurred Frank.

"If you have another drink, you won't be able to see the cards," said Betty.

Frank sat down at the table, his drink spilling on the cards,

"For Christ sake you're worse than a mother hen. Lay off, will you?"

Betty ignored him and said, "Bob, do you want to play?"

"You know I don't like to play cards. I'm looking to see if there's any wet spots around. Mitch must have found where the water's coming in because I don't see any leaks."

After two hours of playing cards, the wind was still blowing at full speed. Betty yawned. "I'm going to bed. I hope this wind lets up soon."

Bob was laying on the couch, Betty's yawn was contagious, and talking through his gaping mouth, he said, "If it doesn't get any worse than this, we'll be in good shape. That is, if the anchors hold. I'm sleeping in the salon. I want to keep a check on the anchors to make sure they're holding."

By morning, the winds were down to forty-five knots and there was still a heavy downpour. The sky was dark with oppressive clouds that reminded Betty of dirty snow piled high in the streets. Scott, Dave and Mitch arrived back from their night out just before lunch smiling, happy but tired. They slept until late afternoon. After cleaning the living quarters, Betty went to her stateroom to read. The whistling wind distracted her. Then she heard voices and knew that Scott and Dave had awakened. They were in the galley discussing their triumphs of last night. She didn't mean to listen, but their boisterous words echoed through the boat. *My God, they sound like a bunch of raunchy sailors*, she thought. She was getting a good view of what men think about women and sex, and it was a bit embarrassing.

"You should have seen the tits on the girl I was with. Wow, like big melons," said Scott.

Dave slapped the table with his hand, "Yeah, your girl really wanted to be with me. I could tell by the way she kept staring at my crotch."

"They didn't stand a chance. We knew we'd have them in bed before midnight and wow, what a fuck she was," said Scott.

"Let me tell you something about women," said Dave. "When I turn a woman on, she lights up like a birthday cake. Hot fire. Who-wee."

"Is that right? How many times did she come?" asked Frank.

"I don't know," Dave stuttered. "I was too busy doing my own thing, enjoying the good stuff. I know she came, because boy, was she juicy."

"Ah, you juveniles," said Frank drumming his fingers on the table. "You don't know what you're doing. When I make love to a woman she climaxes three or four times. I make them beg for mercy, beg me to stop, but I keep humping and humping."

Betty didn't want to hear anymore, it was so vulgar. Walking out to the galley she looked at the three men. They sat leering and drooling, wrapped deep in their conversation.

"You men are disgusting. You're not in a barroom you're on *Destiny*. I don't want to hear your crude stories and I don't want Gregory listening to them either. I wish the women could hear you. Then they'd know to just stroke your little private parts and you'd be at their mercy."

"Who says our private parts are little," asked Frank grabbing his crotch.

"Yeah," said Scott, followed by Dave, and they started to laugh and brag about the exaggerated lengths of their male organs.

"All you think or talk about is that thing between your legs," Betty said, "I should tape your conversation and send it to your girlfriends back home. Go talk somewhere else where I can't hear you. You're so gross and disgusting. I'm glad Greg's asleep and didn't hear you. You're teaching him enough bad habits."

"Why can't we sit here?" asked Scott.

"Because I'm going to fix dinner. I have to set the table."

The three of them walked up on deck. "The way she's acting, you might think we said something about her," said Dave, as they sat in the cockpit to continue their conversation.

It was ten o'clock on their second night at anchor, and the night was as dark and dismal as a haunted graveyard. The wind was still blowing, but now at only thirty-five knots. Five-foot white caps were barely visible, as the drizzling rain lay heavy in the air. Visibility was down to zero, and the fog horn could be heard echoing through the night.

They had just finished watching a video tape and crawled in bed, when Bob sat up. "I think I heard the dingy motor start. Scott and Dave must be off again in search of the night's conquest. It's hard to believe they would go out in these conditions just to find a piece of tail."

"Bob! Now you're sounding just like them," said Betty as she whacked him on the arm.

Laughing, he answered, "What's wrong with that? Isn't that what they're going out for?"

She hit him with her pillow, "Why don't you just go to sleep."

Bob snuggled close to her and they fell asleep listening to the clang, clang of the wind whirling around the mast.

At three in the morning, Betty thought she heard voices. In the background, the rain was beating hard against the decks. Betty was sure now she heard female voices. Sitting up, she said, "Did they bring girls back to the boat in this mess?"

Then she heard Scott's slurred voice, "Come aboard, girls, just climb up."

There was a Philadelphia whine as one of the girls said, "You said we wouldn't get wet. The waves have drenched us and we're cold. We're not climbing up there."

Scott's voice was barely audible above the wind. "Dammit, come on, get onboard. The winds are about to blow me off the fucking deck."

Betty shook Bob. "Wake up, the guys brought girls back in this horrible weather."

He sat up, "What . . . what are you talking about?"

"They're climbing up the stern, right by our portholes."

"Oh for God's sake, what are they, crazy? This has gone too far, waking us up in the middle of the night."

Both girls were angry and screamed, "Take us back. You're damn fools to bring us out here. We should never have let you talk us into this."

Scott tried to calm them down ,"Okay, okay, don't get mad. Dave, take them back."

"Me?" said Dave, drunk and annoyed. "What about you? You're the one that wanted to bring them out here in the first place."

"You're already in the dinghy. See you later, girls," said Scott as he walked away from the railing.

"Like hell you will," the girls yelled from the dinghy.

"I'm going to talk to them in the morning. They're getting a bit carried away," said Bob almost asleep again.

Good news came over the radio the next morning. The worst was over and the hurricane had moved on. It was safe to go back to the marina.

Betty and Bob were having breakfast on deck when Scott came out. "We met some girls last night from Philadelphia. That's close to where you live, isn't it, Betty?"

"I could tell by their accents," said Betty.

Looking puzzled he said, "Did we wake you up when we came home?"

"Wake us up? You blasted us out of bed with your yelling. Besides that, you were climbing up right by our portholes. How could we help but hear," said Bob.

Scott laughed sheepishly and said. "Sorry guys, I guess we had too much to drink."

"I don't want you bringing women back at night," said Bob.

Scott was silent, he knew he was wrong. Joking, he said, "I don't know why not. You run a pretty nice floating motel here."

"Try it again and I'll kick your ass," Bob said seriously.

When they arrived back at the marina, they could see the damage the hurricane had left. Trees were down, windows were broken, roofs had been blown off.

Looking over the mess, Bob said, "I'm glad we were in a safe harbor on *Destiny*."

Bob offered to take everyone out to a restaurant, Frank declined. He wanted to stay onboard and cook. After dinner, Betty and Bob walked down the dock and as they got near *Destiny*, they could smell something burning. Smoke was pouring up from the companion way. Panicking, they rushed down the steps, expecting a fire. Thick smoke burned their eyes as they looked for the cause of the smoke. Frank staggered out from the bathroom. He was holding a glass filled with straight Johnny Walker. "You're back early."

"My God. What's going on? What's causing all the smoke?" asked Bob.

Frank waved his drink in the air and slurred. "I forgot my steak was cooking. It's just a little overdone that's all."

Betty's eyes swept over the galley. "What a mess . . . .Isn't it a little late to be eating?"

106

"No, No. I just wanted a few drinks first to relax. Don't worry I'll clean up my mess. You won't have to clean up after me like you do the other guys," he said waving his hands in the air and splashing the Johnny Walker all over the teak floor.

"Yeah, I know, Frank," Betty answered in disgust, as she grabbed the glass from him. Quickly she wiped the bourbon up before it took the varnish off the teak.

"No kidding, you ought to talk to them guys. They leave clutter around and you're always cleaning up after them." Frank was becoming harder to understand. "I pick up afer me shelf, you don't find my clothes ly-ng round, do ya?'

"You're drunk," Betty shouted at him.

Frank slurred. "I'm going to stop that too, from now on it'll be Mr. Per-fect."

Bob was disgusted with him. "We're going to bed. Make sure you clean up this mess."

Frank staggered after them. "Don't forget now, Betty, I want you to talk to those slobs."

They climbed into bed and listened to the dishes and pans rattling through the door. They heard Frank stagger up to the deck, then there was a thumping sound, some groaning then silence. Frank had fallen on the floor and went to sleep.

"I think the crew's getting a little out of control," Betty said as she rubbed Bob's head. Bob sat up, "Turn over I'll give you a back rub and help you forget tonight's problems." As she turned he kissed her tenderly. "Thanks for not leaving me."

"I couldn't leave you," Betty whispered, "I love you too much."

His hands moved gently down the length of her bare back. The gentle massage sent currents of desire through her. He explored the soft lines of her waist, her hips, her thighs as he caressed her with tender kisses. Gathering her in his arms he tenderly turned her on her back. A moan of ecstasy slipped through her lips as his lips nibbled slowly along each breast, then down to her stomach. She caressed the strong tendons in his neck as she pressed her open lips to his and her body melted against him. His hardness found the warm moist part of her body, and their lovemaking became intense.

Later, they lay together exhausted and satisfied. Betty laughed, "God, it's great to make love in a bed that's not moving.

I don't have to worry about falling off."

When they opened their stateroom door the next morning, they expected to find the galley clean and neat. Instead, they were hit with the sight of dirty dishes and the stove and counters covered with grease and leftover food.

Betty was so angry. "I'm not cleaning this mess up."

"How about bacon and eggs at the club?" Bob asked trying to stay calm.

Betty ran up the steps, "Let's go, I want to get away from here before Frank wakes up."

When they returned, Frank was cleaning and very apologetic, "I guess I had a little too much to drink last night. It won't happen again."

"I know it won't happen tonight," said Bob. "We're all taking Greg out for his farewell dinner."

That night as they gathered at the table, Bob said, "Let's drink a toast to Greg's departure and to the next leg of our trip."

"Here's to Greg jumping ship, the big sissy," said Scott as he downed his drink.

Greg stood up and raised his glass of Coke high in the air. "I have a toast to make."

"Hey-hey Greg, what is it?" asked Frank. "Quiet down. Let the little guy talk."

Proudly he said. "I changed my mind. I'm going to the Azores with you."

"What?" they all said extremely surprised.

Scott stood up and said, "Yeah, let's drink a toast to the Technicolor Yawn."

Betty was both surprised and happy. "Are you sure you want to do this?"

"Yeah, I already called my mom. She said it was okay."

It was their last day and they had to restock the boat. The eight days at sea had put a big dent in the food supply. Finding the things they needed was difficult in a foreign country and the prices were at least double. Betty expected to spend four hundred dollars but she ended up spending seven hundred and fifty. The boxes were emptied and taken off the boat and the food was piled high on the counters, floor and steps. Betty began the job of putting the supplies away. The galley was stifling, and sweat drenched her clothes. It was in the high nineties outside and not a breath of air was coming in through the port holes or companion way.

Bob came down to the salon and Betty asked, "What time are we leaving?"

"We're not. I just found out that the storm that hit Bermuda is hanging out at sea, right where we're heading."

"That's okay. I'd rather be here where it's safe than out there battling a storm. How about putting the air on. I have to put the rest of these groceries away and it's sweltering down here."

"I can't. The air conditioner guy never showed up, so it's not working."

The perspiration ran into her eyes, and she wiped it away. "When's he coming?"

Bob sat down at the table, "He's not. I can't seem to get a hold of him. We'll just have to do without the air."

"What!? I'm not going anywhere in this boat 'til the air conditioner is fixed. You don't know what it's like cooking down here," Betty said as she slammed the cabinet doors in the galley.

"What can I do? The guy didn't show up to fix it," he said defensively.

Betty stamped her foot and banged the table, "I'm not cooking in this fucking hot boat again. I can't and I won't."

Startled by both her language and her tone, he raised his voice in defense. "All right, all right, calm down. I'll call him again and try to get him out here."

He stamped off the boat to a phone. Two hours later, the repair man was onboard and eventually the units were magically humming away. When the groceries were put away, Betty stripped off her sweaty clothes and laid on the bed, letting the cool air blow on her body.

The sky was a robin's egg blue and the rays of the sun glistened on the morning dew that drenched the deck. There was a slight breeze that gently slapped at the flag of Bermuda, high on the mast.

"It's too nice of a day to work," said Scott as he climbed up the mast. He was adjusting the sails and singing a song off tune. "Beautiful beautiful brown eyes, beautiful beautiful brown eyes. Hey, you should see the great view from up here. Let's rent motor scooters and ride around and see the rest of Bermuda."

Dave, who hadn't started his job yet, said, "Yeah, we could take a picnic lunch and swim suits."

"Nice idea, but we have too much work to do. We're sailing off tomorrow," said Bob.

When all the chores were completed, Betty stretched out on the bed. Bob lay down beside her. "The weather fax shows the storm going away from us so it should be all right to leave tomorrow. Are you ready to go?"

Quickly, Betty answered, "No, I'm not ready to sail out in that ocean again."

Bob turned on his side facing her, "We have to leave when the weather's right, you know how quickly it changes."

She got up and walked out to the galley, "I don't want to leave, but I'll be ready. Would you like a glass of wine?" Betty asked, as she poured herself one.

I'm really not ready to go, she thought as she poured Bob his wine. *I'll give it another try and see how the trip to the Azores goes.*

"I won't force you to go if you don't want to," said Bob taking her hand as she gave him his wine.

Smiling, she said, "You're not getting rid of me that easy. This sea witch is hanging around for awhile."

A huge smile came on Bob's face. She loved his smile, and it would be hard for her to leave him. They were so much a part of each other.

"Okay, sea witch, let's take a walk," said Bob, grabbing her hand and pulling her along. "We'll take our last look at Bermuda."

On their way, they passed the Holland cruise ship that was docked nearby. It was a monstrous ship that loomed high above *Destiny*.

"What a beauty," Bob said to the ship's officer, standing at the gang plank. "We're on *Destiny*, the sail boat in back of you. It's just a little thing next to you."

He shook Bob's hand. "I'm Officer Monroe, the ship's physician. That's a nice ketch you're sailing."

"Bob Godfrey's my name. This is my first mate, Betty."

"How long have you been in port?" Officer Monroe asked.

"About a week now, but we're leaving tomorrow," said Betty.

"Good, then you weren't out in that storm. We pulled in last night, it was pretty wild out there. Had to rescue a forty-six foot sail boat that ran into trouble. It was caught in the middle of the hurricane, lost their steering and engine. Lucky for them we were near enough to help them."

Betty got nervous when she heard stories like that and she asked, "Was everyone okay?"

"Yes, there were four of them; two men and two woman. They were wet, cold and scared out of their wits. If we hadn't reached them when we did, the storm would have torn their boat apart. We brought them onboard and towed their boat in."

Later that night, Betty tried to sleep but she kept picturing the people on the boat, fighting for their lives in the rough water. She tried to imagine how she would react in such a situation. The story had really upset her. Shutting her eyes tightly, she turned on her side and thought, *Don't think about it, don't think about it. Just go to sleep.*

Nine

Starting sounds of sailors revving engines, getting ready for departure, was their alarm clock. Bob was already up and the first words Betty heard as she came out of the cabin was Bob giving orders.

"We're leaving today, so let's get moving. Mitch, get those tools put away. Scott and Dave, bring up the dinghy. I want to cast off in an hour."

They were about to depart on their next adventure. All that held them here was Bob clearing customs and getting the guns back.

"I think I'll prepare dinner ahead of time, then if it's rough I won't have to be in the galley very long," said Betty.

She stuffed a turkey and put it in the oven, then peeled the potatoes while they waited.

Bob came back with their papers stamped, the guns and ammunition. "Let's get out of here before they find something else for us to sign or pay for."

Frank, Betty and Greg were standing on the stern deck, looking back at Bermuda, as they sailed out of the harbor.

Greg looked excited. "We're on our way again."

"The sails are set and the winds on our stern," said Frank looking up at the sky. "We seem to be moving at a smooth clip. Hope it stays this way." Then he walked into the cockpit with Greg following behind. Betty stayed to watched the shore slowly disappear. She wondered what was in store for them. *Could she handle the next leg better this time?*

Dave already had his seasick patch on and was writing some post cards. He called out, "Anyone know what today's date is?"

"Yeah, it's the seventeenth of August," said Frank.

Then Dave asked, "And how far is it from Bermuda to the Azores?"

"It's two thousand miles. It should take about fourteen days depending on the weather," answered Bob. "So you might as well settle in and relax."

Bob turned the boat east towards the Azores, and the wind direction changed. It was now pushing against *Destiny*'s bow and they were sailing against a strong head wind.

"Here we go, beating against the wind again and it's getting rough," Betty said as she watched the waves slap the deck. Greg laid down quickly on the bench in the cockpit.

Dave looked over at Betty and pointed behind his ear. "You should have put your patch on. Here's one for you and Greg, put it on now," he said as he handed her a patch that was cut in half.

Just before sunset she went down to the galley to complete the dinner. After twenty minutes, her stomach was churning. "Darn, I should have remembered to put the patch on earlier."

The smell of the roasting turkey filled the air with tempting aromas and the crew was ravenous. Ringing the dinner bell, she stepped aside and the crew came charging down for their evening meal. They made short work of the bird, leaving nothing but skin and bones. Their appetites were not effected in the least by the motion. Working in the galley, even with the air conditioning, the intense heat and the rough motion had taken it's toll on her. After three bites of turkey and a taste of potatoes, Betty broke into the familiar cold sweat and she headed for her bed. Lying there fighting the nausea and churning in her stomach, she kept her eyes closed hoping it would pass. "I'll never cook a big meal again on the first day out," she said as she drifted off to sleep.

Bob felt sorry for her and took her watch, letting her sleep through the night.

There was very little wind for the next four days and they had fourteen hundred miles to go. They motored waiting for a change in the weather. *Destiny* rocked against the waves in a lurching movement and everyone hung on whether they were sitting or moving around the boat.

Bob was at his navigation table where he was checking the course, "Hey, looks like the sun's over the yardarm. Guess it's cocktail time," he said putting his pencil down.

"Sunset is an entrancing time of the day," Betty said, as she fixed a martini. "Look how smooth the water is, it's like a sheet of glass."

Mitch chimed in. "Is that true, or is it the couple of drinks we have?"

"Don't know for sure," said Scott, "but this sure is relaxing. God, look at that sunset, nothing prettier in the world."

"Thought you said girls were the prettiest thing in the world?" Greg said, half sitting up.

"Well, Greg, that's another subject. Now let me tell you about girls," Scott said looking over at Betty with a twinkle in his eye.

Betty threw her book at him and laughed, "Watch what you tell him, Scott."

Greg frowned, "Grandma, how am I going to know about girls if you don't let them tell me?"

Betty patted his head, "Don't worry, you'll find out soon enough."

Scott had told her that Greg had been asking him what it was like to be with a girl in bed. Gregory was getting quite an education from the big boys. She wondered if he'd tell his mother about the conversations onboard.

Six days had gone by and time seemed to pass quickly; they still had eight days before they would arrive at the Azores. The wind was calm and they were still motoring. Stopping, they took a short swim to break the monotony, with Mitch standing shotgun, looking out for sharks. It felt great to be off the boat, getting some exercise.

Bob grabbed Betty's hand and they jumped in the water. First they swam under the boat, so Bob could see how many barnacles had built up on the bottom. Then they surfaced, letting the waves lift them, as they floated on the top of the water. The coolness enveloped them as the blue crystalline water washed over their bodies, leaving a foamy froth. Finally tired but refreshed, they climbed aboard ready to sail off again.

Bob laughed as he climbed aboard. "I noticed everyone was much braver swimming here than they were in the Bermuda Triangle."

"Yeah, no ghosts to worry about," said Betty.

On the seventh day, life seemed to switch gears and the days seemed endless, Betty felt edgy. Looking up at the sky she watched two gray and white long tail birds gracefully drift in the

114

air currents. Picking up air speed, the birds swooped down to the water's edge each catching a small fish in their beaks. Betty wondered how the birds could fly so far from land. How could they land on the surface of the rough water without being knocked over by the peaking waves. She became hypnotized by the gentle motion of their small bodies. The birds rested momentarily, bobbing up and down in the choppy waves. They looked so small and delicate against the vastness of the sea.

"Boy, what I wouldn't give to fly," Betty said. "I would fly home so fast."

"You're not trying to say you'd leave us are you?" asked Scott.

Betty stood up and put her arms out to the sides, "Just give me the wings, just give me the wings."

Scott grabbed her and held her down while he tickled her, making her scream for mercy. Pushing him away she sat on the bench and Greg laid down next to her, putting his head on her lap. "Scratch my head," he said.

Betty gently rubbed his head as he lay quietly beside her. "What are you thinking about? You look like you're in a trance."

"I wish I'd taken that plane home—I wish I could get off this boat right now."

"You're feeling better than you did on the last trip aren't you?" Greg nodded yes.

"Only a few more days and we'll be there," she said, knowing exactly how he felt.

The day crept by and at last it was sunset, cocktail time. Betty took one sip of her martini then threw it overboard. "I can't drink this. I don't feel well."

"You must be sick to throw your martini away," chided Frank.

"That's a shame, hon. What's the matter, seasick?" asked Bob.

"No, I have a bladder infection."

"What are you taking for it?" asked Bob.

"Penicillin every four hours, I hope I get over it soon. I feel cranky and miserable and the burning sensation is driving me crazy."

"We're on single watch now, are you going to be all right with

115

yours?" asked Bob. "Mine starts in a half-hour, if you're not well I'll take it for you."

"No, I'll be all right. I'm not tired. I'll stay up and keep you company."

The sky was dark on the moonless night with only a few stars twinkling far in the distance. The sea mist floated through the air giving off a scent of salt and the brine stung her nostrils.

"You know, we haven't passed a ship the whole time we've been out. I don't think we saw one when we were sailing to Bermuda either," said Betty.

"Well, if we see one I hope it's in the daylight, that way I'm sure they see us. One of the reasons we stand watch all night is because of potential collisions with ships," said Bob. "By the way, how are you feeling? "

"I'm running to the john every fifteen minutes, but I'll be all right."

"If you're sure you don't want me to take your watch, then I'm going to bed, I'm exhausted. He reached down and kissed Betty goodnight. "Call me if you need me."

She sat alone at the helm looking up at the sky. *I know it's the same sky back home. I wonder if my family and friends are looking at it too?* She thought about when her children were little and needed her. How quickly they grew up. Where did the time go? Had she been a good mother? She thought she had been. Now they have children of their own and she was missing their important years. She let her life skip through her mind, reliving past years, then she thought about her days on *Destiny. God, I hate myself for nagging so much, I feel like a shrew. My personality seems to be withdrawing. I'm not as outgoing as I use to be. Even my brain feels useless and numb.* Sitting quietly, she contemplated her thoughts and vowed to be more pleasant and tolerant. Betty got the sudden urge to go to the bathroom again and was glad the boat was on automatic pilot. *Seven days to go* she thought, *before we get to the Azores. Between the motion, the sea sickness and the bladder infection, I feel like jumping overboard.* Gazing out at the black sea, she wondered how it would feel to be adrift and lost in the middle of the ocean. Would she just drown or would a shark eat her? Shuddering, she dismissed the thought. *I know I feel bad but not bad enough to jump in.*

Her watch was finally over and Mitch came up to relieve her. They talked for awhile before Betty went to bed, hoping for a good night of rest.

Bob sat up as she came into the room. "How come you're still awake?" asked Betty.

"I feel exhausted and I really want to sleep. If only that aggravating motion would stop."

Betty crawled in bed and was drifting off when the wind picked up. She could hear Mitch at the helm, adjusting the sails. The wind was building higher as *Destiny* bashed through the increasing waves. Betty slammed against Bob and their heads banged together. Her body screamed to be soothed by a passive motion, but there was no rest.

"Ouch," Bob said. "You gave me an egg on my head. Feel the size of it."

"I'm sorry, I couldn't help it. I have a lump too."

Adjusting her position she fitfully tried to fall asleep again.

At first light, *Destiny*'s motion had subsided. Out on deck, the morning dew was sparkling against the full sails in the sunlight. Bob was on his morning watch.

"The boat's riding much smoother. What happened?" asked Betty.

"The wind changed. It's coming off the stern," answered Bob. "We're broad reaching and doing around seven knots. Look, no storm clouds in the sky; no squalls on the radar."

"Hooray, things are looking up," she said as she went out on the bow to do her daily chore—picking up the dead flying fish. "Fifteen fish today, maybe we should cook them?" Then, smelling them, she said, "Yuck, they're too ripe."

Dave had put the fishing lines out on his early watch and the zing of the reel broke the morning silence. Then another zing as the other reel went off almost simultaneously. Greg grabbed one rod and Frank the other and started to reel in the lines. Greg had trouble landing the small tuna, and Bob went to help him.

They had caught a small dolphin and a tuna. Twenty minutes later, the reels went off again and this time the fish were really putting up a fight.

Awakened by the commotion, Scott and Dave came running

up on deck. "Hey, they're our fish, we'll land them."

They caught two thirty-pound dolphin fish. The bright colors of the rainbow shone from their bodies, sparkling in the sunlight. Then slowly the colors started to fade away as they started to die.

"Throw one back before it dies," said Scott. "We only need one for dinner."

Dave picked up the smallest one and threw it overboard.

"I feel so good today, I sure felt rotten yesterday," said Betty "I think the penicillin's doing the trick."

"If you're full of energy maybe you could make some bread. What we have is all moldy," suggested Bob.

Betty agreed, "I think I could handle it as long as it doesn't get rough again."

"I promise I 'll tell you if we have to change tack," said Bob.

Betty mixed all the ingredients together and then passed the dough up to Scott and Frank to knead. She threw a load of wash in the washer. It felt fantastic to be able to move around the boat, without bumping into things. Her legs and arms were black and blue from the slams and bumps of the last few days. They called Greg the Technicolor Yawn, now they're calling her the Technicolor Body.

After taking the dough from Frank and Scott, she let it rise then put it in the oven. They would have fresh warm bread with their dinner. She walked out on the bow and stood on the bow sprit looking out at the horizon. Bob came out and turned her around to face the row of sails. Their half-moon shapes were in full bloom, with the wind filling each white sail. His arms were around her as he said, "When you're facing this way you can really feel the force of the wind. The whole atmosphere feels so powerful."

"That's incredible," said Betty. "I love sailing when it's smooth like this. It makes you feel so free."

"This boat weighs eighty-five thousand pounds and the wind alone is pushing her through the water. Now you know why I love it so much. Let's hope the weather stays this way. It's so pleasant."

They stood locked in a close embrace feeling the power and magnitude of the wind as it moved *Destiny* swiftly through the water.

In the stillness, they heard a clanking noise—Scott and Dave were attaching the small barbecue to the railing. They grilled the fish in butter, wine and herbs, and the crew dug into the flaky fish leaving nothing but a clean platter.

After dinner, Frank sipped his bourbon and started in with his storytelling. "Did I ever tell you about the first time I went around the horn?"

"Yes," screamed Scott, "many times, and we don't want to hear it anymore."

Dave had been studying his chart, "According to my calculations we have one thousand, one hundred and five miles to go. Despondently he said, "Would you believe we only sailed one hundred and seventeen miles yesterday."

"Yeah, that was a big disappointment," said Frank. "We were hoping to do at least two hundred."

Scott was looking around lifting cushions. "Did anyone see my blue shirt?"

Betty acted nonchalant as she said. "It blew overboard. You left it on deck last night."

"Shit, that was my best shirt. Why didn't you pick it up when you saw it."

Betty pointed her finger at Scott. "I told you I'm not picking your things up anymore."

Scott slammed down the cushion. "That was a very expensive shirt."

"Well, if it was that expensive why did you leave it on deck?" She looked at Scott's red face, and said, "Stop pouting. It's in the dryer. It was soaking wet, along with your shoes and Greg's shirt. Pick up your damn clothes from now on or next time it *will* go overboard."

Trying to change the subject Frank said, "Did I tell you the joke about the man who went to the doctor's because his penis got burned?"

Greg sat up and was eager to listen. "Tell us I want to hear it."

"Greg, isn't it your turn to do the dishes?" asked Bob.

"Yes, but I want to hear the joke first."

"Come on, Greg, I'll help you," Betty said, leading him down stairs. "Clean up your jokes, Frank, by the time we finish the galley."

That night, they sat on deck and Betty remarked, "What a wonderful difference it makes when the seas are calm and the wind is blowing in the right direction. I feel like I'm floating along on the winds of *Destiny*."

Frank jumped up and slapped his head. "Oh God, now she's getting poetic. I'm going to bed."

One day moved into another without much happening. On the tenth day, the sky took on the nasty look that Betty hated to see, and heavy rain came pouring down.

"I just checked the radio and weather fax. Hurricane Brett is ahead of us, to the port side," said Bob. "A new one called Carla is behind us. We should be able to stay away from it, if we keep this speed and stay oncourse. We're doing almost ten knots."

Bob's words echoed in Betty's mind as she stared out to sea. "Here we go again," she said with apprehension in her voice. Remembering what the ship's officer from the Holland cruise ship had said. She knew Bob could handle *Destiny*, but the wind was so severe and the waves were getting higher. *Please God, get us through this safe*, she silently prayed.

Bob looked at the wind gauge and said, "Let's get the genoa down and reef the mizzen and the main. We should still be able to maintain our speed with reefed sails."

Mitch and Scott worked together adjusting the sails as Bob steered through the building weather.

"Goddamn, we're sure getting it now, but we can take anything Mother Nature dishes out," said Frank, acting macho.

Destiny heeled over twenty degrees and thrashed about as the wind seemed to blow from all directions. The whitecaps on the ocean were building to a high of fifteen feet. The rain came down so hard it blocked out all vision as the waves pounded across *Destiny*'s bow, covering her in a waterfall. The dark clouds twirled in ominous turmoil. The storm lasted an hour, but seemed like an eternity. Finally, the wind diminished.

"Whew, I'm glad that's over," Bob said, as he cleaned his glasses. "Couldn't see a damn thing through these lenses."

"You couldn't see anything with or without glasses. That was wild," said Frank. "We must have got some of the side effects of the hurricanes."

With the change of lighter winds, Betty was able to bake two pies without a mishap. Still full of energy, she did another load of wash. Then she settled down in her cabin to read. *Maybe I'll enjoy the rest of this trip after all. I'm getting better at handling the storms*, she thought.

She started to doze off when she heard Scott shout, "What's that over there?"

Jumping out of bed, she ran up to the deck.

"That's a water spout from a whale," yelled Frank from the bow.

"Looks like a big pod of them," said Dave.

Bob changed course to get a closer view. Approaching slowly he guided *Destiny* closer then cut the engine. They drifted along with the family of whales, observing the creatures as they lay on the calm surface. They were so close they could see the barnacles on the whales monstrous backs. Water spouted in jet streams from their blow holes. Their mammoth, gray bodies glistened in the sun. Six adults surrounded two baby whales, protecting and guiding them. *Destiny* and the whales drifted along in perfect harmony enjoying the solitude. The whales soon became tired of the invasion of their privacy. The largest one dove under the water, then came up thrusting its massive body out of the water. Then it thrashed back down into the water, creating a tremendous wake. The rest of the family joined in the breaching and soon the water was turbulent, smashing against *Destiny*.

"Let's not press our luck. Whales have been known to sink a ship when they are annoyed," said Bob as he pushed on the throttle steering away from the pod.

"We're like a pod of people," said Dave. "It takes an experience like that to make you realize that we have our own little world here on *Destiny*. Everything we do involves each other. Our lives depend on one another."

They all sat, quietly thinking about what Dave had said. Then Mitch stood up and slapped Dave on the back, "Boy, that's deep. We need some life in this party. Let's lighten things up and have a crazy hat contest."

Scott eyes brightened as he added, "Everybody make up a funny hat and the winner gets a bottle of champagne."

121

"Sounds like a good idea to me," said Frank. "I can come up with a kooky hat."

Betty was excited, she loved parties, "Okay, let's do it! We'll wear them at cocktail hour."

Cocktail time arrived and they all modeled their creations as Greg stood up wearing a baseball hat. It was covered with pictures from a magazine of young kids on skateboards. "This hat represents the skateboard people of the world."

"Yeah, for Greg," Scott said stamping his feet.

"Boo, terrible, not good enough," said Mitch.

Scott stood up wearing a hat with colorful lures and a tangle of fishing lines wrapped around the brim. There was a funny cardboard flap from a beer carton that hung down in his face. "This represents the fish we have caught and the ones that got away."

Frank scratched his head and asked, "What the hell's the flap in the front for?"

"Damned if I know. I just didn't know what else to put there."

"Boo, throw that hat overboard," said Dave.

"No, throw the *bum* overboard," said Frank.

Bob's hat was covered with American and foreign one dollar bills. "Well guys, this hat is my poor hat. When I stared this trip I had hundred dollar bills in my pocket. This is all that's left."

"We have no sympathy for you, sorry," said Frank.

Mitch grabbed Betty's arm and pulled her up. "Okay, it's your turn."

Betty got up and slowly turned. She was wearing a large brim straw hat. Hanging down on each side was a black lace bra. The top of the hat was covered with see-through bikini panties. Two more pair hung down the back. Dangling earrings and beads made a band around the hat. "These are all the things I've had to give up to go on this trip. I've become a wild sea witch."

Frank broke up in laughter. "Yeah, yeah, we know it's tough on you being here on this luxurious yacht. I'd rather see you wear them, then maybe you'd win a prize."

Next was conservative Dave, strutting his hat covered with old weather fax paper. Charts were rolled up and placed on each side of the brim and pen and pencils hung all around it.

"This is the great navigator's hat. This hat will get us to the Azores. It tells us we still have seven hundred and fifty miles to go."

"If we're depending on that hat, we're in trouble. That shows the weather in Alaska," said Bob laughing.

Frank's hat contained a self-explanatory sign: "I lived through the Bermuda Triangle."

Everyone stamped their feet and booed.

Mitch was last. His hat had tools hanging from it and a water pump on the top. A sign hanging from it read 'Boat Bum.'

Cheers went out from everyone. They cast their secret ballots and the winner was Mitch, the champion hat-maker. Bob presented him with the prize, a bottle of champagne. Mitch gave a little speech of acceptance, telling us what a great hat maker he really was. Then he broke open the champagne for a toast to his hat, and to the seven hundred and fifty miles they still had to go.

Ten

During the night, storms were on each side of them, causing the wind to be very unsettled. Getting around was very difficult again, and the creeks and thumps echoed through the boat. The waves bashed against the hull, causing a loud thrashing noise, that added to the torment. The crew tried to sleep, but it was in vain. Betty heard voices above and knew it was time for her morning watch.

"What are you doing?" she asked Bob, as she sat down next to him at the navigation table.

"Still tracking the hurricanes. They're not a threat yet, but we are feeling their rough effects."

She made herself a cup of coffee, and went up to the helm. The sky was laden with heavy, mystical dark clouds and the strong wind sang a melancholy tune, as they swirled around the tall mast. After her watch was over she went down to see Bob. "Are you still tracking the weather?"

"Yes," he said not looking up. "What do you have planned?"

"Oh, I thought I'd go shopping at Bloomingdale's, then stop off at a good French restaurant for lunch," she joked.

"Don't you wish. No kidding, what are you going to do?"

Betty scrunched her face up. "Make some bread. Doesn't that sound exciting?"

Bob's voice raised a notch. "Are we out of bread again?

"With seven people, it goes fast. I better get started. I don't like to cook in this weather, but today I have no choice," she walked into the galley and started to mix the ingredients.

This time, things didn't go so smoothly. The boat was already doing the *Destiny* rock, and now the boat's bow was slapping down on the increasing waves. The vibration caused the closet door to fly open and a bottle of vinegar narrowly missed her head. Five pounds of flour sailed through the air as she yelled, "Mitch, come fix the damn latches on these doors before I get my head bashed in. I thought you fixed them in Bermuda."

The stifling heat in the galley caused her to feel faint. Her brow was covered with droplets of perspiration that wove their way down into her eyes. Her shirt was soaked from sweat, and stuck to her body like she was in a wet T-shirt contestant. Her auburn hair kept drooping in her face, and it became streaked with white flour as she pushed it aside.

"I can't think clearly," Betty said shaking her head. She knew she shouldn't but she took a chance and opened the porthole. She wanted some relief from the heat of the oven. "Oh, that feels good," she murmured.

Placing her face close to the porthole, she shut her eyes and took a deep breath. *Destiny* dipped low to starboard, and a huge wave splashed through the porthole, drenching her and splashing across the galley. Betty stood by helplessly as the milk and flour flew off the counter, spilling on to the floor. As she reached to close the porthole, another wave came in, washing her down again. She lost her balance and fell on the floor, landing in the middle of the gooey flour and milk.

"Damnit," she screamed. "I want off this fucking boat."

Scott came down and closed the porthole. Laughing, he said, "Is that a new way to make bread?"

"Don't be so damn funny," she said, then she started laughing. "Hey I'm beginning to sound like the rest of you. I'm getting to be a real salty sea witch."

Betty sat on deck waiting for *Destiny* to settle down, and in an hour the boat was back to it's normal slow rock.

"Greg, if you'll help me clean up the kitchen floor, I'll make you your favorite cookies."

A big smile came on Greg's face at the mention of cookies. "Sure, as long as you make peanut cookies."

While the bread and cookies were being baked, the aroma drove the men into a hungry frenzy.

Up on deck in the cool breeze, Betty poured herself a glass of iced tea and relaxed. Everyone was lounging around reading. She sat there in deep thought, then said, "I never used to use four letter words." She was feeling ashamed of her tantrum.

"Four letter words? You mean like *fuck*," said Frank laughing at her.

"Don't be so smart. I never used to cuss, it must be your bad influence."

"Not to change the subject, but there's an eerie quietness all of a sudden. Like the calm before the storm," said Scott. "Can you feel it?"

"I can," said Mitch. "The wind has stopped completely."

Mother Nature allowed them to finish dinner before she let loose. A downpour accompanied the wind as it built quickly to thirty knots, raising the height of the waves to twelve feet.

Bob looked out at the sky. "We're still getting the effects of the hurricanes." *Destiny* was riding high and fast into the waves. "If the winds stay in this direction we'll be able to leave the sails up. If they change we'll have to reef them."

Rather than sit out in the cockpit, Betty went to their stateroom and took a book with her. If she was going to be bumped around, she'd rather be on a soft bed. The Stephen King book she was reading was good and it might keep her mind off the storm. Later, she went up on deck for her watch.

Bob was at the helm. "The autopilot's having trouble holding the course. You'll have to hand steer. Do you think you'll be all right?"

"Yes, sure, I'll handle it. What's our course?" said Betty sounding more sure of herself than she felt.

"Eighty-five degrees. Don't let it go off course or it will luff the sails. We need to keep the sails full of wind at all times. If you have any problems, call me."

"Don't worry, I'll pull you out of bed if I need you."

"Give me a kiss good night; I'll see you when you come to bed."

They stood in their dripping rain gear holding each other, trying for a moment of tenderness. Lately very little time or thought had been given to intimacy, but they felt the strength of their love building each day.

All through the night, the gusty wind fluctuated between thirty and forty knots, slacking only briefly to ten, a moment's peace. Holding *Destiny* on course was difficult, but Betty was able to control the helm. She switched back to the autopilot whenever possible to give her aching arms a break and to grab a cup of coffee. The blackness of the night was like a cocoon around her and she felt so alone. She felt the wind's strength and ferocity as it blew against her body, strong enough to blow her overboard if she went out on deck.

Betty's mind wandered now and then, but her thoughts were mostly on the course she must keep. The radar was like a beacon of safety, and Betty glanced at the screen often, checking for unseen ships. She heard the water washing along the sides, the rocking kept rhythm with the waves. Thoughts of being shipwrecked entered her mind, but she pushed them aside. As the night went on it got harder to keep *Destiny* on course; the wind was getting stronger.

Happy to see Frank come up, she said, "I'm glad to see you." She stood up and bowed. "It's all yours, mate. I'm going to bed."

Frank sat down with a cup of coffee in his hand. "How's it going, anything happening?"

"It's been pretty wild at times. Right now, the winds are about twenty-five knots. There's been nothing on radar, and our course is eighty-five degrees. That's the last of the coffee," she nodded towards his cup. "Can I fix another pot before I go to bed?"

"No, I'll fix some coffee later. Good luck on sleeping, it's rough down there. See you in the morning."

Betty started toward the steps then stopped, "Oh! Bob said to call him if there's any problem."

"Hey, I'm an old salt, I can handle anything. I don't need any sleeping beauties to help me," said Frank, laughing like an old sea captain.

Betty made her way to the stateroom and felt her way in the darkness. She found the door to the head, and just as she opened it, the boat lurched sideways. The movement pulled her back and then threw her forward catching her arm between the door and the frame. A searing pain ran up her arm as the latch jammed into her flesh. She stifled her cry so she wouldn't wake Bob, and soaked her arm in cold water. She waited for the pain to subside, then painfully crawled into bed.

Bob turned over and yawned, "How'd the watch go?"

"I didn't know you were awake. If I had known you weren't asleep I would have screamed out loud when I hurt my arm on that damn door."

"I heard you bang yourself and wondered why you didn't holler. If it had been me, I would have woke the whole boat." They both broke out laughing.

Betty crawled in bed beside him. "Have you been able to sleep at all?"

"I dozed off a little, but not for long. The boat is heeling to your side, and between the motion and the angle it's tough sleeping."

"A-ha! I got the good side tonight. I'm lucky you didn't take it while I was on watch." Cuddling, they drifted off and on in a fretful sleep, just waiting for daylight and a possible change in the wind.

Betty's arm throbbed as she rolled over on it, and realized it was morning. The wind had calmed to twelve knots and they were able to easily move around.

"How's your arm?" asked Bob when she went upstairs.

"It hurts. Look how black and blue it is. Oh, by the way, today's August twenty-second, Greg's birthday. Let's pretend to ignore it, then we'll surprise him later."

"Good idea, we'll fool the little twerp," said Bob. "When the rest of the crew gets up we'll tell them what we have planned for his birthday."

Greg rushed up the stairs in a happy mood and looked around at everyone. "Today's my birthday! Isn't anyone going to wish me happy birthday?" No one said a word, just went on with their conversations.

Feeling neglected, he stood next to Scott. Looking up at him with sad eyes, he said, "How come no one's wishing me a happy birthday?"

"Look, Greg, this whole trip you've been telling us you're one of the big boys. When you get to be one of the big boys, birthdays really don't mean that much. Nobody pays attention to them."

"My mom always celebrates my birthday at home. I'm not a big guy yet."

"On this trip you've tagged along everywhere with us guys, so we're treating you just like one of us."

Greg picked up a book and flopped down on the seat, pretending to read. "Anyone want to play cards?"

They played cards with him while Betty secretly taped the

conversation. Their card playing sounded like a comedy show, as the men cut up each other and laid it heavy on Greg.

After dinner, everyone sat in the salon talking. Greg was still upset and went up on deck. It was his turn to do the dishes and he was hoping they'd forget.

They let him sit up there for a while then Betty called up to him, "Greg, come down and do the dishes."

"Ah Grandma, it's my birthday! Can't I have the day off?"

"Get down here right away," Betty yelled. He dragged himself slowly down the stairs, feeling melancholy.

As Greg reached the bottom step, "Surprise, happy birthday," rang through the salon and they sang out, "Happy birthday to you, happy birthday to you. You look like a monkey and you act like one too."

Betty had baked a chocolate cake with white icing. It was decorated with a picture of a skate board.

Greg sat on the steps and cried, "I thought you didn't care about my birthday."

The candles were lit and they gave him presents. Each person had designed a card, making up their own verses. Mitch created a masterpiece, a card made out of a large piece of cardboard from one of the parts boxes. He drew a globe with a ship in the middle of it, waves surrounded the globe. Inside he artistically printed, YOU MADE A TRANSATLANTIC CROSSING ON YOUR FOURTEENTH BIRTHDAY. Then he gave him his watch he had been wearing.

Greg wiped the tears from his cheeks and said, "Thanks a lot for the watch Mitch, but don't you need it?"

Mitch put his arm around Greg's shoulder. "Happy birthday. I want you to have it. You're a nice kid."

He put the watch on and with tears still streaming down his face he said, "I thought you didn't celebrate birthdays?"

"Well, in your case, we made an exception," said Bob patting him on the back.

"Not many boys turn fourteen crossing the Atlantic," said Scott.

On the other side of the card-playing tape, Betty recorded the party and gave it to him and said, "This will be a great memory for you and because it's your birthday, you won't have to do the dishes."

129

"Let's drink a toast to Greg," said Mitch, as he handed Greg a coke and poured the rest of them wine.

"There's good news tonight," said Dave, rubbing his hands together. "We only have four hundred miles to go, which hopefully, means only three more days at sea."

Betty smiled. "Just three more days until we get to land."

The dangers of the hurricanes had passed and the wind was mild with just enough breeze to keep *Destiny* moving at four-and-a-half knots. There was very little rocking and the peaceful day was enchanting. Several of the crew laid in the shade of the sails, a light breeze fanning their bodies. The massive ocean surrounded the ship, with a far-reaching view of abstract blues.

After dinner, they enjoyed the sunset and Betty said, "I just discovered something!"

"Yeah, what's the big breakthrough?" Frank said, as he sat up and leaned close to Betty. "Tell me your big discovery."

"Get out of my face, Frank, I'm trying to be serious. I've always had problems with allergies, but out here on the water I don't have a problem. I never sneeze or cough and my eyes don't itch."

Scott slapped his leg, "Great discovery. You don't itch or sneeze, you're just seasick all the time. What a tradeoff."

"Stop being so funny," Betty said stifling a laugh, "There's no bugs, flies or mosquitoes to bother us."

"You're right," said Frank. "They're too smart to come out this far. You think they're crazy like we are?"

Bob was sitting on the stern reading a murder-mystery book. "It doesn't take much to entertain you guys anymore. I don't know what's going on but you sure are laughing.

Dave stretched his body, his strong arms raising in the air. "I'm going to take a nap, I can't take anymore of this."

"Me too," said Greg as he slid down the steps. "I don't know what makes me so tired all the time."

It was the fourteenth day at sea when Scott saw the first glimpse of the Azore Mountains. "Land a-ho," his voice echoed through the boat. They had sailed two thousand miles.

Betty started to clean the galley and salon since she didn't want to do it when they arrived at the town of Horta in the Azores.

"Will you men please help me clean up? You helped make the mess. We're almost there, so please, *please*, pick up your junk." No one answered her. Raising her voice louder, she said, "I need help cleaning up the cockpit."

"Okay, after the movie's over," said Dave. They were watching the movie *Scarface* on video, and no one moved. Bob was busy at the helm, and didn't hear what was happening. The more she worked alone, the madder she got. They'd soon be docking and then all the men would jump off and leave, just as they did in Bermuda. She would be left behind to clean up and get things in order while Mitch washed down the boat.

Walking into their staterooms was a mistake. It was complete chaos. The sink, shower and toilets were filthy. She yelled to them, "I'm not touching this crummy mess. I don't think your cabins have been cleaned since we left Florida. I don't know how you can live this way."

"Come on, it's not that bad!" said Dave.

"It's not? Well how come I can't see in the mirrors, and why are the toilets and showers all brown and green? What are all the mildewed clothes doing all over the floor?"

At this point, Betty was talking to the walls. The men were back engrossed in the movie. Giving up, she finished wiping the floors and getting the water marks off the furniture. She picked up the rest of the clothes that were laying around and heaved them into their staterooms. Seeing the room again got her roaring mad.

She walked over to the television and snapped it off. "I'm not putting up with this any longer. Get in your staterooms and clean up your mess. I'll be damned if I'm doing it. I mean *now*."

Shocked, they looked at each other. "I think she's mad," said Greg.

"Yeah, she's really pissed off," said Scott.

One by one, they went into their rooms and started to clean. Betty took her cleaning supplies and put them by their stateroom door. "Here's the Lysol®, scrub rags, and Windex®. Do a good job, not a half-assed one."

When they motored into Faial, in the Azores, they could see the outline of the town of Horta. As *Destiny* sailed closer to the island they could smell the perfume of flowers in the air. The picturesque view of the green hills and palm trees was a perfect back drop for the stark white marina, trimmed in pink with a colorful Portuguese flag flying high above it. Multicolor wild flowers were scattered through the fields, with fluttering butterflies above them.

Betty was spellbound as she gazed out at the island. It had been two weeks since she had a glimpse of land. "Everything is so green and lush, it looks like heaven," sighed Betty, eager to get ashore. "I want to feel the cool green grass beneath my bare feet. I want to roll around in it and lounge under a shady tree for the rest of the day."

Scott had other ideas, "I can't wait to go cruising down the streets of Horta and see the pretty senoritas."

"Ho-lay," yelled Frank clicking his heels as he danced on the decks. Soon they all were dancing and laughing, delirious from the sight of land.

Bob called on the radio and made reservations at the marina. He had been told by other yachtsmen that it was a friendly, clean harbor. Mitch hoisted the Portuguese courtesy flag and also the quarantine flag to let customs know they were entering the country.

Destiny was soon tied up at the customs and immigration pier, expecting to be held up for hours. The officers were there in a half-hour and the paper work took only minutes, then the officers took the guns ashore.

When Betty stepped off the boat, a numbness went through her body, then her legs wobbled like a rubber hose. A surge of energy went from her head to her toes as her feet felt the good earth.

Bob came back from the dockmaster's hut. "Guess how much they charge for the slip?"

"Well, they charged sixty dollars a day in Bermuda, it has to be cheaper here. So I'll say forty dollars a day," answered Betty.

"Would you believe, three dollars and fifty cents a day?"

"Wow, what a difference. I just paid twelve dollars a minute to telephone home and I could hardly hear them."

"That's outrageous. The docks are probably the most inexpensive thing on the island."

"Everyone's fine, it was great talking to my family." Betty smiled, "They said to tell you hello, they were glad we made it safely."

Betty stretched her arms high in the air and twirled around with delight. "God, it feels great being back on land after being out on that rolling sea for fourteen days."

"Lets take a walk. I need to stretch my legs," said Bob. "We'll look for a mechanic to check out the engine."

A short walk was all their legs could take, so after a quick dinner on shore they returned to *Destiny* ready for a good night sleep.

They awoke, ready to explore the town. Horta was a quaint little place with friendly people but very little English was spoken here. After a walk around the small town, Betty and Bob were ready to go up into the green flourishing hills. They rented a car and went off to see the island. They drove along the small narrow streets making their way toward the mountains. Farms framed with beautiful blue and purple hydrangea fences, dotting the hill side. As they drove up the mountains they could see miles and miles of the colorful enclosures. Inside each field was a cow or two, sometimes a horse tied to a tree. Livestock seemed very scarce and precious. It was common to see a man or boy coming down the road, walking a cow on a leash, as you would a dog. Another man sat by the roadside on a stool, milking his cow and selling the milk to the villagers.

Storybook gingerbread houses stood along the roads. Some were built with large colorful stones; others were white stucco. The roofs were made of either straw or red tile, and old fashioned iron pumps at the end of the roads were their only source for water. Each village gave the appearance of days gone by and Betty had the feeling she was in the seventeenth century. They came to a picturesque restaurant, sitting on the side of the mountain, and had the specialty of the day—fish soup and warm rolls.

When they returned to the boat, Greg was playing with a young boy from the village named Tommy. He spent the rest of the day teaching his new friend how to use his skateboard. Scott and Dave were meeting two Swedish girls they had met that afternoon. The rest of the group relaxed in the town square enjoying the music of the guitarist and the friendly atmosphere.

The next day, Scott and Dave were nowhere to be found, last night they had not come home. Mitch was varnishing the bright work and seemed a little haggard.

"Hey, have you seen Scott or Dave?" asked Bob.

He didn't answer for a moment, then looked up. "No. I was with them for awhile last night, but I haven't seen them this morning."

"Where is Frank?" asked Bob.

"He took off, said he was going to do a little touring."

Betty eyed Mitch. "Are you all right? You look sad . . . or are you just hung over?"

"A little hung over, but mostly I miss Diane," said Mitch, wiping the tears from his eyes.

"Did you call her since we arrived?" asked Betty.

Mitch gave a big sigh. "Yes, but there was no answer."

"Well, try again later. We're going to find a travel agent, Greg still wants to go home," said Bob.

There were very few travel agencies in Horta and when they did find one, they were told the plane was sold out. The airline only flew out one day a week and tomorrow was the day. Greg was unhappy when he heard the news. "Ah, darn it. I wanted to go home."

"We'll try again in San Miguel. It's only a day sail and we're going to leave in two days. This way you'll get a chance to see more of the Azores before you leave," said Betty. "We're going to drive out to the other end of the island. Do you want to come?"

"Nah, I'll stay here and play with Tommy."

The north end of the island was completely barren of any greenery. Brown rocky rubble reached as far as the eye could see. It resembled the scenery from *Planet of the Apes*. A volcano stood high, lifting its eerie peak to the sky. It had erupted back in 1957 and 1958, completely destroying this side of the island. The lava had formed large holes by the water's edge and blue water from the ocean filled the holes, making lovely pools to bathe in. Steps had been carved into the rock that gave easy access to the warm salty pool. Climbing down, they submerged themselves into the water as the waves washed around their bodies. The sandy beach was black pulverized lava, and glistened in the sun, making it hot to walk on.

Before they knew it, three days had gone by and it was their last night in Horta.

Having a drink before dinner, Betty remarked, "It's so nice here, I wish we could stay longer."

Scott was laying on the couch and yawned. "I'm not ready to leave either."

Frank jabbed him in the ribs. "Yeah, you only like it because you met a couple of girls. You and Dave never saw much of the island."

"You're just jealous because you didn't meet someone," said Dave.

"I didn't come here to pick up girls. I came to see what the world looks like," said Frank.

"Yeah sure. What happened to you last night, Mitch? We tried to fix you up with a babe and you disappeared," said Scott.

"Don't do me any favors, she was so homely. Besides, I miss Diane."

"Mitch, if you miss Diane so much how come you tried to put a make on my girl?" asked Scott.

"You should have hung around, you might have got lucky like we did," said Dave.

Greg jumped up and down. "Will someone tell me what get lucky means?"

"Let's change the subject. Let's drink to the next leg of our journey. Here's to San Miguel," said Betty.

Bob had two drinks instead of his usual one, and when they left for the restaurant he was feeling no pain. Walking along the pier he met an old sailing buddy he hadn't seen in years. His friend insisted they join him for a drink. Rather than hurt his feelings, Bob had another vodka and tonic. The booze was definitely having an effect on him and he started to slur his words and repeat his sentences.

Betty was getting hungry, "We really have to leave. We have to meet our crew for dinner."

The restaurant was an extraordinary old fort, built with immense gray slabs of rock. Humongous wooden doors, six inches thick, stood at the entrance, adding to Horta's old-world feeling. Renovations had turned the old relic into a unique restaurant that welcomed diners with flaming torches at the gates. Betty could easily imagine warriors crossing the mighty bridge over the flowing moat. Today, the moat is just a dried-up ditch, filled with modern day rubbish of coke cans, newspapers and old rags.

Greeted by the owner, they were led to the table where the crew was waiting.

Everyone had the island special, the only thing on the menu. Fried fish or chicken, greasy potatoes, and two slices of tomato on a leaf of lettuce, saturated with salt. Large bottles of white *vino* were placed on the table, and the waiter promptly filled each glass. The wine was excellent and very reasonably priced.

"This fish might be salty, but I'm so hungry it tastes good to me," said Frank.

"Pass the wine, Dave, my glass is empty," said Scott.

Betty looked over at Bob and said, "Could you pass me the bread." Bob's eyes were closed, and his head was nodding slowly down to his plate.

"He's asleep!" said Betty. "Bob, wake up," and she shook him awake just before his face landed in his food.

Bob's eyes popped open, "What's the matter?... Oh! I think I'm finished," said Bob still slurring his words. "I—I think I better go back to the boat." Then he let out a silly hyena laugh that rang through the restaurant.

Scott pushed his still full plate away, "Come on, Dad, I'll take you back to the boat."

Betty stood up. "Stay and finish your meal, Scott, I'm finished. I can get him back."

Frank reached over and helped Bob up. "You can't tackle him by yourself. I'm through eating, I'll go with you."

They walked down the winding path, heading for the docks, with Bob dragging his feet most of the way.

Bob was in a talkative mood. "What's the matter, do you think I'm drunk? You know I don't get drunk."

"No, you're not drunk," said Frank laughing, "You just wanted to wash your face in your fried fish."

"Well, at least you're a happy drunk," Betty said, as she helped guide him down the path.

"That's right, you got it, I'm not drunk," he said, tripping over his own feet.

"Okay! You're not drunk. You're just sleepy, right?" Betty answered.

Greg caught up with them, and was putting his skate board to some hard use. He maneuvered the board up and down the sidewalks, circling around them chanting, "Bob's drunk, Bob's drunk."

Finally, with much effort, they got him on board and he collapsed into bed, instantly falling asleep, snoring and snorting away.

Frank and Betty sat in the cockpit enjoying the cool breeze that was blowing in from the sea. In the distance, they could hear the strumming of guitars while a soft soprano voice crooned an unfamiliar melody. There was a feeling of serenity on the island that Betty enjoyed. Tomorrow they would sail to San Miguel.

Shopping for food in Horta was an adventure. Since they couldn't read the labels, they would guess at the contents by the pictures. Picking out fresh vegetables and fruit took very little time since the island had a limited selection. The women of the villages made delicious bread so six loaves were purchased along with mouth watering cheese and several bottles of *vino*. They wanted fresh milk but could only find cartons of the condensed variety. The farmers use all the milk they produce for making cheese to export. Now they were provisioned and ready to go.

Since they were leaving tomorrow they thought they would follow the tradition of the marina. Each boat that docks at Horta paints a scene on the wall of the marina, symbolizing their ship. The walls were brightly decorated with symbols, flags and ships. Mitch, with his great artistic talent, drew a picture of *Destiny* riding high on a wave with a silvery moon shining above it. *Destiny* was now imprinted on the walls of Horta for eternity, and it stood out clearly under the moonlight.

Eleven

By eleven the next morning, they were ready to sail to San Miguel, a one day trip. The ship's papers had been checked through customs and the only thing holding them up was Greg. He was not onboard.

Bob was irritated, "Where is he? What's he doing?"

Betty jumped off the boat to look for him. "He can't find his skateboard and he's very upset. We've been looking all over town for it."

Greg came running down the road. "I can't find it anywhere and I don't want to leave without it!" We've checked *Destiny* and all the streets, it's nowhere around."

Dave had been looking too. "Where did you have it last?"

"Tommy and I were riding it last night in the town square, and when I came back to the boat, I left it in the cockpit."

"Someone must have stolen it, or you left it someplace else. Get onboard we have to leave," said Bob.

"I want to keep looking, I can't leave without it," cried Greg. "If I knew I was going to lose my board I wouldn't have come."

Scott grabbed him and put him on board, as Bob pulled away from the dock.

"Calm down," said Bob as they motored out of the harbor. "Everyone, take your last look at Faial."

Betty looked out at that stillness of the ocean. "The sea's very calm, it's always calm when we leave. Then all hell breaks loose later. Where's my patch?"

Their day at sea was uneventful and peaceful as the water rippled by *Destiny*'s hull. They sailed smoothly toward San Miguel, and Betty could almost say she liked sailing. The crew was passive and slept a lot, having spent their energies at Horta. When dinner was over, they passed the night watching videos.

The wind was strong enough to fill the genoa, main and

mizzen. *Destiny* sailed effortlessly through the blackness of the night.

Betty had a good night sleep and was half-awake when Bob came running into the room.

"Get up quick," he said. "Land is near and we have porpoises racing us."

Stretching, she pushed the sheet off, "Boy, did I sleep well last night. What time is it?"

Bob pulled her out of bed, "Come on, get up so you can see the porpoises before they leave."

The water was a clear aqua blue, it made a visual screen to see through. Betty counted fifteen porpoises as they lept out of the water, then flipped in the air. *Destiny's* group watched as the friendly creatures crisscrossed each other in the water, as they kept up with the boat. They entertained the crew for twenty minutes and then went away.

Betty started to walk back to the cockpit. "Look at all the flying fish that came aboard last night." She hadn't noticed them earlier. "Guess my job for the morning is laid out for me." Then she laughed, "Excuse the pun." She counted twenty dead fish as she threw them off the bow.

The crew gathered on deck as Bob steered *Destiny* toward the harbor of Miguel. Bottles, plastic bags and paper were floating in the water. Oil leaking from the freighters covered the surface and a foul odor filled the air. Arriving at one o'clock in the afternoon, they pulled alongside the dock. Bob climbed off and went to inquire about customs and dockage space. When he came back he said, "It will be awhile, so you might as well get comfortable."

San Miguel is a large commercial island and so far they did not like the looks of the place. They sat in the cockpit waiting and watching a large group of people gather near the boat. The fishermen stared and pointed at *Destiny* moving closer as they talked among themselves. The men were dressed in dirty oil and sweat soaked clothes, their teeth rotted, their hair slicked back and greasy. Two tough looking men started to climbed aboard *Destiny*.

Scott jumped up from his seat and shouted "*Nao isto esta errado.*"

The men stopped immediately and stood with one foot on the toe rail, staring defiantly.

Rotten fish, oil and garbage, permeated the air and Betty covered her nose to dull the smell as she said, "There's such a difference in the people and surroundings on this island, compared to the Faial."

"Give us cigarettes, give us Coca-Cola®," the men called out in bits of English as they walked closer to *Destiny*. Three little girls stood by looking like water waifs in their dirty, torn dresses. Their bare feet were covered with dirt and grease. Tangled, stringy hair fell in their faces and their sorrowful eyes almost broke Betty's heart.

Afraid to go below and leave the decks unattended, everyone stayed guarding *Destiny*. For three hours, they waited for customs to come.

"Why are they keeping us waiting so long?" asked Scott squirming in his seat.

Betty stood up and said, "It's after two o'clock and I'm starved. I'm going below to fix lunch."

She brought up sandwiches, beer and iced tea and the begging began again. The fishermen were getting close.

"Give me cigarettes, give me beer," begged the men, and the little girls chimed in with "Coca-Cola®."

At four o'clock customs arrived. When they saw the crowd of people, they yelled at them and scared them off. The officers walked through the boat, inspecting each closet and drawer, pulling up cushions looking for drugs.

They sat in the salon and one of them said, "What a magnifico ship, how much it cost?"

"Mucho money," said Bob as he handed them the papers and passports.

There were a few pens lying on the table with *Destiny*'s name inscribed on the side.

When the officers spotted the pens their eyes widened. "Oh, you have *Destiny* printed on your pens. I take this one, okay?"

"Yeah sure, you can each have one." *Anything to keep them happy*, thought Bob, and he gave each officer a pen. Smiling, they finished the paperwork quickly and left.

"We can dock here for the next couple of nights," said Bob.

"But I don't think it's safe. This is where the freighters dock and it's a pretty rough section."

"No way," said Scott. "I can't stand all these people staring and begging."

"Okay, untie us, Mitch. We'll motor up the bay to the town. We can anchor there. I think we'll sleep better."

As *Destiny* pulled away from the dock the men and children rushed toward the ship shouting, "Give us cigarettes, give us money."

They dropped the anchor just outside of town and when *Destiny* was secured they took the dinghy over to the docks.

Bob pointed at a pier in front of him and said, "We'll tie up there, grab it, Frank, when we come alongside. Use the wire and padlock to tie up with. I'm making sure they can't steal our dinghy."

"The pier is too high and there's no ladder to climb up," Frank said, as he grabbed one of the pilings. Can anyone see anything to climb on?"

"There's some big, black truck tires tied alongside the next pier," said Mitch.

"Okay, go to the next pier, that looks like the only way we can get up," said Bob.

They locked up the dinghy and climbed on the tires and started to pull themselves onto the shaky pier. Broken boards covered with dirt and black grease made their fingers slip each time they gripped the edge.

"God, this is rough. I'm trying to keep my clothes clean and not stab myself to death," said Dave, pointing to the rusty nails sticking out like daggers.

Scott's pants got stuck on one of the rusty nails. "Goddammit, I ripped my pants. These were my best jeans too."

Frank laughed. "You should see the back of your pants, they're covered with grease."

They all had smudges and rips on their clothes and Greg's shoe fell off when he swung his foot on the pier. Frank was behind him and grabbed it just before it hit the water.

Greg whined as they walked along the street. "I really want to go home."

"Stop that whining," said Bob. "That's what you said in

Bermuda. Are you sure this time?"

"Yes, I really am. I've had enough sailing, and it's almost time for school to start."

"Okay, The first thing we'll do is find a travel agent," Betty said, rubbing his head, trying to cheer him up.

When they found a travel agent, they were told the same story. "There is only one plane a week," said the travel agent. "And it just left."

Greg stamped his feet in a tantrum. "But I want to go home now."

Betty grabbed him by the shoulders. "Hey, calm down, don't have a fit. There's nothing we can do about it. Come on, we'll walk around town and see what it's like."

Greg sulked the whole time they toured the town. Their impression improved as they walked farther away from the docks. People passing said hello and smiled and they felt some of the friendliness they had experienced in Horta.

Bob rented a car to see the rest of the island. No one but Betty and Scott wanted to go. They drove around looking for a restaurant that was recommended by the car agent. After driving for an hour, Bob stopped to look at the map. He realized they were lost and would probably never find it.

"There's a couple of guys on the corner," said Scott. Stop there and I'll ask for directions." As the car stopped Scott jumped out of the car. The men were in their early twenties and dressed in tight black pants, blue shirts with embroidered collars. One could speak a little English, but the other two stood quietly, looking at Scott in bewilderment.

"Senor, can you tell us where *Restaurant Francesca* is located?"

"Si, senor, I will show you," he said, and he opened the back car door and climbed in."No, no, that's okay. Just tell us," said Bob getting a bit nervous.

The man smiled and waved his hand. "Please Senor, do not worry, I will show you."

"Oh, let him show us, Bob, he looks harmless enough," Betty said returning the smile of the good-looking Latino.

"Drive Senior, I'll tell you when to stop." The Latino directed Bob down three streets, over two streets and up four more.

"Stop," he said and pointed to a restaurant that was built up against a mountain. "Here you will have the best food, the most delicious vino and fantastic service."

Thanking the man, they climbed the many steps and entered the charming building with its carved porch railings and doorway. An abundance of hydrangeas lined the base of the restaurant, and geraniums hung from the porch ceiling. Inside there were twenty tables with red-checkered cloths. Roses were set in Chianti bottles on each table. The warm air was filled with herbs and spices, making their stomachs growl, as their mouths watered.

The waiters could not speak English and Scott asked aloud. "Is there anyone here that can speak English?"

"I can speak a little," said a young girl with a soft smile. She was seated with a small group of village people.

"Could you help us with the menu?" asked Scott. He was drooling from the mouth this time, not for food though.

"My English is not too good, but I will try to translate for you," she said flirting with Scott. "They have pork, potatoes, and tomatoes or chicken, potatoes, and tomatoes all served with delicious sauces. Oh, also they have fish soup."

The sauces were made from fresh tomatoes, herbs, and garlic, and the savory sauce over the chicken danced on their taste buds. The bread, with fresh churned butter flavored with garlic, just melted in their mouths. Banjos and guitars played lightly in the background as the young girl that had helped them sang a melody unknown to them.

They drove back contented from the delicious food. On the way home they came to a town beaming with colorful lights. Men dressed in white, full-sleeved gaucho shirts and black tight trousers strummed guitars and played accordions. Lively music created a festive atmosphere as men and women danced in the streets and sang songs in their native tongue. Little children weaved in between the dancers creating their own steps. Bob parked the car and they mingled with the happy crowd. The women were dressed in colorful full skirts, off-the-shoulder blouses, wih a rose tucked behind their ear.

Betty caught a glimpse of an American child. "Isn't that Greg?"

"What's he doing here," Scott said, amazed to see him.

Greg was watching Dave dance with a striking maiden dressed in a flowing skirt with layers of ruffles trimmed in lace. Her white crocheted blouse fell loosely off her shoulders. As the girl danced her long black hair lifted in the air like an exquisite mare's mane.

Betty and Bob joined in, locking arms with the dancers, doing a Portuguese version of the square dance. The beer was dark and tangy and quenched their thirst from the activity. It made them feel lighthearted and happy they had come to San Miguel.

Bob was ready to go back to the boat, but Scott wanted to stay. "I'm going to hang around awhile. Never know what might happen."

"Maybe we'll get lucky with the *senoritas*," said Dave with a leering smile.

"If I were you, I'd be very careful; they guard their *senoritas* very closely. I would hate to see you hanging from a tree," Betty said as she took Greg's arm. "Come on young man, we're going back to the boat."

Greg pulled his arm away. "No, I want to stay here with the guys," and he tried to hide behind Dave.

Scott grabbed him by the shoulders, and gave him a teasing shake. "If you come with us, we're going to fix you up with an eighteen year old, and Grandma wouldn't like that."

Dave gave him a gentle push. "You better go home Technicolor, we'll see you later."

Grudgingly, Greg followed them to the car complaining all the way. "Why do you have to treat me like a baby? I'm fourteen, big enough to stay out late."

"Greg, did it ever occur to you that Scott and Dave would like a little time alone?" Betty gave him a slap on the back. "Shut up and stop complaining. You say you're grown up, but you're acting like a three year old."

His eyes started to tear and he sulked for awhile, but soon his mood changed and they talked about the fun they had at the fiesta.

Twelve

They planned their next leg of the trip. It was to Spain and it would take six or seven days—if the weather held out. First, they had to get the boat provisioned and picking out canned goods was like playing a guessing game. Fresh fruits and vegetables were plentiful, and reasonable.

Bob went to get the car while Betty paid for the food. Trying to find a parking space was impossible on the narrow streets. In desperation, he drove the car up to the front of the store and double parked. Horns blew and people shook their fists but he just ignored them. He worked fast to load the car before the police arrived. Scott drove the car to the boat ramp where they had left their dinghy, and proceeded to unload the groceries. Hoisting a large box to his shoulder, he walked slowly down the ramp. As he leaned forward to place the box in the dinghy he lost his balance and fell head first into the water. As he fell, he threw the box of food toward the skiff, hoping to get it in the boat, but the box ripped open. Noodles, coffee, and canned goods went flying into the water. He stood up and grabbed the dinghy just as a wave hit the skiff and it turned over on him.

Falling back into the water, he sat there screaming, "SHIT! SHIT! SHIT."

After loading the seven boxes into the dingy they barely had enough room for the three of them. The food was hauled aboard, they were careful not to bring the boxes on the boat. When they returned for the car, a policeman was waiting for them. He looked suspiciously at all the empty boxes they had brought back. He picked up a few and smelled them.

"*Tem um documento de identficao* (where is your identification)?" he asked sternly.

Scott and Betty gave him their passports, but Bob's was back on the ship. The policeman grabbed Betty's purse and went through it, taking everything out and then pulled out the lining.

145

"Tem um documento de identficao," he said staring at Bob.

"Fala ingles?" (do you speak English?) asked Scott.

The officer ignored him and kept ranting on. They tried to explain their situation in English, but to no avail. Soon more officers arrived with lights flashing and high-pitched sirens blaring.

The policemen brought out handcuffs and walked toward the three of them, saying, *"A esquadra"* (to the police station), as they pointed to the police car.

A large crowd had gathered and Betty knew she had to find someone that could understand English. Walking among the crowd, hoping someone could help them she said, *"Fala Ingles?"*

Heaven was good to them. A young man came forward and helped interpret their situation.

After twenty minutes of explaining, everything was straightened out and the police left. They had parked their car on a restricted military ramp and had not realized it. The police thought that they were smuggling something out of the country and were ready to lock them up.

"Come on, Bob, let's take a ride to the country and get out of this mess," Betty said, jumping in the car and backing off the ramp. "It really feels good to be alone for awhile. Sometimes things get too hectic with everyone around."

Driving along the small bumpy roads, they made their way up the mountain's side, and the view was awe-inspiring. Crystalline lakes were scattered throughout the mountains, surrounded by bushes clustered with red flowers. Daisies, blue and pink wild flowers grew everywhere. There were small villages with picturesque houses, dotted the mountainsides and like Horta, hydrangeas surrounded the farm lands. Stopping for lunch at a restaurant that looked more like a small ornate, vine-covered cottage, they reached for a menu. Hoping for a quick sandwich, what they found was greasy pork, potatoes, and tomatoes.

"Oh no! Don't they know how to make anything else?" Bob said, slapping down the menu in frustration.

When the waitress came over, they pointed to the entree. "Two," emphasizing with their fingers, "and two cold *crevasse* (beer)."

When they arrived back at *Destiny*, they smelled the pungent odor of fried fish. The crew was having dinner aboard ship.

"Come on, join us, it's delicious. I caught and cooked it myself," Frank said proudly as he started down to the galley.

Bob sat down at the table. "Sit down, we can help ourselves."

"I'm not letting Betty down in the galley until I clean it up. It will be my pleasure to serve you."

Betty laughed. "I think they're learning. I better not see a mess down there," she called down to Frank.

"We're leaving tomorrow," said Bob as he sipped his wine. "There'll be an early wake-up call to get our last minute chores done before we take off for Spain."

Technicolor Yawn was already asleep in the cockpit after his busy day, and Frank and Mitch were discussing their day.

"Our first impression of the island was wrong," remarked Frank as he started down the steps to the galley. "It turned out to be a very interesting place."

Bob stood up, ready for bed. "I'm glad we didn't stay at the docks, I'm going to bed. I want to get a good night sleep in this peaceful anchorage. The nights ahead might not be as calm."

The lights of the town flickered brightly. Betty liked the peacefulness of the island. She wasn't ready for the sea and she hated the thought of six to seven more days on the water.

"I wonder what kind of moron puts herself through this torture, when it's so much faster and easier to fly? Why don't I just take off for home, go back where I can stand on familiar land that's steady as a rock?" asked Betty out loud to herself.

Frank had come up from cleaning the galley and answered her, "Why? Because you're beginning to like this search for adventure, the thrill of seeing new land and interesting people. I know that feeling."

"Maybe so, maybe so." Then . . . teasing, she said, "Is the galley clean now? Can I walk through it to my stateroom?"

*   *   *

Getting up early, Betty sat meditating on the bow. A shiver come over her and she walked around *Destiny*. She knew she didn't want to go out to sea again. Trying to convince herself, she said, "You can take what the sea has to offer, you really want to go. Don't be a sissy; it won't be so bad." She thought for a minute then said, "Who are you kidding? You've already been through it, and it can be hell out there on that water."

Scott came up on deck. "Who are you talking to?"

"I think I've lost it, I really have. I'm ready for the nuthouse. Not only am I talking to myself, but I'm answering too."

"Yo, Bob, better get the strait jacket. Betty's off her rocker. We have to lock her up," joked Scott.

"Shackle her in my cabin. I'll deal with the Sea Witch later," leered Bob with expressions of a pirate.

As they pulled up the anchor, Bob gave out a shout, "All hands on deck we're heading out to sea. We have almost a thousand miles to go. Let's set the sails and make sure everything is put away or tied down."

They kept busy doing their last minute jobs and settled down for a quick dinner. The crew swapped stories of what they did on the island, each one bragging about the girls they met, trying to make their stories more exciting.

"I met this sweet senorita," bragged Scott, "she just couldn't keep her hands off of me." Frank snickered. "Yeah, yeah, I know. You pussies couldn't get laid if the girls were held down for you."

"Frank, where did you sneak off to?" asked Dave. "We couldn't find you."

"Yeah we had a girl for you," said Scott.

Frank snickered, "That's for me to know and you to find out. I can get my own woman."

"You men can be so crude," said Betty. "I don't want to hear your lies and wild talk. I'm going to bed."

One by one each person retired to get some sleep. *Destiny* and the wind was good to them as they sailed peacefully until the morning.

It was a very mundane trip for the next two days, and they were averaging about a hundred and twenty-five miles a day. They slept a lot, letting their bodies adjust to the motion, and getting their sea legs back. Greg and Dave were nauseated, but not sick, not until Dave cooked dinner on their third day out, then he was really sick. Betty held up well with the patch on. She sat back and let herself daydream that she was working in her office and talking to her customers. She remembered how loyal her employees were and how they almost felt like family to her. She missed her dog, Shangie, a Lhasa Apso, and remembered how he cuddled on her lap and followed her everywhere. Sighing from her memories, she picked up her logbook and wrote down yesterday's happenings. She liked to keep track of what they did each day.

One day rolled into another, and time seemed to stand still, yet other times it swished by like grains of sand in a timer. Since the seas were calm, she took a chance and made an apple pie. Luckily she had the pie in the oven before the wind picked up. The wind had changed direction and climbed to a speed of forty-five knots with little warning. Making her way up to the deck, Betty found the rest of the crew with their backs and legs braced against the seats. Trying to compensate for the boats twenty-five degree heeling. She sat next to Greg, bracing herself, her arm around him protectively. The wind gauge now read forty-five knots as the wind blew directly on the bow. The boat heeled at a severe angle and Betty was afraid of a knockdown. *God*, she thought, *if the boat turns over on its side and the mast hits the water, it could be ripped away. We'd be in deep trouble then.* A fearful feeling swept over her as she looked at Bob struggling to keep *Destiny* on course.

Betty kept staring at the gauge that showed how far the boat was heeling. "I don't like the way the boat's leaning. It's heeling over twenty-five degrees, it's scaring me."

"What the hell do you want me to do about it?" Bob yelled in pure frustration, his face stern and red with anger. "Goddammit, I'm doing the best I can."

"Don't scream at me," Betty yelled back. "I can't help it if I'm scared."

Bob snapped back, "Go down to bed if it's bothering you that much."

She had one arm around Greg, and she hung on to the seat with the other. Her muscles were taut as she fought to hold her position. Bob struggled to keep the boat on course and there was a look of determination on his sweat-soaked face. The sails were reefed down to handkerchief size and all they could do was ride out the storm.

Frank could see Bob was tired. "Let me take over for a while, chief."

Bob gave him a sharp glance, "No, goddamnit this is my baby. I'll handle it."

"Okay, okay," Frank said as he backed off. "If you get tired let me know."

The winds whipped across Bob's body as he held fast at the helm. At first Betty's feelings were hurt and she sat in a huff. She watched what he was going through, and realized the words of anger were for the wind not her. He showed no fear, just determination as he fought the horrendous weather.

Bob's arms were getting tired. "I can't hold the course in this wind. We have to go off at least twenty-five degrees. Scott, tack the sails to port side, see if she handles any easier."

The waves splashed across the bow and bashed against the windshield. Spray from the waves rained into the cockpit drenching everyone and everything in its way.

"Oh my God! My apple pie! I've got to get it out of the oven before it burns," Betty said, trying to make her way down into the galley.

"Let the goddamn thing burn; it's too rough down there," said Bob.

"No, I've got to get it out or it will smoke up the whole boat." She worked her way down the companionway stairs.

Rough was a mild word for it, it was unbelievable. When Betty got to the oven it was swinging back and forth like a pendulum. She had to get the pie out of the oven but it looked like an impossible job. Her first mistake was to lock the oven in place so it would not swing on the gimbals. This caused the pie to slide back and forth hitting against the back of the oven and door. She released the gimbaled latch allowing the oven to sway back and forth again. Timing her action, she opened the oven on the back swing, and grabbed the pie as it slid forward.

She cried out in pain as hot juice splashed her hand and leg. Almost dropping the pie from the pain, she quickly turned swinging her body towards the sink. "Thank God it's empty," Betty said, as she placed the pie safely down.

"How are you making out down there?" called Scott. "Do you need some help?"

"I burned myself," she said holding on to the counter to keep her balance. Her stomach churned and her hand and leg throbbed. Pulling open the freezer hatch she plunged her burned hand into the coolness and sighed, as the pain eased a bit. The relief lasted only a moment. *Destiny* shifted and the hatch slammed down on her arm. Screaming she pulled her burnt arm free and slumped down on the galley floor. She shoved her feet against the base of the sink, her back against the freezer to keep from sliding. She sat there crying.

Her hand and leg seared with pain and an ugly bruise began to form on her swollen arm. Slowly she stood up and balanced herself. She swayed back and forth, in time with the boat. "Oh-ooh, I'm really feeling sick," she said, grabbing her mouth and heading for the cockpit. Bruised and burned, Betty hobbled up into the fresh air. Scott filled towels with ice and placed them on her hand and leg. Lying down, she closed her eyes feeling utterly miserable.

"Sounds like you were having a party," said Frank. "What was going on down there? Were you dancing the meringue?"

Betty ran to the railing and started to retch, nothing came up so she gulped the air. She stood there waiting to see if she was going to throw up.

After awhile, Frank said, "Come on, don't keep me in suspense, tell me what was going on down there."

"It was a party from hell," Betty murmured. "You should have joined me. We could have slid around the floor together."

"You have to have pretty good rhythm to be able to handle the motion down there," said Frank. "What I want to know is, did you save the pie?"

He finally succeeded in getting her to laugh. "Yeah, I did."

As Scott took the helm, he said, "The winds aren't quite as bad now."

"Yeah, but we're still beating into the wind. Unfortunately, we're not on a course to Spain," said Bob.

"I'm heading for my bunk," Betty said as she went below.

Lying there was little comfort as she rocked roughly back and forth. She was lifted off the bed each time *Destiny* slammed down against the sea.

She flung her hands out in utter desperation as she

screamed, "I hate this, I hate this."

Deep sobs wracked her insides as she pounded the bed, trying to vent her frustrations. *What am I doing here? I must have been out of my mind to stay on this boat.*

Brushing away the tears, she wiped her nose and prayed the weather would change.

There was a knock on the door. "Betty, don't worry about dinner tonight," said Frank. "I'll take your turn. You saved the pie and that deserves a reward."

He really can be nice, she thought, as she fell asleep from exhaustion. She slept until four A.M., and realized she had missed her watch.

Bob was lying beside her, his arm around her. "We didn't want to wake you for your watch. Scott and I took the extra time."

"Thanks, that was very considerate. I'm such a sissy. I really wish I could handle conditions like you."

Bob tucked the sheet around her and kissed her. "You'll get used to it in time."

Dreading another day of strong winds and turbulent motion, she fell into a fitful sleep.

Daylight came and she knew it was time for her watch. The wind was still high she could tell by the rocking and swaying. Betty lay there planning carefully how she was going to get off the bed, and up on deck. Looking around the room Betty located a ledge near the bed and grabbed it making her way to the toilet. Once there, she hung on to the seat to keep from sliding off. Then, moving slowly, she grabbed doors and ledges as she made her way through the cabins. Her aching leg and arm was covered with black and blue marks. The burns had bubbled into blisters.

"You're up!" said Bob. "How are you feeling? You look like you were wounded in action."

Betty hobbled to the seat, "I think I'll live. Look how big the blisters are."

Bob looked at her arm and leg, "Like I said, you look like you were wounded in action. Why don't you rest? I'll handle this for a while."

For two days, the wind stayed almost a constant twenty-five knots and the waves were high. They were still off-course and an extra day had been added to their journey. They had two hundred miles to go before they reached Spain. *Destiny* pushed onward through the heavy wind and seas. Water leaked into the salon again, only worse. Scott and Mitch searched the deck and ceilings to see where the water was seeping in. All the new stereo equipment was completely ruined.

After Scott finished his afternoon watch, he sat in the cockpit looking disheartened. His hands were shoved in his pockets and his shoulders hunched forward. He looked out at the water and said, "Dave and I have been on this boat for six weeks. We were supposed to be back to work three weeks ago. Not only are we not getting paid for the time we have been gone, but we might even lose our jobs. We were determined to complete this trip. Now I think we were nuts."

Dave raised his head from his book, his expression was grim. "Yeah, here we are losing money and getting banged around at sea; somehow that just doesn't make sense."

Scott threw his hands up in despair and screamed at the top of his lungs, "Get me off this fucking boat. I feel like a damn prisoner."

Everyone looked shocked by the sudden outburst, and it was then Betty realized she wasn't the only one that had been suffering the unrelenting seas.

Destiny was only two days away from Spain. The wind and sea died down to a welcome calm, and they sailed in fifteen knot winds. She was broad-reaching, with the wind at their back. The main genoa and mizzen were up, and things felt a little easier. They could move freely around the boat.

Greg decided to cook. Getting some helpful instructions, he served marinated artichokes and mushrooms at cocktail hour. The main course was roast chicken coated in corn flakes with baked potatoes and peas. Dessert was chocolate cream pie, but the graham cracker crust was half-empty because Greg ate most of the pudding.

Shortly after dinner, the wind picked up to twenty knots. They were back on course and making some headway. The waves washed across the bow and pounded against the windshield, making it hard to see.

"We're taking two-man watches tonight," said Bob. "Looks

like it might be a rough one. I'll sleep in the salon. I might be needed in a hurry."

Each one picked a safe spot to curl up on; Greg was on the dinette couch and Betty headed for her safe haven, her bed. She fell into an agitated sleep, only to be awakened by pounding much worse than before. The winds had reached a high of fifty knots, and it felt like *Destiny* was being hammered to pieces. Hearing a commotion Betty went to see what was going on. The boat was rocking wildly as she made her way to the salon. The floorboards over the engine were up, and Bob and Frank were down on their knees. They were peering into the engine compartment that was half-full of black liquid.

When Betty saw the black fluid, she shrieked, "Get away from there, it might explode."

"Calm down," Bob said. "This is diesel; it won't explode. There's salt water in the fuel line and it's leaking somewhere."

"The engine won't start," said Frank leaning deeper into the compartment. "We're trying to fix it."

Glancing around she saw water cascading into the salon, from the ceiling and portholes. Books, stereo, tape deck, everything was drenched. The sea was lashing across *Destiny*, showing no mercy as the water poured through the unseen cracks.

Greg was still curled up on the couch. He looked up with his sad, brown eyes. "Is everything going to be all right, Grandma?"

She sat down and held him in her arms, no longer was he acting like the big, macho teenager.

Kissing him lightly on the cheek, she tried to convince them both as she said, "Yes honey, everything will be fine. Just lie there and keep warm. We'll be in Spain soon."

Walking up the companionway, she stepped out into the force of fifty knot winds that almost knocked her over. Spray from the waves whipped across the boat, lashing her face. Dave was at the helm, only the mainsail was up, and it was reefed to half-sail.

"What's going on?" Betty asked, feeling numb and confused. She watched him trying to keep the ship on course.

She could hardly hear Dave as he shouted above the wind, "We're going through a force eight storm, it's been pretty damn rough."

"How bad is an eight?" asked Betty.

"The worst storm would be a force ten so you see this is no baby. When I had the engine on I had better control, but it fizzled out. The guys are working on it now."

Immense freighters were passing on either side of them, going in different directions. Lights beaming from the monster ships sparkled in the pitch black night like Christmas tree ornaments. Whipping winds howled at fifty-five knots pushing against *Destiny*'s bow.

Frank came on deck. "I'll take it for a while, Dave."

"We're in the Straits of Gibraltar," said Frank taking over the wheel. "The weather is always notoriously bad here. When you're going against a strong easterly wind it's tough sailing. Besides, this passageway is always a busy highway for freighters."

Betty was really confused now. "Gibraltar straits! I thought we were going to Spain?"

"The weather's too rough to go any farther. We're stopping at Gibraltar, that is if we don't get run over by a cargo ship. We've been tacking back and forth all night trying to stay out of their way. It's been a tough night."

Watching the huge ships on radar kept her attention. She could see the center mark was *Destiny*, tacking back and forth dodging the marks of the other ships. Frank kept a distance from the steady stream of ships that kept passing. Betty was caught up in the adventure and too busy to be frightened now. Looking out into the darkness she was sure she could see land.

Bob came up on deck and stood beside her. "How are you holding up?"

"I'm surprised I'm not scared. It's really exciting."

"Look carefully to port side. Can you can make out the silhouette of the Rock of Gibraltar? Once we get past the rock we'll be sheltered and out of the winds."

Betty searched with the binoculars into the stormy night. Then a huge shadow against the black and dreary sky appeared. "Thank God we're close to land and civilization again." Betty went down to the salon and looked at the mess. Everything was ruined, but at this moment she didn't care. Her only thoughts were to get through this horrible mess and back on land.

Bob followed her down, "Help me pull the washer and dryer out from the wall. I want to unplug them, I don't want anyone electrocuted."

Slipping and sliding from the wetness on the floor they pulled the appliances out from their cabinets. Then she disappeared to the warmth of her bed.

They were tacking every twenty minutes. Each time they tacked Betty slid from one side of the king-size bed to the other.

The engine started with a grinding sound, then kicked over. *Destiny* picked up speed and the ride smoothed out. Dave was back on the helm and they headed towards the shadow that stood out in the darkened horizon. "There's the Rock of Gibraltar" someone shouted. The wind came to a standstill, as they motored past the rock that loomed high above them like a mighty protector. A stillness in the air wrapped itself around them and relaxed their ragged nerves.

Betty felt Bob crawl in beside her. He was exhausted and drifted off to sleep, as he said "We made it to Gibraltar."

At daybreak, there was sunshine, peace and calmness. Sails were down and they were motoring, everything was tranquil and under control. Betty placed a frozen casserole of ham and potatoes in the oven. She knew the crew would need something substantial to eat. When the casserole was finished, everyone ate like it was their first meal in days.

She cleaned the galley and mopped up the water in the salon. Pans were placed around to catch the drips that were still seeping through. Feeling the need to freshen up she showered and changed even put on a little make up.

When *Destiny* pulled up to the customs dock Betty knew her nightmare was over, they had made a Transatlantic crossing. The crew was tired and numb, but ready to jump ship to feel the firm land again. They arrived on September thirteenth. It had taken forty-two days to make the crossing from Ft. Lauderdale to Gibraltar. Betty was glad it was over, but she was proud she had accomplished it.

Thirteen

The custom officers quickly checked them in, then Bob motored a short distance to the Marina Bay Club. It was a white square stucco building with blue wooden windows and doors. When they pulled alongside the dock the prisoners of *Destiny* jumped onshore and headed to the nearest bar.

There were many yachts docked in the marina and small bars along the wharf. They were filled with yachtsmen from all over the world. Tables with umbrella's sat outside the bars where sandwiches are being served. The streets are crowded with cars and the airport was right in the middle of the city. Main Street went right across the airfield. There seemed to be a mix of English, Arabs, Spanish and Turkish people.

They made reservations at a nearby restaurant for dinner for all seven. Then located a travel office to purchase a ticket for Greg to fly back to New Jersey. Greg would have to fly out of Malaga, Spain, sixty miles from Gibraltar. After renting a car, they went back to gather the crew. *Destiny* needed a good cleaning.

It would be their last night together as some of the crew were leaving the next day. Their farewell dinner was emotional. They had been together for forty-two days and a deep bond of brotherly companionship had grown between them.

Scott sat by Betty. His shoulders were hunched over and he looked sad. "I have mixed emotions," said Scott. "I want to go home but I'll miss all of you."

"That's how I feel," said Dave. Then his face lit up. "I just can't believe I actually made a Transatlantic crossing. Very few people get the chance to do that."

Betty knew she would miss them, even though she bitched about the mess they made. They had grown so close and been through so much together.

Bob called out, "Hey Frank and Mitch, what are your plans?"

I'm planning on staying and sailing around the rest of the world with you. I'm not one of those pussies that jump ship," laughed Frank.

"I'm going to hang aroung for a few more days, then fly back to California to be with Diane," said Mitch.

"Good, at least I'll have some help, some crew," said Bob smiling.

After breakfast, they said their sad farewells and Scott and Dave took off to tour Spain. Then in two days, they would fly home.

When they arrived at the airport with Greg, Betty and Bob waited for his plane to arrive.

"Thanks Grandma. I had a great time, but I'm happy to go home, I even miss my sisters." Then he laughed and said, "I never thought I'd ever say that." Then he gave Betty a big hug. Shaking hands with Bob he said, "Thanks Captain Bob, it was great. Wait till I tell my friends I made a transatlantic crossing."

They watched him walk across the runway to his plane. He had experienced something few boys his age had ever done.

Betty had tears in her eyes as she watched the plane take off. Her grandson had grown up on this trip.

Bob put his arm around Betty's shoulders and said, "We better head back to *Destiny* and get things in order. Then we can see what Gibraltar's all about."

"I'm going to miss everybody," said Betty feeling a little sad at they're leaving. I'm so used to having them around. What are we going to do about a crew? We're going to have strangers aboard."

"We certainly can't handle *Destiny* by ourselves on long trips," said Bob. "We'll ask around, but let's not worry about that now. First, we're going to see Gibraltar."

When they returned, Mitch was sitting on the deck in tears, his shoulders were stooped over and he was sobbing.

Oh no, thought Betty, *not again*. "Mitch, what's the matter?"

"I'm just so happy. I talked to Diane on the phone and she still loves me. We are going to get married as soon as I get home. I'll never leave her again."

"When are you planning on flying home?" Bob asked with

apprehension. You were going to stay on with us for a few days. There's a lot of work to be done on *Destiny* and we were hoping you'd supervise the mechanics. Betty and I would like to take some time off," said Bob.

"Diane's going to fly here and take a few week's vacation. I'll hang around till the work's done. Then we'll take off and see Europe."

"Great, I'll arrange for the mechanics tomorrow. Today we can take the sails over for repair."

That night, Betty and Bob walked over to the shopping area that was called Main Street. The streets were narrow and the area reminded them of Kowloon in Hong Kong. It was full of small shops selling everything imaginable. The streets were packed with shoppers dressed in a variety of clothing. Woman walked by in saris and veils, followed by young girls in tight mini skirts. A mixture of music echoed through the streets. Chanting from Mosque towers blended with the rock and disco music coming from the music shops. Smells of exotic foods permeated the air from the pushcarts perched at every corner.

When morning came they could hear the mystic chanting from the mosque interrupted by a plane landing two blocks away. When their chores were done they drove around the base of the Rock of Gibraltar and took the tunnel road that winds thirty miles through the rock. Their first stop was a very impressive cave full of stalagmites and stalactites, lit up with all the colors of the rainbow. Bach music played on an organ and the sound vibrated through the cave giving off a renaissance sound. They drove higher up the tunnel and stopped to see the sacred royal monkeys. Several families of monkeys live on the side of the mountain and are protected by the royal guards. Almost too friendly, they approached in groups looking for handouts. The terrain is dry and the tall grass is brown from the hot sun. Squares have been cut through the thick walls for cannons and guns, and at the top of the rock they explored the empty rooms of the old fort.

They started back to the boat and Bob said. "We'll start looking around for crew for our next leg of the trip."

"Okay," she answered with a lack of enthusiasm. She loved it on land and wasn't too happy at the thought of going out to sea again. "Are we going to continue sailing the Mediterranean as you planned?"

"No," answered Bob, "we left Ft. Lauderdale too late. It's the middle of September already and the weather turns cold in October. We'll head back across the Atlantic, and chalk this up as our maiden voyage."

They had only been gone three days and when they returned Mitch's spirits were high. He seemed like a different person.

Giving Mitch a hug, Betty said, "Boy, you look happy, you're almost beaming. Did Diane come?"

He let out a deep breath as he cheerfully said, "No, she couldn't make it."

Surprised at his attitude Bob asked, "How soon do you plan on leaving?"

Mitch was buoyant as he answered, "Eh...plans have changed. I'm staying in Gibraltar."

"You're what?" Betty couldn't believe her ears. "You're staying? I thought you were going to California to marry Diane?"

His voice raised an octave, and he talked so fast it was hard to follow what he was saying. "I met the most magnificent English girl. She's so beautiful, she has long blonde hair and fabulous blue eyes. Wait until you meet Nancy; she's wonderful."

"Wait a minute—wait a minute," said Betty as she stared at him confused. "What happened to Diane? When we left you were madly in love and couldn't wait to be with her."

Mitch sighed. "Diane and I had an argument on the phone the night you left. She said I was unreasonable and I got mad and hung up on her. I went out for a few drinks and that's when I met Nancy. You can't believe how much fun we have together. Then I realized I wasn't really in love with Diane after all."

They stood quietly staring at one another, not knowing what to say. Finally Bob broke the silence, " Eh—I'm glad you're happy for a change." Then he asked, "Is all the work on the boat done?"

"Yes, I took care of everything. Now that you're back I'll move the rest of my things into Nancy's flat."

Betty's voice rose in surprise. "You've moved in with her already?"

"I have most of my things there. Oh by the way, Frank left. He decided he was ready to go back to Ft. Lauderdale."

Bob's face went bleak with disappointment. "Frank left without saying goodbye? I can't believe he'd do that."

"Yep, said to say goodbye for him. Something important came up and he had to leave."

"We better start looking for crew," Bob said, looking at Betty. "I thought if we couldn't find crew, the three of us could always handle *Destiny* until we found someone. With Frank gone, I have to start looking right away."

Betty walked over to the helm and sat down. "I'm going to miss Frank; he was a tease but a lot of fun," Betty said feeling melancholy. "I wish all our men were still here. I don't like having complete strangers onboard."

Bob sat in deep thought, then said, "It's going to be tough trying to check references on anyone we hire."

Mitch interrupted. "Can we have dinner together tonight? I'd like you to meet Nancy."

Bob answered half-listening, "Sure, make it about seven. I want to post signs for crew at the marina and stores."

Meeting Nancy was like being introduced to Diane's sister but she was much younger—barely eighteen. The resemblance was incredible. The two lovebirds talked about their plans together, and Betty wondered what real future they had together.

She laid in bed that night thinking about Frank and Scott and said, "I'm really going to miss everyone. We had so many experiences together." Betty looked over at Bob who didn't seem to be listening to her. "What are you thinking about?"

"I think I know someone who might join us. Remember my friends, the Thomases in Duxbury?"

"Yeah, wasn't that the couple that had the funny red car they kept in their yard?"

"That's right," Bob laughed, "a real rattle trap. Remember how excited their son Jim was about our trip?"

Betty thought for a minute, then said, "Oh yeah, I remember. He said, 'I'd love to go on that trip with you. If you ever need me just call and I'll fly right out.'"

Bob was excited, "I'll call him in the morning, and see if he wants to join us. He used to sail with me from Duxbury to the Bahamas. He's a good sailor."

Betty was tired and her eyes were getting heavy. "We'll both feel better with someone we know, but we'll need more than one crewman."

Bob was up at the crack of dawn. Before he ate breakfast Bob headed for the phone booth. When he came back his face was beaming. "Jim will be on his way next week. I've already wired him money for his ticket."

With the help wanted sign in the marina and stores, many young people came looking for a chance to sail. Some asked for salaries, while others would do it for nothing or even pay their way. But so far no one looked capable or safe. There was a motley group that hung at the local bar that showed interest, but Bob never considered them. Checking backgrounds and references was impossible since they were from all over the world. Bob would have to go on appearance and instinct and that was tricky.

After several disappointing interviews, they began to get discouraged, no one seemed trustworthy. They had heard stories of crew members killing the owners and throwing them overboard. Bob decided rather than have someone on board they couldn't trust, they'd handle *Destiny* with just Jim aboard.

*   *   *

That night as they were heading out for dinner, a young Italian man approached them.

"Hear you're looking for crew," he said.

Bob liked his looks immediately. "Yes we are, come aboard and we'll talk."

"My name is Bob Godfrey, I'm the owner of *Destiny* and this is my first mate, Betty Rennie."

"Please to meet you, I'm Bruno Germaine," he said in a delightful accent. He had straight black shining hair that was neatly cut, and a light clear complexion. "I'm from a place called Positano in Italy." His full lips curled upward when he spoke.

"Tell me a little about yourself. Did you graduate from high school?" asked Bob.

"Yes sir, I have a college degree in teaching. I taught elementary classes for four years," he said, his black eyes gleaming with pride.

That surprised Bob. "Why did you leave your teaching job?"

"I became restless and bored doing the same thing, day in and day out. There was a boat in the harbor looking for crew so I hopped on. I want to tour the world before I settle down."

Bob liked what he heard and asked, "What kind of boat were you crewing on?"

Bruno looked around at *Destiny* with an appreciative glance and said, "The boat was nothing like this, just an old tug. It broke down in the Canary Islands a year ago. It was nothing like your boat. This is a beauty."

"Well, everything sounds pretty good. Can I see your passport?" asked Bob.

Bruno passed it to him. Bob looked through it, checking for the Gibraltar stamp. "Looks like it's in order. What did you do in the Canary Islands when you got off the boat?"

"I couldn't find another ship, so I got a job selling time shares for a year. While I was in the Canary Islands I met a girl, her name is Martha. We've been traveling together for the past year." He blushed a little and added, "We're not serious or anything, just friends. Last week we hopped a ride here hoping to find a boat that needed crew. If you need a girl onboard she would be willing to come for half-salary. With or without her, I want to go with you. That is, if you'll have me."

When Bruno stood up to leave, Betty noticed he was not much taller than she was, about five-nine and a little on the stocky side. He seemed well mannered and intelligent. His clothes were extremely neat, not the average type you see around the docks. Having sailing experience was a plus and his attitude was positive and outgoing.

Bob shook Bruno's hand. "Let me think about it. Stop by tomorrow and I'll let you know our decision." Later, he asked Betty, "What do you think about having a woman aboard?"

"There're pros and cons. It all depends on her personality. It would make it easier on me, we could divide the cleaning and cooking. Bruno looks great. I like the black hair sticking out of his shirt."

"I think you're turning into a dirty old lady," said Bob laughing. "You're right, Bruno looks good. I'm surprised that he's a college graduate. You don't usually find that type looking for crew work. Let's give him a try and if it doesn't work out we'll let him go at the next port of call. We'll interview the woman tomorrow and see what she's like."

"We're not taking her if she's beautiful and sexy. I don't think you're a dirty old man—I know it," laughed Betty as she gave Bob a jab in his side.

Bruno's friend Martha was from England. She was quite heavy, and was five-foot-eight, but seemed taller. She walked down the pier with a manly gait; her long, straight blonde hair flew wildly in the wind. Her face was chubby and pleasant with light skin that drew attention to the freckles that dotted her nose and forehead.

"Blimey, what a bea-u-ti-ful boat!" Her full lips protruded as she spoke with a cockney accent. "Last skiff we were on was nothing like this."

Martha was a friendly, likable sort, but very rough at the edges. She wore a washed out baggy T-shirt with white tattletale gray cotton pants that were worn thin at the seat and hugged her ample rear.

"I'm a good cook. My specialty is shepherd's pie. Me mum taught me what I know about cooking. Don't mind cleaning either," she said beaming from ear to ear. "I don't get seasick, at least not too often. Last boat I sailed on didn't have all this modern stuff, not even a douche or workable loos. Had to go in buckets and throw it over the side. The men all went naked. Us girls went around in just our nickers . . . nobody seemed to mind."

Her frankness was both startling and amusing. She continued to fill them in on her background.

"I'm from outside of London, a place called Southend. Me mum, dad and sisters still live there. I hated high school and when I graduated I just wanted to wander. I took off, backpacking around Europe by myself."

"How old were you when you did that?" asked Betty, wondering how a mother could let someone just out of high school go hiking alone.

"Just seventeen, and I had myself a time. Took a year before I came home. I just had a birthday. I'm nineteen now."

That surprised Betty as she thought she was in her mid-twenties.

"Bruno and I met in the Canary Islands. He's so yummy. We want to sail around for awhile before we settle down in America," she said, as she looked over at Bruno like a love-struck kid.

Bruno sat there listening. His head was leaning on his hands and he never looked up.

"Thanks for coming over, we'll let you know what we decide," said Bob, standing up and shaking Bruno's hand.

"Ta-ta," said Martha as she jumped off of *Destiny*. "Blimey, I almost burst me britches. If you want me to join you, just knock me up."

Betty's mouth dropped open. "What did she say? Did she mean make her pregnant?"

Bob laughed. "That means call her or knock on her door."

Bruno hung back for awhile letting Martha get a distance away. "Look, Martha and I are just friends. I really don't mind going without her if you don't need her."

Was the expression on his face sadness because she might go, or sadness that she would be left behind? Betty wasn't sure.

Bob scratched his head in thought. "We're not sure if we need both of you. If we do take Martha along, she'll have to share your room. There's only three cabins onboard. We have the master stateroom in the stern. In the bow, there's an upper and lower berth in the starboard cabin and the portside cabin has a double-bed. Jim, our other crewman has that cabin," said Bob.

"That's fine. We can make do with that, thank you," said Bruno and he saluted and walked away.

They agreed to take both Martha and Bruno. Her cheery personality would help a lot on the long passages and she sounded like a good worker. Betty thought they made an odd couple. He was so intelligent and refined, while she seemed to be an air head. They arranged for the new crew to move aboard after Jim arrived.

*   *   *

Jim flew in two days later. Twenty-two, clean cut and good-looking, his brown curly hair was flecked with gold and his eyes were the deep blue of a clear Gibraltar sky. His strong body was muscular from years of working out and wind-surfing. Sailing was deep in his blood; he longed to cruise the high seas and Bob knew he was capable.

He was so excited he couldn't stop talking. "I can't wait to go sailing, this is a chance of a lifetime. It's something I always wanted to do. Oh, I brought my windsurfer with me. Is that okay?"

"That's fine. It's great having you here, we really need you," said Bob as they arrived at the boat.

"Wow, what a ship! This is awesome. I can't believe I'm really going to sail on this ship." Betty showed him to his cabin. "You can put your things in here." All he could say was awesome. He reminded Betty of her grandson Greg.

Bruno and Martha came aboard and met Jim, then Betty showed them their room. "Just put your things in here," said Betty. "You can put them away later. Martha, I have to provision the boat, so why don't you come with me? The men can help Bob get *Destiny* ready for departure."

Stocking up on food and supplies was an easy chore as the labels were in English. The store did not have delivery service so they pushed the two carts stacked high back to the boat. The groceries were handed up in a chain-gang effect, leaving the boxes behind. Martha was a great help storing the supplies. She seemed eager to please and was quick at doing chores.

The crew settled into their new quarters and as they put their things away, Betty heard Martha say. "Blimey, look at the drawer space we have, Bruno.

Bruno sounded annoyed as he said, "Don't put your things in my drawer. I have the bottom ones, you can have the top ones."

"Don't be so mean," whined Martha. "I wouldn't take your drawers, I never take your drawers."

"Yes, you do. You always crowd me out," said Bruno in a huff.

Jim was whistling while he stored his things. "This is awesome. My own cabin and head! Wow, I'm in heaven. I can't believe I'm going to sail around the world!"

After dinner, the crew went off to a local bar for a few beers before retiring to bed. They were too excited to sleep.

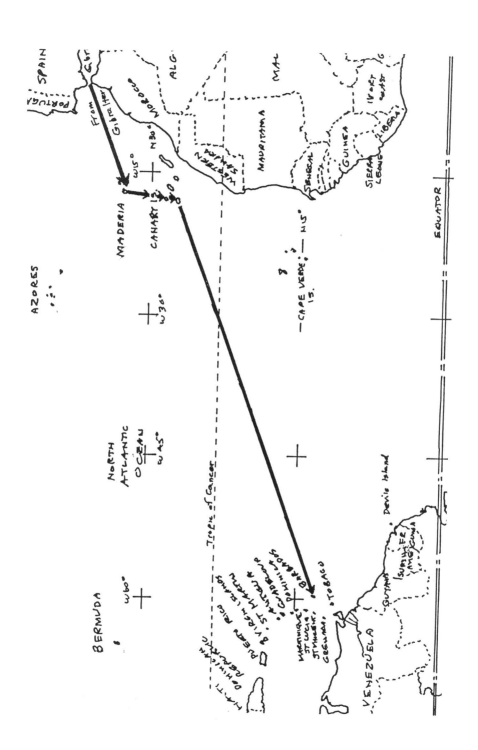

Fourteen

Everything was finally ready and they were on their way to Madeira, one of three Portuguese Islands, six hundred miles away. They were leaving with two perfect strangers and hoped for the best. Bruno and Martha seemed nice enough, but only time would tell if personalities would clash. It was November 9th when they left and they hoped to make it in four-and-a-half days. Betty wasn't looking forward to going through the Straits of Gibraltar again and dodging the heavy freighter traffic.

Leaving the harbor, it looked like the wind would be in their favor, the sun was out and the skies were clear. Once they reached the open seas, they were beating against eight-to-ten knot winds on the bow, but it was bearable compared to their last trip.

When the sails were set *Destiny* heeled a slight ten degrees, and Betty heard crashing glass. "Darn, I forgot to secure the wine glasses," she said rushing below.

She had been so wrapped up in showing Martha everything about the boat that she forgot the last minute tie downs. The glasses broke in slivers all over the dinette area and memories of crossing the Atlantic came back to her mind.

Bob worked with the crew, teaching them how to handle *Destiny*. He had them hoist the sails, tack and winch them, and was pleased how quickly they caught on. He scheduled their watch times; two hours each at night and three hours during the day. Jim, Martha, and Bruno would have the middle of the night till morning watch. Bob would be on-call at any time.

Betty had anticipated that it might be rough so she made chicken noodle soup and chili before they left Gibraltar. She wanted to spend as little time as possible in the galley fixing lunch and dinner that day. After their busy day of training, the crew was ready to head for their quarters.

Betty stayed out on the bow meditating and enjoying a little private time. After finishing her meditation she sat back and looked at the slash of brilliant stars in the sky. She wondered why one star was so low. As *Destiny* sailed closer she said out loud, "It's not a star it's a light on a mast."

She called out to Bob at the helm, "There's a light ahead of us, I think it's a boat."Bob came out on the bow for a closer look. "Seems to be coming towards us, maybe I better steer away from it."

Bob shone a spotlight on it, and saw it was a small sail boat, thirty feet long and cruising slowly.

"The people onboard must have put it on auto-pilot and went to sleep," Bob said shutting off the spotlight. "I'm glad you saw it because I would have run into it. A lot of people are lost at sea that way."

They sat quiet for a while then Betty remarked, "Jim's a great kid isn't he? I'm sure you feel safe leaving him on watch, since he sailed with you before."

Bob put *Destiny* on auto-pilot and sat back. "I'm sure Bruno and Martha will be all right too, but we don't know much about their experience."

"They seem nice enough, and they're good workers." Then Betty laughed, "At least I'm not bitching about the boat being messy. But I don't know about the relationship between them. I get the feeling the romance is over as far as he's concerned."

Bob's eyebrows went up, "Oh really, I didn't pick that up."

They heard a door open downstairs and Martha came up the stairs ready to relieve them.

"We're going to bed," said Bob yawning. "If you need me during your watch, call me."

Martha hopped on the helm-seat. "Don't worry. I took watch on the old schooner. I never had a problem."

For the next few days, the weather was cloudy and miserable. The wind blew a constant twenty knots heeling *Destiny* against the eight foot waves. Sleep was impossible. They went around the boat in a daze waiting for their bodies to adapt to the sea conditions. Martha and Betty took turns cooking and cleaning every other day the first two days, but now with the rough weather, they were too exhausted to do much. They had four hundred and fifty miles to go and were off course due to the strong wind.

Finally the weather turned favorable, bringing an immediate change in moods. Broad-reaching with winds at *Destiny*'s stern, the winds blew at twenty knots. *Destiny* was riding smoothly and gliding through the water like a duck on a sprint. It was making eight-and-a-half knots, but it didn't last. By the fourth day, the wind died down to a trace, and they barely drifted.

"This weather's crazy," said Betty, "It's either too much or too little, now the boat's rocking like a wild cradle."

"Jim, Bruno let's change sails," called Bob. "Take the genoa down and put up the spinnaker. Maybe we can get a little more speed out of this baby. Here Betty, you take the helm while I go out and help."

Working vigorously, they tackled the large sail, watching it balloon out as it sat high on the spinnaker pole. A huge maverick wave thrashed over the bow, pitching *Destiny* sideways.

Bruno yelled. "Look out, the spinnaker pole has come loose."

Bob and Jim ducked quickly, just as the heavy twenty foot aluminum pole came crushing down on the deck. The pole narrowly missed Jim's head, but hit Bob's right leg.

"Goddamnit," yelled Bob at the top of his lungs as he hopped around.

Betty put *Destiny* on auto-pilot and started out to see if Bob was hurt.

She leaned over the cockpit railing and called out, "Are you all right, do you need help?"

"Just stay at the helm. I'm okay. Keep the boat steady at two hundred and forty degrees. Don't let it go into the wind."

It was difficult keeping *Destiny* on course with so little wind. The harder Betty tried to keep it steady, the more it seemed to stray. She realized her hands had a strangle hold on the wheel, and she was oversteering. When she eased her grip, it was easier. The sail was hoisted back up and it billowed out spreading the blue and white stripes of the sail across the bow like a fantasy kite.

"Betty," Bob shouted above the wind, a tenseness in his

voice. "Turn the wheel fifteen degrees to the starboard. Quickly, quickly."

Nervous and flustered from the commotion, Betty turned in the wrong direction to port. As the sails started to flap out of control, she realized her mistake immediately and turned hard to starboard.

Bob's irritated voice screamed, "What the hell's the matter with you? Don't you know your right from your left? I said starboard."

Everyone laughed while Betty sat there feeling stupid, cold, and tired. She reacted angrily to the challenge in his voice. "Don't you yell at me like that. I don't need the aggravation and humiliation." Then sputtering with indignation she said, "I should have stayed in New Jersey where I belong."

Her anger abated some as she watched the spinnaker sway in the wind. It seemed to have a calming effect on her. The billowing sail looked like a huge crescent that filled the whole bow triangle with its gigantic size. Now *Destiny* glided a lot smoother through the water.

Bruno came back to the helm, his hair was standing up straight from the wind. With a sweeping motion, he brushed his black hair back with his hand and said, "Whew, glad that's over with. Here, let me take over for awhile, you need a break."

"Thanks, Bruno," Betty said, and went over and joined Jim and Martha in a game of rummy. She looked over at Bob, her expression was tight and strained. If he looked her way she was going to give him a nasty remark, but he was reading a book. After the game, Betty went out to the stern and sat watching the wake behind the boat.

Bob walked out to her, an uncertainty crept into his expression, as he asked, "You're a little quiet, anything wrong?"

She threw the words at him like stones. "Don't yell at me in front of everyone again. I don't have to take your verbal abuse." Her eyes flashed with anger as she looked right at him.

Bob stiffened as if she had struck him. "I'm sorry, I was just joking."

She stood with both hands on her hips. "Your voice didn't sound like you were joking. If it was a joke, it was at my expense."

171

A shadow of annoyance crossed his face as he backed off. "Okay, okay, I said I'm sorry."

Betty cooked dinner and went to her room to read. She tried to get into a better mood, but she was totally confused by his behavior. Soon it would be time for her watch and she'd have to go relieve Bob. She didn't want to talk or be near him.

When it was time for her watch, she went up on deck, and never said a word to Bob. If he thought he could embarrass her that way, he was mistaken. She didn't get mad she got even. They stared at each other across a ring of silence. His voice grated harshly as he said "Goodnight," and headed down the stairs.

Betty sat against the helm watching the dark sea. Music from her favorite Mantovani tape was filling the night. Trying to pass time and stay awake she did a few sit-ups to the music.

She didn't hear Bob come up. "Oh! You startled me," she said when she saw his shadow in the moonlight.

"Who did you think it was—the boogie man coming to attack you on the high seas?"

"No," she said sternly. "What are you doing up, I thought you were tired?"

"Couldn't sleep, so I came up to keep you company. Thought you might like a backrub," he said as he sat on the bench beside her. She continued to do her sit-ups. He put his arms around her but she pulled away. "You're not still mad are you?"

"Yes," she said coldly. "You made me feel stupid and I didn't expect that from you. Your temper flares without thinking."

Bob sat there with his head down, twisting his hands in a nervous way. "You got me pegged right. I do blurt things out when I'm frustrated. I guess you have to learn to understand me and know when I yell like that I don't mean it."

She swung her legs around to face him. "Maybe you have to think before you scream at me," Betty said, with a little tenderness seeping into her voice.

Bob put his arms around her and this time she didn't pull away. "I love you, you beautiful sea witch." When he kissed her, the kiss was filled with more emotion than she felt possible. His hands explored her body and the touch of his hands sent shivers through her. His mouth covered hers, devouring its softness. They undressed and caressed each other as the soft gentle breeze fanned their naked bodies. Her body arched toward his with an aching desire. They moved in exquisite harmony to the music of Mantovani. Exhausted they cuddled close and wondered why they hadn't fallen off of the narrow seats.

Laughing quietly Betty said, "What if someone had come up on deck and caught us? I would have been so embarrassed."

"Hey, you have to admit making love is a lot better than sit-ups. A much better workout too," said Bob.

He kept her company for the rest of her watch, and they sat looking out at the dark sea. The only light was the glimmer of the little phosphorescence in their wake of *Destiny*.

The first sight of Madeira was the conical peak of Porto Santo, rising in solitary grandeur. Reaching Madeira gave Betty the same elated spirit of the past landings. She wanted to put her feet back on ground again and explore the island. It had only been four and a half days but she still felt anxious. Their port of call was the harbor of Funchal, on Madeira. Anchoring out was their only choice as the harbor was full of freighters. It was known to be a rough anchorage, always crowded with freighters and fishing crafts.

When they anchored, the water in the harbor was choppy with high waves. "Don't open the portholes," said Bob sternly. "The inside of the boat will get drenched if you do."

They went out on deck to get into the dinghy, and Betty grabbed the railing, "We're rolling just as much as if as we were at sea. Look, the waves are splashing up on the deck."

They took the dinghy ashore to find customs, then they tried to find a repairman. The generator was not working again.

Jim held the dinghy while everyone got in, then he asked Bob, "What do you think is wrong with the generator?"

Bob started up the dinghy motor. "I think there's water or bad fuel in the lines."

"If you can't find a mechanic I'll look at it. Maybe I can fix it, I'm good with engines," Jim said with confidence.

Customs and immigration took no time at all, but finding a mechanic was impossible. Finally they gave up and looked for a quiet place to have lunch. There was a bizarre outdoor café on the waterfront.

Martha let out a squeal of delight, "Look over there! What are all those people looking at?"

"They're looking at our boat, and they brought the band to celebrate our landing," said Bob laughing and pointing at the parade coming down the street.

A group of people were marching, dressed in costume with knee pants, billowy sleeves and black hats. The woman were decked out in long, colorful dresses, fluffed out with many petticoats. The scene was very vivid and a full twenty piece band played music the whole time. The crowd stopped at an ornate old schooner that was docked in the harbor, flying decorative flags, plus the Portuguese flag. Martha asked the waitress what was going on, and she said the town was celebrating the discovery of South Africa, by the Portuguese. The ship was a replica of the vessel that sailed to South Africa five hundred years ago.

The day went quickly as they walked through the marketplace and later had dinner. Then they walked into the town square to enjoy the music before ending the night in Madeira. Their sleep that night would be almost as bad as being out at sea. The wind stirred up the water and *Destiny* rolled from side to side all night.

The next morning, Bob called the men together. "Why don't you two see what you can do with the generator? I'm going ashore and buy new hoses and clamps for it."

Betty grabbed her purse. "Martha and I will go with you. We need to shop for some fresh vegetables and fruit."

Bob dropped them off near the market to do their shopping. "I'll be back to pick you up in a half-hour."

They walked down the street, enjoying their freedom from *Destiny*'s rocking, and Martha nudged Betty. "Do ya see how those Portuguese men are staring at us, and in such a brash way? Look, see how they pucker their lips. Blimey, why do they make those sucking noises?"

Betty glanced at the men, they were staring and wrinkled their foreheads at them. Their eyebrows moved up and down in a grotesque way. "They look like their undressing us with their eyes."

"Cheeky creatures, aren't they?" said Martha.

"The women seem friendly, they nod and smile," said Betty, "The Portuguese women all have dark hair. Maybe they stare at us because of your blonde and my red hair."

When Bob picked them up, they rode back to *Destiny* laden down with fresh string beans, okra, peppers and bananas. Their bags also included eggs just laid that morning, freshly made bread and cheese that was a Madeira special.

The next day was Sunday and they awoke to the sound of church bells. "I'd like to go to church, Bob," Betty said, getting dressed to go. "I haven't been there since we left Florida. I never missed a Sunday back home."

Bob had just finished his breakfast. He wiped his mouth and said, "I'll take you in. I have to go to shore anyhow. I'll rent a car and drop you off at the church."

Betty entered the ancient gothic Catholic church in the center of town. Bob went off to pick up more parts for the generator, he would return for her in an hour. As she listened to the service, it brought a sense of unity to her. Near the end everyone shook hands saying what she believed was, "Peace be with you." She felt the warmth of the people as they shook her hand, she returned their friendly smiles.

Betty went outside after the service with a spiritual inner-peace blossoming inside her. The crowd had disbursed and she stood alone waiting for Bob. She was intrigued with the magnificent steeples that seemed to pierce the sky. Saints and angel faces were carved into the gray stone walls. She decided to capture this architectural wonder on film and focused her camera snapping several shots. From the corner of her eye, she noticed four men edging towards her. Their eyebrows twitched as gross sucking noises came from their puckered lips. She looked around and there was no one else around. Chills went through Betty as they started to encircled her. *Why were they doing this?* she thought as she looked to see how she could get away. They circled in closer, nudging her with their shoulders, and knocking her off balance. Betty's camera was knocked out of her hands as she tried to get past one of the men. He stiffened his body against her and she pushed him away and tried to get around him. Another one grabbed Betty's arm and she slapped at him, yanking her arm away he closed in on her and grabbed her blouse. Betty pulled away as she felt her blouse ripped open. Holding it together, she ran up the street. The men let out a big laugh and started after her. Betty could feel the tears welling up in her eyes. Fighting back the tears she kept control of herself. Her pulse began to beat erratically at the threatening sound of the men's footsteps behind her. Betty had to think, *Where could she go? All the shops are closed.* She continued to run praying Bob would show up. The men followed her closing the distance.

A horn blew and a car pulled up to the curb a short distance away. Betty came to an abrupt stop, her heart jumping in her chest. Then she realized it was Bob and ran to the car. The men stopped and watched. When they saw Bob get out they turned and ran. Betty couldn't control her emotions, and she broke down, crying hysterically.

"My God," said Bob as he reached over and took her in his arms. "What's the matter?" In a tear smothered voice she told him what had happened.

Bob was furious, his face was red with anger and the muscles tightened in his biceps as he started up the street after the men. He could still see them and he yelled at the top of his lungs, "You sons of bitches, if I catch you, I'll kill you."

She ran after him and grabbed his arm, "Please get back in the car. There's four of them and only one of you."

"I'm going to try and find your camera," he said pulling his arm away. He walked up the street as the men retreated, then he spotted her camera lying by the curb and picked it up.

Bob helped Betty in the car, as she tried to keep her fragile control. "I'm taking you to the police station, you're going to report this."

A shadow of alarm touched her face, and taking a deep breath Betty said, "What can I prove? Nothing. The police won't believe me, we're strangers here. We don't even speak the language . . . Let's just go back to the boat."

His tone of voice infuriated her as he asked, "What were you doing when you were standing there by yourself?"

"What did I do? What do you mean what did I do?" She spat out the words in an angry tone. "I was taking pictures of the church while I waited for you." She was so furious she could

176

hardly speak, "What do you think I was doing, lifting my blouse and showing off my boobs?"

He shook his head regretfully and put his arms around her. "I'm sorry, honey, I didn't mean it that way." Bob let out a long audible breath and said, "I don't want you and Martha to go anywhere without one of us men with you. This is not a good area to walk around by yourself—are you feeling calmer now?"

Her voice sounded tired as she answered, "Yeah, I'll be fine, I'm just shook up. Let's go back to the boat." Later, after she composed herself, she asked, "Did you get the parts for the generator?"

"No, all the shops are closed," His voice was rough with anxiety, "We'll have to patch it up and hope it works."

Bob arranged to keep the car for another day so they could see what the island was like. They marveled at the abundant groves of banana and orange trees, also the innumerable vineyards. There was very little grass anywhere. Everywhere you looked, the island flourished with fruits and vegetables, and every house was surrounded with gardens. The countryside reminded Betty a little of the Azores, with the small wooden farmhouses. There were rain forests with a lot of waterfalls tucked away in the mountains. The crew went with them in the car as they drove the narrow roads of the countryside.

Water poured down the wall of the mountain on to the road and they had to drive through it. Bruno laughed and said, "This must be a Portuguese car wash.

They planned to leave the next day, so Jim and Bob tried to fix the generator. They were busy working beneath the salon floor while Martha and Betty made sandwiches. Suddenly a loud blast shook *Destiny* and the salon and galley filled with smoke. Startled, Betty screamed. "Get off the boat, get off the boat."

Martha yelled, "Oh Lord, I'm going to burn to death," and headed for the steps.

"Get off the boat," Betty screamed again, as she rushed toward the companionway. Bruno and Bob had already made it up on deck. Then, they heard Jim laugh and say, "Hey, troops calm down. I accidentally stepped on the lever of the fire extinguisher."

Bob came back and looked down into the opening where they

177

had been working. The large halon extinguisher was spewing foam all over the engine and generator. A white cloud had filled the cabin and small flakes drifted down, as if it was snowing.

"Whoa, Jim, let's be a little more careful where you put your feet," said Bob a little more composed. "Those canisters are expensive, and it's almost impossible to get it refilled out here."

An hour later, Martha asked, "How is the repair job coming on the generator?"

"We're not doing so well," answered Bob in a disgusted voice. "We'll have to wait until we get to the Canary Islands to get it fixed." Bob was annoyed as he added, "There's always some damn thing going wrong."

Betty couldn't help but jab a little dig at him. "Hey grumpy, this is your dream trip, cheer up."

Sounds of large freighters leaving the harbor woke them early. After breakfast, Bob called the crew together. He leaned back in his chair and slowly sipped his coffee, as he said, "Our schedule's changed, we can't leave until tomorrow. With the generator broken, we won't be able to use the watermaker, so we have to fill our water tanks here."

"Think the water's any good to drink?" Betty asked in a serious tone.

Bob thought a minute then said, "We'll buy some bottled water for drinking and when we run out of that, we'll boil the water."

Arranging for water was not an easy task, especially with the language barrier. The only place to get water was at the commercial fishing dock. After three hours of dickering, Bob finally got the message across to the man in the office that they needed water.

The man had a way about him that Bob automatically didn't like. He spoke in a nasal twang, "I want four packs of cigarettes and twenty American dollars. Then I'll okay the sale of the water."

"What!" yelled Bob. "That's highway robbery."

The man shrugged his shoulders and coolly said, "You want water, I want cigarettes and twenty dollars."

Bob thought a while then said, " Shit . . . they got us again, Betty. Okay, you win. Here's your twenty and I'll give you the cigarettes when we move the boat to the dock."

The man sneered, then picked up his phone. Soon a huge dark-skinned man came out dressed in pants that were stiff from brine, and smelling of rotten fish.

He greeted them with a big smile and a greasy hand-shake. "*Buenos Dias*. I am Captain Hernandez. I understand you need water."

Surprised that he spoke English, Bob said, "Yes, we need to fill our tanks on the boat."

His voice had a degree of warmth and concern. "No problem senor, my men will help you."

They moved *Destiny* over to the fishing dock and waited. Two men arrived with three huge rusty containers filled with water. They trickled the water from the containers through a skinny hose into *Destiny*'s water tanks.

They were finally finished at sunset and in a grudging voice, Bob remarked, "What a long, frustrating day this turned into. It's taken four hours to fill two water tanks." Then he paid the man an additional thirty dollars for the water.

Fifteen

After a good breakfast of sausage and eggs, they sailed off into the wind. Their next port would be an overnight stop at Tenerife, the first island they would come to in the Canary Islands. Then, they would go on to Las Palmas on Grand Canary Island. *Destiny* flew through the water at ten knots. The weather turned cold and the day, gray and damp. Changing into warm clothing, they took their turns at the helm.

Betty liked to watch Bruno and Martha. They seemed like such an odd couple. He treated her indifferently while she followed him around like a sick puppy. They were sitting together, then Bruno walked over to sit at the helm with Bob.

Bob glanced at him then said, "How do you like this weather? The wind's mild, but we're still beating against the wind."

Bruno didn't answered, he looked out at the horizon like he was deep in thought.

Betty looked up from her book and shivered. "I'm glad we only have fifty miles to go. I'm chilled to the bone. I'm going down to my bunk, and cuddle under the warm, cozy covers."

Reading in the warmth of the room, she drifted off until the wind changed to a furious, forty knots. *Destiny* felt like she was going wild, bucking like an untamed bronco.

"Betty, get up here," yelled Bob. "We need you."

Rushing up on deck, she saw Jim and Bruno changing the sails.

Bob looked sternly at her and said, "Take over the helm and hold her steady. Don't let it veer off course. I'm going to help reef the sails."

A huge wall of water came crashing over the side, knocking Betty off the helm seat.

"Oh God, I hope the boat can handle this. I sure can't swim in this mess," Betty said, as she worked to keep *Destiny* steady.

Beating against a strong wind is the most uncomfortable sail and they had been doing it for hours. *Destiny* might be a good size, but she was like a pea pod out there in the middle of this ocean. When the wind is high she is tossed around like a twig. The boat was heeling twenty-five degrees to the starboard and the railing was submerged in the sea. Water rushed onboard clear up to the edge of the cockpit. The men were having a tough time getting the genoa and stay-sail reefed, as the sheets had tangled and the sail was stuck on the track. Finally the main sail was reefed and *Destiny* was once again under control.

Bob was at the helm and stood mute. Betty could see something was bothering him.

"What's the matter," asked Betty. "You seem worried."

"The crew is so new and the weather could get worse. I think we better find a port to get into until this blows over," said Bob. "Jim, take the helm."

Bob went down to the navigation desk to study the charts and Betty followed.

"We're way off course. We won't get to Tenerife until four in the morning. It's just too rough to stay out here. We'll pull into the first point of this island," he said pointing at a speck on the chart. "That's Santa Cruz."

It was a dragging four hours as *Destiny* beat against the harsh wind. Santa Cruz, at the harbor of Gourda was a rough anchorage, but calmer than the sea. Worn out, and cold they looked for a sheltered spot and anchored for the night. It had taken them nine hours to go thirty-three miles dead against the wind.

Betty handed Bob a bourbon and soda. "Here, you look like you could use this. God, that was rough."

"Damn weather just won't give us a break. All we do is beat, beat, beat," said Bob despondently.

After a couple of sips, he relaxed. "The crew is holding up well." He looked over at the three of them resting at the end of the cockpit, enjoying a beer. "Hey guys, you did good today."

"That bloody wind almost knocked me knickers off," laughed Martha.

"Will you speak proper English?" said Bruno looking annoyed. Then he said to Bob, "It was quite an experience. I've

181

never been in weather this rough. I was sure the boat was going to overturn."

Jim burst out with a weird laugh, "What a way to go, wow-ee, what a trip."

Later that night Betty laid in bed thinking of her family. She wanted to call home but she couldn't get through on the ship to shore radio. Longing for home and family, she began to wonder again why she was here. *Stop thinking of home, you're here to see something of the world. Besides you gave your word you'd do it,* she scolded herself. Finally she fell into an erratic sleep, feeling the rocking and jarring of their vessel against the waves.

The anchorage was calmer in the morning, but the sun was hazed over from orange sand floating in the air. They could barely see the sun peeking through the heavy dust cloud. It looked like a tiny glowing ember. *Destiny's* decks were covered with the orange sand that the strong wind blew in from the Sahara desert, eighty miles away.

Hoisting the anchor they made their way out of the pro-tected haven, not knowing what to expect. The wind was waiting for them just around the bend murmuring. "Here comes *Destiny,* let's beat her up again."

Destiny struggled against twenty knot winds and heeled fif-teen degrees. The boat's speed was eight knots and not on course. Bob tacked to the starboard side to see if he could get closer to the course he needed on the compass. As soon as he did, their speed cut down to five knots.

"What's going on here?" yelled Bob. "Bruno, tighten up the sheets on the genoa and loosen up the sheet on the mainsail. See if that helps."

"We only have seventeen miles to go, why is it taking so long?" asked Betty in an irritated voice.

"Be patient," Bob barked back. "Between the wind current and position of the island, it's going to take us at least eight hours to get there."

"Eight hours to go seventeen miles?" Betty said in despera-tion.

Bob tacked the sails again to gain back the speed. "We'll cut back in as we get closer to Las Palmas at Grand Canary."

Destiny was still heeling fifteen degrees. The crew sat rigid hanging on for balance, wishing they were anyplace else but here.

At long last they could see Las Palmas on the horizon, their oasis in the storm. When they entered the harbor a wonderful calm fell around them, and a sigh of relief went through the boat. Sailboats were as far as the eye could see. In the harbor of Las Palmas, flags were strung all over the docks and buildings, and people were swarming everywhere. There was a sailboat race that time of year from Las Palmas to Barbados and was called the ARC Race. Yachts that have spent their summers in the Mediterranean met there for the race back to the Caribbean.

Bob pulled *Destiny* into an open spot along the wall. Once the boat was tied up, Jim said, "Whoa, that was one long trip."

Betty jumped off and laid down in the grass, "This feels marvelous. I love the sweet aroma of earth," she said laughing.

Bob laughed at Betty's actions, then said, "I better check in with customs, then we'll register for the race." Bob gathered his documents. "This is quite a big event."

Bob and his crew went to the meeting and met some new people. At the meeting, the captain of the ARC group explained the rules of the race. Boats up to thirty feet would leave first and boats up to forty feet would leave second, followed by the larger ones. Prizes would be given to the first of each class to arrive in Barbados. There was to be a lead boat and one on the rear. They would monitor the air-waves, and give assistance if and when it was needed.

A dinner dance was given by the ARC race sponsors and steaks were served from the grill, with corn on the cob and red baked potatoes. Beer and wine flowed freely in monogrammed cups and glasses. The next few days were filled with meetings on navigation and safety, and every night was party time.

Marvin and Bridget from the boat *Marbid* were there. They had been in the Azores the same time as *Destiny*. Bridget was always seasick. From the moment she left port she would remain in her bunk, until they reached the next port. Her husband managed to do everything on their forty-foot boat alone. At night he'd put the boat on auto-pilot and sleep. Bob tried to explain how dangerous it was but they were willing to take the chance. Seeing them again was like meeting old friends.

Before *Destiny* could leave for Barbados, they had to make the necessary repairs. The list was longer than the one in Gibraltar. Among other things, the generator, engine and bow thrusters all needed work. Plus there were electrical problems. Water still leaked into the salon, and the bilge pumps ran almost continually. All repairs had to be finished within two weeks, as the larger boats were scheduled to leave then.

Las Palmas was lively with music and the town was decorated both for the race and for the Christmas holidays. One of the largest department stores Betty ever saw was *Cortes Inglas*. The five floors had items from food to furniture and everything in between. The grocery department had food from around the world and the meat counter was loaded with prime cuts.

After shopping, Martha and Betty hailed a cab. The driver put their groceries in the trunk.

The driver smiled, his gold teeth showing. "*Boa tarde*, where you want to go?"

Speaking no Portuguese, Betty said, "We want to go to the ARC Race Yacht club."

The cab driver shrugged his shoulders. "*No comprenda?*"

"You just asked us in English where we wanted to go," said Martha.

"*No comprenda*. Where you want to go?" The driver asked with a big smile.

Martha broke out laughing, "Blimey, the only English he knows is, 'Where you want to go.'"

Betty reached for the door handle. "Let's get another cab."

There was a click, and the doors locked. "No," the driver said. Then he handed Betty a pad and pencil, and made drawing motions with his hands.

Surprised, Betty said to Martha, "He wants us to write where we're going."

The cab driver laughed, and shaking his head up and down he pointed to the paper.

Betty drew a picture of a sailboat and the name ARC and handed it back to him. His face lit up with a huge smile and he started the car. As he drove the cab, he blew kisses and winked at them through the rear view mirror.

He pulled up in front of a shipyard. "No, no," said Betty.

"This is the wrong place." She underlined the word ARC on the paper.

"*Sim sim, oue!*" The driver said smacking his head. "*Exactamente.*" He finally understood and he drove further down the road.

When they returned to the boat, Martha had a letter from her parents waiting for her.

"Oh me God, me mum's here in Grand Canary. They hoped they would still be here when I arrived. I'm so excited."

Martha called the hotel where her parents were staying and went to see them. Later they joined Betty and Bob for dinner. During the meal, Bob told the crew that they were planning to leave for three days to drive around the island.

Martha pulled Betty aside and asked, "Would it be okay if me mum and dad live aboard while you're away? They think it's such a cushy yacht."

"I don't see why not. They can sleep in our cabin while we're gone. Take a couple of days off and spend some time with them."

"I wouldn't ask, but they have to get out of the flat they're renting. They'd like to stay a few more days."

"That's fine," said Betty patting Martha's hand. "There's plenty of food onboard. Make them comfortable."

"Thank you ever so," Martha gushed. "I'll let them know the good news after dinner."

After Betty and Bob gave the crew last minute instructions they left for a few days of privacy. Their first stop was the Grande Playa, a beach resort that was just loaded with hotels and restaurants. A beautiful room was reserved for them at the Casa Grande hotel. They walked the black sandy beaches and drank rum-berry drinks. They cuddled and made love on the beach and in the motionless bed, a just reward for the rough voyage.

It was a bright sunny morning so they decided to drive to the other side of the island. When they found the road to the other side of the island, they found that cars were turning around and coming back. They signaled for Bob to do the same. They said the road was too torn up and not safe to use. Betty waited for Bob to turn the car around, but he kept driving straight ahead.

"Bob, turn around, it's not safe to go up any further," Betty said as she tugged his sleeve.

"I want to see it for myself," said Bob still driving ahead. "If it's no worse than this, we can make it, it can't be that bad."

The road was extremely narrow as it climbed almost straight up. It was full of ruts and holes, and there were no guard rails. Some areas were so narrow a car could barely fit on it. Betty looked at the long drop along side of her and shivered. "We better turn back, it doesn't look safe. We're up pretty high and it's a long drop down if we go over."

"I think we can make it, I'll go slowly," said Bob, determined to get to the other side.

"Now it's raining, that's an omen to turn around and go back." When he wouldn't stop she yelled, "You're hard-headed and never listen to me or anyone. You'll get us both killed." He didn't answer. He just continued to drive carefully up the steep narrow stretch. Betty sat in her seat chewing her fingers until they were raw. There was no use complaining. He wasn't listening anyhow. All morning they bounced and bumped jarring their insides. He was determined to make it to the other side.

Finally the road smoothed out. Bob had a smirk on his face as he said, "I told you we'd make it, and it looks like we've landed on the moon."

Stuttering from the roughness, she said, "You bounce me around on the water, then you bounce me around on land." She shook her head in desperation and said, "Man, you're something else."

They walked around the ragged plateau, examining the wavy and grotesque formations the molten lava had created. Here and there, little specks of life could be seen as some green plant tried desperately to survive. They drove back through the narrow countryside, stopping at the shops where lace, carvings and baskets were sold. When they returned to *Destiny*, they felt more content from the much needed privacy.

Everything was in good shape; the crew had completed the work Bob had assigned, but Martha was crying in her cabin and Betty went in to comfort her.

"Mother and Dad's gone back to England," Martha whimpered. "I'm gona miss them. They loved *Destiny* and sleeping in your room . . . Oh, me mum left a gift for you in your room."

Betty opened the gift. "This is a terrific cookbook. It's from

Harrods department store in London. Give me your mother's address as I'd like to write and thank her."

Then, Martha added, "I took the turkey out of the freezer like you asked me to. It's defrosting in the sink."

"Oh, that's right," said Betty. "Thanksgiving's tomorrow. I've lost track of time."

While Bob and the crew were working on *Destiny*, Betty prepared the Thanksgiving meal. She stuffed the bird and put it in the oven, then made a pumpkin pie. The turkey turned a golden brown and the aroma reminded her of Thanksgivings at home. The table in the dinning area was set with table cloth, crystal and porcelain dishes. When dinner was ready, she called everyone to eat, but no one came. They were in the middle of installing the mainsail back on its track.

Martha came down and gasped, "Upon my word the table sure looks bea-u-tiful and the bird looks scrumptious."

Betty went on deck, "Come on guys it's Thanksgiving and the turkey's getting cold."

"Bruno, get your knickers down here now," yelled Martha.

A half-hour later they appeared in the galley with their clothes, face and hands filthy.

Betty growled, "At least wash your hands before you sit down."

Bruno said grace, before they dug in like hungry vultures.

Their days were taken up with repairs and the nights with parties and fireworks. Martha and Betty went back to *Corte Inglas* for their final provisioning. A large amount of supplies was needed for the long trip across the Atlantic to Barbados. They filled six baskets with food, toiletries, and booze. She was a thousand dollars poorer.

A small artificial Christmas tree caught Betty's eye and she couldn't resist it. She picked up little wooden sailors decorated in red green and blue, along with lights to decorate the tree. Betty found five small Christmas stockings to hang on the wall, in case St. Nick came to visit. The Christmas song, *Felize Navidad* filled the air, giving off holiday spirit. Betty bought Christmas presents to send home for the family and also some for Bob and the crew. She could hardly wait to get back to the boat to put the Christmas tree up.

Securing it tightly to a table with duct tape, she decorated the little tree then pinned the stockings to the wall. Now the salon had a festive look.

Bob walked in the room. "Wow, it looks great in here. Where did you find such a small Christmas tree?"

Betty was jubilant. "Doesn't it make you feel like it's really Christmastime?"

"Yes it does. You did a great job," he said giving her a big hug.

Betty hung on to him not wanting him to go back to work, as she asked, "How's the work coming along?"

Bob sat down and pulled Betty on his lap, "Well, it looks like we're ready to head for Barbados. All the repairs are done and *Destiny*'s fuel and water tanks are full. I'm waiting for the mechanic to come and collect his money for the final repairs." There was a knock on the side of the boat. "This must be him now."

When the man handed him the bill, Bob looked at it in surprise. "What's this? This price is too high. Almost twice the amount." He pulled a paper from his back pocket and shoved it at the man. "This is the price you quoted me."

"Well, mister, it cost more than I expected. This is the new price," the mechanic said.

Bob threw the bill back at him. "I'm not paying this, no way."

The mechanic sneered. "You better pay it. I'll have you locked up and your boat confiscated."

Bob stared the man in the eye and studied him for a while. "Go get the police, let them try to take my boat. You're just trying to cheat me."

The man's face went red, he raised his fist in the air and shouted, "You're a cheap American, that's what you are. A bully, cheap American."

Bob handed him the money and he grabbed it and walked away.

The excitement was really building as the first group said goodbye. The race started at two-thirty, and two hundred boats were scheduled to leave. The harbor was one big traffic jam with boats running into each other as they tried to back out of their slips. The water way was so crowded the boats couldn't pass each other.

Martha and Gary grabbed Betty and Bob and gave them a hug. "See you in Barbados. Godspeed you safely across," said Gary.

"Goodbye," they called out as they watched their friends climb aboard their crafts.

The group from *Destiny* walked along the dock waving to the boats heading for the starting line. A cannon sat high on the hill. At the wave of the white flag, it shot off with a tremendous burst, as black smoke weaved through the air.

The boats motored out of the harbor, the start of the two thousand, six hundred and forty mile trip from Grand Canary to Barbados.

"Boy, that's a hell of a long way to go," said Jim.

"They've taken all precautions they can," said Bob anxious to go. "Including constant radio contact for safety reports on bad weather or breakdowns."

Betty looked out at the horizon. "I wonder what the wind is like out there?"

"The winds are reported at twenty knots just outside the harbor, and thirty-five knots, after they get around the island," answered Bob.

Martha shuddered. "I hope they calm down before we leave."

Four days later, it was *Destiny*'s time to join the larger ships. What lay ahead was uncertain, but all precautions had been taken to make the trip as safe as possible. The life rafts had been repackaged and extra water and fuel was aboard, with life vests at easy access.

Sixteen

The cannon echoed through the air as the group of boats fifty feet and up started off. Surrounded by fifty other boats, *Destiny* headed out of the harbor. The wind was gentle until they passed the island. Then thirty knot winds thrashed waves over the decks. They were back fighting Mother Nature again. Betty didn't feel frightened; she had been in worse conditions. A reprieve from the stormy seas came the next day, although they were still beating against a light wind. They were forced to put the motor on or drift nonchalantly at one-and-a-half knots.

Several days went by as the balmy breeze continued. Still motoring, *Destiny* was riding smoothly through the rippling glassy water. Everyone felt relaxed as they moved around the decks looking for things to do. The women took turns doing the wash and preparing gourmet meals. Things turned even better when the wind shifted to southeast. Bob called it the trade winds, and it blew on the stern of the boat.

Bob was overjoyed and yelled, "Just what we were waiting for!" Full sails were flying and it felt like they were floating on air.

Betty lay out on the deck reading. She put her book down and said, "It feels like heaven after the hell we've been through on the other trips."

Bob looked up from the helm and called out, "*Destiny*'s moving at four-and-a-half knots in seven knots of wind. It's not fast but it's peaceful."

On watch the nights were moonless with shooting stars. They seemed to dart through the sky in celebration of the race. The smell of the salty air tingled Betty's nostrils and made her sneeze. Phosphorescent lights danced in the waves from the small organisms in the water, giving *Destiny* a weird glow of a ghost ship lost in the night.

During the day, they passed time playing cards and finding

small jobs and repairs to do. Nothing threatening was happening, and they enjoyed the tranquillity.

Staring out at the vast horizon and the endless sea, Betty's eyes searched for sealife. "Where are the fish that should be chomping at our fishing lines? Where are all the birds or the other ships we took off with?" She talked loudly and didn't expect an answer. Her mind was just glad to relax and talk about simple things. Weary of worrying about survival tactics, she just let her thoughts go free in these tranquil moments. She visualized the sharks circling below, grabbing the tuna and dolphins that try to take their hook. *That's why we're not catching any fish,* she thought and giggled to herself.

Martha was in the galley fixing dinner. She always came up with a mouth-watering meal. "It's great not having to go down in the galley to cook when the weather is wild," said Betty.

"Somehow it's always my turn to cook when it's rough," laughed Martha.

Bob chimed in with, "Funny how it works that way."

Martha woke up the next morning, with a cheery, "Good morning." She was wearing a bright yellow extra large T-Shirt with a huge picture of Minnie Mouse in red polka dots. Her jeans seemed extra-tight as she climbed out of the cockpit.

Bruno took one look at her and said, "You have my jeans on! Can't you wear your own clothes? You'll stretch mine."

"Don't be such an old crab," she said pouting. "I don't have none to wear. Mine are all dirty."

"Keep your hands off my clothes. You wear my underwear, now you're taking my jeans," said Bruno, really miffed.

Betty started to laugh. "You wear Bruno's underwear?"

"Well, we were a little short on money. We just bought men's bikini knickers and we both wore them."

"You weren't this fat when I first met you, now you stretch them out of shape," said Bruno, shaking his head.

His attitude towards her was very abrupt and at times he acted like he didn't even like her.

Martha pouted for a while, but kept the jeans on and soon she was singing, "London bridge is falling down, falling down, falling down."

"Oh, for God's sake," Bruno said as he walked out to the bow.

Going through the cookbooks, Betty looked for great ideas to make their meals more interesting. The men loved the aroma that seeped from the galley and it was magnified tenfold by the pure air.

"I don't know what you're cooking but it's driving me crazy," said Bruno. His salivary juices ran full flow as the tantalizing smell flowed up the companionway.

"Is that apple pie I smell?" Inhaling the aroma, Bob's stomach went wild with gurgles. He moaned and groaned with ecstasy. Eating has become their greatest pleasure and they constantly asked, "What's on the menu tonight?"

Each day, Martha and Betty tried to outdo each other in meals. They searched for something exciting and different to serve.

"Guess what we're having for afters tonight?" said Martha as she came up from the galley.

"Afters? What's afters?" Bob said with a quizzical look.

"Afters, you know . . . After you eat your meal you have a sweet, that's afters."

"Oh, you mean dessert," said Betty. "Great, what did you prepare?"

"Plum pudding just like me mum makes at home."

The pudding was superb and a great ending to the shepherd's pie.

Days blended together and clear skies added to the beauty of the tranquil weather. They relished every minute of the perfect day. They had two thousand and ninety miles to sail before they reached Barbados. Each night, they made radio contact with the lead boat to let them know all was well. So far there had been no mishaps. *Destiny* had passed a few of the yachts hoping to make it to the lead boat.

There was no "Good morning" from Martha today when she came up for her morning watch. She looked sad as she came on deck.

Betty looked over at her and asked, "Are you feeling all right?" Martha didn't answer. "Are you getting homesick?"

"No, that's not the problem. It's Bruno. He don't love me anymore. He hasn't touched me in months and he used to be so loving."

This was not what Betty expected to hear. "I'm sorry. It must be hard for you to stay in the same room as him. Why did you come on the trip if he feels that way about you?"

"I thought he was just having a tizzy and would get over it. I love him so."

Oh God, Betty thought, *I just went through this with Mitch.* "Would you like me to ask Jim to sleep in Bruno's room?"

"No! no! Please don't do that. I want to be near him. Maybe after a while he'll change."

Martha got up and danced back to the cockpit where Bruno was reading. She flopped down next to him, grabbed his hand and kissed it.

"For Christ's sake Martha, why can't you be more gentle?" he said, pulling his hand away.

Martha pouted, "Don't fuss with me. I just want to sit with you."

Bruno put his book down and let out a perturbed sigh. "Why don't you shave your legs? They look like gorilla legs. I can't stand the sight of them."

Martha, half in tears answered, "I forgot, all right? I'll do it tonight in the douche."

"No you won't. You'll forget, just like you forget to clean up the room and pick up your clothes."

The rest of the people onboard tried not to listen. It was embarrassing both to her and to them. They could see now why Bruno had talked about coming alone. There was no romance left as far as Bruno was concerned. Listening to her talk drove him up a wall. He used perfect English while she had the cockney slang and didn't want to correct it.

Betty and Bob walked out to the stern of the boat. "I'm not sure what's going to happen between those two. Their behavior is interfering with the harmony of our lives," said Bob.

Betty sat down on the deck and looked up at Bob. "Bruno seems fed up with her, how about having a talk with him. Ask him to keep whatever problems he has with Martha quietly between them."

"I will, but I don't know if it will do any good. Everything she does aggravates him. Well, it's my watch, I better go take over," said Bob.

Betty laid down on the mat on the stern deck and fell asleep. The sunlight danced on her face as she awoke to the sound of Bob's voice, calling her.

"Look at the large school of dolphins that are swimming alongside. They're incredible," Bob said hanging over the side watching them.

The glorious mammals were entertaining and breaking the monotony of the trip. They jumped out of the water making clicking sounds, as if to get attention. They jumped across each other, then landed back into the water. It was a scene from *Water World*. They enjoyed seeing the dolphins and hoped they would stay for awhile. The dolphins hung around for an hour, then the show ended as they swam out of sight.

Time had passed by without Betty knowing what day it was. She didn't really care. All she knew for sure was they still had eighteen hundred and nine miles yet to go. After her night watch she always checks the miles before going to bed. Then the first thing in the morning, she'd race to the navagation table to see how many miles they sailed during the night.

It's her day watch now and she stared out at the horizon that seems to kiss the ocean. Waves ripple by in monotonous motion as her eyes search constantly for something to see. Another ship, sealife, anything that would give a spark to their daily existence.

A lost seabird appeared out of nowhere and her brain came alive. A feeling of excitement ran through her as she jumps to her feet.

Betty shrieked with delight and ran to the stern. "There's a bird," she called out to everyone. "It's only a scraggly seagull but it's beautiful to me."

"Blimey! There really is a bird. What's the poor little thing doing out here so far from land?" asked Martha.

Bruno and Jim looked upward. Their eyes are fixed on this feathery creature. The bird was making huge circles in the blue, cloud speckled sky. His circles got smaller as he flew around the mast, trying desperately to land on the top of it. Mesmerized by the poor creature's determination, they cheered him on. After several minutes, the bird was exhausted, and landed on the white-capped water to rest. *Destiny* sailed onward and soon their cherished little creature was out of sight.

The wind shifted, but it was not a strong wind and caused a wrenching uncontrolled motion. One moment, the sails are full pushing them along smoothly, then quickly the wind changed directions. It played with the sails causing loud cracking noises, as the wind spilled from the sails. They flapped back and forth then billowed out again. *Destiny*'s speed went from two knots to six knots, then back down again. They tried to sleep but to no avail. The motion and the night seemed endless.

Betty tossed back and forth with the constant movement. Her nerves were on edge again. She felt like she was in a torture chamber; her body craving stillness.

"Please God, let this motion stop. I just want to lie still for awhile," Betty moaned.

The only one up was Jim. It was his watch and he was scanning the horizon on the pitch-black night for ships. Everyone else had gone to their cabin hoping exhaustion would let them sleep. The only sound was the rushing of the waves as it lapped against the side of *Destiny*.

The stillness was broken by a wind change and Jim called out. "Bob, come quickly, the wind has shifted. We have to get the spinnaker pole down."

Bob staggered out of bed. It was two in the morning, but he wasn't sleeping. "Damn, when is this wind going to settle down and make up its mind?"

"I hated to call you," said Jim. "But the wind changed to southwest. I can't hold our course."

"That's okay," said Bob yawning. "I can't sleep anyhow. Get Bruno up and we'll change the sails."

Drizzling rain filled the air, making the dark decks slippery. They worked over an hour with only the stars and a small spotlight to see by. The men struggled against the frustrating wind to get the spinnaker pole to portside. Jibing the main and mizzen the task was finally accomplished.

"What an awful job that was. I'm soaked through to the skin. I'm going back to bed," said Bruno as he headed to his bunk.

"Wait a minute Bruno—I don't believe it. I just don't believe it," said Bob in an irritated voice. "How can this be happening?"

"What's the matter?" Bruno said coming back up.

Bob threw his hands up in the air. "The damn wind has changed back again."

"Oh no," they moaned, each dreading the thought of going back out in the strong wind. "Let's wait awhile and see what happens," said Jim. "Maybe it will switch again."

After ten minutes, Bob climbed out of the cockpit, "Okay, let's get the damn thing changed. I hope this time it stays."

They finished just as the orange glow of the sun crested over the distant horizon. Painting the sky with glorious hews of pink, orange and gold.

With all the noise on deck, Betty had come up to see if she could help out. When everything settled down she asked, "Bob do you know Christmas is just three days away?"

"Only three days? How far are we now from Barbados?" asked Jim.

Betty checked her log, "As of this morning we have fourteen hundred and eight miles to go before we reach Barbados."

Martha's face was all smiles. "I think we should get a little holiday spirit going around here. We're all a bunch of sticks in the mud."

"I'll put some Christmas carols on the stereo." Jim who was always looking for a way to have fun, said, "Let's have a half-way party and break open the champagne."

"Yeah, that would put some life in this group," Betty said with excitement in her voice. Then she added, "One thousand fourteen hundred, and eight miles to go. It seems like an eternity."

That evening at cocktail time, they broke open the champagne. Before they drank a toast, Jim handed each of them a large sheet of paper.

"What's this you're handing us?" Martha asked, looking at it curiously.

"They're certificates. I made one for each of you. It states the time, day, year and latitude when we crossed the half-way mark," Jim said with a proud smile. He had printed each certificate and put a gold seal on them.

"Thanks, Jim. This is a special gift worth keeping for a long time," said Bob.

A few more days passed and their sailing speed had been five knots. Eight foot seas sloshed against *Destiny* making her waddle like a fat goose. Betty felt like she was in a trance as she lay on the stern deck. She was reading and felt exhausted. The heat along with the sleepless nights had sapped her strength. Betty read the same page over three times before she gave up and shut her eyes.

What always snapped everyone out of a depressed mood was Mother Nature's tantrums. The wind picked up rapidly and swirled around *Destiny,* ripping the spinnaker to shreds. The sail flared in the air for a moment, as if in a freedom celebration. Then it cascaded downward as the tattered spinnaker fell into the sea. It dragged heavily in the water as it twisted around and around like a mop being rung out. One sheet was still attached to the pole, and it kept the sail from going completely overboard. All hands were on the bow immediately, struggling to haul the heavy drenched and tattered sail back onboard. Without the spinnaker up, *Destiny* rocked violently back and forth.

"Haul the sail in as quick as you can," yelled Bob above the wind. "I don't want it to wrap around the prop."

The rocking made it difficult to pull in the sail. Soaked with saltwater, the spinnaker seemed to weigh a ton. The four of them worked with team effort tugging and pulling to retrieve it. Bruno and Martha were pulling on one side as Betty and Jim yanked and pulled on the other. Betty's foot slipped and she slid along the wet deck, getting close to the open railing. Jim reached out with one hand and gripped her arm. With his support on one arm and her grip on the sail, she regained her stance and started to help again. After retrieving the spinnaker from the water, they sat on the deck exhausted.

Bob called out. "We're going to lose speed without the spinnaker. We better put the stay-sail and genie up wing to wing."

"Come on, Bruno," said Jim. "The sooner we set the sails, the sooner we can rest."

When they were finished, *Destiny* was sailing at four knots, still rocking, but not violently.

It was Christmas Day and Betty walked the deck singing, "Deck the halls with boughs of flying fish, la la la la la la la la." The flying fish lie stiff in the sun.

As Betty threw them overboard she called to Bob, "Look what Santa left you, an extra large fish, filled with a special cologne." She took it over and dangled it in his face. "It's a new fragrance called, 'L' Puko."

Grabbing it from her hand, he chased her out on deck. "I think it's more your fragrance," he said trying to rub it on her face.

Betty screamed, "Throw it overboard. Stop! Don't rub it on me." He held her down but she wiggled free, and ran back to the helm.

She sat and listened to the Christmas carols. Sighing, she said, "This doesn't feel like Christmas."

"Why not?" said Bob. "We have our own tree and Santa put something in your stocking."

Betty jumped up from her seat. "Really! There's something in my stocking? How would Santa find me way out here on the ocean?" she said hurrying down to the salon.

Bruno and Martha came on deck and half-asleep, said, "Merry Christmas."

Then, Jim staggered up, and yawned. "I can't sleep with all the racket going on. You might think it was Christmas or something."

Betty returned with her stocking and her arms full of gifts. Singing carols and wishing each other Merry Christmas, they sat around in their bathing suits in eighty-five degrees, exchanging gifts. The crew gave Bob and Betty a brass ship's bell. The clapper had fallen off the old one. Jim received new shorts, Martha shirts, and Bruno jeans. When Betty opened her gift from Bob she found a gorgeous butterfly pin. It had small diamonds for the eyes.

Hugging him, she said. "Thank you, honey, it's lovely, Merry Christmas."

When she handed Bob his gift, he shook it and squeezed it. Finally, he unwrapped it. He was all smiles as he said, "Just what I need, a diver's watch." Then he kissed her and said,

"Merry Christmas, my butterfly."

"Hey guys, I saw Santa on the radar last night," said Jim. "He only had one red running light, so it had to be Rudolph."

Betty left the merry group to prepare the turkey for dinner. The galley was extremely hot and would get worse as the turkey cooked. She listened to the Christmas carols and the songs brought back memories. She thought of the times when she cooked holiday dinner back in her own kitchen. Betty's eyes watered both from the onions and homesickness. After the turkey was in the oven she rolled the dough for the pumpkin pie.

Thoughts of her grandchildren drifted through her mind. She could hear Ryan saying, "Oh Grandmom you're making pumpkin pie, I love pumpkin pie."

They were always into the cookies that Betty made every Christmas. She pictured them coming down to see the tree and toys, and she longed to be there. Placing the dough in the pie plate, she poured the pumpkin sauce into the crust. *Destiny's* rocking set the filling in motion and it spilled over the crust. Betty picked it up to place it in the oven. That proved to be a big mistake. The rocking made the filling sway faster, and the sticky orange gob ran down her arms and on to the floor.

Angry and frustrated she threw the pie in the sink. "The hell with the pumpkin pie."

The melody of *I'll be home for Christmas* echoed through the boat, and that made things worse. Snapping the stereo off, Betty went to her stateroom to beat the mattress and have a good cry. After she released her frustrations She listened to the laughter above. She felt silly crying, they must miss their families too. She wondered why she overreacted so. *It seemed like tension builds up inside of me*, she thought. *My body needs a release and crying seems to be the safety valve.*

Betty went back to the galley and put on livelier music. Then, she continued to cook the holiday meal. The Christmas feast was served the usual way. At the ringing of the new bell, everyone rushed down to fill their plates and take it up to the cockpit table.

Bob opened a bottle of wine and as he poured each glass he said, "We're getting closer. Only have nine hundred and fifty nine miles to go. We should be in Barbados for New Years Eve."

"New Years Eve! Man, am I going to party," said Jim.

Everyone agreed that it would definitely be party time when they finally arrived.

When Bob came on watch the next morning they were way off course. Switching the auto-pilot off he steered *Destiny* back on course. When he tried to put it back on auto-pilot, it wouldn't stay. Bob switched to the backup Robertson auto-pilot. It wouldn't hold either. Frustrated, he continued to hand-steer for the rest of his watch.

When Betty came up to relieve him she took one look at his stern face and asked, "What's the trouble now?"

"Both auto-pilots are out. We've never used the back-up one before. Take the helm, I'm going below to see what's wrong." When he came up a half-hour later he was frustrated. "The gear on the auto-pilot is worn out and we don't have a replacement part. Also the wires on the Robertson had been severed. The mechanics in Las Palmas must have cut the wires when they worked on the boat. The bastard, not only was he trying to cheat me, but he wrecked the Robertson auto-pilot. We'll have to steer the rest of the way."

Bob broke the news to the crew when they woke up. They groaned knowing with the wind and wave action, it was not going to be easy.

"I'm changing the watch. Two people must be on deck at all times. Each one will steer for two hours, and sleep or rest on deck for two hours," said Bob. "That way there will be an extra person to help with the sails in case of wind change."

"Blimey, me arms will break off," moaned Martha.

"Stop complaining and for God's sake go shave your arm pits and legs," said Bruno.

"Leave me alone. I'll do it when I go to bed," whined Martha.

Today was December 29th, Bob's birthday. His celebration was a huge squall building behind *Destiny*. The sky swirled with black brooding clouds, ready to break loose as they grew closer. Their nostrils burned from the salt-laden air, and they could tell by the eerie atmosphere that it would be a wild one. The wind picked up pace to twenty knots as torrents of rain come plummeting down. *Destiny* rode the waves like a race horse, moving ahead strong and steady at nine knots.

"Get those sails reefed," yelled Bob above the wind. "The wind's up to thirty-five knots and it's still rising."

Once the sails were reefed, they felt pretty secure until a sheet broke free. It snapped in the wind like an uncontrolled whip, lashing back and forth like an angry snake. Jim ran out on deck and tried to grab it. The sheet thrashed across his bare back raising huge red welts. Twirling around to escape the rope he lost his balance and fell against the guardrail. His feet slipped and he dangled over the side, holding on to the slippery rail.

"Hold on, I'm coming to help you," Bruno called as he ran out into the raging storm.

"Watch out, Bruno," Betty called out, "the sheets coming back around."

Just as he reached the bow, the sheet whipped back, then wrapped itself around the search light, ripping it off the side of the boat. The light slammed down, narrowly missing Bruno's head. He pulled Jim back on board and helped him regain his balance. The rain had become a wet screen and they were unable to see through the torrential rain. Waves were splashing high on the deck making it treacherous for both of them. Bruno blindly thrust his arm forward and caught the sheet before it whipped Jim's body again. The wind had risen to fifty knots and it drew the sheet upward pulling Bruno up off his feet.

Betty took the helm as Bob reefed the sails. Then he went running out to help. He grabbed the sheet pulling Bruno back down. He was able to secure the sheet, then the three struggled back to the cockpit. Lightning slashed across the sky cutting through the brooding clouds like Zorro's sword. It was followed by thunder roaring like a sonic beam. Wind and waves thrash across *Destiny* with unmerciful strength and Bob wondered how long he could stay on course.

Looking back, they could see the clouds scattering and the sun trying to break through. An hour later, the squall had passed over *Destiny*. It was like a miracle, the rain stopped and the wind died down to fifteen knots. The rays of the sun glistened on the rain drops. *Destiny* appeared to be covered in a sheet of crystal, reflecting the rainbow.

"Jim, let me look at your back," asked Betty. "It's pretty raw. I'll put some ointment on it."

Making light of his injury, Jim answered, "Nay, I'll be okay. It just stings a bit."

Before the first storm hit, Bruno had put out two fishing lines. As the wind died down, both reels went off at the same time.

"Looks like we lost one fish," said Jim, reeling in the empty line. "Hey, Bruno's got a winner, an eighteen pound tuna."

"This is Neptune's birthday gift to you, Bob," Bruno said, as he proudly hauled in his catch.

"Well, we certainly had enough fireworks today for anyone," said Bob. "Don't bake me a cake, Betty. I want a cherry pie instead for my birthday."

Betty looked at him in surprise, "Who said I'm baking you anything?"

"Come on, it's my birthday. After all I went through to bring us through that mess, I think I deserve a cherry pie."

"Well, maybe you're right. It depends on how rough it is in the galley."

The boat was heeling ten degrees and the movement was mild enough to make the pie. Martha cooked the tuna and they celebrated Bob's birthday in proper style.

Two days later, Betty woke up earlier than usual, she was still half-asleep as she went on deck. She sat sipping her morning coffee looking out at the horizon. The day was so clear she could see for miles.

At first, she wasn't sure what she was looking at. "Is that a ship?" she asked as she grabbed the binoculars. Betty focused on a small brown spot on the horizon. "It's land," she yelled in great excitement. "Oh, I don't believe it. We're finally here." Betty squealed and danced up and down in absolute bliss.

"We spotted land at six bells," said Bob, laughing at her overzealous actions. "Looks pretty good doesn't it?"

"Looks good? It looks wonderful. God, I can't wait to get there. Tonight's New Years Eve and we are going to celebrate," she said as she planted kisses all over Bob's face.

"Cut it out, save it for when we dock," said Bob laughing and feeling just as happy.

Eighteen and a half days, twenty-two minutes and thirteen seconds is the time it took to get to Barbados from the Canary Islands. As *Destiny* sailed close to the island, aromas from shore drifted out to them. They gloried at the sight of civilization after being on the vast ocean for so long. There was never a more welcoming sight and their bodies ached to stretch out in long walks.

Destiny arrived at Barbados late in the morning. They pulled up against a wall in the commercial marina and waited to be cleared. Anxious to get off the boat, they tried to be patient but waiting was getting to them.

"What in the world is taking them so damn long?" said Bob. "Jesus Christ, we've been here for two hours."

Martha paced up and down the deck, "I want to get off this fricken boat."

"Oh, shut up and be patient," said Bruno. "I'm sure there's a lot of boats checking in."

Jim was more laid back. He just sat on the deck with his hat over his eyes not saying a word.

At four o'clock, the customs officers showed up. "Sorry we're so late. Ten boats came in almost at the same time. Two of them were freighters."

"We understand," said Bob. "We're just eager to go ashore. Here are all the passports and ship's papers."

The officers studied each passport, taking their time. Then they leaned back on the couch in the salon and said, "It's so hot out can we have a drink of water?"

Betty brought them glasses of ice-water and they drained them immediately.

Martha came down the steps and said impatiently, "Aren't they done yet?"

Betty shook her head and signaled for her to go back up. She didn't want the officer to be aggravated and hold them up any longer than was necessary.

"May I have another glass of ice-water," asked one of the officers. Betty refilled both glasses and waited patiently.

Wondering why they were taking so long, Bob asked, "Is everything in order?"

"Yes, it is. We're just enjoying the coolness of your boat. I see that you have declared guns aboard. We'll have to keep them until you leave."

Bob eagerly signed the release papers and surrendered the guns. He was used to giving them up at each port. Now they were clear to go ashore once they found a place to dock.

The small marina at Barbados had no available slips. They anchored offshore in front of a bar and restaurant called the Boatyard. Seven boats were there already, but they managed to squeeze *Destiny* in. The Boatyard was situated on a long, wide golden beach and people were milling in and out of the bar. Calypso music was playing and laughter could be heard all the way out to their ship. It made them impatient to get ashore. Lowering the dinghy, they scrambled aboard, ready to talk to the many yachtsmen and be part of the New Years festivities.

As they tied the dingy to the Boatyard's broken down dock, they heard a large group of people yell, "Here's the *Destiny* crew."

"How was it, any problems?" asked Harvey from the boat, *Reprieve.*

"Our auto-pilot went out, but other than that we're in good shape," said Bob. "When did you get in?"

"Six this morning, you were pretty late," said Harvey.

"Why do you say that?" asked Bob.

"There's only three boats left to come in out of fifty."

"Well, I never said *Destiny* was a race-horse," Bob laughed. "Did everyone arrive safe?"

"No," answered Harvey. "One of the smaller boats judged his distance wrong and got caught up in the surf. He went aground and the boat tipped over. He and his wife are safe but they've lost everything."

"We're glad to be here, safe and sound. That was a long trip," Betty said, her feet danced in time to the music. "Wow, the music's great."

"Here, have a cold beer," said Yancy, from the boat *Willing Way*. His wife Coretta grabbed the beer from Betty and said, "Get her a rum-punch, she's in Barbados now." Then she added,

"There's a barbecue on the beach tonight. Are you coming?"

"Wouldn't miss the party for the world," said Betty. "We've been waiting eighteen days, four hours, and eighteen minutes to celebrate New Year's Eve, and we're going to have a blast tonight."

The crew met up with a young group and were already dancing.

New Year's Eve was celebrated on the beach under the full moon and stars. Everyone was in bathing suits or shorts. Hot dogs and hamburgers were plentiful. Wine, beer, and rum-punch flowed like water

"How did you like the wild squall we went through," asked Helen from *My Girl*. "Wasn't that terrifying? I got so sick I threw up for hours."

"Which storm?" asked Betty. "We went through several."

"The worse one. The one with the twenty-foot waves and the lightning. Damn, I was scared shitless."

Mary from *Talooth*, was dancing in the sand. "I'm hot as hell," she said, slurring her words.

"You're hot?" asked her husband as he picked her up and threw her in the water. "There, that ought to cool you off."

Mary was mad. She staggered out of the water and threw sand on her husband. "There, now you have to go in and wash off."

Grabbing her arm he pulled her back into the water and they both shrieked and laughed with glee.

The rhythm of music was so vibrating, Betty couldn't keep still. She put her arms around Bob and said, "Let's go into the bar and dance."

They ate, drank, and danced the night away. Then the fire works went shooting into the air at midnight, lighting the sky in multicolors. Martha was dancing on top of the bar and feeling no pain.

A man at the bar yelled to her, "Hey good-looking, I like your t-shirt. Want to trade?"

"Sure," Martha said. Without missing a beat, she whipped her shirt off and tossed it to him. She continued to dance while her bare breasts jiggled to the music.

The man's mouth fell open as everyone laughed and cheered.

"Come on give me your jumper," said Martha. "I'm getting cold."

"No, I'd rather look at your titties," said the man. Then he took off his shirt and threw it to her. She never missed a step as she pulled it over her head.

Betty's mouth fell open, "My God, she took her shirt off, and she had nothing on underneath."

Bruno gave Martha a disgusted look, "For Christ's sake Martha, what's wrong with you? Where's your modesty? I think you're drunk."

"What did I do wrong? He wanted my shirt and I liked his, so I gave it to him. You're such a prig." Martha said as she danced around Bruno. "Come dance with me." Bruno walked away disgusted, and sat down at the other bar.

"Come on Jim, you dance with me," said Martha as she grabbed his hand, and pulled him out on the dance floor.

Jim's face turned red from shyness as he stumbled around the dance floor in a drunken stupor.

By two A.M. Bob and Betty was ready to go back to *Destiny*. They staggered back to the boat, leaving their crew to come back when they were ready. The swaying movement of *Destiny*, bobbing in the tropical breeze, sent them into a deep rapturous slumber.

Seventeen

It had been a long time since they had a hangover; they had forgotten how bad it could feel. The morning sunlight hurt their eyes and their heads felt like huge drums, beating a conga. Their mouths were dry, stomachs upset, but the celebration was worth it. The long palm-fringed beaches helped them remember they were in Barbados, the island of the sun.

The landscape was patterned with plantations of sugar cane, dry valleys, and luxuriant growth. The people were warm and delightful. The native women that strolled the streets wore long flowering cotton skirts of bright colors. Turbans of flowered material decorated their heads.

Betty and Bob wandered the streets taking in the sights. An old man came up to them. "Mon, are you a little lost?"

"No, we're just trying to find our way around town," answered Bob. "Could you tell us where we could rent a car?"

"It's just around the corner," said the old man. "Everything's just around the corner."

"Is the airport just around the corner too?" asked Bob laughing.

"No, mon. That's a bit further. Just follow this main road and you'll come right to it. Say maybe a half-hour away."

Betty was excited. Her son Clint had left a message at the boat yard restaurant. He was coming to Barbados to see them. She had called last night to verify that he was definitely coming.

They arrived at the airport just as his plane came in.

Betty saw him get off the plane and her heart started to pound. "There he is. Clint, Clint, we're over here."

He saw them and waved as he walked towards them. He wrapped his muscular arms around her, lifting her off her feet. His hazel eyes were lined with veins of red and he looked tired.

"You look a little hungover. Looks like you were celebrating last night too," said Bob.

Clint laughed and rubbed his bloodshot eyes. "Well, New Year's Eve only comes once a year. You got to get out there and enjoy it."

Seeing one of her family again was overwhelming. "It's good to have you here. Happy New Year," she said as she hugged him again.

Their day was spent exploring the island in the rented Land Rover. They went to visit the old sugar plantations where the sugar cane still grows tall. Old mansions furnished with the original furniture were open to the public. Then they went back to *Destiny* so Clint could meet their hungover crew.

The next morning at breakfast, Bob asked, "Clint, did you bring your certification card for diving? If you did, we could go diving today."

"I sure did," said Clint all smiles. "I wouldn't leave home without it."

"Are you stealing the American Express slogan?" laughed Betty.

They went diving in the harbor, going down sixty feet to a sunken ship. Fish scattered as they approached, and a moray eel poked it's head out from under a corroded anchor. Searching further away from the ship they found old antique bottles, a good treasure to take home.

Life was carefree and exhilarating as they drifted into the tranquil island mood. Clint fit right in with the crew swimming, hiking and partying together.

Before Clint left for home, Betty went shopping with him for gifts for the family. Then they had lunch out on the verandah of an old plantation.

"Mom, you must be having a super time, I wish I could do what you're doing."

"It is fun when we're ashore. It gets pretty miserable when you're out to sea for so long. I miss the activity of the business. You know, being around lots of people everyday. I miss having something to challenge my mind. Most of all I miss you and the rest of the family."

"We'll always be there for you, like you are for us. We miss you too but, hey, this is your time of life. You raised us and did a good job. Now it's your turn to do what ever you want."

"Yeah, I know. Maybe I'll get used to it. Bob's been good to me and we get along well."

Clint looked at her with caring eyes, "Do you love him?"

"Of course I do. I wouldn't stay if I didn't. Hey, those are questions I should be asking you about your love life." She laughed and hugged him.

*   *   *

There was a farewell party for Clint the next day on *Destiny*. Some of the people from the ARC race were invited. Murphy, who owned a sleek sixty-foot ketch called *Black Horse* was there. His boat was built for speed, and he constantly bragged about how fast his boat could go.

Murphy came aboard *Destiny* and looked around, "Look at all the equipment you have on this boat. You can't possibly make any speed with this overloaded tug."

"Don't call *Destiny* a tug," said Bob indignant. "Just because you want to sail your boat stripped to the bare essentials with no convenience, doesn't mean it's any faster."

When his wife Rose came aboard, she walked through the boat looking at everything. "This boat is so pretty. You have a microwave, and a gimbaled ice maker! Oh my, you even have a washer and dryer. I'd love to have just a few of these things onboard. Life would be much easier for me on the long voyages."

Murphy turned to his wife, "I told you I don't want the added weight, I want speed."

"It wouldn't hurt to have a washer or just some little drapes up at the portholes," said Rose looking timid.

"No, I told you. If you don't like it, go home." Then turning to Bob he said, "I'll challenge you to a race and we'll see who has the tug."

"When?" asked Bob, excited to do it.

"Right now, buddy. Right now."

"You're on," said Bob. "We'll meet at the head of Carlisle Bay."

Starting and finishing lines were designated by the big rocks on the beach. The rocks were four miles apart. *Destiny* and *Black Horse* took their positions at the first rock, ready for take off.

They had to sail down to the second rock and back again. Bussie Williams, a native of Barbados, heard about the race. He offered to referee with his seventy-foot catamaran, *Joyride*. Of course Bussie thought his boat was faster than both *Destiny* and *Black Horse*, and it was.

"When I fire my pistol, that will be the signal to start the race," said Bussie, trying to project great authority.

Two minutes later, the gun went off and the race was on. Bussie sailed his Cat between both boats rooting them on.

Joyride was light and fast. It could maneuver with ease between *Destiny* and *Black Horse*. His boat made the other crafts look clumsy and awkward.

The crew on *Joyride* shouted reassurance to both boats, teasing whoever was lagging behind. "Hey Betty! How about passing a little vodka over to us, we're all out," yelled Chris, the first-mate on *Joyride*.

Bussie's catamaran glided close to *Destiny*'s starboard side. Chris reached out to grab the vodka. He stretched too far, and almost fell overboard.

"Get a little closer Bussie, I can't reach it," called Chris.

This time *Joyride* got so close it almost collided with *Destiny*. "Goddammit Chris, forget the vodka," yelled Bob.

"Forget the vodka? I might as well forget the whole race if I forget the vodka," yelled Bussie. Betty reached farther out and Chris grabbed the bottle.

Destiny passed *Black Horse* on the starboard side and blocked the wind from *Black Horse*'s sails, causing it to loose speed. As *Destiny* neared the finish line the cheers went out in full force.

"Hey Murph," Bussie called on his loudspeaker. "I thought your boat was the fastest thing on the water. What's holding her back? You gonna let that overweight *Destiny* beat you?"

No comment came from *Black Horse*. Bussie didn't give up, "Yo, Rose! Go for it baby. Order the washer and dryer, it can't make it go any slower. No excuses now, Murph."

"Yeah, champagne's on us," yelled Bob, surprised that *Destiny* had won.

Everyone was teasing Murphy, "Yo, Murph, bet you won't hear the end of this for awhile," yelled the group on *Destiny*.

When they anchored back in the harbor, the party continued, but Murphy wouldn't come over to join them.

"Just a sore loser," said Bussie as he downed another vodka on the rocks.

One by one the couples left and the day came to an end.

"I still can't believe *Destiny* beat Murphy's boat. I don't think we would have won if I didn't block his wind," said Bob as he climbed in bed. Betty was already asleep.

Ten days had flown by and Clint had to leave. Betty and her son hugged each other as they said goodbye.

"Take good care of my mom," he said shaking Bob's hand. Then he walked out to the plane. After Clint left, Bob put his arm around her, "I know you feel bad about him going, but at least you had him with you for awhile. Now we have to start planning for the next leg of our trip. Come on, the two of us will go shopping."

Betty was rested and in good spirits. Even Martha and Bruno seemed to be getting along better. *Destiny* was ready to go except for the part for the auto-pilot. Bob had ordered it from California when they first arrived. It was supposed to be expressed out the next day.

"As soon as Air Express delivers the part we'll head out," said Bob to the crew. 'Finish up whatever needs to be done."

Betty was having lunch with Murphy and Rose at the boatyard when Bob came in looking for her. She knew from his face something was bothering him. "Sit down and have a cold beer and tell me what's wrong."

"I just called California about the part for the auto-pilot. It won't be in for another week," Bob said.

"Why don't you sail on without it," said Murphy. "I'm going to be here for a week or so. When it comes in, I'll pick it up for you. We'll keep in touch by radio and rendezvous at a convenient place."

"Great idea, we do have one working auto-pilot, so we're okay. Let's meet in Grenada," said Bob. "Betty, if you're finished with your lunch we can go find the crew. I want to tell them we're leaving in the morning."

That night in bed, Betty had a hard time sleeping. *Here we go again* she thought. *The next leg would be a short easy trip, so it shouldn't be too bad.* She tried to spruce up her confidence. *I'm a seasoned sailor*, she thought, *and I've crossed the Atlantic not once but twice. I almost feel the call for the adventure of the sea that Frank talked about.* It didn't work; she still hated the idea of going.

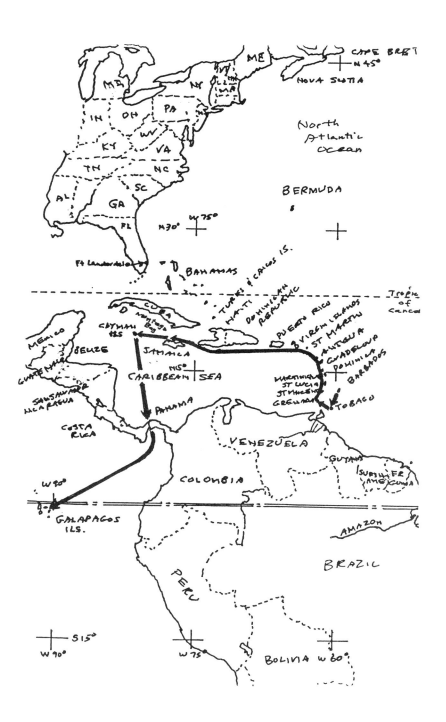

Eighteen

The Caribbean Islands stretch almost twenty-five hundred enticing miles, surrounded by blue, clear water. They sailed to Tobago, and anchored in the small harbor. It was a stop off spot to rest before sailing on towards Grenada.

Something in two small moored fishing boats caught Betty's eye. She got out the binoculars for a closer look. Betty let out a loud giggle. "The boats are filled with pelicans. Look at them, Bob. They're sitting on the seats four abreast. Lets tow them around the harbor. They looked like they were waiting to take a ride."

"No, let's walk around the town and get some exercise," said Bob.

The crew went with Betty and Bob to explore. The small island had a few small homes, and a couple of stores that were dark with open screenless windows. They explored the island and hiked the rain forest that was filled with birds of paradise growing everywhere. Heavy fields of ferns filled in the bare spots under the palm and eucalyptus trees. A mist sprinkled their warm bodies as they hiked the flowering paths. Snorkeling was exciting as schools of barracuda swam by them. Octopus tried to bury themselves in the rocks, then started to turn different colors. Feeling annoyed that they were being watched, they sent out an inky liquid.

Two days later, they reached Grenada. The island entranced them with it's mystic charms. "Blimy, I know why they call this the spice island," said Martha. "I sure can smell it."

The wind whipped the fragrance through the air. Their nostrils flared with delight at the wonderful scent of cocoa, cinnamon and nutmeg.

Betty took a deep breath and said, "Smells like cookies baking in the oven."

They hired a guide and hiked through the dark terrain. It was an abundant lush, rainforest that sprayed them with a light misty perfume of tropical flowers. The small birds sang melodious songs, while others screeched loud startling calls.

"I feel like I'm lost in paradise with all these birds chirping away," said Jim.

At the end of the trail, Bob asked the guide, "How far have we hiked?"

"About six easy miles," answered the guide.

Bruno was fascinated with the forest. He was able to name many of the plants. "You don't mind the walk with the mist spraying you. It keeps you cool."

Bob looked at his watch. "Do you realize it's five o'clock already?" Then looking at the guide, he asked, "Where is a good place for dinner?"

"Mamma's is my favorite," answered the guide.

Mamma's would never be forgotten by the crew of *Destiny*. They sat on carved wooden chairs made out of the logs of the trees. Checkered curtains made up of a sheet of cloth was stretched across and thumb tacked on the window. The table was made with two by fours nailed together and served the purpose.

Mamma served the island food of possum, snake, and curried mangoes. They sampled everything. The snake was bony and tough but the taste wasn't bad. Possum had too strong of a taste for Betty and Bob, but Bruno seemed to like it. Mamma brought a steaming dish of chicken and rice. The taste was scrumptious.

Sailing the serene Caribbean waters was an unbelievable experience. The wind and seas had been perfect. Beautiful blue waters caressed the sky, and the white sandy beaches seemed endless. Island hopping every couple of days, they visited as many islands as possible. The crew wandered along the beach soon discovering that the women went topless on the island. Bruno and Jim thought they had died and went to heaven. Their eyes roamed everywhere, yet tried to pretend they weren't looking. Seeing their enthusiasm made Martha jealous, so she took off her top letting her bare breasts flaunt in the sun.

Bruno looked at her in disgust. "For God's sake, what did

you do that for," he said walking ahead of her.

Martha paid no attention to his remark, and went strutting along behind him.

When they sailed off to another island, Martha sat on the bow. She was watching Bruno and Jim work on the sails. The men paid no attention to her so she took off her top. She lay back against the mast as if basking in the sun. Bruno still paid no attention to her. Jim on the other hand had a hard time keeping his eyes off of her. Her bare breasts were getting to him.

Betty watched from the cockpit. "I think Martha's hoping to make Bruno jealous. She's only succeeding in giving Jim an eyeful, and he loves it."

Laughing and leering, Bob said "She's giving me an eyeful too."

Betty laughed and said, "You're such a dirty old letch," and she whacked him with her book.

Later, Betty had a talk with her. "Martha, I don't care what you do ashore, that's your business. I'd like you to keep your top on when you're onboard."

"I'm sorry" she said, lowering her eyes and put her top back on.

Later Bob was sitting at the helm, teasing Jim. "Hey, you were getting quite a view of Martha. Maybe you're looking to take over Bruno's girl."

With a sly grin on his face, he said, "She puts on a good show, but she's not my type, too fat for me. I like them slender, tall with dark hair. I'm not much for blondes."

"Is that right?" sneered Bob. "Then how come you're looking all the time?"

Jims face turned red, "Hey, if she wants to show it, I'll look. I'm a red-blooded American boy." Then he added, "She's a nice girl. I don't like the way Bruno treats her."

"Oh I see. Hum . . . ? If you say so," Bob answered coyly.

St. Vincent and Young Island were across from each other in a small harbor. As they entered the harbor, Bob remarked, "A prettier anchoring spot would be hard to find."

Young Island gives the appearance of being top-heavy. A

towering mountain takes up most of the island. There's a fort sitting very majestically on top of the mountain.

"Let's climb to the top," said Jim. "The book says there's two hundred and fifty steps. It would be a good workout."

Martha stretched her neck to look at the top of the mountain. "Blimey, you got to be kidding me. That's more than a work out."

Going ashore, they started the climb. The group of steps circled around and around until the final bend. There they walked into four huge cannons. Each iron monster was pointing out across the water like the guards of the century.

"My Lord," said Bob, "How did they ever get them up here?"

Betty was panting as she climbed the last few steps. "The view alone made the climb worth it. She looked down into the clear unpolluted water. The coral reefs below the surface stood out as clear as an abstract painting. They formed mystic designs and Betty could see many islands in the distance.

They spent their time between the two islands, drinking paw-paw daiquiris and napping lazily in hammocks.

"Is this paradise or am I dreaming?" Betty said as she swayed in the tropical breeze.

Mesmerized by the tranquil surroundings they didn't notice four island boys taking an unauthorized joy ride in their dinghy. When they were ready to go back to *Destiny* the dinghy was nowhere in sight. After reporting it to the local constable, the dinghy was found and the boys were brought to apologize.

The constable had two of them by the ear, "Go ahead, apologize to these people."

The four boys stood shaking. "*Hey mon, we weze jst haben a littabita fun mon. No haam, mon.*"

"Trouble with the young ones around here," said the constable. "They think they can borrow anything they want. I'm gonna put them to work. Take up their free time." He walked off with the four boys in tow.

When they left the next morning for St. Lucia, the crew was suffering another hangover, they always seem to get smashed the night before *Destiny* left the harbor.

"You three are not much help to me hungover," remarked Bob. "I'm going to lock you in your staterooms on our last night in

217

town. That will fix you."

"Don't do that, Captain," they all hollered in unison, and they started to act more alive.

Eight hours later they completed the sixty-mile journey, and glided into a small lovely harbor.

Jim was on the bow, ready to drop anchor when Bob called out. "The current's too strong here. We'll anchor our bow first. Then we'll tie our stern with lines to a tree on shore. Wait till I get *Destiny* lined up then drop it when I signal."

A crowd of boat boys in carved out canoes came rowing out. They were shouting and hollering. "Hey mon. We tie ya up. No trouble mon just ten e.c.(5.00 U.S.) Mon."

The first canoe that reached *Destiny* got the job. Jim threw the lines and the natives quickly rowed to shore and secured the boat.

It was beginning to get dark so they had a quick dinner and retired for the evening

A cool breeze blew across the deck while Betty was having her breakfast. She was captivated by the panorama view of thousands of palm trees. The spectacular Pitons that pierced the sky were awesome. One mighty peak was over two thousand feet high. Martha came up and joined her for coffee and they sat quietly enjoying the serenity. Betty noticed something large and gray moving on the shore. She rubbed her eyes and looked again. Standing in a clearing of the palm trees was an elephant.

"Martha, look over at the island to your right. Tell me what you see," said Betty questioning her sanity.

Martha let out a squeal, "I don't believe me eyes, how could there be an elephant out here?"

Betty called down to Bob, "There's an elephant over on the island. Let's get ready and go ashore."

Bob came up and looked, "You're right. That's crazy. We'll pack a lunch and spend the day there. I want to see if the elephant's real."

An hour had passed by the time everyone was organized, and when they got to shore the elephant was nowhere in sight.

"Maybe it was just a mirage," said Betty looking all around.

Disappointed, they walked towards the highest Piton, completely caught up in the fantastic surrounding.

Betty felt a hard nudge on her back. Screaming, she turned around, "My God, the elephant just hit me with his trunk."

The baby elephant weighed about eight hundred pounds and he had smelled the food in their backpacks. His huge trunk groped wildly trying to get the backpacks. They started to run, but the elephant trotted after them. His loud, shrill, trumpeting let them know he was closing in on them.

"No sense running," said Bob. "He can outrun us. Here let me grab the bananas out of your pack, Bruno. Maybe it will distract him."

He grabbed the bananas and threw them over his head. The elephant's attention went immediately on the bananas.

Two native men came over laughing in glee, "Mon, you sure got lucky. It's good you threw those bananas. The other day he picked up a woman and threw her down to de ground. Whamo!!! Mon this your lucky day."

Laughing. Bob said, "Yes, I guess it is our lucky day."

"Whew, I'm glad that's over," said Jim. Now let's do something really macho. Lets climb that high Piton."

"I think Martha and I are going to walk around. We'll see you back at the boat," said Bruno.

They started up the hill to climbed the steep rocky Piton. After a half hour Betty became dizzy and short of breath. Still determined to climb the peak, she continued on.

A third of the way up, they met a native coming down the trail. "Mon, you not thinking of going up there are yea? It's too rough for you mon."

"Nay, it's not too rough for us," said Jim sounding macho.

"Take a long time, Mon. Five, maybe six hours. Better change your mind."

Hearing this, Betty said, "He's convinced me. I still feel a little dizzy, I'm going back."

Seven and a half hours later, Bob and Jim returned. They were covered with dirt, exhausted and bruised, but thrilled with their accomplishment.

"That was the hardest climb I've ever taken. I'm glad you decided not to go," said Bob.

They were full of aches and pains the next day, but still bragging of their conquest.

The weather has been perfect as they sailed on to Martinique, and Iles de Saintes. Each island was just as lovely and breathtaking as the last. They picked up their mail at the American Express office and sailed off again.

Their trip across to Guadeloupe came just as the weather changed. It was cold and windy. White caps appeared as they beat into the wind and fought against the current. The sea lashed angrily at *Destiny* making it difficult to stay on course.

"We've had it too good, I knew it wouldn't last," said Bob.

Bruno was looking out at the horizon when he said, "There's something in the water on the starboard side."

Bob looked through the binoculars, "Looks like a couple of kids on a small sunfish. What are they doing out here on a day like this?"

Betty was concerned. "I think their boat is sinking. Go alongside Bob and see if they need help."

As *Destiny* got close Jim yelled, "Do you need help?"

They couldn't make out what the boys were saying, but they could see the boys had problems.

Bob slowed *Destiny* down, "Lower the dinghy Jim, and go get them."

Getting the dinghy off the davits in the rough weather was not an easy chore. Jim and Bruno worked as quickly as possible to rescue the young boys.

They came aboard dressed only in a pair of bikini swim trunks. "*Merci beaucoup,*" they said shivering. Goose bumps covered their entire slender bodies. Their faces were white with fright, their lips quivered, blue from the cold. Their eyes were glazed from shock and they were near exhaustion. Betty wrapped large towels around them and Martha gave them hot coffee. They were French and it was hard understanding them. Slowly the crew from *Destiny* understood their story.

They had started from Guadeloupe to sail across to the island of Iles de Saintes. They were on a homemade surfboard and an old sunfish. The weather had taken a sudden change, and the boys were caught in the high winds and strong current.

Unable to handle the conditions they had put the surfboard underneath the sunfish, hoping to keep it afloat.

Jim tied the sunfish behind *Destiny* and Bob started off again. "Weather conditions are getting worse. We better pick up our speed," he said as he pushed the throttles forward.

The French boys started to scream, "*Non! non! ca ne va pas.*" Jumping up and down they pointed to the stern.

Destiny's wake had caused the sunfish to flip over. It was being swamped and pulled under. Bob idled the boat as Bruno lowered the dinghy again. He went over and moved the line to the stern end of the sunfish. Bob eased *Destiny* slowly ahead as he watched until the sunfish flipped right side up. Then carefully headed for shore.

Anchoring in the harbor of Guadeloupe the boys thanked them over and over again. They knew if help hadn't come, they would have been on their way to Panama.

Destiny continued on through the Caribbean. Each island filled with wondrous sights and delights. Repairs were made as they went along, as something was always breaking down. The boat seemed like an endless money pit. Perfect weather conditions surrounded them for weeks and time flew by like feathers in the wind. Time had no meaning. Their only clock was the rise and set of the sun.

Trouble stirred in paradise as Martha and Bruno argued constantly. Their nights on shore usually ended in fights with Jim bringing Martha back. She was jealous of Bruno's attention to other girls and the evening ended in tears.

In the middle of the night, a screaming plea echoed across the water, waking Betty and Bob from a deep sleep.

They heard a girl's voice plead, "Don't leave me! Please don't leave me."

Betty sat up with a jolt, "What in the world is that? What time is it?"

Looking at his watch, Bob yawned, "It's three in the morning."

They leaned out the back portholes, "Do you think someone needs help?" asked Betty puzzled and confused. "It sounds like someone's being murdered."

Bob laid back in bed. "I can't hear them now. Maybe it's over."

Betty heard the voice again, "Bruno, come back. Please don't leave me, I'm frightened." Bruno's voice was nasty and sharp, "If you don't leave me alone and stop nagging I'm going to swim back to the boat. You can bring the dinghy back yourself."

Betty gasped. "For heaven's sake, it's Martha and Bruno."

The yelling continued. "Please don't leave me here. I don't know how to operate this thing by myself. Please, Bruno. I'll shut up, I promise." Betty could hear the pleading in her voice.

Bruno's voice got louder, "You never leave me alone. You follow me around every minute. I can't stand it anymore. I just can't stand the sight of you."

Martha was crying, "Please, Bruno, don't say that. I love you. You love me, I know you do."

"Just shut up, dammit," shouted Bruno. "I don't love you. You're driving me crazy."

The outboard started up and soon they were climbing aboard. Not a word was said between them. The next morning everyone acted like it never happened. But tension was heavy in the air.

* * *

Destiny needed her bottom scraped and painted. Finding a place to do it was more of a problem than anticipated. First, they couldn't find a boatyard with a lift big enough to handle the boat. Then they couldn't find a yard that had the space and time. Several weeks later, they arrived in *Virgin Gorda*, at Spanish Town. The boatyard there could take *Destiny* right away.

"This is a good time to work on the bright work," said Bob. "While they're doing the bottom we can all pitch in and take all the teak down to the bare wood."

"Where will we get the sandpaper and varnish?" asked Bruno.

We'll have to put on seven coats of varnish. I'll check the marina. What they don't have they can order," answered Bob.

They worked diligently in the hot tropical weather that showed no mercy. The scorching sun glared down on them, as it burned through their thin clothes, baking the moisture from their bodies. Jim and Bruno worked bare chested; their rippling muscles glazed with sweat as they scraped away at the faded varnish. Bent over in an awkward position, they sanded the wood carvings of the bowsprit as the sun fried their back a beet red. Martha worked in swim top and shorts. The sweat rolled down her body as the sun burned her back and arms. Her bare feet were covered with flaking old varnish that fell from the railing. Betty was in a swimsuit and Bob in shorts working along with them. It was too hot to work, but the job had to be done. They would dress *Destiny* up in shiny new paint, repair her sails, then they would continue on.

Nineteen

It had been six months since they had been home, and it was time for Bob's check-up. He had been in excellent health; sailing seemed to agree with him. Despite the beauty of the islands, Betty was still homesick. She longed to see her family, and sleep in her own bed. She wanted to steep in all the familiar feelings of home life. The work on *Destiny* was almost finished and the crew could handle the rest while they were away.

Bob said goodbye to Betty when they arrived at the Philadelphia airport. It was their first separation in ten months. He had to fly to Boston to see his doctor and visit his son Dan while he was there. Then, he would fly down to New Jersey.

Betty felt good being back in familiar territory. Walking into her house, she was greeted by her daughter, Debbie. They hugged and kissed and broke out in tears of happiness. Her dog Sanchey jumped into Betty's arms, licking her face and whining.

Debbie went upstairs to get her five-year-old twins, Brittany and Ryan. They had been so much a part of Betty's life before she left.

Hesitating at the top of the stairs, they stared down at Betty, "Come on, Grandma's here. She has a present for you," said Debbie.

Betty heard Ryan whisper, "I forget what she looks like. I don't remember her."

Betty's heart ached when she heard that. Slowly, the children walked down the stairs, looking strangely at Betty. At first they were a little distant, holding back shyly. But soon she had them hugging her and fighting to sit on her lap. Betty's heart felt heavy. They were growing up so fast and she was missing so much of their formative years. No longer a focal point in their lives, it was easy for them to forget her. Betty vowed to write to them often and send pictures and presents. They would not forget her again. She wanted to be important to them and have them know they had a grandma who cared.

Spending time with Loretta and her three children was another delight. Janine and Kacey, ages eight and nine, remembered her. They hung on their grandma's every word.

Gregory was beaming, excited to hear all that had happened since he left *Destiny*. Bob arrived a week later, his report from his doctor was excellent.

Bob's mood was buoyant as he talked, "The doctor said he's never seen anyone recover they way I have. My heart is ninety percent repaired."

Betty's smiled, "The salt air must be good for you."

It was Saturday night, and they had just returned from a party. Cuddled in each others arms, Bob caressed Betty's back and kissed her neck tenderly.

She sighed with happiness and said, "It's so nice to be with everyone again. It just feels *so* good to be home."

"I hate to break the news," Bob said as he hugged her a little tighter. "It's time to head back to *Destiny*. Our plane leaves Monday morning."

"This Monday!" Betty laid there silent for a moment. "Bob, I'm not ready to leave yet. Time went too fast."

Bob kissed her on the ear and whispered, "It's been three weeks. We have to leave if we want to keep on schedule."

"It seems like we just got here," she answered quickly with determination in her voice. "I'm just not ready to leave."

Tears crept down Betty's cheeks. She wiped them away trying to hide her tears.

Bob sighed and in a gentle tone said, "Honey, we really have to go, and I don't want to go without you. I wish we could stay longer but we can't."

She laid there thinking. *What should I do? I love this man and I promised to make the trip. But I want to stay home with my family, and be part of their lives.*

"Is that tears I feel running down your cheeks?" Bob asked as he kissed her. "I love you, please say you'll go."

"No, I'm not crying," she lied in defense. "I want to go with you. Its just that I'm torn between you and my family."

Gently, he turned her to face him, his blue eyes stared at her as he said "They have their own lives and we have ours. I know you miss them, but you won't be gone forever."

Betty kissed his forehead and cheek softly. Then passionately, she kissed his lips. Holding her closer, he returned her kisses with sincere emotion. Her feelings for him were overwhelming, she felt her heart would burst. They made love with a wild passion, their bodies melted into each other, like a flowing of souls. Completely exhausted, they drifted off to sleep—each knowing they would be leaving Monday.

Twenty

When they arrived in Spanish Town, *Destiny* was in the water, looking bright and new.

Betty walked along her decks. "Now, that I'm back it feels good to be aboard again." Surprise reflected in her voice. "I thought I'd hate it, but I'm raring to go." Betty laughed and twirled around the decks. Her arms were spread out in the wind and a contented feeling spread through her.

"You goofy nut," said Bob as he picked her up and swung her around. "I'm glad you're not upset."

During dinner, the men were very talkative as they told Bob about the work that had been completed. Martha sat playing with her fork, something was bothering her.

Betty looked at Martha and asked, "You're awfully quiet tonight, is there a problem?"

Martha's eyes started to water. "I'll let Bruno tell you."

Bruno looked sheepish. "Well, I was going to talk to you later—but since you noticed something's wrong, I'll tell you now. I'm leaving *Destiny*."

"You're what?" Bob stopped eating and glared at Bruno. "Where are you going? When did you decide this?"

Bruno hesitated then said, "Murphy, from *Black Horse* dropped off the part for the auto-pilot. He asked me if I would like to be captain of his boat—I told him I would."

Bob slammed the table with his hands, "I'll be dammed. I go away and a friend steals my crew." His jaw clinched and his eyes narrowed as he asked, "When are you and Martha leaving?"

Martha's eyes darkened with sadness, "Captain, he didn't ask me. I'd go if he'd want me."

"It's just you leaving?" Betty asked as she watched a relief pass over Bruno's face.

"Please, Bob, don't let Bruno go," Martha pleaded. "You want to stay with me, don't you?" Teary-eyed, she grabbed

Bruno's hand and stared into his eyes.

Bruno cleared his throat, his voice husky from emotion. "Look, Captain, you've been good to me. I had a great time on your ship, but it's time for me to better myself."

Bob's tone softened, "I understand, it's just a shock to me. When do you plan on leaving?"

"As soon as possible." Bruno pulled out a piece of paper from his pocket. "Murphy sailed ahead. Here's a phone number in Tortola where we can contact him."

"Okay," Bob answered taking the paper. "Darn sorry to lose you, but if that's what you want, guess we head for Tortola."

"Martha, what are your plans?" Betty asked, not sure what she wanted her to do.

Martha kept staring at Bruno with sad puppy dog, eyes "Guess I'll just go home. Me mums been after me to come back. I just don't know what I'll do without Bruno. It's not Bruno that don't want me, it's that darned Murphy. He loves me I know it," she wrapped her arms around Bruno's neck.

Betty felt so sorry for her. Martha refused to see that it was over between the two of them. This was Bruno's means of escape. She idolized this man who had come to think of her as a ball and chain.

The brief sail to Tortola was a torment to them all. They watched as Martha hung on Bruno's arm, begging him not to go. They could see the torment on his face, his teeth gritting with tension. He held his temper looking at the horizon, waiting to reach shore, to break away.

It was more than Betty could bear, "Martha, don't you have some work to do?"

Martha smiled up at Bruno, her face as close as possible to his. "No, Mam, I got it all done first thing this morning, so I could be with Bruno."

The whole scene was getting a bit disgusting as Martha practically laid on Bruno. "Martha, why don't you go below and fix something cold to drink for all of us?"

Bob caught on to what Betty was doing and added, "Bruno, go forward and clear the lines off the deck, and secure the sails."

They said their sad goodbyes to Bruno the following Saturday. "Tell Murphy if he doesn't treat you right, he'll hear from me," said Bob. Martha walked Bruno to *Black Horse* crying all the way. When he reached Murphy's boat, Bruno jumped aboard. Waving goodbye, he sailed away.

Peace and quite at last, Betty thought, as she relaxed on the aft deck. She was enjoying the light tropical breeze and dozed off with the sway of the boat.

Martha came aboard and plopped heavily down beside her. Tears were in her eyes as she said softly, "Betty, are you awake?"

Annoyed at being disturbed, Betty half-opened her eyes. "Yes, I'm awake. I was just enjoying the quietness of the harbor." She closed her eyes again and tried to stay relaxed.

Martha edged close and in a half-whisper said, "If you could talk Bob into paying Bruno more money he'd come back, especially if he gave him Jim's job of authority."

Betty sat up sharply, "Martha," she said sternly, "he's not coming back, he's gone. He wanted to go. Money has nothing to do with it." Betty wanted to say he wanted to get away from you, but she couldn't be cruel. Instead she said, "When are you planning on leaving?"

Martha sat twisting her long blonde hair, "Changed me mind. Thought I'd stay on if it's all right with you. I'm not ready to pop home yet. Besides, Bruno might come back for me, then we'll get married and go to America."

Betty shook her head in bewilderment. "You're welcome to stay, but no more moping around. If he comes back fine. If he doesn't you'll have to face it and get over him." Martha stood and shrugged her shoulders and without another word she walked away.

Bob heard a knock on the hull. Standing there was a young man who was the spitting image of Michael Wilding, the movie star. "Hi, I'm Harvey Grant," he said, holding his hand out. "I heard you're shorthanded, and might need a new man. I'd like to crew for you if I qualify."

Betty broke out laughing, "Talk gets around fast."

Bob shook his hand, "To tell you the truth we hadn't thought much about it yet. Come aboard and tell us something about yourself."

He was a little guy not more that five-four with black tight curly hair and mustache. He had a short body, but powerful arms and legs. He wore knee-length white shorts and a white knit shirt. Stylish and spotless, a clone of Mr. Clean—with hair. It was hard to believe he could be a sailor.

Bob gave him a doubtful look, "What kind of experience have you had on sailboats?"

Confidently, he said, "None whatsoever, but I learn quickly."

Bob laughed, "Pretty sure of yourself aren't you. What are you doing here in Tortola?"

Hr stuck his chest out and proudly answered, "Biked through every state in America. Now I'd like to try my hand at sailing to foreign ports."

"That's amazing," said Bob shaking his head, "You mean you have your bike here?"

"Yes sir," he smiled. "I take it everywhere."

Bob sat down and crossed his legs, "Sit down, Harvey, you're interesting. What makes you think you could handle life at sea?"

He wiped the seat first with his handkerchief, then sat on the edge of the seat. He crossed his legs like Bob and said, "Let's take into consideration that I . . . Number one, have been on a few boats. Number two, I've never been seasick. Number three, I learn extremely fast. I'm also an avid reader, good listener, and can do a job after being shown once. I've also shown my determination, and perseverance through the success of my cycling background. Put all this together and it shows I can accomplish almost anything."

Both Betty and Bob sat back with their mouths wide open. They were impressed by his manner of speech and his extreme self-confidence.

Bob slapped his leg, and let out a hoot, "I've never heard an approach like that before. Let me think about it and I'll let you know in two days."

It was late in the season and they knew there was no one else available. They'd have to give him a chance.

Two days later, bright and early, a knock came on the hull. There was Harvey standing at attention. "Well Mr. Godfrey, I mean Captain—do I get the job?"

Bob stood silently for a while then said, "Here's how it goes.

We try it until we get to the Cayman Islands. If you work out, you can continue. If not, I'll pay your fare back to Tortola, and we part friends. How's that?"

Harvey's face beamed, "Sounds terrific! You won't be sorry. I'll work hard."

"When can you come aboard?" asked Bob. "We're leaving for St. Thomas in the morning."

Harvey jumped off of *Destiny* and said, "I'll be back this afternoon. I have to get my bag and my bike."

"Your bike? Good Lord, he's bringing his bike," said Bob, shaking his head.

Bob worked with him, explaining the lines, sails and techniques. He taught him the routines and had him work hand in hand with Jim. Diligently, he listened and read, but in spite of what he had told them, he was a slow learner.

Harvey was able to stand his watch as long as the auto-pilot was on. Steering manually was like having a drunken sailor at the wheel. Much worse than Snake Wake Rennie. He was obsessed with keeping his hair and clothes neat, and wore hat and gloves for every chore.

Betty watched how Jim and Martha kept ignoring him most of the time, and asked, "Why aren't you two more friendly with Harvey?"

"I think he's weird," said Martha making an odd face.

Betty looked at Jim and said. "He might catch on a little quicker if you worked a little more with him." Jim just shrugged his shoulders and walked away.

"It makes me sick to talk to him," said Martha as she left to join Jim.

When they arrived in St. Thomas, Bob felt sure Harvey wasn't working out. But he had promised him he could sail on to Jamaica, then the Caymans for his final try.

On their way to Jamaica, they ran into some rough weather. Bob was on the bow trying to release the spinnaker before the wind blew it apart.

Bob needed Harvey and called to him, "Come out here I need your help," he said as he continued to try to control the sail, as it whipped in the wind.

Harvey was laying in the cockpit reading. "Okay," answered

Harvey as he slowly stood up, put on his hat, and started to pull on his gloves.

"For God's sake, what's keeping you. I need you now," yelled Bob, infuriated with his slowness.

Betty was sitting at the helm, "Harvey, if you want to keep your job, you better get out there fast. Hurry. Bob's in trouble."

In a prissy voice he squawked, "Betty please, I've got to get my gloves on to protect my hands."

His answer made Betty raise her voice, "Put them on while you're going."

By the time Harvey got out on deck, Bob had things under control. All Harvey had to do was help wrap the spinnaker and put it away.

Bubbling with enthusiasm he came back to the helm, and with a smile he said, "I love my job, the sea is perfect for me. I feel so at home and I'm doing a really good job."

Betty almost burst out laughing. *He really doesn't have any idea that we won't be keeping him*, she thought. *He's like a kid at the circus, enjoying every minute of it.* "What do you plan on doing with your future, Harvey?"

"Not what my Dad's doing, or my sister or brother," he answered, with a thoughtful look on his face.

Betty checked the radar, then asked, "Why is that?" She was curious.

"My dad's a Vice President at our hometown bank," Harvey said a little nervous. "My brother's in his last year of college, he wants to be a banker too."

Betty kept looking ahead for ships, and asked, "What's your sister doing?"

"Mom's a school teacher, teaches fourth grade. Becky wants to be a carbon-copy. He sat staring out at the water, then added, "Me, I want to do my own thing. I love biking and I want to enter as many marathons as I can. I've won two races already."

Betty was intrigued by the story, "Wow, that's great, but you can't make a living riding bikes."

"After I finish this trip, I'm going to enter a triathlon in Australia. There's big money there if I win," he said standing tall and looking proud.

Going down to the salon he posed in front of the mirror. Flexing his biceps he struck a pose as he admired himself.

So far the weather had been delightful and *Destiny* stopped briefly in Jamaica. Then they sailed off through the blue calm waters. The mild tropical wind was on their stern as they continued on to the Grand Cayman Islands. *Destiny* arrived safely, and after clearing customs they were ready to go ashore. Jim had told us he wanted to go home for a week and he left immediately.

Dan and Scott, Bob's sons, flew in for a visit. It was good to have Scott back on board with his fantastic sense of humor.

"Hey Betty give me a hug! I missed your bitching," laughed Scott.

Dan had a warm friendly personality that would win anyone's heart. "Hi Betty, still putting up with my old man I see," and he hugged Betty.

Until they came, Martha had been quiet and sad, but being around Scott and Dan was a tonic for her. That night she giggled and laughed, and she told funny stories at the delight of everyone. Flirting and playing up to Dan was a definite sign her mood had changed.

*   *   *

The next morning, Harvey saw the *Destiny* group ready to go diving and he ran out to the dinghy and asked, "Would you mind if I came along? I'm a certified diver and swim like a fish."

"I'll be dammed," said Bob. "I didn't know you could dive. Okay, grab some equipment and hop in."

They dove the gigantic, magnificent walls of the Cayman waters. It was the most fantastic underwater life they had ever seen. Each dive more superb than the last and diving with the stingrays was a real thrill.

Nights were spent drinking margueritas, and dancing the night away. Martha was spending a lot of time hanging around Dan and Dan was making the most of it. Ten days were gone before they knew it and off Bob's family went, back to reality.

Martha took them to the airport and came back crying. "Every man I love leaves me."

Betty gave Martha a funny look, "You've just known him a

233

short time. I don't think you're in love."

Martha got all moony, "Well he was so nice. I'm going to miss him so . . ."

"Oh my God," Betty said, shaking her head. "Another Mitch."

Two days before they were scheduled to leave, Bob pulled Harvey aside. "I have to let you go, you just aren't working out."

Harvey was stunned, "What! I thought I was doing so well. What's wrong?"

Bob sat down on a beach chair and studied Harvey, "To be truthful, I don't feel you're what we're looking for. You move too slowly, you don't want to hand steer, and you worry more about your gloves than you do the boat."

Harvey looked sad as he pleaded. "Can't you give me another chance? I'll improve."

"Afraid not, we'll be heading through the Panama Canal. I need someone who works fast and digs in on his own. I'll buy you a ticket back to Tortola, thanks for giving it a try." Extremely disappointed, Harvey mumbled, "I thought I was doing such a good job."

Betty liked the little Wilder kid, he was sincere and honest, but Bob was right, he wasn't fitting in. The crew didn't like him and made fun of him behind his back. There went another crewman from the chapters of *Destiny*.

Knowing they were heading for the Panama Canal sent a whirl of excitement through everyone. They were all looking forward to the great experience of going through the canal. Bob sat at his desk, checking the mileage to Panama. "We're going to look around for another crewman."

Martha overheard and asked, "Why do we need someone else? We can handle things ourselves."

"Jim, what do you think about that?" asked Bob. "That would put a lot of extra work on you."

Jim just shrugged his shoulders, making no comment.

Bob studied Jim's face for a minute then said, "No, I think we better find another crewman."

Friends from another boat recommended Jamie. He had

lived on the island for three years, and they said he was honest and a good worker. Jamie came aboard on the same terms as Harvey. Trial run until they were through the Panama Canal and reached the Galapagos Islands.

Jamie was a youthful twenty-one, short, slight in build and wiry. His slick black hair was worn long on the neck, framing his tan complexion. The expression in his eyes gave off a cocky as hell attitude. Jamie jumped aboard giving every one a big salute when Bob introduced him. He grabbed his gear and thanked Bob for having him aboard, then headed to his stateroom to unpack.

Betty saw Martha staring at Jamie and asked. "What do you think of him?"

Martha sneered, "I don't like him one bit. We don't need him."

Betty was surprised at her answer. "Come on, give him a chance. He might work out. It's too much work for the four of us, going through the canal."

Bob chimed in, "He *does* seem a little cocky, but that might just be his way. What do you think of him, Jim?"

Shrugging his shoulders again Jim said, "I guess he's okay!"

Bob sighed at his answer, "Well at least we'll have an extra hand to help with the lines when we're going through the Canal."

They all worked together preparing for departure. Jamie was a hard worker, pulling his own weight. He seemed to know boats and was right at home. Martha and Jim worked with Jamie, but ignored him. Pitching right in with the work, Jamie stayed in good spirits. He tried to be friendly but he could see the crew didn't like him.

Twenty-one

Five days was their anticipated time of arrival at the Panama Canal entrance. They were hoping for good weather all the way. Like always, the first day out to sea was an adjustment. Betty had finally reached the point where sailing for days didn't bother her as much. The engine had been on for two days and they were gliding along at five knots. Not a hint of wind filled the sails, and the air was stifling.

Jamie was trying to learn the routine required to handle *Destiny*. He was doing well at first, but three days later, he seemed to lose interest. He sat by himself while the crew ignored him.

Bob noticed the change in Jamie, "Lately you have an 'I don't care' attitude. You don't even listen to what I'm saying anymore."

Jamie stood there looking out at the water, not saying a word. He flopped nonchalantly down on the seat in the cockpit and picked up a magazine.

"Come help me put the sails in their bags. Then you can clean up the foredeck," said Bob walking ahead.

"Okay, okay," Jamie said, annoyed. He put his girlie magazine down and meandered out to the fore deck. Shoving the sails in the bag, he quickly sat down again to read.

Bob looked at him lounging on the sail bag while everyone else was working. "Jamie, snap to it. I told you to clean up the foredeck. There's lines to be coiled, sails to be tightened, stainless to polish."

Jamie stood up twirled a few lines and sat back down and listened to his walkman.

Bob looked over at Jamie, when he saw him sitting there his forehead wrinkled and his voice became curt, "For God's sake man, get off your ass. Don't you see Jim and Martha working? Get up and help them."

"Yeah, sure man, okay!" He answered with a smirk on his

face that made Bob's blood boil. His hand moved slowly as he made little effort to polish the chocks.

Betty was amazed at the change in Jamie's attitude. *What happened to him, he seemed so different in the beginning. Harvey was bad, but this one seems plain lazy.*

The nights had been stifling with very little breeze coming into the staterooms. The humidity laid on their bodies like a heavy wet cloud. Sleep was impossible. Tossing and turning in her sweat drenched bed, Betty felt like she was suffocating. The air-conditioning could not be turned on, they had to conserve fuel. Sitting up in bed, Betty reached for a magazine to fan herself.

"What's the matter, you having trouble sleeping too?" Bob asked in a sleepy voice.

"Yes. God, it's two in the morning and I haven't had a wink of sleep. I'm going up on deck for some air. Jim's on watch, I'll sit and talk with him for awhile."

Trying not to wake the rest of the crew, Betty walked quietly through the salon. She could feel a cool breeze blowing from above. She climbed the stairs to the deck and when she reached the top step she froze. Martha was straddled across Jim's lap. They were so engrossed in heavy lovemaking they never knew she was there. Her blouse was unbuttoned and her breasts were fully exposed. Martha moaned as Jim fondled and kissed her nipples. Her shorts were off with her bare ass showing. Jim's pants were pulled partway down, as he wiggled back and forth. Not knowing what to do, Betty started to hum and pretend to accidentally bump the companionway door. Martha looked up at Betty, then pulled Jim's head up and gave him an openmouth kiss. She made no movement to get off his lap or to acknowledge Betty's presence's.

Feeling extremely awkward, Betty walked out to the stern and looked out at the sea.

When she heard them whispering she returned, "I didn't know you were up here, Martha. Aren't you suppose to be resting?"

"Couldn't sleep the whole bloody night, so I thought I'd keep Jimmy boy company. My watch is in an hour, maybe Jim will keep me company."

Jim's face was red, "Maybe I won't," he said, pushing her roughly off his lap.

"You don't have to be so bloody rude," she said sharply.

Feeling completely out of place and not knowing what to say Betty went below.

Martha stood up. "Upon my word, she is the sneakiest one. Did she have to come up and spoil our fun?"

Jim walked out to the stern, "Shut up and go on down to bed."

Martha stood up with her hands on her hips and yelled, "Don't tell me what to do. Besides it's almost my watch."

"Well I'm not staying with you," he said as he started down the steps. "We're probably in big trouble."

Betty climbed in bed mumbling to herself. "What an out and out hussy she is. She sure has changed lately."

"What did you say?" Bob asked half-asleep. "Are you all right?"

"Yes, I'm all right, I'm just livid. When I went on deck, I found Martha straddled across Jim's lap half-undressed."

Bob sat up, "She was what?"

"Yes. The brazen hussy just stayed on his lap even after she saw me. No apologies, no, oh, I'm sorry we didn't hear you. She acted like it was natural for me to find them that way. He finally pushed her off his lap. At least *he* seemed embarrassed."

Bob started to laugh. "I knew she had the hots for Jim. Let's hope we don't end up with a pregnant crew on our hands."

Suddenly, Betty started to laugh and couldn't stop. "What are you laughing at?" Bob asked, laughing with her.

"I was just thinking of the times we made love. We were worried about being caught, but they sure weren't." Then she turned serious. "Ever since we left the Cayman's she's been coming on to Jim. She's out for a man, and now that Bruno and Dan aren't around, she's set her sights for him. Oh well, let's try and get some sleep."

The next morning, nothing was said about the experience of the night. There was definitely a feeling of defiance and tension in the air.

Betty could see the Cristabal harbor through her binoculars.

It was an outline of dilapidated buildings.

As they sailed closer, Betty asked, "What's that long gray and white building on the dock?"

Bob slowed *Destiny* down a bit, "That's the Cristabal Yacht Club."

"That's the yacht club!" Betty exclaimed, 'It sure is a run-down mess."

They were greeted by the dockmaster as they approached the pier, and he assigned *Destiny* a slip. Aztec Indian women were sitting on the dock. They were dressed in colorful striped clothing of deep reds, burnt orange and shades of green. Their hands moved rapidly as they crocheted mats and doilies. An array of finished articles lay at their feet. No prices were marked on them. The price was quoted and the bargaining began the minute you walked by. Adorable children with long black hair and starkly cut bangs played along the porch. Makeshift toys of wood and cardboard were their playthings. Their happy laughter rang out as *Destiny* sailed in.

Cab fare into Colon was one dollar, an unheard of small amount. As they walked the streets, they were surrounded by rundown buildings. Not a screen or glass covered the windows, the place looked like a warzone.

The stench of the city was overwhelming as they breathed in the hot polluted air. The poverty broke Betty's heart as she looked at the children in tattered rags. They played in the pot-holed streets with no shoes, badly in need of a bath.

People hung out of their windows in search of whatever breeze there might be. The heat was unbearable in their tiny apartments. Streets were torn up and traffic was heavy, causing a constant turmoil. Warned not to go into town alone especially at night, they traveled in groups everywhere.

That night after returning back to the boat they drifted off to sleep. They were awakened by a muffled scream then all was quiet again. The next morning a man was found stabbed to death outside the Yacht Club.

Eva, a thirty-two foot sailboat was tied up at the dock. Hanz and his crewmen were working on their engine. Betty and Bob dove with them in the Caymans.

Hanz was a gynecologist who took off from his practice for two years. He was like Bob, he wanted to sail around the world, but he could never talk his wife into going with him. Hanz was in his early fifties, six foot tall with a sturdy big-boned physique. His full lips and ruddy complexion enhanced the shiny Yul Brenner bald head. When he spoke, his words were heavy with a thick German accent. His lips slashed on an angle each time he smiled. Hanz eluded an air of staunch hard military intrigue. Underneath it all he was kind and gentle.

The crew of *Eva* were in their thirties. Both men were lean and had light color hair. They had very little expression in their faces. Tom appeared like a mama's boy, meek and mild in every way. Ryan was a bit flaky, boisterous, and had never been able to hold a job for very long. Their boat was stocked with more booze than food and they stayed drunk most of their sea voyage. *Eva's* nickname was, 'The booze soaked boat.'

The next day, Bob was approached by a small dark-skinned man in his forties. He was dressed in a dirty flowered shirt with large sweat marks under the arms. His black-soiled pants were tight and shiny from wear. The dirty black pointy shoes he wore had seen better times. The man took a comb out of his pocket and combed through his slick black hair. It was shinning from an overdose of hair-oil. As he thrust his hand out to shake hands his arm pits reeked with body odor. Decayed teeth tainted his breath as he broke into a big smile.

"Hello sir, let me introduce myself. I am Fillip Santiago. I know everyone around here. Ask anyone and they will tell you I am an honest man."

"Please, to meet you," said Bob, not taking his hand. "What can I do for you?"

"It's what I can do for you. Are you interested in going through the canal soon?"

"Yes, we are. I can't seem to find anyone who can put us on the right track."

"Aha Senor, I have come to help you. I can take you to the proper place and introduce you to the right man," he said with a wink. "I'll help you fill out the necessary papers. Then arrange for the day and time you want to leave."

"Terrific. We'd like to leave Tuesday, if that's possible."

"Oh Senor," Fillip said shaking his head. "Tuesday is quite soon and it all takes much time. With my—how you say eh—influence, maybe I can do it. My fee for my service is two hundred and fifty dollars."

"Two hundred and fifty dollars!" shouted Bob. "That must include the canal fee."

"No Senor. That's just my fee. It takes work and influence to get things done right."

Bob was a bit suspicious at this point. "Well, I don't know, Fillip. That sounds a bit high to me. How about letting me think about it. Come back tomorrow."

"You must hurry if you want to go Tuesday. Give me some money and I'll start—"

"No, Fillip. Come back tomorrow," Bob said walking away.

Bob climbed on *Destiny* and shook his head in bewilderment. "This can't be right. I think that guy is a con-artist."

Betty agreed with him. "I think he is too. Although he's the first person that has tried to help."

"Maybe the ship's chandler can help us. They might be able to tell us about the canal fees. Come on Betty, walk over with me."

A tan-skinned man about mid-twenties was behind the counter. He was dressed in clean white ducks, and spotless clean sneakers. His black wavy clean hair glistened in the sunlight that streamed through the window. Ricardo was on the name tag, pinned to his shirt.

Bob walked up to the counter. "Ricardo, do you know a Fillip Santiago?"

"Why, sir, what's the problem?" he asked.

"We're trying to go through the canal with our boat, and he says he can help us. Wants to charge us two hundred and fifty dollars for his services, is that usual?"

Ricardo's handsome Latin face lit up with a huge grin. "Old Fillip is at it again. I will take you to the port captain tomorrow. You can fill out the papers yourself. They'll charge you one hundred and fifty dollars and you can leave any day you choose."

"Are you kidding? That's great—wait a minute, what's your fee?"

"Fee? I don't charge a fee," said Ricardo. "It's part of the service of the yacht club. Come tomorrow at nine and I'll take you over."

Fillip arrived bright and early in the morning. "Are you ready to go senor?"

"No way, Fillip, you tried to rip me off."

"No senor, I'm just trying to make a living," sadly, he walked away.

Destiny had to prepare for the trip through the canal and the long voyage afterwards. Everyone was deeply engrossed in their chores except Jamie; he snuck off to the local bar.

Bob looked around for him. "Dammit, where is that man? He's never here when I need him."

"I'll go get him, I know where he is," Betty said, as she put down her brush and walked to the bar. Jamie had a beer in one hand, and a pool cue in another. Betty went up to him and asked, "What are you doing here, Bob's been looking for you. There's still a lot of work to be done."

Jamie lined up the balls as he said, "Oh, I thought I finished my job."

Betty took the cue stick from his hand, "You better come back with me, Bob's pretty upset. So is the rest of the crew. No one's finished their work until *Destiny* is ready to leave."

Jamie trailed behind Betty in a slow lumbering gait. "Bob's going to send me home because they don't like me."

Betty turned to him, "Who doesn't like you?"

"Martha and Jim, they want me off the boat," said Jamie climbing aboard and before Betty could question him he looked at the crew and said, "What's so important that you need me to do."

The crew looked at him in disgust and Bob made sure he worked the rest of the day.

* * *

Tuesday morning on May twenty-fourth was their fourth day at the harbor and now *Destiny* was ready to go. Tanks were filled with water and fuel, and the boat had been measured by the port authorities. Rubber tires had been tied along both port and starboard sides to protect her from the canal walls.

Eva and another sixty-foot boat, *Saga* were going through the canal with them. The only hold-up was waiting for the professional pilot to arrive. Each boat going through the locks had to have a canal pilot onboard. He was due at eight that morning and he arrived at ten.

All three boats took off in a line motoring toward the entrance of the Panama Canal. Looking ahead, they could see huge container ships and freighters going though the locks. Martha and Jim were out on the bow and Betty and Jamie were on the stern. As *Destiny* entered the canal, they saw several men on each side of the high huge walls. Once they were in the locks the canal workers threw light ropes with a ball on the end. On both starboard, and port sides, first to the bow then to the stern. *Destiny*'s crew grabbed the ropes and tied them to their heavy lines. The men above pulled the heavy ropes back up and secured them to the wall on each side. They wanted to keep the boats in the middle of the canal, so they didn't bump against the walls.

After the three boats were secured in place they closed the locks, and the water poured in. Quickly, the crew took up the slack in the lines as *Destiny* rose higher and higher. Fish caught in the locks jumped high in the air, as if to see what was going on. The workers called down from the walls making friendly remarks while school children on a day's outing waved down to them. The feeling was overwhelming in these huge surroundings. It made them feel insignificant and small.

When the water reached the proper level they opened the gate and the men walked along the wall with the lines, guiding *Destiny* into the next lock. Each lock was a repeat of the one before. They would go through three of them today.

After the third one, they motored to Gambia on Gatun Lake. The pilot left them and *Destiny* was anchored for the night in the heavy jungle surroundings. The three boats rafted together and enjoyed dinner on *Saga*.

That night while they slept they could hear the howler monkeys in the distance, screaming in the trees. Branches snapped as they jumped from tree to tree not ready to settle in for the night.

Eight-thirty sharp, the new pilot arrived and they were on a new day's adventure. Approaching the canal, *Destiny*'s engine started to make a weird noise. They smelled a burning odor.

Bob radioed to the boat *Saga* ahead. "Tom, we have a problem. Our engine is acting up and we have to check it out, any chance of towing us in?"

"Sure," answered Tom Orland. "I'll slow down and you can throw us a line."

Jamie threw a line to Tom and they towed *Destiny* into the lock.

While they were being towed, Bob called out to Jim, "See if you can find the trouble."

Jim lifted the floorboards and looked down the opening over the engine. "Yeah, I see it. It's a broken fanbelt."

Bob handed him a new belt. Jim looked puzzled, "It's a difficult spot to get at, but I'll try it."

The heat was unmerciful as he squeezed into the narrow opening. Sweat drenched his shirt and he pulled it off as he continued to work. The diesel smell emanated from the hot engine and he started to gag. Gasping for air, he worked quickly to replace the belt before he threw up.

The procedure through the locks was the same. This time they were in high water going down. As the water in the lock lowered, they eased out the lines keeping the lines secure. They went through the three locks quicker than expected and they were out of the locks by noon.

Twenty-two

When they came out of the last lock, Bob was overjoyed. "Welcome to the Pacific," he shouted with glee. "We made it this far and it's only a thousand miles to the Galapagos."

Only a thousand miles didn't seem to faze Betty. "Look, even the wind is welcoming us." A cool marvelous breeze sped *Destiny* on her journey.

Bob was in his glory. "We're on a broad-reach guys, let's get the main and mizzen up."

The sails billowed out rising in the air like beautiful white clouds. "Looking good," said Bob. "Now lets try the spinnaker. Here Betty, take the helm while I help get the spinnaker pole up."

Bob was elated. Crossing the Atlantic and Caribbean was one thing. Heading to the South Pacific definitely meant his dream was about to become a reality.

As they sailed along peacefully, life aboard ship was serene. They were lulled into a feeling of contentment. It's like having a baby; you forget the pain and torment you went through until it's about to happen again. They drifted off like babes in a cradle, rocked into a light easy sleep.

Dinner was over and the galley cleaned in fast time. Everyone was weary and waiting for their bodies to adjust to the open seas. Lying in the cockpit Betty watched the skies change like a kaleidoscope. The blue sky turned gray and dismal. Streaks of red and orange ran through the twirling storm clouds. Suddenly, she heard the shrill whistle of the wind picking up speed. A squall lashed out sending thunder and lightening through the air. It slashed fire across the sky in wild angry designs. Thunder roared through the night, sounding like a massive bowling alley, giving Betty a frightening feeling.

Shivering, she stood at the helm watching the wind gauge climb. Twenty-five knots then up to thirty-five then back to twenty-five.

"Reef the sails," she heard Bob yell as all hands got busy.

"It feels like all hell's broken loose," Betty said. "I hope this isn't any indication of how the weather's going to be. I wouldn't want this mess all the way to the Galapagos."

The auto-pilot kept going off; the conditions were too rough for it to handle. Betty wrestled continually to keep *Destiny* oncourse.

"Bob, take the wheel for a moment. I'm drenched and I want to go below for dry clothes and rain gear. I'll get some for you too."

Going below was no easy chore. *Destiny* was heeled twenty-five degrees and the ride was fast and turbulent. After many hours of torture, the wind shifted to a calm fifteen knots. Betty was alone for her night-watch. She sat in the darkness and thought she saw a small shadow. It ran quickly along the port side deck.

"Oops, what was that?" she said out loud. Feeling nothing could be there she chalked it up to her imagination. Then, she remembered noticing that shadow several times before on her nightwatch. She'd have to ask the other crew if they saw anything. By the time Jim came up to relieve her, she had forgotten all about it.

The boat settled down to a slow rolly rock. Not wild but still nerve-wracking. The staterooms were stifling and they were back to sleepless nights.

"One thousand miles," she mumbled as she climbed into bed. "I must be out of my mind. I must be nuts. I should have left with the pilot and flown home from Panama."

Mornings come and go, but where do the days go? They had been out to sea now for six days. Betty was cranky and irritable as she sat at the helm. She tried hard to keep her mind off of the rocking. The auto-pilot was not working again and the wind was constantly shifting.

"I can't keep on course, and I'm oversteering this damn thing," she screamed at no one in particular.

"Here, let me help," said Bob, as he adjusted it for her. She took over the helm again and still couldn't hold the course. Bob corrected it again and was getting impatient with her. Giving up before his temper blew, he went below.

"For some reason I just can't do it," she shouted into the air. Tears rolled down her cheeks and she shook with shear frustration. No one was on deck so she let go and cried uncontrollably. The sound of the wind muffled her sobs, and she felt better after the cry.

Mother Nature provided them with a variety of wind. Some that sent *Destiny* sailing fast and smoothly through the vibrant sea. Others stirred the seas making the waves leap ten, fifteen feet high in the air. The strong wind pushed against her bow as the waves lifted *Destiny* out of the water. Then the boat slammed down against the water with a powerful thud. That night they were being thrashed and the force lifted Betty's body off the bed. With each movement, her insides jumbled and she searched for a more comfortable spot. Betty went out to the cockpit but it was windy and wet. Then the salon, but the gushing noise of the waves bashing against the hull was loud and thunderous. Returning to her stateroom she tucked pillows around her body and curled up in a fetal position. Lying there she waited for sleep to overtake her. It finally came at four A.M.

Bob was as tired as the rest of the crew. He's lucky he didn't have the squeamish feeling the rest of them had. Everyone else was on the edge of throwing up. They quietly waited for time to pass, and land to come in sight.

Added to the horrific conditions there was tension onboard. Jamie and the crew were not getting along. He was doing less and less work; irritating the crew's already bad moods.

Betty was sitting at the helm with Bob watching Martha and Jim. "I have the feeling they are going to ask us to let Martha take Jamie's place."

"Yeah, Jim has been training Martha for the outside deck work."

Betty went out on the bow. "We must be getting close to land. Looks like I'm back to my favorite pastime counting dead fish. Makes me feel useful again," she laughed.

Jamie came up from below and watched Betty throwing the fish overboard. "Hey, that's always a sign we're getting close to land."

"How would you know," Martha said sarcastically. "You ain't

been on a long leg before."

"No, I ain't," Jamie said making fun of her. "Don't you know ain't isn't proper English?"

"Shut up, you ignorant fool. You stop picking on me," said Martha, her cockney accent flaring out.

"Picking on *you*! *Me* picking on *you*! You haven't liked me since we first met. You didn't even want me onboard," said Jamie, hot under the collar. "All you and Jim want to do is be by yourselves so you can fuck around."

"My God, I never heard such a flipping mouth," said Martha, pushing her hair from her face.

"Oh yeah, well I sure hear plenty from your bedroom. Oh Jimmy-boy fuck me, oh oh oh, I'm coming, Jimmie-boy, I'm coming," he mimicked shaking his hips. "I see him sneaking in your room. You're a pig."

"Well I never—Betty, Bob make him shut up," cried Martha, in tears.

Betty almost laughed out loud at Jamie's demonstration. "That's enough out of both of you. Stop the bickering now." She walked out to the stern to get away from them.

Everything went quiet, and Jim just kept on reading while the other two stared darts at each other.

It was peaceful sitting on the stern and Betty started to meditate. The sky was full of billowy clouds and she watched them float by. A gracious white bird seemed to be floating above the mast. They hadn't seen a bird in a long time.

"There's a white bird circling above us," shouted Betty. "I think he's trying to land on *Destiny*."

Everyone's attention went on the tremendous struggle the bird was having as it tried to land. After several minutes of fighting the wind, the bird landed, clutching the railing in desperation. His chest moved vigorously from the exertion and they let him get his breath before scattering bread. They took great pleasure in watching another living creature survive life at sea. The bird rested for a few hours, then tucked its head under its wing to sleep. An hour later, the bird groomed himself and flew off into the horizon

They had been sailing for eight days and they should have

reached the Galapagos by now. They still had a hundred and sixty miles to go. Wind and current just would not let them back oncourse. *Destiny* sailed along in moderate seas at eight knots, and the wind had been a steady fifteen knots. To make it even better the temperature dropped to seventy-eight degrees. A great relief from the ninety-seven degrees they had been living with.

"Ah, this is what I call sailing," said Jim lying down on the bench seat.

Bob looked at the wind-gauge, "I can't believe it. Everything is near-perfect for a change."

Just as the words were spoken, they heard a loud rip and pieces of the genoa sail went flying in different directions.

"Jim, Jamie, get that sail down. I'll get the stay-sail ready to put up. It's small but it's better than nothing," said Bob rushing to the bow. Jim came running but Jamie slowly took his time.

"I never did see anyone as bloody lazy as you," said Martha, pushing past him and rushing out to help.

Jamie jabbed at her with his fist but missed, "What the hell's bugging her, what's she got, a bug up her ass or something?"

"If you take any longer getting out there, the work will be done. What's the matter don't you want your job?" Betty asked, staring angrily at him.

"Yeah, sure I like my job. I don't like the crew. Besides, what's the hurry?"

"What's the hurry? Well, if you don't know, then you really don't understand sailing."

Jamie had a sneer on his face as he said, "Let her do it if she wants to. Here let me take over the helm," he reached for the wheel.

"Oh no, you don't. You were hired to help, now get out there and do your job."

Reluctantly, he went out, and Martha came back fuming. "Lazy bloody, no good bum. I feel like kicking him in his knickers. I'm going down and start supper."

Twilight was beautiful. The glow of the setting sun cast a shadowed beam upon *Destiny*. Jim was on the bow watching an immense bird circling and on an impulse he put his arm out as a welcoming gesture. The bird landed on his arm.

He called out. "Hey guys come look at the bird on my arm."

They watched the blue-footed booby nibble on Jim's hand, it seemed very comfortable. Betty reached her hand out to pet the bird, and the bird pecked hard at her hand, "Ouch! Looks like he's a one-man bird," said Betty rubbing the spot.

Jim was delighted with this heavy strange creature with huge blue feet. He rested his hand on the railing to help support the weight of the bird, until his arm got tired. Then he placed the bird on the bowsprit. Later that night, another bird joined it, staying for the rest of the night.

Santa Cruz appeared on the horizon at first-light. When they lowered the sails, the birds flew away. *Destiny* had given them a ride home. They were probably as happy to see land as the crew of *Destiny* was.

It was seven-thirty at night when they pulled into Academy Bay at Santa Cruz. They could see the sun beginning to set. Bob had been on the radio all afternoon trying talk to the dockmaster. He needed to know where he should dock. Because of the language barrier, he was having trouble communicating. Amidst all the confusion, an American interrupted and helped translate the conversation. Finally, Bob received permission to enter and tie up along the town wall.

After doing a quick clean up on *Destiny* the whole group hit the sack. Sleep would come easy tonight as they were exhausted. Their bodies craved a peaceful night's rest.

The noise of people walking along the town wall woke Betty early. She drank her coffee out on the deck, enjoying the early morning. She gazed ashore at the primitive small buildings lining the dirt streets. *What are those weird things covering the roofs*, she wondered. She peered through the binoculars. Each roof was covered with large iguanas, there were thousands of them. Oblivious to the world, they laid there letting the sun soak their long scaly bodies. Impatient to explore the town, she woke Bob and they went to clear *Destiny* through customs.

The customs officer asked, "Where is your visa or cruising permit to visit the Galapagos?"

Bob was showing his frustration, as he stuttered, "I applied several times for one, but I never received an answer back. Can we purchase one here?"

"No, they have to be purchased ahead of time at the Embassy. We only allow so many boats a year in the Galapagos. There's a long waiting list. We'll allow your ship to stay in the harbor for forty-eight hours. Then you must sail on."

Betty interrupted, "Officer, we traveled all this way to see your beautiful country. It's filled with such wonderful unusual creatures. Can't you give us a little more time?"

The officer smiled as he fumbled with their passports. "Okay, I will give you seventy-two hours, not an hour more."

They thanked him and went immediately to see a local travel agent. They hoped to schedule a short cruise of the islands. The only ship available was a very small one, not very impressive. They were told the cruise was for two-and-a-half days, and would visit three of the islands.

When they returned to *Destiny*, the crew was having breakfast. Bob sat down with them and said, "We're going on a cruise for two-and-a-half days. The ship leaves this afternoon at one. I'm putting you in charge, Jim. Jamie, you make sure you listen to him. I've made a list of the things that have to be done. As soon as the work is finished, you can go off and enjoy the island."

The three sat there listening and Jim looked over the list. "This shouldn't take us long." Bob pulled out his wallet. "I'm leaving your wages and a little extra. Have a good time when the work is done."

Betty had never let Martha go shopping on her own before. She took a chance and said. "Martha, I won't have time to do the shopping myself and take the cruise. Here's a list and money for the food and supplies we need. If you see anything else we need, get it."

Martha looked over the list, "No problem, I'll take care of it."

Betty and Bob walked over to the cruise ship. It was badly in need of a paint job as rusty streaks ran down the sides making abstract designs, around the peeling paint.

As it motored up to the pier, Betty said, "We're giving up the comforts of *Destiny* to ride on this tub."

Captain Alfonso greeted them in Portuguese as they went aboard. His first-mate translated his message to them

Fourteen passengers and nine crew were onboard. They were shown to their stateroom and found it tiny but clean. It was sparsely furnished with double bunks, and they shared a dilapidated bathroom with the next room.

"I love the decor." Betty said laughing. "Look at this fashionable crack in the toilet seat. That will get your attention if you sit down wrong."

The showerhead hung over the toilet. Bob chimed in with, "How clever. You can go to the toilet and take a shower at the same time."

Betty laughed so hard she couldn't stop. "Bob, you're so gross."

"You'll stop laughing when you take a shower. The water is brackish and cold."

"You mean there's no hot water? That's okay. I'll put up with almost anything to see the islands," answered Betty.

Traveling to Floreana, Espanola and Seymour, each island held a different kind of wildlife. One island was barren, but they were greeted by herds of friendly sealions. Others were covered with hundreds of blue-footed boobies and albatross. Nests were built everywhere along the ground. Eggs or babies nestled under the mother's wings. Sometimes the young birds would wiggle out to squawk and flap their wings. Male boobies would dance back and forth squeaking disapproval as people walked along the path. Male frigate birds flew everywhere. Their bright red chests expanded like huge balloons, as they tried to attract a mate. It was a birdlover's paradise. The surroundings were overpowering. Water sprayed high in the air through blow holes in the mounds of rocks. As the ocean crashed against them.

Thousands of iguanas lay dozing in the sun, moving only when the visitors cast a shadow on them. Everything was breathtaking, beautiful and primitive. Mammoth turtles scurried down the beach to the water as the group approached. Salmon-colored flamingoes stood on spindly legs, feeding on the tiny bugs and fish in the outlet of grassy water.

Breakfast was sometimes unrecognizable, but lunch and dinner was fresh fish caught that day. Despite the meager accommodations, it was a great way to see the Galapagos.

* * *

Arriving back at *Destiny* a little earlier than expected, they were not happy with what they found. Dirty dishes lay all around the galley and salon; trash was overflowing and the boat smelled like a brewery.

"What's going on here?" yelled Bob. "This boat is a mess."

Jim was asleep on the salon couch. He sat up at the sound of Bob's voice. Surprised that Bob was back so soon, he stuttered. "Jamie wouldn't help with the work."

Martha came walking in the salon from her stateroom looking hungover. In a muffled voice, she added, "Yea, and he brought strangers back to the boat last night and partied 'til the wee hours."

Betty was listening as she walked in the galley, and looked in the cupboards. "As far as I can see, none of the work has been done. Martha, where are the supplies you were supposed to buy?"

They stood there like a couple of kids caught playing hooky not saying a word.

Bob walked out on deck and looked down at the dinghy, "How did the tether on the dingy get broken?"

Jim shrugged his shoulders and said, "I don't know. Jamie took it out last."

Bob's face was red with anger. "We gave you chores to do and they're not done."

Jamie came walking in from the dock. "Got back early," he said with a smile on his face.

"Yeah, and we're not too happy either. The work's not done and the tethers broken on the dinghy," said Bob.

"Hey, I didn't even have the dinghy. They took it out," he said pointing at Jim and Martha.

"You're a dirty liar. You did it, not us," yelled Martha.

Betty went over and stared Jamie in the eye. "We heard you had people onboard while we were gone."

"*Me*, just *me*?" Jamie started to laugh. "Yeah, blame it all on me. I get blamed for everything. Martha and Jim were there and they had people over too. Look at how hungover they are, you can see how much they enjoyed the party. Go ahead, Martha, tell them about the friends you had over."

"You shut your mouth, Jamie. He's lying," shouted Martha, but Betty could tell she was lying.

Bob was so mad he was ready to fire them all. He walked around the deck cooling off.

Listening to the three squabble among themselves, he yelled, "All right, that's enough. Get this boat cleaned up and the work done now."

The crew moved around the ship in lightning speed, trying to get their jobs completed, each blaming the other as they worked.

An old lady selling homemade bread came strolling up the docks. The aroma was tantalizing and Betty bought a loaf.

She placed the hot bread on the counter in the galley and said. "I'm going to the store to get the supplies you were suppose to buy, Martha." She looked at Bob and asked, "Want to come with me?"

Bob looked around at the crew. "We're going to the store. Don't dare leave this boat until the work's done."

When they returned, there was a big chunk missing from the bread. It looked like someone had ripped a piece out of the center.

Betty was angry and she called out, "Who tore open the bread like this?"

Another argument started as each blamed the other for doing it.

"No one takes the blame for anything around here," Betty said as she bent over the galley table to put the groceries under the seat.

A gigantic rat the size of a cat jumped from the seat and scurried up on deck. Screaming, Betty ran into her stateroom shutting the door behind her.

"What's going on?" everyone said rushing into the galley.

Peeking out of her door she said, "There's a monster rat on board."

"Oh Blimey," Martha said. "You scared me out of me knickers."

"Now I know what that shadow was I saw each night on

watch," Betty said, still shaking.

"I saw that shadow too," said Jamie. "I bet it's been onboard since Panama."

"Let's go buy a rat trap right now. We can't let that thing stay on board," said Bob.

Buying a rat trap was not easy. All they could find were huge complicated contraptions. They settled on the smallest one, then the clerk suggested rat poison along with the trap. They baited the trap with cheese, and after many tries were finally able to set it. Betty cut a large piece of bread and coated it with poison. Then she laid it on the seat where the rat had been.

Even though they were mad at the crew, they took them to dinner. There was a small but clean outdoor restaurant on the corner. They were serving huge lobster dinners for only four dollars per person with potato, vegetables and homemade bread included in the price. They washed it down with homemade wine that was smooth and cool.

After dinner, Bob took Jamie over to the bar. "I'm going to let you go. I'm not satisfied with your work, or your personality."

Jamie's face turned red, "I knew this was coming from the second day I came aboard. They never liked me from the start," he said pointing towards Jim and Martha, and they sneered back at him

Bob stood listening then, "You might be right but I still have to let you go. I can't have contention among the crew."

Jamie's voice was calm but forceful as he stared Bob in the eye. "You think the whole thing is my fault don't you? They had people over and laughed and talked about you behind your back, even drank your good wine. How come you're not sending them off too?"

Bob felt like a football coach having to bounce a player, "I'll pay your way back to the Caymans. I'll arrange for the ticket tomorrow." Bob started to walk away but stopped to listen as Jamie continued.

Jamie was flustered his voice raising in pitch, "They never wanted me here. I tried real hard in the beginning. It didn't take me long to see they didn't like me. What was the use of working hard when I knew they were planning to get rid of me? I heard them talking about it. Why don't you just give me the money? I'd like to hang here for a couple of weeks."

Bob felt sorry for him. "Look, I can't do that. By law, I'm responsible for getting you off the island. I'll pay for your ticket. You can pick it up at the travel agent whenever you're ready to leave."

Going back to the table, he looked sternly at Martha and Jim. "As for you two, I'm really surprised at you. You've been with us long enough to know what's expected of you. We are really disappointed with your actions."

Martha and Jim sat with their shoulders slumped over. "We're sorry, but it's Jamie's fault it wasn't . . . "

"Stop," yelled Bob. "Don't make excuses or blame someone else for what wasn't done. Jim, you were in charge and I come back to a filthy boat and you hungover. I need crew, so I'll give you both one more chance. If it ever happens again you're out."

The unhappy crew walked back to *Destiny* still arguing among themselves.

When they went down to the galley, Betty looked at the trap. It was still intact, but the poisonous bread was missing.

"Maybe he got off the boat and went ashore," said Martha.

They looked around, but there was no sign of the rat or the bread.

Reluctantly, Betty crawled in bed wondering where the rat was hiding. She heard Martha let out a bloodcurdling scream, and they rushed to her stateroom.

Martha was standing on her bed with a towel wrapped around her body. "Oh me god, oh me god," she kept saying. She stood on the bed shivering and pointing to the bathroom.

The rat was on the toiletseat and Jamie was hitting it with his shoe. The rat fell on the floor, staggered forward and collapsed.

Martha was still shaking, "I . . . went in to take a douche. After I turned on the water, I went to go to the toilet. There was this big monster thing sitting on the edge of the toilet. The bloody thing scared me." Letting out a sob with tears streaming down her face, she added, "It could have bit me."

"Man, that's the biggest rat I ever saw," said Jamie. "It must be at least twelve inches long and look at the length of his tail."

Jim poked the rat with his foot. "It's dead. I guess the poison made him go for the water in the toilet." Picking it up by the tail, he threw it overboard.

"Come on, Martha, calm down, the rat's gone now," said Betty, helping her off her bed. As Betty climbed into bed again she said, "I'm glad to be rid of the rat."

Bob pulled the covers over him as he said. "This has been one hell of a day. We had such a nice time on the trip. Then, we come back to this. I should have let them all go, but it's so hard to find a crew, particularly out here."

Betty turned over to face him and rubbed his arm. "I do think they wanted to get rid of Jamie. Martha didn't like him from the very first day. Jim seems to go along with whatever she wants."

"You might say he's pussy-whipped." Ducking, he hid under the covers as she hit him with the pillow.

"You are so crude. You didn't talk like that when we first met, you hardly even said a cuss word. The longer I know you, the worse you get."

Bob laughed as he peeked out from under the covers, "Well, I never said I was perfect. Goodnight Sea Witch, I love you."

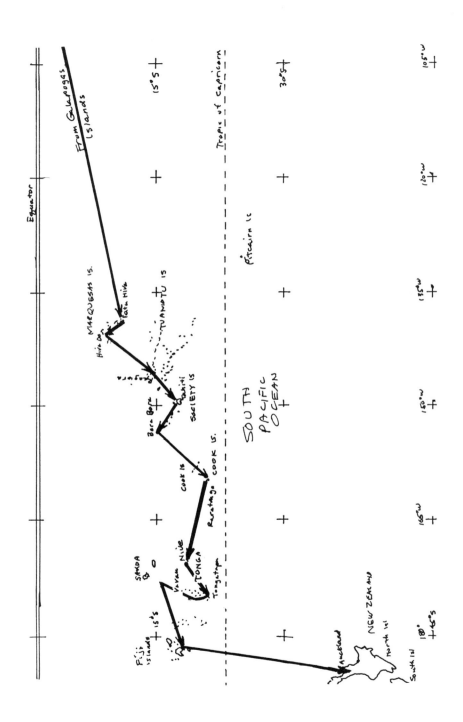

Twenty-three

Their day was busy as they prepared to leave for the Marquesas Islands. Jim was cleaning the decks. He pulled out the canvas that was stored behind the gear box.

"Hey, come look at this," he said, holding up a cover. It had big gaping holes chewed in it. Hidden under the cover were bones from flying fish that the rat had eaten.

Bob examined the canvas covers. "Looks like the rat had plenty to eat out to sea. Once *Destiny* was in port he had to go below for food. Might as well heave all of the covers. They're no good to us with holes in them."

*   *   *

It was three thousand miles to the next port of call of Fatu Hiva. It would take eighteen to twenty-four days. Betty was pleased the ocean was calm, with very little wind.

Nothing much was happening as time drifted slowly by like the seaweed floating in the ocean. Betty laid on the deck in the peaceful surroundings, thinking of her family and friends. Her mind drifted to things that happened when she was a child. Her memories were crystal clear as she relived the past, remembering a toy sail boat here father had given her.

Blue crystalline water gave off a mirror image. It was an easy pace, and restlessness sent her in search of things to do. The boat was riding so smoothly, she's able to spend time painting the birds of the Galapagos.

Bob was examining the sails and he walked over to Betty. "I've got a great job for you."

Betty put down her paint brush, "Yeah? What is it."

"Come with me and I'll show you." He had set up the sewing machine on the bow. "See, if you can repair this blown-out genie."

Betty's mouth dropped open. "You're kidding, aren't you?"

She felt the thick material, "I don't know if it will fit under the foot of the machine."

"Well, try it and see what you can do," said Bob pulling the sail to the machine.

Betty sat down, determined to try. "Jim, come over here. I need your help. I'll guide the sail under the foot and run the machine while you pull it slowly through. Together we might be able to mend the sail."

Betty held the edges of the sail together with one hand. Then she laid mending tape on the top and bottom. She forced the material under the foot of the sewing machine, expecting it to break off, but it held. Jim pulled the sail as Betty kept the sewing machine going. The material bunched up several times and she stopped to rearrange it. Two hours later, the sail was repaired, and the genie was ready to fly again. All they needed was some wind.

Destiny continued to churn through the water, her engine purring away. They are getting closer to their destination. Feeling the change in wind, Bob called out to Jim, "The trade winds have arrived. Hoist the sails, *Destiny* is a sailing vessel again."

Betty stood beside Bob her arm around his shoulders. "Look at her glide through the waves. Like she's been set free."

The engine was no longer running and the quietness was a blessing. Lying on the deck box, at the stern, a peaceful reverie spread over Betty. The stillness of the surroundings lulled her to sleep. It was her daughter Debra's birthday. Betty dreamt she was celebrating it with her. It seemed so real she could smell the waxy perfume of the candles. Her daughter's laughter rang in her ears. She woke with a start and realized it was just a dream. It was Martha giggling.

Bob was at the helm and Betty walked over and sat next to him. "Is something bothering you?" he asked. "You look a little sad."

"Today's Deb's birthday and I just dreamt I was home with her. I could hear her laughing so clearly, but it was Martha laughing up on the bow."

"Why don't you call her on the ship to shore radio?"

"Good idea," Betty said going down into the salon. Picking up the receiver she said, "*Whiskey Oscar Oscar* this is *Destiny*

WTJ3231 come in please." There was no answer. She repeated it over and over again for an hour before finally giving up.

Going back upstairs she said, "It's a good thing we're not in trouble. We'd sink before we got help."

"Take over the helm, Betty. I'll give it a try," said Bob. He called three other stations and finally got through. "Come on down, Betty, I got Debra on the radio."

Betty rushed downstairs elated. Grabbing the receiver she sang, "Happy Birthday to you."

There were still two thousand miles to go before they reached land. The seas were churned into large swells that back-lashed against *Destiny*'s hull. The waves swerved the boat sideways with each thud.

Feeling lightheaded and nauseated, Betty put on half a patch, something she had not needed for days. "Do you need me up here for anything?" she asked Bob.

"No, why don't you go lie down, you look a little green."

When she attempted to climb into bed, *Destiny* reared sideways. Betty was thrown on to the wall and her arm rammed into a clothes hook. She let out a scream from the pain as the hook punctured her arm.

Martha was in the galley and came rushing in. "Oh my God, you're bleeding."

Blood rushed down Betty's arm from the long gash just below her elbow.

"This damn swerving is going to kill me yet," said Betty, sobbing.

Martha ran and got the first-aid kit, setting it down on the bed. Betty held the cut together as Martha applied a butterfly bandage.

"What happened down here?" Bob asked as he walked into the room. "Wow! That looks bad. I'll get the ice pack and a couple painkillers. Then, I want you to lie down."

Night watches had been pleasant. The evening was dark and moonless, except for a few stars twinkling in the sky. Music from Betty's walkman helped the night pass quickly. Watching the radar helped keep her alert. Alone in the darkness she sat on the portside deck staring blankly at the horizon. There was nothing in sight. She could feel the overpowering gust of the wind from *Destiny's* speed. Chills ran through Betty at the thought of *Destiny* swerving sideways, knocking her overboard. The frightening thought sent her to the safety of the helm chair. Nothing was showing on radar and she closed her eyes for a minute. Then, on the far corner of the screen, a small dot appeared—the first ship they have seen in days. Betty felt so tired and her arm ached. She could hardly wait for Jim to relieve her.

When her nightwatch was over, Betty couldn't wait to get to bed. She was just dozing off. when she heard voices coming through the hatch above their bed. It was Martha's voice that woke her.

"Jim, I don't want you to just fool around with me. I want you to be serious about our affair. I'm in love with you."

"I don't want to be serious with you," answered Jim. "I just want to fuck you, that's all."

"You're so bloody horrible," said Martha and started to cry.

"Ah, for Christ sake, now you're pulling a crying act on me. Just like you did to Bruno. You like to do it as much as I do."

"No I don't. If I can't be your girl, I'm not going to let you touch me anymore. I'm not staying up here with you either." She went below and slammed her bedroom door.

Their arguments went on for days. Martha did her best to sway him to her way of thinking—going topless whenever she and Jim were alone, and waiting on him hand and foot. It was Jimmie boy this and Jimmie boy that until Betty wanted to throw-up. Mornings soon found Jim creeping out of Martha's room. One of them had won.

On Bob's early watch, Betty said, "I'm a little uncomfortable with what was going on with Martha and Jim. Do you think we should say something?"

Bob put the helm on auto-pilot and turned his chair towards her. "We're going to be at sea for a long time, and it's important to keep harmony on the boat. Let's wait and see what happens. Let's hope she doesn't get pregnant."

"I guess—they're not doing anything more than we are," said Betty, "but they're just kids. Maybe since we let her and

262

Bruno sleep together, she feels we wouldn't care if she sleeps with Jim."

"It's tough when you're young and your hormones are really flowing, she's the only act in town," Bob laughed.

Betty gave him a kick. "There you go being crude again," she laughed.

Bob got serious, "Jim's been very conscientious up 'til now; been able to do almost any job." Bob leaned over to check the radar.

Betty smiled, "He's a cute kid and you've taught him everything he knows about sailing. He can handle the navigation equipment and do the readings almost as well as you can."

They both sat thinking. Bob had grown to love Jim as a son, and would do almost anything for him.

Betty broke the silence, "We pay them well, including all their needs, take them everywhere we go on shore. They're almost like our own kids."

Sighing, Bob looked out at the sea. "I don't know. There's a fine line between treating them like employees or like family. Living so close together, I think we crossed the fine line."

"Well, do we close our eyes to the things that bother us, let them have their personal life?" asked Betty.

Laughing, Bob said, "There's no way in hell we could stop them."

They heard a noise downstairs, "Jim's coming to relieve us."

The morning was perfect with tame wind and puffy white clouds, drifting lazily in the sky. Bragging lately about the light winds was a mistake, because by afternoon the wind direction changed.

Snapping sails gave Bob a warning as he screamed out, "Good lord, the winds too strong for the spinnaker. Lets get it down quick before it's blown out."

Rushing to release the lines, the wind gusted to forty knots. It's force and strength bent the sturdy metal spinnaker pole into a U-shape. Hanging almost in limbo before it came crashing down on the deck. All hands worked diligently to get the spinnaker down before it blew out.

The squall cast shadows over the sails as it passed overhead. The seas increased to twenty-foot swells, causing an extremely unbearable motion. Waves washed over *Destiny*'s decks, pounding the sides with a thundering sound. They held on and waited for the storm to pass, hoping that it wouldn't get any worse. No one said a word and they sat in silence knowing if they make it through the storm, there would be an end to their torment. Tomorrow they would see the first island, Fatu Hiva, after eighteen days at sea.

A heavy mist hung over *Destiny*, as they neared the land. They could barely make out the jagged rock formations that form the beginning of their landfall. Gliding through the water under motor they could make out shadows of high hills. As they moved closer to the island, the air cleared and they spotted mountain goats grazing on the jagged cliffs. Lush foliage covered the mountain in multi-colors of green. Their eyes relished the beauty as they breathed in the fragrance that lingered in the air, intoxicating them with its sweetness. Far ahead, two huge spires jutted up into the sky. They stood in front of the mountain backdrop that surrounded the island. The spirals appeared like gigantic soldiers, guarding the village nestled in the valley.

Four boats were in the small harbor. They recognized two of them, *Gypsy Rover* and *Good Times*. Ashore they were greeted by native fishermen as they cleaned their catch and children ran to meet them. The group from *Destiny* walked along the dirt road that led to the village, fruit and flowering trees were everywhere.

There was a sign posted that said *Gendarmerie* (police) on a rickety old shack, and they were greeted by a friendly Polynesian man. His white stained shirt stretched tightly across his huge stomach. A few buttons were missing, leaving large gaps between the buttons. A broad grin of welcome appeared on his face, his tongue flapped between the huge gaps in his teeth. Black stringy long hair kept falling in his face and he swept it back with his huge brown hand.

"*Bon Jour*," he said, extending his hand. "I am Peppy the Gendarmerie and this is my daughter, Camellia."

Camellia gave a shy smile baring beautiful white teeth. Her shining hair was the color of ebony as it flowed down to her hips.

"She is absolutely beautiful," Betty said, as she looked at her tawny skin and high cheek bones. Her eyes were almost as dark as her hair.

"Hello, Peppy. Hello, Camellia." The *Destiny* crew said as they shook hands. Giggling, Camellia ran from the room.

"Don't mind her, she's shy. Camellia doesn't see many strangers."

Bob looked around, "Where is the customs office?"

"There is no customs here. You sign my book," Peppy said, "that will make you legal, until you check in at Tahuata.

Bob signed the book, "That makes life easy."

Peppy started out the door and signaled them to follow. "Come, let me show you around our island. You will find our people friendly and very smart. There are only fifty people on the island and each family must build their own home. See those two small huts? They are the school rooms where all the children study together."

"You seem to have every fruit imaginable growing here," Betty said, enthralled with the many tropical fruit trees.

The sun was shining down brightly, but a cool breeze dried the moisture from their sweaty bodies. They walked in the shade of the lush growth trying to stay out of the hot sun.

"It feels great to be back on land again," said Jim as they walked around a thicket of green. Around the bend was a cascading waterfall that emptied into a small pond. A fence of tall flowering bushes lined the banks, screening the pond. Several people were naked enjoying the coolness of the water.

Peppy hurried them on, "Come away from there, this is the village bathing area."

As they walked to the center of the village, people were sitting in what seemed like a town square with carvings, tapas and baskets in front of them.

Bob asked, "Are they selling their crafts?"

Peppy laughed, "They don't want your money, but they'll trade for your T-shirt."

Betty and Martha bartered T-shirts, cologne and hair ribbons for the tapas and baskets that the women made. Before they went back to the boat, they were given a basketful of luscious bananas, papayas and mango. The basket was made from braided palm fronds and crafted by the children.

Three young men approached Jim, "Do you want to go boar hunting tomorrow?"

Jim got excited, "Yeah! That would be great." Then, he turned to Bob and asked, "Can I borrow one of your rifles?"

Bob slapped him on the back, "Don't see why not."

Jim was ready at six in the morning when they came in their dugout canoes. He returned late in the afternoon proudly showing off a huge boar's leg. It had been skinned and wrapped in banana leaves.

Jim was all fired up, "Man that was great. You should have seen the size of this thing. I didn't shoot it, but the tall one with the scar on his face did." His face glowed, "Wow, are those guys gutsy. Wait till I tell my friends at home about this."

Martha took the meat down to the galley and then seasoned the boar's leg in several herbs. Later, she roasted the boar meat for dinner.

Bob invited friends from *Gypsy Rover* and *Good Times* to share the meal. As they sipped cocktails and watched the setting sun, Betty said, "These past three days have gone so fast. It feels like a small paradise here, so peaceful and serene."

"Enjoy it tonight cause we're shoving off tomorrow," Bob said as he made another drink. "We'll head for the island of Tahuata. Hit the sack early tonight."

"Hey, where can we go?" laughed Jim.

"I don't hear any jam sessions going on," chimed in Martha.

They left bright and early the next day. After eight hours of calm weather sailing, they anchored at the island, in the harbor of Tahuata, another lavishly green secluded place. A few boats were sprinkled here and there but none that they recognized.

Jim was washing the salt off the railing when Bob asked, "How about taking Betty and I to shore? We have to find the customs office. You and Martha can catch up on your work while we're gone."

"We'll be gone an hour or so. Keep an eye out for us so you can bring us back," added Betty.

266

Jim lowered the dinghy in the water. "Do you have a list of things to be done?"

Bob climbed in the dinghy, "Yes, it's on my desk. Do your regular work first, then the few things on the list."

Jim dropped them off on the pier and they started along the dirt road. It was bordered with heavy tangled overgrowth of blackberries. They walked for an hour in the hot scorching sun eating the blackberries as they went along. They started to get discouraged, and wondered if they were going the wrong way. Small houses started to appear, each dwelling had an abundance of flowers along a white picket fence. Soon, a pleasant town came into view.

Weary from the walk and thirsty, Bob said, "There's the custom office, hope we can get some water there."

French customs officers stood at the counter in military style, hands outstretched for their passports.

The officer checked each one thoroughly, then said in a French accent, "You have to purchase insurance for each person."

Bob had a questionable look on his face as he asked "Is this something new?"

"No," the officer answered, "it is a standing regulation. It is to guarantee that you have enough money to leave the Marquesas islands."

Bob shook his head, "I've never heard anything about needing insurance. How much is it?"

The officer looked at each passport, "A two thousand dollar bond is needed for the person from England. An eight hundred and fifty dollar bond is needed for each one from the United States. All money will be returned when you leave the last island."

Bob was flabbergasted, "That's highway robbery. That will take all the money we have. You can't do that to us."

"The choice is yours," shrugged the officer. "If you don't pay it, you can't stay in the country." Then he turned his back as if to dismiss them. "Pay or go home."

Bob had little choice, "Can you give us till tomorrow? We'll have to go back to the ship to get it."

The officer smirked. "You have until tomorrow at noon."

When they got outside, Bob let loose. "Goddamnit they did it to us again. Everytime you think you have everything under control, a bombshell hits you. That's going to take almost all our money."

"Two thousand dollars for Martha! We should have sent her home back in the Caribbean," said Betty.

They hitched a ride in the back of a rickety pickup truck with broken springs. It was a rutty, rocky road and they were bounced around as they sat on the floor. By the time they got back to the harbor their rear ends were sore. They saw Jim and Martha sitting in the dinghy by the pier, with uptight expressions on their faces.

Before Bob could say anything, Jim snapped sharply, "What took you so long? We've been hanging around waiting for you."

Bob looked at Jim in surprise, "Hey, wait a minute, we had no way of knowing how long it would take."

Jim started the engine without another word and took them back to the boat. Then he zoomed away with the dinghy.

"Whoa," remarked Betty, "who's working for who?"

Bob got up early the next morning, he knew he had to take the money to the customs office, or they would be asked to leave.

Opening the safe, he started to count the money. "Damn, I hate to give them all this money. Suppose something happens, and I need it before we leave the islands."

After breakfast, Bob called Jim, "Run us over to shore. We have to pay the insurance money to customs."

"Insurance money! What's that for?" asked Jim.

Putting a dig in Bob said, "I have to pay it so you and Martha can stay in the islands. You're an expensive crew, especially Martha. It's two thousand dollars for her to stay."

Jim scratched his head and said, "That's a lot of money."

"Take us over to the shore," said Bob. "When you finish your work, you and Martha can go off. Leave the dinghy tied up at the pier for us."

Jim climbed into the dinghy. "Whoa, the harbor is a little choppy today." The white caps were standing high in the harbor.

Bob and Betty climbed into the swerving dinghy. "The guy on the next boat told me about a short-cut to town," said Bob pointing across the way. "Drop us off at that large rock over there."

Jim steered the dinghy close to a huge flat boulder. It was almost covered with water. Betty looked in fright at the choppy waves washing over the rock. "There's no way we can get off here, it's too rough."

Bob stood up in the dinghy, "It's a piece of cake. Get closer, Jim and we'll jump off."

Jim maneuvered the rubber dinghy close to the rock. With each rush of the waves, the boat swept sideways. It bashed against the rock, almost washing up on top of the boulder.

Betty cringed. "I can't do it, I'll fall in the water."

"No you won't, watch me." The boat washed against the rock jarring everyone in it. Bob jumped off and slipped, one foot went into the water. He did a balancing act on top of the rock, until he regained his footing.

"Jump! Jump now," said Bob, reaching his hand out to Betty.

Betty stood up and was barely able to keep her balance. The dinghy kept slamming into the rock. She leaned over ready to jump but hesitated.

Jim was white as a sheet, "If you're going to jump, do it fast. I can't hold this thing much longer. I'm afraid it's going to overturn."

Bob reached over and grabbed her arm, pulling her towards him as she jumped off. She lost her balance and fell on her knees, drenching her slacks. Jim backed the dinghy off immediately, eager to get away from the crashing waves.

Carefully they made their way off the wet rock, their pants and shoes dripping wet.

Betty was shook up and mad. "Damn you and your crazy ideas. Now where do we go?"

"We're going just behind these bushes. There's a long flight of steps that will take us up to the road and close to town," said Bob, leading the way.

As they walked through the thick, tangled trees, the branches pulled at her hair. When they stepped out from the bushes, Betty gasped. "There's no steps! There's no way to get up to the road from here. There's only fallen trees and tangled vines."

Bob hoisted himself up on the trunk of a fallen tree. "Look, the fallen trees are crisscrossed and form a ladder up to the top. We'll climb up."

Betty couldn't believe what he was saying. "Are you crazy! That's a darn steep hill. I can't do it . . . I won't do it."

She ran back to the rock and she spotted Jim out on the water. She called and waved to him but it was useless. He couldn't hear her against the wind.

"Come on, it won't be that tough. You're stuck here now, so you might as well give it a try."

Betty was furious. "You get me into the damnedest toughest situations. Sometimes I think I hate you." She stood there fuming, watching Bob climb up the fallen trees. He used the trunks like rungs on a ladder. It looked pretty risky to her. There was no other way out, she had to try. Finally she conjured up enough nerve and started to climbed with caution. She held tightly to each vine and tree. Betty talked to herself to keep her courage up. She mumbled a few cuss words at Bob for thinking up this fool idea.

As she climbed the fallen trees, mud clung to her clothes and branches scratched her arms. Her shoes were soaked and weeds hung from her wet pants.

Betty was completely exhausted when they reached the top. "Tell me again why we had to take this so-called short-cut?"

Bob brushed his clothes off and said. "It cuts at least three-quarters of an hour off our walk."

"What about the twenty-five minutes it took to climb this cliff? Have you considered the risk-factor of possibly breaking our necks."

"Don't bother me with such details," laughed Bob. "We made it, didn't we?"

A man was watching them from across the road. He walked over and pointed just a short distance away, "Why didn't you take the stairs?" he asked.

Betty could see in the distance the path leading to the stairs. "I could kill you, Bob Godfrey. We got off the dinghy at the wrong place."

Bob laughed, "Never mind the threats. Come on, we have to get to town before noon."

They reached the customs office barely before noon, and Bob grudgingly paid the bond money and obtained a receipt.

"You are free to explore the Marquesas Islands. Please enjoy our country," said the officer.

The next few weeks were spent island hopping to places where the names were hard to pronounce. *Hiva Oa, Fatu Hiva, Ua Pu, Ua Nuku* and finally, *Nuku Hiva*. They explored and savored each one. The final island they stopped at was Nuku Hiva, the largest and most populated island of the Marquesas. The harbor was larger than the others, and there were more boats here than they had seen in a long time.

It was the Fourth of July, and the *Destiny* group decided to celebrate. "We have fire-crackers that we bought in St. Thomas. All we need is some beer and liquor," said Bob.

As they looked at the prices, Bob whistled and shouted, "Forty-two dollars for a quart of Smirnoff® vodka, fifty-six dollars for a fifth of some unknown scotch?"

"We can really do without it and just have beer," said Betty. "Whoa, beer is thirty-five dollars a case!"

"If we're going to celebrate, we might as well do it right," said Bob pulling out his wallet.

Hanz's boat *Eva*, was in the harbor. They decided to invite them to the party. Jim grilled the steaks and potatoes while Martha rustled up a salad. They celebrated the Fourth like it was New Year's Eve, everybody drank a bit more than they should have. They sat on deck telling sea-stories, laughing and joking at the many happenings. *Destiny* gently swayed back and forth in the cool breeze, creating ripples in the still water. Soon the moon and stars came out and the fire crackers filled the air with colorful sparkles. Hanz was filling his glass with scotch and gulping it down in one mouthful. The bottle was almost empty.

"Hanz, are you getting plastered?" Betty asked, as she watched him dribble his drink down his shirt.

"Are you kidding me, I'm a man of the sea," Hanz said, as he thumped his chest and slurred his words. "I can handle the seas, my we-man and my . . . (hiccup) . . . booze."

He staggered against Betty as she said, "Sure, Hanz. I heard that one before. Hey guys, you better take your Captain back to the boat. I think he's far gone."

Grabbing Hanz's arms his crew guided him to the stern ladder. Hanz shook himself free and said, "Thash okay. I can make it on my own."

Tom, his crewman, stood in their dinghy and held onto *Destiny*. The other crew man helped Hanz make his way down the ladder. He missed a step and landed in the water, disappearing completely.

They waited for him to surface. "He's not coming up. Where is he?" asked Martha.

After a few seconds, Hanz's head shot out of the water. He laughed as water sprouted from his mouth.

"Get in this boat," shouted Tom as he tried to pull him over the edge of the rubber dinghy. Hanz stayed in the water with a big smile on his face.

"Come on," said Tom. "What's the matter with you? Why aren't you helping us?"

Hanz sputtered more water as he said, "Cause ... Ahhh ... I'm taking a pee."

Loosing their patience, they started to holler, "Get the fuck in the boat, Hanz, or we're leaving you."

This time, Hanz was more cooperative and he helped as they yanked him in the dinghy.

Everyone was suffering from a hangover in the morning and they laid around most of the day.

After breakfast, Bob yawned, "Hey Betty, let's take the dinghy ashore. We can walk around the island. I need the exercise."

As they walked along the country road, they came to a shanty surrounded by a marvelous vegetable garden.

The owner was weeding as Betty asked. "Can we buy some of your vegetables?"

"Sure, tell me what you want." The man picked everything Betty pointed to. Then he put the large variety of fruit and vegetables in a palm basket for her.

"How much do I owe you?" asked Bob.

He was amazed when the farmer said, "Five dollars pays for everything."

They walked across the street to a banana plantation. A lovely French woman was in the field cutting back the weeds. She was wearing a flowery piece of material with bursts of orange, blue, and purple colors. The material was tied tightly across her breasts and draped down her body in folds. She spoke to them in French until they asked for bananas. Then she answered in perfect English.

The woman picked up a sharp machete and whacked off a large stalk. It had at least six dozen bananas on it. "Three dollars please," she said.

Loaded down with their bounty, they made their way back to the dinghy. The tide had gone out and their craft was high and dry on the beach. They piled the food in the corner of dinghy, putting the bananas on top. Then they started to pull the dinghy towards the water, and noticed a man sitting on the wall. He was built like a wrestler, and he had a bottle of vodka in his hand. He started to wave his arms in the air, and then he staggered over to them. They could see he was drunk and tried to ignore him. The man grabbed the dinghy and started pulling it back up the beach, as he grumbled in French.

"*Non, Non,*" Bob yelled as they tried to pull it away from the hefty man.

The drunken fool continued to pull the dinghy. His massive arms almost covered the stern. Sweat covered his dirty body and he bumped against Betty, almost knocking her over.

"*Non, Non,*" Betty yelled this time.

Bob and the wrestler had a tug of war, pulling the dinghy in both directions. Betty could feel the anger rising in her. She was seething as she grabbed the drunk's arm and pulled with all her might. She was hoping he would lose his balance and fall. The drunk looked at her and laughed. Then he screamed in her face, his whiskey spittle spraying all over her. His hand shot out and grabbed the bananas from the boat.

"Stop! No," Betty yelled, and grabbed the bananas back. He reached around her and grabbed them back again.

Losing all thought and control, Betty shook her finger in his face and started to holler. Saying all the angry thoughts that came in her head. The drunk stopped and stared at her, confusion glaring in his eyes. He stood motionlessly trying to understand what she was saying.

Bob took advantage of the opportunity and pulled the boat to the water's edge. Seeing the drunk's confusion, Betty grabbed the bananas and ran to the dinghy. They motored away as the big brute stood up to his waist in the deep water. He was yelling at the top of his lungs, shaking his fist high in the air.

Betty was breathless. "Good God, that was frightening. What was he trying to do?"

"Damned if I know. I'm just glad we got away."

*   *   *

They were ready to leave the beautiful Marquesas islands, the only thing holding them up was customs. It was ten o'clock in the morning when customs finally arrived to return their guns and money. No sooner had they left the tranquil harbor when the wind was there to beat on *Destiny*.

"No, not again," said Betty dreading the strong winds.

Bob looked at the wind gauge, "Twenty knots, and we're not even out at sea. Let's stop at the end of the island. There's suppose to be a great hiking place there," said Bob. "Hanz was telling me about it."

"Are you sure it's not like that short-cut we took before?" laughed Betty.

Bob couldn't help laughing too. "Don't remind me. No really, the hike's even in the Pacific guidebook. They say it takes three hours and it's incredible."

Jim rubbed his hands together, "I'm for that. I'm always ready for a challenge."

The sail to the north end of the island was supposed to be just a half-hour. With the winds against them, it took two hours. Anchored in a little cove out of the wind, they took the dinghy ashore. Their first sight as they reached the shore was a magnificent waterfall tumbling down a mountainside. The cascading crystalline water flowed on to the beach, making its way into the ocean.

"If this is what the hike is going to be like, it will be worth it," remarked Betty.

Jim was checking the place out. "Hey Bob, there's a stream

back here. I'm not sure how far it goes. If we pull the dinghy over the sand bar we can paddle it up stream. It's not deep enough to use the motor."

"Sounds good Jim, come on girls, give us a hand."

The pulled the dinghy upstream until it was deep enough to float. Then they paddled up the stream to a dilapidated shack. Outside, an old wrinkled man and woman were knee-deep in the water, spreading their fishing nets.

"Hello," they called out. "Would you like a cold drink?"

"No, thank you," said Bob. "Could you tell us how to get to the big waterfall?"

The old man pointed to a trail just barely visible through the palm trees. "It's over there but its too late to go for a trek now. You have to go early morning. It's a rough trail and takes a long time."

"Bob, maybe we should wait and go in the morning," said Betty ready to go back to *Destiny*. "He must know what he's talking about."

"Nah, we can make it. It's only four miles," said Bob walking on.

Waving goodbye they followed the trail that was heavy with palm trees. It grew denser as they walked on.

After twenty minutes, Bob said, "This doesn't look right. This is not a trail. We've missed it somehow."

Veering to the right, they came upon a woman gathering coconuts. "I think we're in a copra field," said Jim. Then he asked the woman, "Could you tell us how we get to the waterfall?"

"Don't go up there now," she answered waving her hands in the air. "It's too late, and very dangerous. There's gonna be heavy rain."

"Maybe they're right. Maybe we should go back," said Martha.

Bob was confident, "Listen, with the speed we walk it will take us no time. We'll be up and back way before sunset."

"I don't really want to go," said Betty. "It doesn't sound safe to go up this late. That's the second person that told us not to go."

"You can come or stay here, but I'm going," said Bob as he walked ahead.

Betty thought a minute. She didn't know how she'd get back

to the boat by herself. Against her better judgment, she went along with them. The dry terrain was turning to mud, and soon they were ankle deep in slimy muck.

"Whose crazy idea was this," Betty asked as the mud squished down in her shoes.

"Sure as hell wasn't mine," Martha answered. "Crimey, it's bea-u-ti-ful in here, but I'm not sure it's worth it."

They traveled on and crossed a rocky, ankle-deep stream. It snaked along the disappearing trail. The deeper they went, the rougher the trail got. Unsure of where they were going, they trudged on. The trail was marked with piles of rocks, and they became their landmarks. Soon there were no markers and no trail. Only a mass of trees surrounded them.

"Jim, you go off to your right and I'll try my left. See if we can find the trail," said Bob.

"Martha and I will stay here and wait for you. That way we won't get separated," said Betty.

"No, I'm going with Jim," said Martha, running after him.

Betty stood there alone and waited. It seemed like hours before she heard Jim holler. "I found the trail."

"Jim's found the trail, Bob. Come on back," yelled Betty as loud as she could. There was no answer. Waiting for a while she called again, but still no answer.

"What's keeping you?" Jim yelled. "We're going to walk ahead."

"Don't go yet," screamed Betty. "Stay where you are, Bob's not back yet."

Waiting for Bob was driving her crazy. As time passed, she visualized him falling in a deep hole, hurt and bleeding. Then she heard the crackle of twigs. She looked to her right as Bob came walking towards her.

"Oh my God, I'm so glad you're safe. What took you so long?" she said hugging him.

"Damn, It's thick in there. I almost lost my way. Oh no, it's raining." They ran to catch up with the others, then continued on.

The trail was a mass of fallen trees. The path was full of rocks covered with slippery mud. They had to go slower than planned because of the obstacles on the trail. Despite the diffi-

276

culties, the forest was breathtakingly beautiful, peaceful and tranquil. A little farther up they saw the tip of the waterfall. The panoramic view of thick tropical foliage was spell binding. Their first glimpse of the waterfall was astounding. The misty rain made the scent of the tropical flowers more noticeable.

They crossed two streams, one knee-deep and one ankle-deep, and stepped carefully on the slick rocks beneath the water. The drizzle continued covering them with a wet coating as they walked for two and a half hours. When they reached the magnificent falls, they let out a shout of joy. Beneath the falls was a bather's paradise. The roar of the water was overwhelming as it poured down the mountain. It threw off a misty spray that bathed them in cool moisture.

"Last one in is a ninny. I'm going in with my knickers on," said Martha gleefully. She ran and plunged into the water. "Ah, this feels won-der-ful."

"I'm in," said Jim, following her. "Come on, Betty, what are you waiting for?"

Betty started toward the water, but Bob stopped her, "We've got to start back right now,"

There was urgency in his voice. "We have no time for a swim," yelled Bob. "Come on get out."

"We just got here. Can't we take a swim and rest awhile?" asked Betty.

"We have to get back before sunset," said Bob looking at his watch. "It'll be too dark to find our way out once the sun goes down. If we leave right now, we'll make it."

As they started back, the light rain became a heavy deluge, the streams had overflowed.

The trails were distorted and they couldn't find their way, and couldn't afford the time to be lost.

"Whoa," said Jim, surprised by the depth and current of the water. "This can't be the stream we crossed? It's thigh-high."

"It's the right one. I'll go in the water first and test it out," said Bob.

He walked into what seemed like a roaring river. The force almost swept him off his feet. Stumbling and sliding on the rocky bottom, he came back on the shore. "We've got to figure out a safe way to cross." Bob thought for a while then said, "We'll hold hands and make a human chain. That way we can support and help each other."

They grabbed each other's hands and stepped into the water sideways. That way the current wouldn't pull them off their feet. Slowly they made their way across in the torrential water as they supported and braced each other. The rocks were slippery and jagged under the water as they stumbled along.

"Wait!" Martha shouted. "My freaken foot is caught."

She wiggled her foot free, then continued the slow pace across the swollen stream.

"We made it," said Bob as he rushed ahead. "Lets hurry. It will be pitch black in here once the sun goes down. Then we'll never find our way out."

As they hurried along the trail, Martha slipped on the muddy rocks. She fell head first in the mud, scraping her face on the hidden rocks.

"Are you all right?' Betty said, stopping and going back for her. "Give me your hand I'll help you up," she said, as she wiped the mud and blood from Martha's face. "Come on, we have to catch up to the men or we won't find them."

Betty hurried along the trail until she slipped on a pile of rocks. Her feet went out from under her and she fell, bruising her arm and leg. "For God's sake Bob, stop walking so fast, we can't keep up with you. I'm never going hiking with you again." Then she looked at the river ahead. "Wait a minute, we never crossed water that deep."

"That used to be a stream. We're going in the right direction," said Bob.

"It can't be the same stream we crossed earlier, it was only ankle deep. This one's past my hips and it's like white water," said Betty, worried about crossing.

Jim was studying the stream. "I know it's the same stream. I'm just not sure we can cross it. It looks pretty treacherous."

They surveyed the terrain while standing under a tree for shelter, each trying to figure the safest way to cross the rapid waters. White water flowed down the banks with torrent force, swirling angrily around the jagged rocks

"There's some rock heads sticking out of the water," said

Jim. "They go almost all the way across. Maybe we can get over by hanging onto the rocks as we walk through the water to the other side."

"It's worth trying, let's hope it works," Bob said feeling nervous about the whole situation.

"I'll go first this time," Jim said as he stepped in and grabbed the first rock. Bent over, he edged across grasping each rock. His feet slipped occasionally but he kept his balance.

"It sure doesn't look easy," said Martha.

Once he was onshore, Betty stepped cautiously into the rough current, grabbing the rocks one by one as she inched across. Nervous and unsure of herself she stepped slowly, feeling for hidden rocks with her foot before she put it down. When she reached the half-way mark, she began to feel confident. Then one of her hands slipped off the rock and she lost her balance. The current swept her off her feet. Betty's chest hit a submerged rock, and she was stunned for a moment. She could see the wild force of the cauldron water surrounding her. It was pulling her, stretching her straight out into the white whirling water. Her other hand held fast on the ragged rock that was slicing at Betty's fingers. Water washed over her body in a steady stream, pulling her shirt from her shoulders. "My arm's getting tired. I don't know if I can hold on much longer!" she shouted.

"Try to reach for another rock with your free hand," yelled Bob.

She lunged forward with her last bit of strength. Betty sighed with relief as her fingers wrapped around the rock. She forced her legs down and tried to stand. Her feet kept sliding off the rocks that lay hidden on the bottom. Wedging her foot between two of the rocks, Betty regained her footing.

As she grabbed each rock, she forced herself to continue across. "Please God, don't let me get swept away."

Jim stepped into the water and held out his arm encouraging her on.

When she was close enough, he pulled her safely to shore. "Here, sit on the rock and rest while I help the others."

"Going white-water rafting without a raft is not my idea of fun," said Betty breathlessly. Jim reached out to help the others when they were near the shore.

"We can't afford to rest. We have to get out of the forest before the sun sets," said Bob puffing from exertion.

They could see the sun getting lower in the sky as they rushed on. "That looks like the trail we started on," said Jim, excited.

"It is, there's the old ladies' shack," shouted Martha with glee.

As they stepped out of the jungle into the clearing, the darkness surrounded them. It was like some one turned off the light switch when they took their final steps. Tired and bruised, they headed to the dinghy, and pushed off in the total blackness.

Destiny was a welcome haven. Their bones ached. They were all looking forward to going to bed.

Twenty-four

Destiny left for the Tuamotu Islands. As soon as they were out of the harbor, they were met with thirty-knot winds. The sails were stretched to their fullest as large swells splash against *Destiny's* hull. The boat rocked harshly from side to side, and they wondered where the gentle trade winds were.

"Here we go again," shouted Betty over the wind.

Their speed was tremendous as they made faster time than expected.

Betty held on tight as *Destiny* heeled over. "With this wind, we should make it in three days instead of four."

"Jim, reef the sails, we've got to slow this boat down. No point in getting there in the middle of the night."

Jim reefed the sails as he said, "Why? The sooner the better, as far as I'm concerned."

"Come here, I'll show you why." Bob ran his fingers along the chart. "The Tuamotu Islands are flat coral. See the jagged edges extending way out? It's tough enough to spot the jagged edges in daylight. At night, it's about impossible. The passage into the harbor is too dangerous to go through in the dark."

Arriving in three days, they pulled into the harbor of Rangiora at about eight in the morning. They were greeted by the sight of a lavish resort hotel.

Betty couldn't believe her eyes. "Look at the grass huts. This looks like a sailor's dream. Pinch me—I want to make sure I'm awake."

They anchored off the hotel beach and walked the white sandy shore. Languishing by the pool, they sipped delicious banana daiquiris. Management more than welcomed them as they made reservations for dinner.

"This is great. We can use their facilities and sleep on board," said Bob.

"Good heavens, look at this brochure! The bloody rooms are five hundred and fifty dollars a day, and that don't include eats," Martha said. Smacking the side of her head, she continued, "How can any bloody person afford it?"

"A lot of people can," said Bob as he stood up and stretched. "I'm going back to *Destiny* for a well-deserved nap."

That night, Betty dressed up for dinner. She wore slacks, and a halter top with a light shirt jacket of royal blue and white. Curling her hair with hot rollers, she put on makeup for the first time in weeks.

"What a change, you look like Betty instead of the sea witch," Bob said, as he looked her over. "Wow, you look pretty nice."

The four of them went for cocktails, then enjoyed a fabulous dinner. They served chicken marinated with brandy and island spices and a banana sauce.

"These sweet potatoes are something else," said Jim. "They have some kind of a pineapple dressing on them."

"I'm saving room for the French pastries," said Martha. "They look yummy."

They listened to the magical music of the electric guitars and glowed from the atmosphere and the wine. It was a great reprieve from life at sea.

"Well, Betty, are you ready to go back to the boat?" asked Bob.

"No, let's take a walk." She took his hand and they walked out to the moonlit beach, and wadded in the warm ocean water. "Doesn't this remind you a little of our walk in Ft. Lauderdale?"

"Betty, this doesn't look the least bit like Ft. Lauderdale, Florida."

"God, you really are seaweary. I mean the night of our first date—you know, our first walk on the beach."

"Oh that, oh—yeah, it was a night like this," he said laughing.

"What happened to the loverboy I use to know? Here I'm trying to be romantic and you're an old frump," Betty said, as she left him and ran up the beach.

Bob ran after her and grabbed her arm. He kissed her long and hard. "Is that a kiss of an old frump?"

"I'm not sure," she said rubbing her lips together. "You'll have to do it again."

He kissed her again more passionately this time. "Well now, maybe I woke the old frump up."

They walked farther up the lonely stretch of beach, the moon and stars their only light. Bob pulled her over to a white woven hammock that was swaying in the soothing breeze. They laid in the hammock, swaying under the palm trees. The moonlight embraced them with its magic light. They forgot everything except their cravings for each other.

Betty woke at six in the morning to the sound of splashing water. She looked through the portholes to see where it was coming from. Fish were jumping out of the turquoise, translucent water of the beautiful lagoon. Fascinated, she watched as the large fish tried to catch their breakfast while the little fish jumped high in the air so they wouldn't be eaten. Betty made coffee and took a cup up to the upper deck. She was taken back by the indescribable beauty and serenity.

White sand and palm trees were everywhere, surrounded by crystalline water. It was as blue as she'd ever seen. The pure clean air opened her mind to the freshness of the morning. The scent of dew-kissed flowers wafted through the air.

Off in the distance, she could see a ship entering the harbor. "*Eva's* sailing into the harbor," Betty shouted down below.

Bob came on deck and called out, "Hey *Eva*, glad to see you made it."

Eva anchored nearby and Hanz came over to visit. "Would you like to go diving?"

"Sure would," said Bob, "I hear the best place to dive is in the passage of the lagoon. An hour after the incoming tide, the water rushes through the passage at five knots. They say it's an incredible dive. The current is fast and it's full of fish."

"Then let's do it. It's incoming tide now and by the time we get our equipment and get over there, it will be perfect timing," said Hanz.

Decked out in their scuba gear, Jim, Bob, Betty, Stan and Martha took the dingy to the mouth of the lagoon. Everyone but Martha jumped in, descending as quickly as possible. Martha stayed in the dinghy and would drift through the passage. She'd pick everyone up inside the lagoon when they surfaced.

They drifted along weightlessly in the cooling water. It gave them the feeling of being in outerspace. Like astronauts, they floated swiftly along sixty feet below the surface. Manta rays with a wing span of twelve feet swept by them completely unconcerned. Three feet away, a six-foot reef shark was pulled along with them. Betty froze for a minute, not knowing what to do. Then realizing he was not interested in her, she relaxed, and let her boggled mind enjoy the experience.

Moving along at uncontrollable speed, Betty wondered if everyone was all right. She grabbed a piece of coral and her body swung around like a flag on a staff. Jim was bouncing off the bottom into an upward somersault in the fast moving water.

On the surface, Martha was drifting at the same speed. In an hour, they were through the pass and surfaced right by her. They enjoyed the dive so much they did it four days in a row.

On the fourth dive, as always, they checked each other's equipment before going down. This time, someone accidentally turned Betty's air off and she didn't know it. She had descended down to thirty feet and had been breathing slowly. Suddenly there was no air coming through her regulator. She kicked ferociously to get to the top. Then she swam against the strong tidal current toward the dinghy. There was no air to inflate her vest, and she couldn't reach the valve on her tank.

Martha was floating towards her and called out, "What's the problem."

Betty reached for the rope on the side of the dinghy. She was puffing from the exertion as she said, "Turn my air on."

Martha leaned over and turned the valve. After taking a few breaths to make sure the air was flowing freely she sank into the depth. Her buddies were all hanging out waiting for her, their bodies waving like human flags.

Rangiora is the largest atoll of the Tuamotus and people live mainly from the copra fields. With a population of only a thousand, it is very secluded, clean and friendly. Scrumptious French bread was baked fresh each day, and the smell was luscious. There were a few small stores scattered here and there, with only bare necessities.

The hotel arranged a barbecue and boat tour for their guests, and the group from *Destiny* and *Eva*. They went by speedboat to a secluded island about twenty miles away.

"We're taking you out to snorkel, and you can watch while we feed the sharks."

"Feed the sharks?" everyone said in unison.

"Hope we're not the food for the sharks," said a very fat gentleman in the group.

"No, but you'd make a mighty good meal for them," laughed someone in the crowd.

When the motor boats stopped, sharks seemed to come from all directions. They swam around the two boats as they anchored. The sharks knew they were going to be fed.

"Don't be afraid, they won't hurt you. Put your snorkel gear on and jump in the water. Follow me," the guide said getting in first.

Betty grabbed Bob's hand. "I don't want to be shark food. Let the others go in first."

"Come on, there's nothing to be afraid of," said the guides.

"Easy for you to say," Betty joked back and finally jumped in.

The group of snorkelers swam behind the guides while the eight sharks circled around them. The group hovered on top of the water, watching through their masks. As each guide speared a fish, he held it out to the sharks. One by one, the sharks tore viciously at the fish on the spear.

Feeling uncomfortable and apprehensive, Betty asked, "What if they want to try one of us for dessert?" No one answered or laughed. Then she climbed on a huge piece of coral to get partway out of the water, "If there is a grab for dessert, I don't want to be it."

When the guides stopped spearing the fish, the sharks started to swim away.

"Everybody back to the boat," said the guides.

Betty looked over at Bob and said, "I'll race you back to the boat," and she swam swiftly ahead.

"Slow down, Betty," called Bob. "I want to get a picture of this big shark."

He held his yellow underwater Nikon to his eye, and snapped away. The shark swam slowly toward him when it saw the yellow camera. The shark must have thought Bob had a fish and was getting too near for comfort.

When Betty saw what was happening, she yelled with fear in her voice, "Bob, put your camera down. The shark thinks you're holding a fish. Put it away."

"Good lord," Bob said looking up. "I wondered why the shark appeared so close."

Tucking the camera in his swim trunks, he swam towards Betty. The shark stayed still for a second before swimming away.

"Man, that will be a story to tell when we get home," said Bob.

"Hey, I'm glad you'll be alive to tell it," Betty said, laughing with relief.

Twenty-five

The weather gave them a break and *Destiny* sailed on to Tahiti in a fast two days. The strong wind was behind them all the way. They pulled into the marina in the heart of Papeete. Noisy civilization hit them smack in the face. They had been in quiet, serene unpolluted areas for months. Definitely not used to the heavy traffic that was rushing by their stern-to slip. The foul smelling pollution lay heavily in the air. Horns blasted away as if in celebration of their arrival, and trash littered the streets.

"This is not what I expected," Bob said, saddened at what he saw.

"Blimey, this is Tahiti? It's not much to look at," said Martha.

Busy shops and restaurants lined the streets and a carnival was going full swing. People were rushing around like New Yorkers. They stayed just long enough to clear customs. Then, they motored off to a small harbor called Maeua Bay.

It was more the type of surroundings they had grown accustomed to. Bob found an anchoring spot in front of another luxurious resort. Just like before they went ashore to enjoy the facilities.

As they walked into the lobby, Betty spotted a National Car Rental office. "Let's rent a car and go see the real Tahiti," she said gleefully.

"Okay, but let's check with Jim and Martha—see if they want to go with us," said Bob.

"They sure have been acting odd lately. It seems like they want to stay by themselves, but sure, lets ask them."

Martha and Jim were already gone when they got back to the boat.

"It's just as well. It will feel nice to be off on our own," said Betty putting on her bathingsuit. "I'll make a couple sandwiches to take with us."

Driving through the tranquil part of Tahiti, the green plush foliage covered the dark rich soil. They stopped at a path that led into a forest of ferns, red ginger, and birds of paradise. "Want to take a hike and see where this leads to?" asked Bob.

Betty laughed and said, "Sure, as long as it isn't anything like the last hike." They started down the path and Betty said, "This is what I dreamt Tahiti would look like."

Walking for an hour, they were surrounded by all the tropical plants people paid so much money for at home. They could hear the roaring of a waterfall and soon came upon a tremendous one. Big rocks surrounded the pool of water under the falls. Pretty tan-skinned children giggled and splashed in the water. They watched teenagers dive from the high sides of the falls into the cooling waters.

"Lets go in," Betty said, not waiting for an answer.

The water was wondrously cool and invigorating as they swam around. They sat under the falls letting the water massage their backs and shoulders as it cascaded down the rocks.

After a while, they laid down on the large rocks that compassed the pool. They dried themselves in the afternoon sun. After a lush week in Tahiti, they continued on to their next spot of paradise.

Cook Harbor in Moorea was a lush island with astounding beauty. They lowered their anchor in front of the Bali Ha'i Hotel. After lunch, they rented scooters and drove the island in search of adventure. The only adventure they had was getting a flat tire. Then, they ran out of gas followed by the scooter breaking down completely. To ease their frustration, they relaxed by the pool and sipped Pina Coladas.

The next few days, they island hopped to Huahina, just an overnight trip. Then *Destiny* went on to Raiatea, just five hours away. These islands were not as lovely as the others but still interesting in a placid way.

They were eager to get to Bora Bora and motored out of Raiatea harbor. Suddenly, they felt a heavy thud and heard a loud swishing sound.

Falling sideways against the helm from the unexpected collision, Betty yelled, "What was that?"

"Good Lord," said Bob. "Look at the size of that whale. He's almost as big as *Destiny*."

Along their portside was an immense gray whale that had rammed into the boat. It had surfaced and was spouting water from his blowhole. Its mammoth body was close enough to touch. The whale laid in one spot for twenty minutes, startled as much as they were.

"I wonder if he's hurt?" asked Betty. The whale breached just as she spoke, then surfaced again behind them. The whale lay basking in the sun as *Destiny* continued on.

"I'm not sure who was scared the most. What an awesome sight," Martha said staring back at the superb creature.

"Let's be thankful he didn't damage the boat," said Jim.

"He could have killed himself," Betty added, still awed by the whale.

Jim and Martha were inseparable at this point, and were off by themselves as often as possible. They no longer hid the fact that they were sleeping together.

As they were sailing towards Bora Bora, Jim sat with Bob and talked about his future, "What I'd like to do someday is be Captain of a charter boat. I love life at sea. This is me."

"There's a lot more to sailing when your doing it as a career, a lot more responsibility. The first thing you need to do is log your sailing hours. When you have enough hours, you can apply for your captain's license. Keep a logbook and I'll sign it when we've finished the trip."

"I've been keeping track of them. I've learned a lot from you about navigation. Yep, I think I'd like to do that," said Jim dreamy-eyed.

"Well maybe when we've finished this trip I'll set you up in business. I'll turn *Destiny* over to you as a starter. We can see what happens from there," said Bob.

Jim was surprised when Bob said that. Betty could see the admiration and respect he felt for him. Sitting there listening, she thought, *I only hope Martha doesn't pull him too far away and break this bond.*

They reached Bora Bora in three hours. Repeating their pattern, they anchored in front of another hotel, nothing as luxurious as the last few. The island did not impress them—it was rundown and unkempt. Several of the big chain hotels were boarded up.

Bob was anxious to see the artillery World War II memorabilia on the island. He rented a car and the two of them drove for miles. They looked everywhere for the military artillery. When they asked the natives where they could find the artillery, most of them just looked at them strangely. They were too young to know or remember. They continued to search and found some cannons rusting away and overgrown with weeds.

"Looks like they want to forget the past. They are leaving what's left of the memories to rot away," Betty said, as she climbed a hill to look at the view. "Look, there's Mount Pahia. Let's climb it. It doesn't look that high."

"It is a great day for a hike and it's still early," said Bob. "I'll check the South Seas handbook and see what they say about it." Bob took the book from the car, "It's only four hours round trip and they say it's not difficult."

"Good, then we won't have to go back to the boat and change. Our shorts and T-shirts we have on should do fine," said Betty, pulling on her hiking boots.

For a while, the climb was fairly easy and gradual. They were walking among incredible surroundings. The scenery was like watching a jungle movie. Colorful birds of all descriptions flew low through the trees, shrieking loud calls to each other. Flowering bushes and trees were scattered everywhere, their fragrance like an expensive perfume.

"It's starting to drizzle. Do you want to go back?" asked Bob.

"No, the drizzle feels good, it's cooling me off. Besides, it's so pretty out here. Lets keep going. We've come this far, might as well make it to the top."

The closer they got to the top, the more difficult the terrain became. They had to kick holes into the dirt to make foot holds. They grabbed roots to boost themselves up the side of the mountain.

"This last part is almost straight up. How far would you say it is to the top?" Betty asked, as they pulled and tugged their way up.

"It's only about a half a mile, not too far. Looks like someone dug steps in the dirt wall here. That will help make it easier," said Bob tugging away.

"I hate to think about coming down this thing later," said Betty, finally making it to the top. "Wow, what a fantastic view. I'm going to take pictures, but I don't think I'll capture the beauty."

Ominous clouds closed over the blue sky, misting over the fantastic scene. The drizzle turned into a heavy downpour.

"Shit," Bob said in disgust. "We better start down. This looks like it could get pretty nasty."

"I have to rest before I go back down, I'm dead tired. I didn't expect the trip to be this tough," said Betty still panting.

"Sorry, we have to go, or we might not get down. Look, the sides are washing away." "Damn, why does it always have to rain on every fantastic hike? How do we always get into these situations?" Betty screamed.

Going down looked extremely difficult. The side of the bank had become slick mud and the foot holds were washed away.

Betty stared at the earth turning into mud, as it washed down the bank, "Oh my God, how are we going to get down?"

"There's some long vines hanging almost all the way down," said Bob. "We can grab one and slide down gradually.

"What! Are you kidding?" Betty asked as she stared at the vines.

Bob had a hold on one of the vines. He tugged hard on it to make sure it was secure. "Hold the vine in one hand and keep it between your knees," he said. "Keep your stomach toward the wall. Use the roots that are sticking out as a hand and foot hold."

"I can't do that. I'll slip in that muddy mess," said Betty.

"Do you have any better suggestions? We have to get down," Bob said as he started down the long six-foot vine. "Just follow me and do as I do."

Betty watched him as he slid off. He had gripped the vine with one hand and also held it between his knees. The other hand he used to grab the roots as he dug in with his toes.

Mustering up as much courage as she could, she took the plunge. She grabbed a vine and slid off. "I feel like I'm in a Tarzan movie. Me Jane, you Tarzan. Tarzan carry Jane and swing on vines?" Betty said trying to ease her tension.

"Yeah, me Tarzan, all right. Tarzan scared shitless. Jane swing on own vine," Bob laughed.

They lowered themselves at a snail's pace as they grabbed roots. While they worked their way down, Betty talked to herself, *Please little root be strong enough to hold me. I don't want to fall. Nice root, good vine don't pull out.* She grabbed each root and tested it before she put her full weight on it.

When she looked down at the straight immeasurable drop below her, she shuddered. Closing her eyes she murmured, "Please God, get us down safe. Please God, please God."

Slimy red mud covered them from head to toe as they slid gradually down. Betty was still talking to herself trying to keep her cool.

"What are you saying Betty? I can't hear you," Bob asked.

"I'm talking to the roots and vines. I'm not going crazy, I'm just trying to keep my sanity."

It seemed like forever before the treacherous half-mile was over. Now they were able to stand, but the rest would be far from easy. At least there was an occasional rock to help support them. Bob ran down at a faster pace, hopping over each slippery rock like a mountain goat. Betty was still unsure of herself and afraid she'd fall in the slippery mess. She sat down and rested for a while. Then putting her arms behind her and her legs stretched out, she bumped her way down on her bottom.

Bob started to laugh. "What kind of position is that? You look like a huge crab climbing down a hill."

"I may look funny, but this way, if I fall, I won't fall far," answered Betty. "Don't make fun of me."

The sun had just set as they made it to the bottom. They were completely covered with mud and barely able to move. Bruised and scratched, they limped towards their dock.

Jim was waiting for them. "I was going to send someone out to look for you, you were gone so long." Then he started to laugh, "My God, what happened to you? You're both a mess."

"Yeah, I look like a Philadelphia Bag Lady, I feel like one too. It's a long story that we'll tell you later."

"Will I ever learn not to believe those books? The four-hour trip took us six hours," said Bob.

292

After a few days, their aches and pains from the climb subsided. They began to feel rested again.

"If I'm not beating myself up sailing, I'm doing it hiking. Maybe I've becoming a masochist?" said Betty to Martha.

"Beats me why you do it," answered Martha, really not interested.

Rain and heavy winds continued for three days. They had to move *Destiny* to a sheltered cove for protection.

"It's impossible to leave in this weather, " said Bob looking at the weather fax. "We'll just hang in till the weather changes."

"Let's put on our rain gear and take the dinghy over to the marina," Betty said getting bored.

They took the skiff to the pier and the four of them went into a small bar. They were greeted by a few other yachtsmen who were passing time. Exchanging books and videos, they drank beer and told tales of the sea. Each one embellished their story with each beer, meeting each day to continue their stories until the weather cleared.

After three days of heavy monsoon rain, they woke to the welcome sight of the sun. It was shining brightly through the portholes.

Bob got up at five-thirty in the morning. "Get up, everyone," he said as he started the engine. "We have to be on our way."

"For heaven's sake Bob, can't you give me time to make breakfast?" Betty said, trying to wake up. "I'm still half-asleep."

"We can eat after we leave. It should be smooth enough for you to fix breakfast while we're sailing out of the harbor," said Bob, as he pounded on Jim's door. "Up and at em, I need you to handle the anchor. We only have time to stop at two islands on our way to New Zealand. Maupiti is the first one and it's five hours away," said Bob, running in high gear.

True to his word, five hours later, they were there, heading toward the entrance to the Maupiti lagoon, where he planned to anchor.

Bob looked at the entrance to the harbor. "The pass is not only narrow, it looks pretty treacherous and shallow." He slowed the boat down to a crawl, "Jim you go out on the bow. Betty, you

293

and Martha get on each side of the boat and help guide me in. Yell if you see any shallow water."

He started the approach. The cross currents caused the waves to pound on both sides. "It's hard to keep the boat on a straight course," yelled Bob.

"Look out, we're coming too close to the coral on starboard side," yelled Betty. The jagged edge stuck out like a spear. "Stop, we're almost crashing against it."

"Goddammit Betty, give me more notice than that," he said pulling to portside.

"Stop yelling at me. I would have told you sooner if I could. Look out, you're coming too close again, the current's taking you."

"Watch it, you're getting to close on portside," said Martha.

"How does it look out there, Jim? Is it clear of the coral?" asked Bob.

"Keep coming slowly," called Jim.

A welcoming voice came over the radio. "*Destiny*, this is *Dalcenia*, switch to channel eleven."

"*Dalcenia*, this is *Destiny* switching to channel eleven," answered Bob.

"Hi, *Destiny*, this is Roger from *Dalcenia*. I'm anchored in the harbor, can you see me?"

"There he is," Martha pointed at a forty-eight foot sailboat.

"Glad to see you, Roger," Bob answered, more confidence in his voice.

"I'll help guide you through the shoals. I can see the reefs better from here. It's a bitch of a pass to get through. The currents will wash you ashore if you get too close."

They breathed a sigh of relief when they dropped anchor off the beach. "Thanks for your help, Roger. I don't think we could have made it without you. Come over for a cold one later. We have ice aboard."

"Ice! You've got to be kidding, nobody has ice. We'll be over for sure."

The island was covered with palm trees and there was a ghostlike stillness around them. Betty looked around, "There's no one on this island. The houses are all empty. It doesn't look like anyone has lived here for a long time."

They walked closer to the vacant properties. "There's an

abandoned weather station," remarked Bob. "Wonder why they closed it?"

Betty's mouth dropped open when she saw the size of the crabs crawling all over. She called to Bob, "Come see these gigantic crabs, they must be twelve inches across. I don't believe the size of their right claw, it's enormous."

There were hundreds of the brown creatures, crawling in and out of large holes along the beach.

"I've never seen anything like them before," Bob said as he stooped down to get a closer look at one.

The crabs were ripping open the fallen coconuts and eating the meat.

"That's incredible. I sure wouldn't want them to get a hold of my fingers. They could chop it right off," said Betty. "This is an old copra plantation. I wonder why they abandoned it?"

Bob took her hand and continued to explore the island. Then he looked out at the water and said, "We'll have to leave early tomorrow at high tide, if we want to get out of here in one piece."

When they left the island, the wind gods blessed them with mild winds. They sailed one hundred and nine miles to the next destination. Entering the pass at the island of Mopelia was almost as treacherous as the last one. With the morning sun exposing the hidden coral, they made it with little difficulty. Several boats were in the harbor, all waving welcome. It felt like old home week. Mopelia was another copra plantation, but this one was active. It was occupied by five men and one woman.

Michael was the designated chief, a huge French Polynesian with a barrel chest. His thick black, greasy, hair stood straight up. Michael's clothes were dirty from days of wear. The powerful musk of his body permeated the air around him. From a distance his large boned face seemed to scowl, as his black eyes looked right through you. His eyes darted from side to side with a glassy look.

"He doesn't look too friendly, does he?" said Martha.

Jim turned and walked away. "Looks mean as hell to me."

When he approached, his eyes took on a friendly sparkle

that chased away the frightening feelings his appearance portrayed.

Putting his huge hands out in welcome, he said *"Bon jour, comment vous appelez vous?"*

"Parlez vous anglais?" Bob said.

"Petit," he said. Holding two fingers slightly apart and making a face. "Welcome, welcome. How long you—stay here?"

"We'll be here a couple of days, depends on the weather," said Bob shaking his hand.

"Good, then I take you lobster hunting, we meet after dark. You bring lights," said Michael, fumbling over his words.

"Lights?...Oh—you mean *flashlights*," said Jim. "Yeah, sure."

"You must. How you say...eh...shine light down. Then big lobster come and you swoop him up," Michael said using hand motion, as he spoke.

The group from *Dalcenia* was invited along. Following Michael's instructions they came away with fifteen lobsters. The group ended the night with a moonlight barbecue.

The beach that surrounded the island was lovely and the day was a sheer delight. The sun was so strong and bright it bleached the sand and shells to a Clorox® white. Strolling along, they stopped to collect shells. They rested on the beach mesmerized by the surf—as it rode over the ragged coral. A whiff of salty seaweed lingered in the air. Michael came by breaking the spell. He entertained them with stories of his many wives. Life was in limbo and Betty wanted this serenity to last forever.

Betty liked Michael; he had a great sense of humor. "Would you like to come to dinner tonight?"

"Oui, I like that. What time I come?"

"Why don't you come out to the boat at six?"

"Merci beaucoup. I will see you at six," he said, strutting off into the green mass of palm trees.

Michael arrived on time in a clean unpressed shirt. His hair was slicked back and shining. They could smell the aroma of soap—he had bathed for the occasion.

Handing Betty a large bucket, he said, "Here, I catch this big bugger for you. Dis is a coconut crab."

Betty looked into the bucket. "It's one of those monstrous crabs. Is it dead?"

"Dead? She is dead from my grill. I cooked it for you. Ze meat from dis crab is tout sweet," he said smacking his lips.

"*Merci beaucoup*," said Bob. "Can I get you a drink? How about a bourbon and water or gin and tonic?"

"*Oui, Oui.*"

"Eh!—which drink do you want?" Bob said, trying not to laugh, "bourbon or gin?"

"*Oui, oui.*" Then looking puzzled, he slapped Bob on the shoulder. "I take what you drink."

Bob brought him a bourbon and water. "Have a seat, Michael. Welcome to our floating home."

Michael took his first sip of the drink and his face cringed. "*Oui,*" he said as his eyes rolled round in his head.

"You don't have to drink that if you don't like it," laughed Betty, taking the glass from him.

"Ho, ho. Is powerful stuff you give me. What you call that?"

Bob laughed, "That's old Grand Dad. I'll bring you some wine."

"Wine would be better," he said with a twinkle in his eyes.

The evening was delightful and Michael ate whatever they served him, smelling the food before he ate it. He kept them laughing with his island stories. They said goodnight to Michael about midnight. When he left, Betty knew he would always be a special part of their memories.

Mornings were a reverie with the birds singing wake-up calls. They had just finished breakfast on deck when they received a call on the radio.

"*Destiny* this is Jeff from *Deseria*, want to do some diving?"

"We've been thinking about it. Michael told us about a good spot last night," said Bob.

"I'm not certified but I know how. I'd like to come along with you if you're going?"

Bob hesitated for a moment. "I hate like hell to take someone down that's not certified."

"I'll be fine. I've done it many times," said Jeff pleading.

"Okay. We'll pick you up in the dinghy in an hour."

They searched and found the clearing on the southside of the lagoon that Michael had told them about. The four of them—Bob, Betty, Jim and Jeff, donned their equipment.

"Stay close to us, Jeff. Don't go off on your own," said Bob, a little leery about taking him with them.

Descending to fifty feet, they found very little plant or sealife, but visibility was good. They were in the water for about twenty minutes when a six-foot blacktip shark appeared. He turned in their direction and followed them. Signaling each other, the divers gathered together for protection. Jeff was not there; he had wandered off and was far ahead.

Swimming at a faster pace, they caught up to Jeff and pointed towards the shark. Bob was worried about the shark and signaled for everyone to start back. Jeff seemed completely unaware of the shark or what Bob was trying to tell him. He went off on his own again.

Jeff swam off to the left, lengthening the distance between the other divers. Seeing this, the shark swam towards him. A dreaded feeling came over the other divers as they watched the shark. They had no way of knowing what it might do. Bob signaled in the direction of Jeff. The group swam fast towards Jeff, narrowing the gap between him.

Once they reached Jeff, they circled him, and headed back to the dinghy. The blacktip shark swam to the top for a moment then came back down, and circled the divers.

Oh my God, that's a signal sharks give when they are about to attack, thought Betty. *Don't panic, don't panic* she kept repeating to herself. *Just get back to the safety of the boat.* Reaching the dinghy in unison, they quickly slipped off their tanks. Then, they climbed into the boat, trying not to splash too much. The shark swam back down under the water, but they clearly saw his form in the water.

They all started talking a once. "Jeff, why didn't you stay with us? You kept swimming away. Didn't you see that shark?"

"Shark! No I didn't. I'm sorry I didn't know I was swimming that fast."

"I thought you were going to be shark food for a minute there. Didn't you ever hear of the buddy system?" asked Bob.

Jeff had been completely unaware of the whole situation.

His face turned white. "You're kidding me!"

The shark surfaced again and swam near the boat. "Look in the water," said Jim. "That's no Walt Disney character."

Jeff glanced in the water. "Holy shit," he said as they drove off.

Tired from the dive, they relaxed on the deck of *Destiny*. The cool tropical breeze lulled them to sleep until a knock came on the side of the boat and woke them.

They couldn't see anyone but a voice called out, "Hello, anyone aboard?"

Three men in a small wooden boat were hanging on to the side of *Destiny*. "Do you have any painkillers?" one of the men asked.

"Why, what's the problem?" asked Bob.

"One of our men just had his calf bitten by a shark. He needs pain medicine to relieve the pain. The helicopter can't get here until tomorrow morning to take him to the hospital."

"Sure, we have some codeine," said Betty. Then she turned to Jim, "Go get it for them. Where was he diving?" asked Betty.

The natives hung on to the side of *Destiny*, and continued, "He was spearing fish just past the reef where the water washes in."

"That's where we were diving," said Betty as goosebumps waved up and down her body. She looked at the others and said, "It could have been us."

When the men left they sat quietly on the deck thinking of the man that was bitten by the shark—Jeff had been lucky.

Martha rang the dinner bell, "Come on, dinner's ready," she called. Then, slowly one by one, they went down for their food. They had lost their appetites.

After dinner, they went into their rooms to read before bed—thinking how lucky they had been.

Twenty-six

In the South Pacific, the hurricane season was from November to April. It was already the 8th of September and it was a long way to the safety of New Zealand. The Cook Islands were on the way, so the next stop will be Rarotonga, four hundred and twenty-four miles away. They left in miserable weather and it was still raining, high winds were making the passage rough. The only good part was they were not beating against the wind. Four days later, they arrived in the Rarotonga harbor. The water was choppy with high swells, it was as bad as being out to sea. Bob pulled *Destiny* alongside of a pier and went in to meet the harbormaster. He had a scowl on his face and a voice that could rip someone apart.

Despite the man's personality, Bob greeted him with a friendly smile, "I'd like to know where we could anchor?"

Nasty and inhospitable, the harbormaster said, "I don't want your ship anywhere near the docks. If you plan on staying here, I want you at the far end of the harbor."

Furious, Bob said, "We can't anchor out there. It's too rough; we need some protection."

"That's not my problem. I don't want you in the way of the freighters coming in. If you want to come ashore, that's where you'll anchor. Another thing, I want you gone by five tomorrow morning. I have supply ships coming in and I need the room."

"Don't you worry," answered Bob sarcastically. "I don't want to stay where we're not wanted. We'll leave as soon as we get supplies. Thanks for nothing."

The harbormaster puffed his cigar and blew smoke in Bob's face. "Suit yourself. I don't care if you leave or stay."

It was almost unbearable where they anchored. They put out two anchors to secure *Destiny* before they went ashore. The dinghy was swamped with water as they cut through the harbor. The groceries they brought back were soaked even though they were wrapped in plastic.

At five in the morning, they heard the sirens blowing. The loudspeaker hailed all yachts out of the harbor. One by one, the yachts moved out and bounced against the rough seas. The cargo ships came in as the yachts waited for them to unload.

"What are we hanging here for?" asked Jim. "This is damned uncomfortable."

"You're right," said Bob. "Let's head for Tonga."

Betty was reading the South Seas handbook and she asked, "How far is Niue?"

"Niue! Never heard of it, why?" asked Bob.

"Well, if this book is not exaggerating, it sounds too good to be true. It has caves and grottos. It's something completely different than we've seen. If it's not too far out of our way, I'd like to stop there."

"I'll check the charts." Bob went to his navigation table. "It's right between the Cook Islands and the Tonga Islands. Let's see, it's five hundred and eighty-eight miles from here. It's not too far off course."

Betty got all excited. "Since we're not spending any time here, let's head for Niue."

When they changed their course, they were broad-reaching. The wind was coming from behind. The seas were calmer as they pleasantly sailed for four days.

When they sighted land, it was one o'clock in the morning. The night was so black they couldn't find the passage to the harbor. Bob found what looked like a safe spot and anchored for the night.

When they awoke at early dawn they were in Alofi harbor, just outside of Niue. They were delighted by the pleasant atmosphere and the charming people who lived there. The island itself was not much to look at. Small clean houses dotted the countryside, and little bed and breakfast places were on Main Street. Only one hotel was on the island and it had just been built for a hopeful up and coming tourist business.

Australian Airlines serviced the island, but they were on strike. There is no way in or out of the island except by boat. Consequently, the hat shaped coral island was quiet and undisturbed by tourists. They asked about the caves and grottos as they walked in and out of the few small stores.

Each person gave them a blank stare and said, "We don't know where they are."

Betty pointed across the street, "There's a rental place. Lets rent motor bikes and do some exploring. I'd like to find the caves the book describes."

They went back to *Destiny* and grabbed some food to take with them. Then they started on their journey. Betty and Bob rode on a motor scooter, following the directions in the book.

"This is worse than finding a needle in a hay stack," said Bob, carefully scanning and back-tracking the area.

"That looks like a washed out sign over there," Betty pointed at a small white board, barely visible.

"Oasis," read Bob. "That's the name of the place we're looking for."

"We found our first site. That was pretty easy," said Betty, getting off the bike.

A jagged cliff overlooked two palm trees that were surrounded by golden sand.

Bob looked down the side of the cliff. "Here's the orange rope the book talked about. Come on, let's climb down."

When Betty looked over the cliff, her mouth dropped open. "Climb down there? Are you crazy! That's got to be twenty-five feet and look at the jagged sides. You'll rip your skin open."

"No, no. Watch me," he said as he grabbed the rope. "See, it has hand knots tied on it, all you have to do is boost yourself over," he said as he swung over the side. "Then, brace your feet on the wall. See how I'm doing it? Lower yourself, see it's easy."

Betty stood there watching, "Looks too dangerous to me." She wanted to try it, but she was afraid she'd fall. "No, I don't think so." She sat on the edge and stared down at him.

"Come on, Betty. Look, I'll hold the rope and steady it for you. Don't be chicken. *Cluck cluck cluck.*"

"Stop making fun of me. Just because you don't have enough brains to be scared, doesn't mean I'm chicken," shouted Betty.

"It's so beautiful down here," Bob said trying to tempt her. "Look, there's a cave we can go through. Come on, at least try it."

Betty wanted to see the cave; she loved caves. "Well, make sure you hold the rope."

Bob waited for her to get up enough courage, then he steadied the rope while she slowly lowered herself off the edge.

She squealed as she hung in midair, "I'm going to fall, I know it."

"No you won't. Work your way down, now brace your feet on the wall," he encouraged. She slowly maneuvered herself down. When her feet were on the sandy ground she said, "Oh my God, I did it. I'm down."

Behind the oasis was a cave that was a sight to behold. Exquisite breathtaking stalagmites and stalactites in multi colors were abundant. They walked through cool channels and entered onto an orange colored coral plateau. Waves gently washed ashore from the emerald blue ocean. Not able to absorb all this spender at once, they sat on a rock letting their eyes drink in the surroundings. It seemed like minutes but they were in the cave an hour.

"If we want to see anymore caves today, we better climb out of here," said Bob.

Betty nervously grabbed the rope as Bob steadied it, and she struggled to the top. Of course, Bob climbed with ease.

He hugged her and said, "You're getting pretty good at climbing ropes. Let's try to find one more before we go back to the ship," said Bob. "I think I see the sign ahead. Yep, Matapa chasm."

"This is supposed to be a former bathing spot for royalty. Let's pretend we're royalty," said Betty strutting around, acting like a Queen.

They walked through the large rainbow striped chasms that surrounded the watering hole. Cool waters rushed in from the sea into a rock formation shaped like a swimming pool. They were shaded from the sun by massive, high coral walls that enclosed the bathing area. They stripped off their clothes and enjoyed their private recluse.

Back on *Destiny*, they talked to Martha and Jim about their experiences. They exchanged directions and went to bed early, eager to seek out all the hidden wonders tomorrow.

They next day, they packed sandwiches and rode off to explore. They found a magnificent petrified coral forest. Vast sculptures that were designed by Mother Nature stood everywhere. How the trees and foliage grew in this rocky terrain was a mystery. The limestone ground was uneven and jagged, tearing at the soles of their shoes.

"What's the name on the sign we're looking for?" asked Betty.

"It's called Vaikona chasm. It's marked with red paint at the top of a small opening on a rock," answered Bob.

"We've been walking for two hours. We must have missed it. Wait . . . what's that over there?" Betty asked as she watched a spray of water spewed high in the air.

"I don't know, let's go see," Bob said as they climbed over a huge boulder wall.

Betty let out a deep breath, "What a fantastic view." She stared at a shelf of bleached white coral, overlooking the ocean. Steplike shelves lead down to the water, an open invitation to climb down. Betty started down and was stopped when a gigantic wave came rolling in. Peaking high, it pounded down on the steps with a turbulent force. Gushing underneath the plateaus, it seeked out the hidden holes. Then, the water blew full force high into the air. Showering them with cool foaming water. The hot sun gleamed down on the bubbly water casting fantasy colors across the rocks. They sat among this splendor while they ate lunch and watched Mother Nature's water show.

"Even if we can't find the cave, I'm happy. This is an unbelievable sight," Betty said as she laid down on a ledge. She let the cool mist in the air settle on her body. "That was a hot exhausting walk we took, and this shower feels refreshing."

After resting for an hour, they felt rejuvenated. Betty stood up, "Are you ready to head back?"

"Let's try to find that cave we were looking for. It's got to be here somewhere," said Bob, walking ahead.

"Maybe we ought to head back. We've already looked for two hours. It's just not here," said Betty lagging behind.

After another hour of walking she was tired and her feet were dragging. "It's hot walking in the sun, let's go back to the boat."

Bob let out a holler, "Here's a small opening and it has a red mark over it."

Betty caught up to him, "That can't be it, the hole's too small."

"I'm going to crawl inside. All the places have an orange rope. If I find it I'll call you."

Waiting, she prayed, "Please don't let him find it. I'm tired and I want to go back."

Minutes passed then she heard, "I found it. Can you hear me? I found it."

Betty stamped her foot in aggravation, "Damnit," she was tired and didn't feel like going in that dark hole. "Are you sure you found the orange rope?"

"Yes. Come on, squeeze in. Be careful and walk slowly as there's a big slab of rock that slants down. Brace your hands on the rocks above. The slab is rough, so you won't slip."

"Thanks a lot," she grumbled, crawling in. Betty was barely able to see him in the distance. She inched herself along, knowing one wrong step would send her sliding down into the black crevasse between the huge ledges.

"Here's the orange rope," she heard him say.

When she found Bob, she let out a shriek, "What, are you out of your mind? That's a thirty-five foot drop."

"This one's easier than the one yesterday, all you have to do to grab the rope . . ."

"Yeah, yeah, I know. You always make it sound easy."

"No, listen to me. All you have to do is grab the rope sit on the edge and slide off. Then brace your back against the wall and your feet against the rock. It's just like walking down." She knew he could talk her into almost anything, "Okay, you do it first and if it looks too hard, I'm not doing it."

He slid off and shimmied down. He looked awkward and clumsy, yet it seemed like very little effort.

"How do you always make things look so simple? Especially when I *know* they're not," she said as she grabbed the rope.

Edging herself over the side, Bob called to her, "Brace your feet, that's it. Now lean back. See you're wedged in you won't fall."

He kept rooting her on until she was down. Betty gasped, "Look how beautiful it is down here. I love it."

Massive flattop boulders stood in circles around two fresh

water pools. The ceiling of the cave was like a ruined Gothic castle. The walls soared high and there was an opening that the sun's rays swept down through. Thick cascading greenery swept through the opening and down the walls. A splash of white flowers sprinkled about sent off a scent of honeysuckle. Standing in the coolness of the cave, they were in awe. Was it real or a mirage? She knew then there was a God, because only God could create such beauty.

"Let's go skinny dipping," Betty said, pulling off her clothes. They dove head first into the invigorating water. Swimming deep into the chasm, they floated on their backs, oblivious to the rest of the world. When they were tired, they climbed out and sat on one of the boulders at the edge of the pool. They watched a tiny black bass stay in one spot, peering at them.

"I think that little fish is in love with you. Look at the way its big eyes are staring at you," said Betty.

"The fish has good taste. I'll bet it doesn't see many people."

"I don't want to leave this place," said Betty as she stretched out on the boulder. "I've never seen anything like it and I'm afraid I'll never see it again,"

"We don't have to leave right away," said Bob, leaning over and kissing her nose. "We can stay awhile longer. Aren't you glad I was persistent and found this place?"

Pulling Bob down she kissed him passionately. "That's your reward."

"Is that all the reward I get for finding this incredible paradise?"

"Let me show you my real appreciation," and she wrapped her long legs around him. Locked in a wondrous embrace they made love in paradise. After bathing again in the freshness of their private pool, they climbed back up to the rest of the world.

Betty and Bob went searching the next day for the Arches of Talva. They found massive peaks of coral carved by tides and currents that had been thrust to the surface by an unseen force. It now stood as a monument to King Neptune. Enthralled with the surrounding, they stood among the many gargantuan arches, absorbing the stately beauty. This was the last place listed in the South Pacific book. The book had not lead them astray; this island was perfect. They climbed up into each cave and searched through the caverns. Each cave exited out onto a pink coral plateau where the blue water of the ocean washed gently ashore. They took their shoes off and walked along the rough coral, letting the gentle waves caress their feet. The smell of honeysuckle and gardenia mingled with the salt air, soothing their nostrils. They ate their lunch sitting in the shallow water basking in the tropical sun.

Bob pulled Betty to her feet. "Come on, we have to get back to town before the bank closes. I need to cash some traveler's checks."

He parked in front of the bank and went in while Betty waited outside.

A lady in a lovely vivid flowering dress asked Betty. "Are you on that big boat in the harbor?"

"Yes, we came to visit your caves and grottos. They're incredible. My favorite one is the one with the hole in the ceiling, and vines and flowers growing down into it."

She listened to Betty rave on then said, "I've never been to the caves. I just never take the time to go. My son has been there once or twice. Maybe I should go to see them."

Betty was dumbfounded. How could there be so much beauty here, and no one enjoying it?

Jim walked up as Bob came out of the bank. "Tomorrow is our last day here. What do you want to do?" asked Bob.

"Let's go on a dive," said Jim. "I talked to one of the men at the bar. He said there's great diving right here in the harbor."

"Fine. That's what we'll plan to do. Then we'll stock the boat with whatever we need and leave," said Bob.

"Let's have dinner at the little restaurant on the hill," yawned Betty. "Then turn in early. I feel tired."

It was a perfect morning weatherwise, and again they enjoyed breakfast on the deck. Taking the dinghy just a short distance from *Destiny*, they searched for the dive spot. Jim and Betty were the first ones in, and they descended to sixty feet to wait for Bob. It took him a little longer because he always had trouble clearing his ears on the way down.

Reaching the bottom, Jim saw a dozen curious sea snakes swimming towards them. He pointed them out to Betty. Their reaction was like the kind you would see in the movie *Twenty Thousand Leagues Under The Sea*.. Horror, fright, then mystified as they stood on the bottom, not sure what to do. Long and slender, the snakes were about eight inches around. They had black and yellow rings around their white bodies. The snakes kept their distance but as Jim and Betty swam ahead, the snakes followed them. Betty remembered what she had read about the poisonous creatures. They're as poisonous as a cobra, but as long as you don't torment them, they leave you alone. As soon as Jim and Betty realized they weren't going to be harmed, they felt more at ease.

Bob was deathly afraid of snakes, and when he finally made it down and saw the snakes, his eyes popped wide open. His skin went white as he watched the twisting forms squirm by him. Then he went ridgid as he stared half in shock. Seeing that the snakes kept their distance, he relaxed. The curious creatures liked their company and followed them everywhere. That would be their last exciting experience on that fantastic island.

Twenty-seven

The sea beckoned *Destiny* with fifteen knot winds and they started on the three hundred and eighteen mile trip to Tonga. Their routines were the same and they move about the boat freely. Good weather, peaceful sailing and beautiful days made the time fly by. Before they knew it, they could see Tonga on the horizon. Betty handled the days at sea like a regular sailor now, as long as she kept her mind off her family.

Arriving in Tongatapu at ten-thirty in the morning, they were eager to go ashore. Customs, immigration and health officers came aboard to inspect and search the boat. Then, they sat down to enjoy the coolness of the salon. Bob presented their passports and the officers put them on the table and sat smiling.

"What's going on?" Betty whispered to Bob.

"I don't know," he whispered back, waiting for the officers to start the paperwork.

After a few silent minutes, the immigration officer said, "We're hungry, we had no lunch yet. What do you eat for lunch?"

Betty looked at them curiously. "Well, we usually have a sandwich."

"Can you make us American sandwiches?" asked one of the officers.

Betty looked at the five men, "For all of you?"

"Yes, yes," the five said in unison.

Betty smiled as she said, "Is a ham and cheese sandwich okay?"

"Yes," they said, shaking their heads and smiling.

"Oh, you have VCR," said the health officer. "You put a movie on for us?"

Hoping they wouldn't stay long, she partially rewound the tape that was in the video. She forgot to check to see what it was.

Turning on the video, she whispered to Bob, "I think they're taking advantage of us."

Grudgingly, Betty went into the galley to fix the officers lunch. Then, she heard their voices become boisterous and excited. She glanced into the salon to see what the problem was. Their eyes were glued to the screen watching *Fatal Attraction*.

"Oh my God, it's the sexy scene in the elevator," she said as she hurried to shut it off. "Let me change that."

"No, no lady, leave it on we want to watch it," the officers said, deeply engrossed. They were almost drooling and their eyes bulged from their face. They sat and watched Michael Douglas and Glenn Close make wild passionate love in the elevator scene. They were speaking in Tongan and by the tone of their voices, Betty was glad she couldn't understand them. She waited for a less sexual scene before she served the sandwiches and cokes. When the officers finished, she took the dishes away, hoping they would start the paperwork.

"You have more cokes and maybe some cookies?" the officers asked without taking their eyes from the screen.

The health officer left and Betty whispered to Bob, "Good, maybe they'll do the paperwork and we can get off the boat."

Martha came down to the galley annoyed, "Haven't they done the paperwork yet?"

"No. Go back on deck. We're stuck here until they decide to do it," said Bob.

They heard the thud of someone coming aboard. It was the health officer returning and he brought a buddy with him. An hour later, the movie was over and the paperwork finally completed. They now had permission to go ashore.

Betty's son Clint was flying in to spend two weeks with them. He would sail with them until they reached Fiji. She was excited about him coming, and they rushed to the airport to meet him. When Clint's plane arrived, they toured the city and found Tongatapu to be a busy commercial place. The men walked around in long skirts and sandals, their masculinity shining through the long outfits. Sightseeing and going to the Royal Palace was one of the many delights as they walked through the streets near the Palace.

"Phew, what is that horrible odor?" Bob asked.

"Did you forget to shower this morning?" Betty teased.

310

"Wow, the stench hurts my nose."

Hearing what sounded like a mass of birds screeching, they looked up into the trees.

"Man, there must be thousands of them." Clint held his nose and asked, "What are they?"

"I think they're Flying Foxes," answered Bob. "You know, bats."

The bats were hanging upside down covering every branch, and the smell was unbearable. Bob watched them for awhile. "These little bats with fox-like faces are sacred to the Tonga people. Only royalty can hunt them."

"Well, I'm moving on. I can't stand the smell. Besides, they look weird," said Betty, crossing the street.

Tired from all the walking, they returned to *Destiny*. They sat on the deck and watched the glowing orange sun drift slowly below the horizon. They drank a toast to Clint and the trip to the Tonga outer islands tomorrow.

"Clint, you've never been on a four-day trip out to sea, have you?" asked Bob.

"No, I'm looking forward to the experience," said Clint. "It should be exciting."

Bob laughed, "If you're anything like your mother, you'll get seasick."

"Not me, I'm tough like you," said Clint acting macho.

"Ho, ho, ho, time will tell," laughed Jim.

Dreary weather greeted them in the morning as heavy rain drenched *Destiny*. When they left the harbor, they were hoping the weather would improve. The stormy weather battered *Destiny* with prodigious waves as once again they beat into the intense winds. The skies were gray with storm clouds and thrashing rain. The boat lifted high on the waves like a surfboard, then slammed down with a smash.

Betty braced herself against each impact, "I'm glad I put the patch on before we left, or I'd be sick now." She looked over at her son lying in misery, white as a sheet. "Did you put the patch on I gave you?"

Clint looked sick, "No. I didn't think I'd need it. I feel horrible."

Holding firmly to the railings, she edged her way down to the salon, and grabbed one. "Here, put the patch on. Maybe it will help a little."

He was so sick he could hardly move. "I don't understand. I never get sick in my boat," he said groaning.

"You've probably never been out in twenty-five knot winds," Bob said as he adjusted a sail. "Too bad you're not an old salt like me."

The pounding and beating went on for hours and Jim was thrown from his seat. "It feels like we're getting nowhere. We're just getting knocked around."

Bob was steering, "It's hard to stay on course, the current is pushing against us."

Jim felt miserable, "It's taken us all day to go fifty-five miles."

Bob yelled above the wind, "The weather's just not letting up and things are getting a little too nasty. We'll stop at Nowaka Island, it's fifteen minutes away."

Happy to hear that, they all gave a cheer—except for Clint, he couldn't even lift his head. When they pulled into the sheltered bay at Nowaka harbor, Clint sat up almost immediately.

He came out to the bow where Jim was getting the windless ready to drop the anchor. "Man was I sick. I never felt so bad in my life."

"Stick around awhile, you'll get used to it," said Jim with a knowing smile.

They anchored at last light between two small islands in a cove. The water was dead still, and everyone was completely exhausted. Lying in a motionless bed was going to feel great after the beating they took.

As the sun shone brightly in the early morning hours, *Destiny* was bathed in early morning dew. The fresh clean air was scented with the fragrance of the briny sea. They ate breakfast and looked across at the islands on each side of them. One island had a small village with children playing on the beach, while the other looked uninhabited.

"Anyone want to ride over to the village?" asked Bob.

Betty stood up from the table, "I'm ready."

Jim and Martha were still drinking their coffee. "We'll stay here and go over later."

Bob lowered the dinghy and started the motor, just as Clint came running up from below. "Hey, wait for me."

When they reached the shore, there were at least twenty children on the beach. The little ones ran into the water to help with the dinghy. They ranged in ages from three to ten years and were dressed only in their underwear. They were so excited to have visitors, and giggled and shouted, "Hello."

"Hello, what's your name?" Betty asked. She shook a shy little tike's hand, and he stood giggling. Turning from side to side, he then hid behind the other children. As they walked along the narrow dirt road towards the village, they felt like the Pied Piper.

The crowd of children trailed behind them saying, "Hello, what's your name . . . Hello, what's your name," like parrots that had learned a new word.

Clint glanced around, "There sure are a lot of kids here. Wonder where the adults are?"

"I don't know, maybe this is a child's sanctuary," Betty said, as she pulled a pack of balloons from her pocket. When the children saw them, they squealed with delight. She threw the balloons in different directions and the children scrambled for them. One little girl about three stood crying, she had been pushed away and didn't get one. Betty knelt down beside her and wiped the child's tears. Then she pulled a red balloon from her pocket and blew it up. "Don't cry. Here honey, this is for you." The little girl grabbed it, then rewarded Betty with a bright smile.

Most of the houses were sheets of plywood, hammered together with rusty nails. Some were painted, but most were just weathered wood. Makeshift curtains of colorful cloth hung at the windows. The dirt floors and streets were swept unbelievably clean.

A man and woman came out of a yellow painted house and said, "Welcome to our island."

"They're the first adults we've seen," said Clint. "Wonder where the rest are hiding?"

"You are from that boat?" the native man asked pointing toward the water. "What a big boat!"

Almost like magic, people appeared from fields and houses . . . soon the whole town was there. They brought bread, vegetables, shells and wood carvings to trade. They didn't want money, they wanted to trade their goods. Clint traded the T-shirt off his back for a wood carving. Betty traded her barrette from her hair for a loaf of bread.

An old man walked out from the fields with a two hundred pound pig on a leash. He walked up to Bob and said. "I give you my pig for your little boat."

"My dinghy for the pig?" Bob asked in surprise.

"Yes, my pig for your little boat and motor."

"Oh, you want my motor too," laughed Bob. "How would I get back to my big boat?"

"I take you and pig back to big boat. Then I'll help push the pig on boat." The old man said proudly. "Then I bring the little boat back here."

"No, I don't want a pig on my boat. He'd be too messy."

"I will kill the pig and cut him up for you. You'll have lots of meat for your trip." The old man said, trying to put the pig's leash in Bob's hand.

"We better get back to the boat before I lose the dinghy in this deal," said Bob, walking toward the beach.

The old man ran after him. "My pig for your boat is a good deal, no motor just the boat." Bob kept walking. "Hey, mister wait," called the old man.

The children ran to help pull the dinghy into the water as the entire village waved good-bye.

After lunch, Betty relaxed on the back-deck, enjoying the tropical breeze. She stared over at the other island and the white sandy beach. It looked so pristine and seemed to beckon her.

Bob had dozed off in the cockpit, and she called to him. "Let's go over to the other island and walk on the beach. I'm getting a little restless."

"Why?" asked Bob raising his head a bit. "There's nothing over there."

"It's a beautiful beach. Maybe we'll find some shells to add to our collection. Besides, I want to walk off my lunch."

"Okay," he said reluctantly. "Go put your bathing suit on. Anyone else want to go along?"

"Yeah, Martha and I'll go. We need to get off the boat for awhile," said Jim.

"You're not getting away without me," said Clint as he jumped in and released the painter. They walked along the fine white sandy beach, stepping over large pieces of driftwood. Then a splash party began. Laughter filled the air as they dove into the waves of the warm clear water. Among the lovely palm ridged surroundings, they played volley ball with a coconut, tripping in the sand.

They were so preoccupied they never noticed the man that came over the dunes. He was dressed in a blue shirt and pants that looked like a uniform.

He walked up to them and asked in a stern voice, "What are you doing here?"

Startled, they stood looking at the man, wondering where he came from.

"Oh! We didn't know there was anyone on the island," said Bob. "We were just enjoying the beach. Is there a problem?" asked Bob.

His voice had a nasty ring to it as he said, "No one's permitted here. This is a prison island, didn't you see the no trespassing sign?"

"A what?...A prison island?" Betty repeated. "We're sorry we didn't realize. We'll leave immediately."

"You can stay for a while, but I want you to know," and his voice got harsh, "there's no trespassing past this point," he said pointing to the dunes.

"Okay, thanks for letting us know, we won't stay long," said Bob.

"Blimey," said Martha. "Who'd a thunk it."

"Let's get out of here now," said Bob staring at their skiff anchored in the sand.

"Someone might try to escape with our dingy. If they make it to *Destiny*, we're in big trouble."

Everyone was nervous about the situation and hurried back to the dinghy. They started to drag the boat to the water's edge when another uniformed man came running toward them. "Wait, I want to talk to you," called the other man.

"Now what's up?" remarked Clint.

"I'm Warden Fresco," he said putting his hand out. "I heard you were here on the beach. I've been admiring your sailboat. It's

315

a beauty. We didn't mean to scare you away. Stay and let me show you around our plantation."

"Plantation? We were told it's a prison," said Jim.

"Well, I like to call it a plantation," said the warden politely.

"No, I think we better leave," Bob continued to pull the skiff.

"Please stay. We don't get many visitors. It would be my pleasure to show you our facilities."

Bob looked at Betty, and then the others, "What do you think?" Reluctantly, they agreed to stay, not sure what they were getting into.

"We had no idea there was anyone on this island," said Bob. "We didn't see a single light last night."

"Everyone was on the other side of the island spear fishing. We had a barbecue with the fish we caught, then stayed the night."

"What a tough life the prisoners have," said Jim. "How dangerous are they?"

"They are here for petty crimes. Burglary, assault, maximum three-year sentences. They're not dangerous and there's no way they can escape," answered the warden.

He escorted them through the dunes to a row of huts. Much like the ones on the other island. Groves of fruit trees stood in lines behind the houses, laden with succulent ripe fruit.

Twenty men were standing near the huts. They were stripped to the waist, their muscular bodies shining with sweat, from the outdoor work. Wearing tight jeans, they stood with their legs spread apart. Their hands were on their hips in a tough-looking stance. The men couldn't take their eyes off of the women. Martha and Betty were still wearing their skimpy bikinis. The men's eyes flared with fiery passion as they gawked up and down the lightly clad bodies. They had not seen a woman in a few years, and the lust and desire was clearly visible. They undressed Betty and Martha mentally. Their eyes wandered up and down the women's bodies. The prisoners murmured among themselves, and the murmuring got to a high pitch as the men took several steps toward the women.

Without saying a word, Jim and Clint went on each side of their women and Bob stood in front. Their adrenaline was churning, as they held their arms away from their sides. Hands clenched and muscles protruded in their biceps they were ready for action.

The prisoners licked their lips and weird sucking noises filled the air. Excitement built in their voices as they talked among themselves. A feeling of fright came over Betty and Martha as the prisoners raped them with their minds. The women wrapped their towels around their bodies and turned to go.

Bob shouted furiously, "What did you do, invite us up here so your men could rape our women?"

The warden stepped forward and shook his fist wildly in the air, yelling commands at the prisoners. Three guards that were standing nearby, walked in front of the prisoners with long clubs. Suddenly, a calm fell over the men and they turned and went back to work.

The warden looked bewildered as he said. "I apologize for their behavior. It is my fault. I should have asked the ladies to cover up. It's been awhile since they have seen females, especially such attractive ones. I would never have let the situation get out of hand."

"Maybe we should go," Betty said feeling apprehensive.

"No, don't go. Everything is good now. Here, let me show you our banana plantation."

"I still don't feel comfortable," said Martha.

"I give you my word you are safe," said the Warden

Bob stared at the prisoners, watching to see their reactions. "Okay, we'll give it another try, but first sign of trouble we're out of here . . . How many men are on the island?"

"There are twenty prisoners, five guards and myself. We keep our men busy working in the fields and sell the produce to the mainland. A freighter comes every week to bring supplies and pick up our fruits and vegetables."

Two prisoners approached Betty and Martha smiling shyly, "We apologize for our actions. We didn't mean to offend you. We'd like to present you with this basket of fruit and these rare shells."

Betty accepted the gifts, "Thank you very much. We accept your apology. Let us give you something in return. Is there anything you need?"

"Beside your freedom or our women," laughed Bob.

The men roared with laughter, and one of the men spoke up. "Do you have any spare slings for our spear guns?"

Another chimed in, "Any music tapes or cigarettes?"

"Yes, I think so," answered Bob, glad that everything was peaceful.

"Do you have a recorder that takes American tapes?" asked Jim.

"Yes," they all answered simultaneously.

The group from *Destiny* started toward the beach. "We'll go back to our boat and see what we have. We'll be right back."

The woman put on shorts and tops and then the group returned with everything the prisoners had asked for, including some blueberry muffins that Betty had baked and a bag of fresh oranges.

"You are much too generous," said the Warden.

The prisoners approached in a friendly group, "We'd like to entertain you and show our appreciation."

Forming a circle, they sang Tonga folk songs and danced. A few did acrobatics. There were no instruments, but the harmony was excellent.

When they left to go back to *Destiny,* the prisoners said goodbye. Their eyes were sad with longing, "Wish we were going with you," they called out.

Back on the boat, Betty said, "What an experience! We weren't thinking. We should have covered up before we went into the camp."

"I thought I was going to get me knickers torn off," said Martha.

Jim broke out laughing, "Yeah, and you would have loved it too."

Clint breathed a sigh of relief, "I'm just glad it turned out the way it did. For a while, I wasn't sure what was going to happen. It turned out to be great."

Bob looked nervous as he went to bed. "I don't know if I'm going to sleep tonight, knowing the prisoners are so close."

Twenty-eight

Bob was checking the weather for their next leg of the trip. "According to the weather fax, the winds should be out of the southwest. We'll sail today for American Samoa. You'll like it there, it's a fun place," said Bob, going over his charts.

Betty always wanted to know how far away each port was. That way, she could track the miles as they went along. She walked over to the navagation station where Bob was sitting and asked, "How far is it?"

"If we stay on course it's about three hundred and twenty-nine miles, approximately three days of sailing. It should be an easy trip."

Bob went up to the helm and they motored out of the harbor. "Hey Jim, when we get past the two islands, get the sails up."

Jim came into the cockpit, "What do you want up?"

"Put the main, genoa and the mizzen up, until I see how the wind is."

When all the sails were set, *Destiny* glided through the water with ease. They felt airborne and free, moving at eight knots.

"Wow!" Betty said, "what a fantastic day. There's not a cloud in the sky and the trade winds are behind us."

Completely relaxed, they lay around reading, occasionally glancing up to watch the birds circle above. *I don't mind this at all,* Betty thought to herself as she lulled the hours away, feeling lazy and content.

Three hours later, she heard Jim say, "Oh no, I knew it was too good to be true."

"What's up?...Never mind I can feel it, the winds have changed," said Bob. "Guess what, Betty? We're beating again."

"So, what else is new? We're always beating," Betty said half-asleep. She could feel the change of rhythm on the boat. *Destiny* was no longer sailing smoothly.

"Okay! Let's get the sails changed," said Bob loosening the sheets.

Jibing the sails, they prepared themselves for the uncomfortable sail. The wind was still beating against *Destiny* that day and all the next. Their nerves were skyrocketing from the constant rough twisting motion. Martha and Betty were not feeling well, and Clint had turned green and was throwing up.

Then, just like someone turned off the fan, the wind died down to nothing. Another change of sails was ordered.

Bob flipped on the motor and a loud clang echoed through the air. "What the hell is that noise?"

"Sounds like the drive shaft, let me check it out," said Jim, lifting the floorboards. "Yep, we have a big problem now. Better turn off the engine or we'll ruin it. It's something I can't fix."

"Damn, now we're really behind schedule," said Bob.

They drifted for hours at three knots, and way off course. Bob made a hard turn with the wheel as he said, "We're turning around and heading for Fiji. The wind will be in our favor going in that direction. Jibe the sails, Jim."

As they circled around, the sails billowed out into perfect silhouettes. *Destiny* picked up speed, dancing on the waves like a pup set loose to run. They felt exhilarated, they were on a roll with everything set for perfect sailing. It lasted a day and the wind gods toyed with them again.

Bob beat the wheel with his fist, "I don't believe this. The wind direction has changed again and we're back to beating. You just can't win."

Trying to adjust to the tormenting conditions, everyone sank into a somber mood, wondering how long this would last.

"Looks like we'll be four days out at sea instead of three," said Betty looking over at Clint who was lying there in a green hue.

Martha was trying to write a letter. "I've lost track of what the date is. Does anybody know?"

Clint looked at his watch. "It's October 9th."

"Put the generator on, we'll make some water," said Bob looking at the water-gauge.

Jim started the generator but it squealed and conked out. He tried to start it again, when it wouldn't go he climbed down to check it out. "The damn water pump to the generator is broken."

"Goddamnit, what else can go wrong," screamed Bob. "How are we going to make water? They're doing it to us again, Betty, they're getting us." Bob banged his fist against the helm.

"Who's getting us?" Betty snickered, not meaning to laugh at his frustration.

"The sea-gremlins, that's who. They got us again."

"Calm down, Bob," said Jim. "I think I can repair it when we get to Fiji."

Another day passed and still there was no wind. Frustrated, Bob called out, "Jim, put the spinnaker up. See if that's any help."

Jim and Clint put the spinnaker up, "Not doing much," yelled Jim, as he watched it flap around searching for wind.

'All right, let's get it down. Put up the yankee and genie wing to wing. Maybe it will stabilize the boat and cut out some of this Goddamn rocking."

That was a good move. The motion eased a bit and it made the trip a little more bearable.

Everyone was out on the bow except Jim and Bob, who were in the cockpit. Bob noticed an odd look on Jim's face, "Something on your mind?" he asked.

Jim looked sad, "I think I'll go home when we get to New Zealand."

"Just for a visit?" asked Bob.

"No, for good. I think I've had enough sailing. I'm ready to go home."

"Well, that's too bad. I was hoping you'd make the whole trip with us. Any problems we can work out?" asked Bob.

"No," Jim shook his head. "You've been more than fair with me. I'm just ready to go home."

Bob put *Destiny* on auto-pilot and relaxed for a moment. "Okay, but if you change your mind, you're welcome to stay."

Coasting at half-a-knot, they drifted along with the current. The hot sun beat down relentlessly, draining their energy and spirits. Going down below was like stepping into a hot sauna, not a breath of air anywhere.

Martha was fanning herself with a magazine. "Good thing

we have the bimmi top, at least we have some shade."

Jim crept up behind her and poured a bucket of seawater on her. "There, that should cool you off," he laughed.

"You bloody pig," Martha shrieked and ran for revenge.

That started a water fight between them, each grabbing a bucket and dousing the other. Bob sat deep in thought at the helm. He was the only dry body aboard.

"Got to cool you down," Betty laughed as she threw a bucket of water on him.

"Damnit Betty, did you have to do that?" he said, biting out his words.

"Don't be such an old grouch. You need to cool off." As she laughed, a pain shot through her tooth. Grabbing her jaw she said, "Wow, my tooth hurts. I don't know what's wrong with it."

"Has it hurt before?" asked Bob, concern showing in his face.

Betty held her jaw, "It's been hurting a little for the past two days, but now it's worse."

Bob was sympathetic. "I'm sorry to hear that, but there's not much we can do for it out here. Put some ice on it."

Before Betty took her night-watch, she numbed her tooth with aspirin, and tooth drops. That night she was anxious for Jim to relieve her and was glad to see him at the end of her watch.

Their three-day trip had turned into nine days and the wind had not increased.

Clint was feeling better and took his turn at the helm, "What a miserable day. It's so bleak and cloudy you can't see very far."

"We're near the harbor. Here, let me take over," said Bob as he took the wheel. "I'm going to start the engine and see if we can use it long enough to get in."

Bob started the engine and they waited to hear the horrible clanging noise again. They could only hear a slight grinding sound. "Get the sails down and hope the motor holds up until we get into port."

Their three hundred and twenty-nine miles had turned into eight hundred and thirty-five miles. *Destiny* finally made it to the harbor of Suva, in Fiji, arriving at six in the morning in a downpour. Bob notified the officials of their arrival and they were kept waiting all day.

At four o'clock, the officers climbed onboard, and the first thing they said was, "Do you have a VCR?"

"Yes we do, but it's broken, "Betty said smiling.

The officers moaned in disappointment. She wondered if the officers from Tonga had called ahead, and told them about the movie.

Suva was very commercial but interesting; a potpourri of nationalities. There were Indians, Orientals and English, everyone more than friendly. Again, Betty was taken back by the men in long skirts. She couldn't seem to take her eyes off the tall muscular men.

"I must be turning into a dirty old woman, or I've been at sea too long," said Betty, eyeing the men.

"Mom, is that anyway for you to talk? Especially around your son," laughed Clint.

"Shut your ears. I'm a sailor too long at sea, and if men can get away with it, why can't I?"

Restaurants were in abundance. The scrumptious Chinese food was the best they had ever tasted. Walking around town, they went to see the cultural centers and gardens in Suva. Again, they smelled the vile odor in the air and knew there were flying foxes around. They hiked through the Cocoa Forest smelling the fragrance from the cocoa blossoms. Then, they sat under large ferns eating their lunch. They felt like kids again when they swung from ropes that were tied to a tree into an emerald lake. Refreshing their bodies from the long trudge, they did it over and over again, challenging each other to see who could swing the farthest.

Finally, it was time for Clint to fly home and they reluctantly took him to the airport, knowing they were going to miss him.

Betty lay awake all night with a severe toothache. She knew something had to be done before they sailed away for eleven days.

While they were having breakfast, she said to Bob, "I think

I'd better find a dentist before we head for New Zealand. My jaw's swollen and my tooth is killing me."

"Lets walk over to town and ask around for a dentist," said Bob.

They were directed to a clinic, an old dilapidated building in the center of town.

"Oh, Bob, I don't want to go in here," Betty said, looking at the crowded poor facilities.

"You have to do something about your tooth," said Bob, pulling her into a large room.

Every chair was taken, so she stood nervously against the wall.

A man offered his seat. Before she could sit down, she heard a soft voice with a British accent say, "Can I help you?" Turning, she saw a short Oriental man coming towards her. He was dressed in a white medical jacket.

"Yes, please. I have a horrible toothache, and I need someone to look at it."

The doctor smiled, "Please follow me. I'll take you right away."

Looking around, she could see that hygienic conditions were lacking. The equipment was way behind times, she was worried.

"First, we should take x-rays. Then, we can see what your problem is," he said politely.

He took her into a room and she sat in a torn leather chair that belonged in a barber shop.

The metal arms and foot-rest were rusty, and Betty whispered to Bob, "What am I getting myself into?"

The x-ray machine was an older version of the one her dentist used. At least she knew it was an x-ray machine.

After he checked the x-rays, he told her, "You have an abscessed tooth. It should be treated immediately."

Betty grabbed hold of Bob's hand, she felt squeamish. When the doctor walked out of the room she said, "I don't want my tooth fixed here. I want to go home to my own dentist."

When the doctor returned, he smiled at her and said, "Maybe you would be better off with a private dentist. We are quite busy here."

Betty's eyes lit up, "A private dentist! Do you know one?"

"Yes, I'll give you his name and address," the Oriental doctor said, as he took out a notepad and pencil. Writing down the name and address, he said, "It's just around the corner and he's well recommended. Here are your x-rays, he will need to see them."

"Thank you very much," said Betty as she started to leave. "Oh, how much do I owe you?"

The nurse stepped up and said, "Your charge is one dollar for the exam, and two for the x-ray."

Bob paid him and they went outside he said, "Wow, what a bargain!"

They walked around the corner to a two-story building. It was a bit neglected with dirty newspapers and cigarette butts covering the floor. As they entered the doctor's office, they were happy to see that it was spotless. The furniture was modern and the walls were painted a soft white. They were greeted by a lovely Indian nurse with long black hair. Her dark almond shaped eyes sparkled with friendliness. She wore a light blue chiffon sari. A red dot was prominent in the middle of her forehead.

"Can I help you?" she asked with a sweet smile. Her accent was spoken with a slight lisp.

"I'm here to see Dr. Nuji. I was sent over by the clinic," Betty said, feeling better in these surroundings.

"Please be seated. I'll tell the doctor you're here."

The nurse came out and led them to his office. The doctor stood up as they entered. "I am Dr. Nuji," said the striking man from India. He was six feet tall and his high cheek bones arched out sharply. A kindness glowed from his black eyes while his full lips broke into a friendly smile.

"I was sent over from the clinic," Betty said shaking hands.

"Ah . . . Americans! Welcome to our country. How can I help you?"

She handed him her x-rays and waited while he looked at them.

Then with a click in his voice, he said, "Yes, you have a bad abscess. You will need a root canal." His broad chest stood out proudly as he said, 'I am the only doctor in Suva that can do root canals. This will be expensive, but you must have it done."

"How much will the root canal cost?" asked Betty, knowing whatever it cost, she'd have to have it taken care of.

A little reluctant he said, "Seventy-five American dollars."

"Seventy-five dollars?" Bob answered not believing what he heard, knowing back in the states it would be at least five hundred.

The doctor looked apologetic, "Please let me explain how much work it will take. Then you'll know why it is so expensive."

"When can you start and how long will it take?" Betty asked still feeling uneasy.

"We can start tomorrow, if that's all right with you. I'll do it four days in a row."

"Only four days? That's great, we'll still be able to stay on schedule," said Bob.

The doctor looked at his appointment book, "We can start ten o'clock tomorrow morning."

When she agreed, the doctor said, "Good, I'll see you tomorrow morning at nine."

*   *   *

Betty was nervous when she went into the office. She was greeted by a young Indian receptionist, "Good Morning. What are you here for?"

Betty sat down at her desk and said, "I'm here for a root canal."

"Oh!" The receptionist said, her eyes opening wide. "That's going to hurt you."

Laughing with false bravery, Betty said, "I certainly hope not."

Dr. Nuji was very gentle as he applied the welcomed novocain. Betty waited for the numbing effect to take away the pain. The friendly nurses kept her mind occupied with stories of their Hindu customs.

As Betty sat in the chair, she asked, "Dr. Nuji, are you going to give me an antibiotic for any infection that might be in my system?"

"No. I will apply some antibiotic in the tooth when I kill the nerve. That's all you'll need," he said as he started to drill.

Betty thought she remembered getting a prescription for an antibiotic when she had a root canal before. *I hope I don't have any problem later*, she prayed.

Dr. Nuji had a light touch as he worked. He kept her entertained with stories of his life. He had completed his dental education in Australia.

When the root canal was finished, Betty still felt she needed an antibiotic. When she went back to *Destiny* she searched her medical books. She found the best medicine for gum infection was penicillin. There was no penicillin in their medicine box, they were out of it. *Maybe I should have insisted on a prescription,* she thought.

Hearing a commotion in the staterooms, she called out, "What's all the racket?"

Jim was coughing and answered in a disgusted voice "The toilets are backed up. We'll have to clear the lines before we can leave."

"Boy, that's a smelly job," said Betty wrinkling her nose. "Will we be leaving today as planned?"

"No, it will take all day, might even go into tomorrow," said Bob as he continued to pull up the floorboards.

They worked all day and were sick to their stomachs from the stench that swept through the boat.

Martha and Betty went shopping for supplies and found a fantastic assortment of fresh vegetables and fruit. The outdoor market was chaotic, with everyone shouting and trying to sell their wares. Meat was hanging on racks in the open air, with flies flocking over it. They were dining on the pungent carcasses.

Betty held her nose and whisked the flies away, "Let's not bother with meat. We'll make do with what we still have in the freezer. Come on, Martha, I want to get out of here before I throw up."

Men sat in groups in the corner of the market, drinking kava. It was made from the roots of the kava tree. They ground the roots then mixed it with water and drank the gritty mess. It made their mouth feel numb, as if they just had a shot of Novocain. It's a popular drink that they had instead of beer or alcohol. It's a custom to present it to the chief when visiting one of the outer islands.

Martha seemed quiet all day, "Are you feeling all right?" asked Betty.

"I feel okay," said Martha with a sad look on her face. "I just hope Jim is serious with me. I really care for him."

"You haven't known each other very long. Don't rush him."

"You're right, I know. I love him so much," she said, her accent not quite so noticeable.

Betty tried to change the subject. "Do you think you'll always want to work on yachts?"

Martha's face lit up, "Yeah, I like it and Jim likes it too,"

"You know, with your experience in travel you could get a good job. You could work as a tour guide or travel agent. You're looking good since you've been on a diet. If you could polish up your English and lose your cockney accent, you'd do well," Betty remarked kindly.

"I know. Everyone makes fun of me when I talk. All the British men I meet get me to talk, then they laugh at me."

"Your mother and dad don't have the cockney accent. How did you get it?"

"I hung around with a group of cockney kids in school and thought it was hip. Mum used to get so mad at me when I talked, but she couldn't change me."

"Oh well, at least you're trying to change it now." Betty felt sorry for Martha. She was in love again. Sometimes she could be so sweet, but lately she'd been snippy and curt.

When they returned to *Destiny,* the stench inside was unbearable. They used two cans of Lysol® deodorant to get rid of the sewage odor. The toilets were finally repaired late that day.

They were leaving for New Zealand the next day. It was the nineteenth of October and hurricane season started the first of November. They were cutting it close, and didn't want to be caught out at sea in unpredictable weather. Once they make it to the Auckland harbor, they'll be well out of the way of the hurricanes.

Betty was ready to go, she just needed another good night of sleep before *Destiny* took off. She hadn't caught up from the last nine days at sea.

"It's one thousand, one hundred and thirty-two miles from here to New Zealand. I already alerted Martha and Jim that we're leaving in the morning," said Bob. "We have to get an early start."

Betty became a bit anxious. "We're not going straight through without stopping, are we?"

"Yes, we are," said Bob. "Sorry, but we'd have to go way out of our way to stop."

Twenty-nine

Betty woke at sunrise feeling very nostalgic. Today was October 20th, her birthday. It was hard to believe that she'd been sailing for over a year. *I have changed in so many ways, I no longer get so homesick, and I can handle the motion of the boat much better. That's a big accomplishment, I don't even dread going out to sea . . . well not as much,* she thought.

I always said I never wanted to get married again. Yet I don't like the feeling of just living with someone. She got up and went into the shower and thought, *It makes me feel like what I heard the yachties refer to as pier bitches. They're girls that hang around ports looking to be picked up. Then, they sail away with men they don't even know. I know I'm nothing like that, but I get tired of hearing, 'Oh, you're one of Godfrey's crew, or you're his first-mate.' It made me feel cheap.* Drying herself with a towel, she continued thinking, *Probably it's my old-school up-bringing—living with a man without being married.* She laughed to herself, *I certainly am past the stage of loosing my virtue, but the feeling still haunts me. Even when I went with my ex-boyfriend, I never lived with him. Always thought, if I didn't love him enough to marry him, I wouldn't give up my freedom. Now here I am in the middle of the ocean, living with Bob.* Betty came out of the bathroom with the towel wrapped around her, and flopped on the bed, continuing to reminisce. *We're together twenty-four hours a day, everyday. God, I never thought I'd ever be able to stand anyone around me twenty-four hours a day. Well it's a good way to find out if you're compatible—a damn tough way. It's got to be love, not sexual infatuation. The sea has a way of taming your sex life down.* Her mind kept twirling, as she thought, *How do I know how we'll feel at the end of this trip? Will I be able to adjust to the hectic business world again? We are by ourselves so much and I'm so used to the quietness.* Oh—well, she sighed, *we're all set to leave for New Zealand. I'll have plenty of time to think things out.*

Bob startled her as he walked in. "How come you're still in bed? Are you lazy or are you day-dreaming?"

"No, just contemplating. Isn't that what you call it when *you're* goofing off?" said Betty, snapping out of her mood.

"Hey, I *don't* goof off. When you see me lying down with my eyes closed, I'm in deep serious thought."

As Betty got out of bed, she laughed and said, "And the snoring I hear is your brain grinding away? Hmm, I see."

"Here...I bought you something," he handed her a lovely package. "Happy Birthday."

Tearing open the gift, she squealed, "Two bottles of Giorgio®! Thanks, I'm almost out of it." She laughed as she read the funny card. It was signed, 'To my sea witch from your gypsy.' "Thank you for remembering my birthday," she said as she kissed him.

"I'd never heard the end of it if I hadn't," said Bob in a teasing voice.

"You're right, you wouldn't."

"Hurry and get dressed we're leaving in an hour."

Their passage out of Fiji was calm and scenic as they watched the land slowly disappear. Motoring since they left Fiji two days ago, the drumming of the engine had become background noise that ground into their minds.

Hearing the change in rhythm, along with a loud squeal, Bob turned off the engine. "I don't like the sound of that noise. I bet they didn't fix it right in Fiji. They got us again, Betty. They got us again."

Jim put up the spinnaker, hoping they could catch a breeze. Later that day, the wind shifted head-on and they were beating again.

"The damn wind gets us every time," yelled Bob. "Can't we ever get away from this fucking beating?"

Mother Nature heard his cuss words and took revenge. Twenty-five knot winds whipped *Destiny*, and waves reaching heights of fifteen feet washed across her decks. The horrific conditions lasted days and they made very little headway. The boat had an exaggerated rock that was driving them all crazy.

331

Betty was checking the logbook and said to Jim, "We've only gone three hundred and forty-four miles in five days."

Jim looked up from his book, "Did you say something?" he asked.

"No, nothing important," she didn't feel like repeating herself. Her body was starting to rebel against the aggravating motion, she could feel a scream building. Instead of going down to the stateroom to beat the mattress, she jogged in place. It was time for her watch so she sat at the helm feeling depressed. Betty watched the horizon and wished desperately she was back on land . . . somewhere . . . anywhere would do. She was shaken out of her mesmerized mood by a swift pull to port, *Destiny* had gone off course.

"Bob, the auto-pilot just went out. I'm switching over to the Robertson," she called out.

"Is everything going to break on this damn boat before we reach land?" growled Bob. "I'm going below to check it."

Bob came back on deck. "We have to steer manually. For some reason, the Robertson and auto-pilot are drawing too much electricity. If we lose our power, we lose our navigation equipment."

They took turns at the helm, an hour on, an hour off. They fought not only the wind but the current, too. Clouds overshadowed the sun and rain was intermittent. The temperature dropped and they had to change to heavy pants and jackets. Three days later, the wind and waves calmed. They were back to making very little progress.

"Let's try the engine again. I want to see if we can motor slowly. At least we'd make some headway," said Jim.

Listening to the purr of the engine, they waited for the squealing to start. As long as they kept it at slow speed, there was no noise. When they gave it power, the noise was deafening.

"I'll run it at slow speed. At least we can charge the batteries enough to use the auto-pilot," said Bob.

They had a hundred miles to go. They were under sail with the spinnaker flying high. There was only eight knots of wind, but every little bit helped get them there. On deck they could see a silvery full moon high in the sky. The stars twinkled like a mass of lightning bugs. Betty felt miserable and restless. She thought about all the romance and loving feelings in the movies. The hero and heroine sail off into the sunset making passionate love. Weather, of course, was always perfect. *All I feel is irritable and bitchy,* she thought. *The constant slapping motion saps away any sex drive I might have. I don't need to plead a headache, the captain already has one, and we're both sea weary.*

Finally after eleven days at sea, they pulled up to the docks in Auckland harbor. Their endless trip was finally over. Customs told them to tie alongside a twenty-foot high wall, the only spot available. A metal ladder anchored on the wall was the only way they could get up to the pier. Testing the ladder to make sure it was secured, they started the twenty-foot climb to the top.

"This is a hard way to get to town," Betty said, not wanting to look down.

"Piece of cake," said Jim following close behind.

"It's the only way to town, and I'm climbing," said Martha. "Hurry up, I want to get off this fricking thing."

"Wow, this is Auckland?" Betty said, as she looked at the great shops lining the streets. "This could be any city in America"

Betty's brain rattled as it absorbed the hustle of the excessive traffic that roared by. Walking through town, Betty began to get dizzy and lightheaded.

Grabbing Bob's arm, she said, "What in the world is the matter with me? I feel like I'm going to faint."

Bob took her hand. "Sit down for a minute and rest."

She lowered her head to her lap, hoping the feeling would pass. "Maybe I'm not used to land."

After several minutes, they started to walk again. Every twenty minutes, she would feel ready to pass out. "Let's get back to the boat. I want to lie down for a while."

When they reached the ladder, Bob climbed down first. Betty turned to take a step down onto the first rung. Black circles spun in her head and she grasped an iron ring in the ground and pulled herself back up. She lay there in a cold sweat; her head was swirling. A sickening feeling grew in her stomach.

Bob yelled up, "What's the matter? Climb down, I'll be here to help."

The spinning stopped and she crawled over to the edge, ready to try again. Betty put her legs over the side, and started down the first step. Her head went into a whirl of circles. She almost blacked out, subconsciously she grabbed for the iron ring and hung on.

As long as she laid still with her eyes closed she didn't see the black circles spinning by.

She called out to Bob, "I can't do it, I keep getting dizzy. I'm afraid I'll fall," she said starting to weep.

Jim and Martha came up on deck. "What's wrong with her?" said Martha. "Why can't she climb down, she bloody can't be scared?"

"Betty, try it again. I'll come up the ladder and help you," said Bob. "I don't know how we'll get you down if this doesn't work."

This time she kept her eyes closed and slid over the edge. Gradually she lowered herself to the first rung. She opened her eyes to see where the next rung was and circles began to twirl. This time she hung on leaning against the ladder, waiting for it to pass. Bob had come up the ladder and held her. With his arms around her they went down slowly. One step at a time until she was on *Destiny*'s deck.

"What is causing this?" asked Betty, really worried.

"Go lie down. Maybe you should go to a doctor," said Bob, concern in his voice.

The next morning, Betty felt pretty good as she lay in bed. When she stepped out of bed, she was lightheaded again. Crawling back in bed, her mind searched for an answer. *Maybe my equilibrium is off? If I take a seasick pill, it might help.* Sure enough, an hour later after she took the pill, she was able to stand up and walk around.

"How are you feeling this morning?" Bob asked as he came into the stateroom.

"I took a seasick pill and it helped. I still don't feel right. I know by my clothes that I've lost weight."

"Why don't you go to a doctor and get checked over?"

"Let's see if the pill keeps it under control. We're going home in a couple of days. I'd rather see my own doctor. I'll get checked out as soon as I get home. It's going to be wonderful, being home for Christmas."

They left expense money and gifts for Jim and Martha. "We'll be gone for three weeks. Here's a list of things to be done; it's not too long of a list, considering. What have you decided, Jim? Are you leaving for good when we get back?"

"No. I'll go home for a couple of weeks, then I'll be ready to return. I just got homesick."

"If you and Betty don't mind, I'd like to take a trip home. I need a break and I miss my mum," said Martha.

"Sure, it's all right. It's been a while since you've seen them," answered Betty. "We've got to go, see you when we get back. Have a Merry Christmas."

Thirty

They were met at the airport by her family. The first one she saw was her beautiful daughter, Debra.

"Mom, I'm so glad you're home," she said as she hugged Betty.

Britt and Ryan, her grandchildren, were there and remembered her. "Did you bring us something?"

Bob caught a flight out to Boston to see his doctor. He was feeling great, but he promised he'd get a checkup every six months.

As soon as Betty got home, she called her doctor for an appointment.

Dr. Whitaker gave her a full examination. "I want you to go on Mevacor. Your cholesterol is three hundred and forty, much too high. You've lost five pounds since I saw you last, but everything else seems okay. Are you still having dizzy spells?"

"No, not for a while, maybe I just had a bug. Could I try a no fat diet first instead of taking the medication for my cholesterol?"

"Well, you can give it a try. I'll give you a menu to follow."

Betty wondered why he couldn't find anything wrong. *Why had she lost five pounds?*

She picked Bob up at the airport. He had a good report from his doctor and they celebrated his good health at dinner.

When they returned home, they were shivering. They weren't used to the cold weather. Betty and Bob cuddled in bed. A fire blazed in the fireplace. Bob kissed her cheek and asked, "What would you like for Christmas?"

"I've been a really good girl. I think Santa should give me something very special."

Bob acted like he was thinking. "How about a new bathrobe?"

"A new bathrobe? You got to be kidding, that's not special," said Betty pouting.

"Well...how about a pair of fuzzy slippers for this cold weather?"

"Now you're being silly. I don't want that sort of thing for Christmas. I want something wonderful, exciting and romantic."

"How about a diamond ring, would that make you happy?"

Betty's eyes sparkled, "A diamond ring! That would mean we're engaged?"

"Why else would I give it to you, you beautiful sea witch?" he said, kissing her with his warm moist lips. "Do you want a diamond engagement ring?"

Betty stared into his blue eyes. The flickering light from the fireplace danced on his face. "Well I don't know if I want to be engaged to a gypsy," she laughed.

"What," he said in surprise. He grabbed her and started tickling her.

"Yes, I do, yes, I do," she giggled and managed to pull away. Then, Betty kissed him passionately. Their bodies pressed tightly as his fingers slid the gown off her body. His hands moved magically over her smooth breasts. Their lips met and she drank in the sweetness of his kiss. Deep in this rapturous feeling, his hands crept across her breast in slow lingering movements. Instinctively, her body arched toward him. The hot tide of passion surged through them, making up for all the celibate nights on *Destiny*.

"I love you so much. I can't bear the thought of being without you," Betty said breathlessly.

"Don't worry. I'll never let you get away. I love you and always will," said Bob breathlessly.

A pleasant exhaustion filled their bodies, and Betty said, "This is the kind of rocking I like. I could put up with this anytime."

Teasing, Bob answered her, "You don't like the *Destiny*'s shuffle and drag?"

"*That* I could definitely do without."

Christmas and New Year's was wonderful. It felt great being home for the holidays. Trimming the tree and spending time with her grandchildren was exhilarating. Betty watched their expressions of joy. Cooking the turkey under normal conditions was a treat in itself. Family and friends were around the table laughing and enjoying the festivities. Everyone raised their glasses and drank a toast to Bob and Betty's engagement.

Time went by swiftly, and their last week was spent buying parts and supplies to take back to *Destiny*.

Martha and Jim met them at the airport. "Betty, what's that goo—gous babble on your hand, is that new? Are you two engaged?"

"Yes, we are. Got it for Christmas," Betty said showing it off.

"Are you feeling all right? You look thinner," asked Martha.

"I did lose a little weight. I had a checkup, but they couldn't find any reason for it. I'm a little tired and occasionally dizzy, but it's probably from jet lag."

"We know you're dizzy, don't try to blame that on jet lag," Bob laughed.

The next day Martha and Jim left. They went home for their much needed vacations.

Bob's sons Scott and Dan came to visit for a month and Bob was happy to see his family again. He gave each a hefty pat on the back. "We're really going to explore New Zealand. I have a motor home lined up for us."

"Hey Betty," said Scott, "you're still sticking it out. What a trooper."

"This is my reward," said Betty, showing off her diamond. "Hi Dan! It's good to see you again," she said as she hugged them both.

"The motor home is fifteen feet—not too big. It doesn't have a toilet or shower, but we'll make out," said Bob.

They toured the north and south islands of New Zealand and loved every part of the country. It was close quarters in the motor home with Bob and Betty sleeping on single couches on each side of the motor home. Scott slept over the driver's cabin and Dan hung from the ceiling in a hammock.

There wasn't anything they missed. Hot springs, sheep shearing, trout fishing, glaciers and whitewater rafting were some of the things they saw and did. It was a unanimous feeling—if they had to live anywhere other than America, they would live here. Soon time ran out and regretfully, Dan and Scott flew home. While waiting for Martha and Jim to return they met some wonderful New Zealanders on a trek at Milford Track. They were invited to their homes and were made to feel so welcome.

Destiny had been hauled and repairs made while they were away. The boat was ready to go and Jim and Martha were back from their vacations feeling in good spirits.

"There's still a few more weeks of hurricane season," said Bob. "But I can tell by the weather fax, it's clear where we're headed.'"

"No chance of running into bad weather?" Jim asked, studying the fax sheets.

"There's always a chance, but it's very slim. We had to rush away from the Fiji area. We never had a chance to see the outer islands. I think we'll backtrack and spend some time there," Bob said, looking over his charts.

Betty was glad they were going back, "I really enjoyed Fiji." Then she thought for a second and added, "We better buy some Kava. Remember, we have to present it to the chief of each island."

"I almost forgot about that," Bob said as he checked his charts again. "It will take eight days to get there if the weather holds."

Leaving the harbor, they encountered the same bad conditions as the last sail; high cold winds, rough seas and terrible motion. They hoped each time they sailed it would be different, but it never was.

Bob was studying the weather fax. "It shows a cyclone off the southwest. We are heading northwest, so we'll be able to avoid it."

For days strong winds, up to forty knots, pounded against *Destiny*. They stood two-man-watches to ensure their safety. High seas and winds left them no rest.

Betty sat at the helm, looking out at the horizon. "Do you know it would only take three hours to fly to Fiji from New Zealand."

Bob looked up from his book, "Yeah, but look at all the fun you would have missed."

She threw a towel at him. "You're not going to convince me you think this is fun."

Betty looked around to see where Jim and Martha were, "Have you noticed since our crew has been back their attitude has changed?"

"Yeah, I did," said Bob putting down his book. "They've kept to themselves most of the trip, and the chores are falling behind."

"They're either up on the bow or in one of their rooms. Martha is like Jim's shadow, never letting him alone," said Betty deep in thought. "Let's hope it's just the sea conditions causing their mood."

"We'll be arriving at one of the outer islands of Fiji, called Lautoka. We should be there by eleven tonight," said Bob, picking up his book again.

"Great," said Betty. "I'm looking forward to my first peaceful night sleep in eight days."

After they cleared customs the next morning, they provisioned *Destiny* and rested. After two days of relaxing, they went island hopping, in the intriguing beauty of the Fiji outer islands.

They anchored outside a lovely resort that was sparsely covered with thatched huts.

Betty climbed in the dinghy. "I'm going ashore," she said. "You can catch me at the pool drinking banana daiquiris."

"Whoa, wait for me," yelled the crew as they climbed aboard.

While lounging by the pool, Bob looked up and saw Martha in the water. "What's she doing?"

"She's taking diving lessons," Betty answered half-asleep.

"My God, when she first came aboard, she could only swim with a life preserver," reminisced Bob.

Betty sat up to watch, "Now, she wants to learn to dive. That's pretty good for someone who was afraid of water."

Bob laughed, "I think Jim has something to do with that. He keeps teasing her and calling her a sissy. Have you noticed? Ever since they've been back, she's been doting on him more than ever."

"How could I help but notice," chuckled Betty. "She mothers

him and caters to his every wish and he loves it."

Bob sounded a bit miffed as he said, "The problem is they're spending less time doing their chores."

"Martha doesn't have that much to do. I keep our stateroom clean, cook every other day and do our wash. If I think she's busy, I clean up the galley and salon. Lately, after I've done her work, I find her up on deck scratching Jim's back. There's definitely something wrong with this picture." Betty turned over to sun her back.

"Who's working for whom?" added Bob. "We have to do something about this situation. It's just so hard finding crew out here. I should have let them go home in New Zealand. It would have been easy to get crew there. I really like Jim and his parents and I don't want hard feelings."

Betty saw how upset he was and said, "Maybe you should have a talk with Jim."

Two days later, they sailed to a more remote island. The trip was short and the weather super. They had just anchored and Betty went down to the galley. She could smell the odor and knew what was cooking.

Betty walked over to the stove, "Are you cooking fried rice again for lunch, Martha?"

"Yes, you know how much Jimmie-boy loves it."

"Jim might like rice every day for lunch, but Bob and I don't. For the past week whenever it's your turn to cook, you prepare rice."

Martha flipped the rice and sarcastically said, "Tell me what you want and I'll fix it after we're done with our lunch."

"What! You've been preparing lunches for us for six months," Betty snapped. "There's a lot more food onboard beside rice."

Martha stood there stirring the fried rice with a defiant look on her face. She never answered.

"What's this, a new thing? Jim gets what he wants and the hell with our lunch?" Betty added fuming.

Her face turned red as she continued to stir, "It's not like that at all. It's just Jimmie-boy likes his rice."

Gritting her teeth, Betty said, "When you're done with Jimmie-boy's lunch, I'll get ours. Looks like that's the only way we'll

341

get something besides fried rice." Betty didn't know how long she could take this.

Martha prepared a plate for her and Jim and together they sat at the cockpit table eating. Betty fixed their lunch and they sat eating their meal at the helm.

Betty looked over at the two lovebirds, then leaned over to Bob, "This is crazy. We used to all eat the same thing and sit together. They're at the table and we're scrunched here at the helm."

"It *is* strange, and it really makes things uncomfortable," agreed Bob.

The next few islands they anchored at were uninhabited. When they arrived, it was just as they expected—serene and lovely with white sparkling beaches. Water so blue and smooth, it looked like an artist's dream. The aroma in the air was a pungent brine of the sea mixed with flowering fragrances. They snorkeled and dived each day, and were mesmerized by the wondrous sights of the coral and fish below. *Destiny* was the first cruise boat to arrive after the hurricane season. They found the beaches loaded with shells of all descriptions.

Betty was looking over the chart. "Our next stop is Blue Lagoon, is that the little island where the movie was filmed?"

"According to the South Pacific book it is," said Jim.

"Wait 'til I write home about this," said Martha, "it's just as bea-ut-iful as in the movie. Who was the girl that played in it?"

"It was Brook Shields," Betty said. "Can't you just picture her diving into this magnificent lagoon?"

They spent the day in the romantic atmosphere. Jim and Martha walked off in the opposite direction. Betty and Bob lay together under the fanning, whispering palms. Then, they swam in the gentle surf and swirled with the caressing water as the waves pulled them to and fro. They drank champagne in the surf as the water washed over them. Placing lingering kisses on each other's body, they made love on the white pearly sand, cooled gently by the ocean breeze.

"It's times like this that make the whole trip seems worthwhile. We are as close to paradise as we'll ever be," murmured Betty.

Islands were everywhere, with odd names like Maloloailai, Nananuira, Soma Soma and Taveuni. Some had small villages of maybe two hundred people. Others were uninhabited with nothing but goats that ran from their sight. They drank fresh coconut milk and picked ripe papayas and bananas right off the trees. They were beginning to feel like natives.

Betty was still losing weight and she was tired all the time, sleeping a lot. Not one to miss anything, she pushed herself to see and do it all. Anchoring out each night, the cool tropical breeze lulled them into a peaceful sleep.

Always exploring, they took the dinghy ashore to a small island and looked for shells. A baby goat staggered toward them, bleating in desperation.

"That's odd! Goats always run from us," said Jim.

"Look at the poor thing," said Martha, picking up the tiny creature.

The small starving goat sucked at her finger with all its might. They searched around through the thickets for its mother, but there was not another goat in sight.

"The poor little thing must be hungry. Let's take it back to the boat and feed it," Betty said, taking it in her arms.

Back onboard, they found a small plastic bottle with a squirt top and filled it with diluted milk. It wouldn't accept the bottle at first until Betty placed milk on her finger. She rubbed the milk against its lips until the goat finally licked it from her finger. Seeing this, Betty placed the pointed top in its mouth. After consuming four bottles of milk, the goat was content. Betty laid him on the seat in the cockpit, where he went to sleep.

The women were ecstatic. All of their mothering instincts came out, as they fussed over the little creature.

"I better get rid of this thing quickly. You'll be so attached to it, you'll never give it up," said Bob, watching the attention the goat was getting.

"He's so adorable. Can't we keep him for our mascot?" Betty asked, petting his rough coat. His big, gentle eyes looked up at her.

"Look at him lying there, so safe and secure. He's not the least bit afraid," said Martha. "He can't be more than three months old. Please, Bob, can't we keep him? We'll keep him out of your way," pleaded Martha.

Bob started the engine, "We can't keep a goat onboard, they're messy. No, we're finding a home for it right now."

They stopped at the first village they saw and the whole village came out in waist deep water to greet them. The native men lifted the dinghy on to the sand. Children giggled and hid behind their mothers' skirts. They peeked out with their huge gentle brown eyes and friendly smiles. Women offered gifts of gigantic trumpet shells, fruit and cakes. Then, they were led to the chief's hut.

Suddenly, the heavens opened up with torrential rain. Thunder and lighting went through the sky, like bolts of roaring fire. All the natives gasped in surprise, looking at the *Destiny* group, as if they had brought the thunder gods.

Entering the chief's hut, they were given sarongs made of a soft, flowery material. Large hibiscus flowers were placed behind their ears.

"Never saw you in a skirt before, guys. You look pretty sexy with that flower in your hair," Betty said looking over at Jim and Bob.

"No funny remarks," Bob said as he tried to adjust his skirt.

"You do look pretty fetching," said Jim, making funny eyes.

Seeing them laugh sent the villagers into a giggling frenzy. The chief was sitting on the floor with his legs crossed in front of him.

He put his hands up to silence them. "Be seated. I am Chief Latoga, and this is my wife Malina, my son Ohwa, and Junno."

The chief's sons sat smiling, most of their teeth were missing. They wore soiled T-shirts, including one from the New York Yankees, and *Rambo*.

"Very pleased to meet you," the *Destiny* group said. They shook each mud crusted hand as it came towards them.

"We would like to present you with kava," said Bob, placing it at the knees of the chief. "And for your lovely wife we offer this little baby goat," he placed it on Malina's lap.

Chief Latoga went into a ritual, raising his hands to the gods. Bowing low to the ground, he chanted a few words. Then looking at Bob, he placed his hands on the kava, the sign of acceptance.

"Thank you for such wonderful gifts," he said. "Also for bringing us much needed rain. You will stay and celebrate with us. Quick, Ohwa—make the kava so that we can all drink."

He ground the kava root with a stone mallet then added water, stirring and mashing it until it looked like muddy water.

"Are we going to have to drink that?" Betty whispered to Martha.

"Bloody hope not, it'll make me ill."

"I thought only men drank kava. Look, his wife left the room. Maybe they'll bypass us," Betty said hopefully.

Placing his blessing over the drink, Chief Latoga picked up an old coconut shell. He filled it with the kava and passed it to Bob. "Drink Captain," he said, face beaming with delight.

It was a high honor to be asked to join a celebration, but they did not want to drink the muddy goo. Bob gulped it down and tried not to make a face. Then he handed back the shell. The chief immediately refilled it and drank with delight, savoring the taste and smacking his lips. Refilling the coconut shell, he passed it from person to person.

When it was Betty's turn, she whispered to Bob, "I hope we don't catch anything. They're not washing the shell after they drink." She took a drink and it almost gagged her. She gulped it down anyhow and handed back the shell.

Bob started to rise, "Thank you for your hospitality."

The chief raised his hand in a command. "Sit, the celebration isn't over," and he refilled the community shell.

After the second drink, Betty's mouth was numb and her ears were ringing. When the third shell came, she knew she couldn't stomach it. Looking at Latoka with a sympathetic smile she placed her hands on her stomach. "No more please."

The chief smiled with an understanding look, "Okay, lady, no more."

Finally the last drop was scooped out and the *Destiny* group got up to leave. Giving back the sarongs, they said farewell as they staggered to the dinghy. Helping hands were everywhere as the natives lifted the skiff back in the water. Their goodbyes could still be heard as they sailed away.

"They sure made us feel welcome," Betty said, feeling woozy.

"I feel a little sick to my stomach," said Jim, flopping down on the seat. "I'll take a good cold beer anytime."

"We'll motor around the bend out of sight, then we'll drop anchor," said Bob. "I think we all need a nap, I'm seeing double."

No one was hungry; they just wanted to sleep. They were done under by the kava.

Sun rays were shining through the portholes. The cool morning breeze woke them from a drugged sleep. The smell of bacon and eggs weaved its way into Betty and Bob's cabin. The aroma aroused their stomach juices and drew them quickly into the galley.

"Morning, I'm just fixing Jimmie-Boy's breakfast," she said as she took the full plates up on deck.

"Don't know who's working for who around here anymore," said Bob.

"Oh well, I'll cook ours. How does eggs, bacon and toast sound?" asked Betty.

When she served the food, Bob consumed his in no time. Three mouthfuls was all she was able to eat, she was sick to her stomach.

"Must be the effects of the kava," Betty said. "Lets take a swim."

Cool waters enlivened their bodies as they dove into the deep blue sea. The cool water seemed to soothe Betty's stomach. They swam over to an island that was only visible at low tide. As they searched for shells they saw something flutter in the distance. Approaching with caution they found a seagull in trouble. A piece of plastic was tangled around the bird's neck and wing as it struggled desperately.

"Hold him, Bob. I'll try to untangle his wing," said Betty grabbing the plastic.

The bird was frightened and pecked Bob's hands. "Hold still you little varmint, we're trying to help you. If we don't get you free before high tide you're a goner."

Pulling the plastic off, they released the bird and watched him fly safely away.

There was very little work being done on *Destiny* and she looked neglected. Bob gave the crew a list of jobs to do to get them back into a routine. When Bob and Betty completed their chores, they got in the dinghy and went snorkeling. When they returned, Jim and Martha were sulking on the front deck and didn't hear them come aboard.

"They have their bloody nerve going off and leaving us. They didn't even check to see if we had plans," whined Martha.

"Why are we doing all the work while they leave us stranded?" added Jim.

"You ought to good and well tell him when he comes back," urged Martha.

Bob was furious when he heard them. He walked toward them and asked, "Is there a problem?" Bob asked staring at the two of them. "Do you have something you want to talk about?"

Startled, Jim's face turned red and he stammered, "No, everything's fine. We're just about finished."

Martha stood up and swept her long blonde hair back and asked, "Is it okay if we take a ride in the dinghy?"

Bob stood with his hands on his hips and stared at them, "Sure, as long as your work is finished."

After they left, Betty shook her head in disgust. "They're acting like two spoiled brats. We should treat them like employees rather than family."

Bob was angry, "I pay them a salary and we include them in everything we do. I've given them three raises since they came aboard, and this is how they act."

"I know," said Betty, feeling down. "Jim's attitude has definitely changed towards us. Maybe we've been together too long."

"Don't let them get the best of us," said Bob. "Hey, isn't it time for lunch?"

"Yeah, how about some fried rice?" laughed Betty.

'No, no, please. I can't stand the smell of it anymore," Bob laughed, grabbing his stomach.

As the days went by, Betty was still not feeling well. She could only eat a few mouthfuls of food. Fighting a bladder infection wasn't helping either. She had lost so much weight, she looked skinny. Trying not to complain, she kept up with everyone. Keflex® was the only antibiotic they had onboard, but it was not helping her. They were in malaria country and took malaria pills. Those gave Betty severe cramps and she refused to take them.

Bob decided to go back to the city of Suva for much needed supplies, and to the American Express office for their mail.

As Betty climbed off the boat to go shopping, Martha approached her. "Would you mind if we went with you?"

"You don't need to come. I'm just buying a few things," Betty answered. They followed her anyhow as she pushed the cart down the aisle. Martha and Jim walked along side her in the store, putting things into the basket.

"We don't need ten pounds of rice, we have plenty on board," said Betty putting it back.

"Jimmie likes rice and I don't want to run out," said Martha in false sweetness as she placed it back in the basket.

They kept placing unnecessary and personal things into the basket as they went through the aisles. When Betty checked out, she had spent more than she expected. Fuming, Betty paid the bill, vowing it would not happen again. She felt too ill to fight about it now.

They had pleasant weather in the Fiji outer islands, and now it was time to head out. Next stop, Vanuatu. Gray clouds filled the sky, blocking out the sun and a dreary day loomed ahead. The bustling wind beat against *Destiny*, determined to hold her back. Betty felt so bad she slept through the rough conditions.

Drizzling rain kept them damp and miserable, and they were pleased to hear Bob say, "We're pulling into the harbor ahead. It's a French island halfway to Vanuatu, called Ouvea. We have to get out of this mess."

They were motoring close to shore, ready to drop the anchor, when they heard a siren. A French Army craft came along side of *Destiny*. Some of the soldiers were dressed in uniforms, others in skimpy bikinis. All were young and handsome. Their magnificent bodies, tan from the sun, glistened in the misty rain. Betty thought she was turning into a lecherous sea witch.

Requesting to come aboard, they climbed on deck with automatic rifles. They inspected the documents and passports, then thoroughly searched the boat.

"What's the problem, Sergeant?" asked Bob.

"We had an uprising. One of our diplomats was murdered last night," said one of the soldiers as he continued to search the boat. "Our troops were flown in from France to control the island." Reexamining one of the passports he asked, "Why are you here?"

"We're on our way to Vanuatu," said Bob. "The weather got so bad, we came in for shelter."

The soldier looked at him, "You can't stay here. The people will sneak aboard and rob and maybe kill you."

"What a horrible thought. It's too rough to go back out there and we planned to leave in the morning," pleaded Betty.

Using his portable radio, he talked to his superiors. Then he said, "You can anchor in front of our barracks. I'll put two men on duty to guard you through the night."

"We'll anchor wherever you say," agreed Bob.

A soldier walked the beach in front of *Destiny* all night, another lay bivouac style in a trench. Crowds roamed the beach arguing among themselves, shouting and pointing at the *Destiny* with raised fist. Chills went through Betty at the thought of what could happen while they slept. Bob and Jim took turns keeping watch and at two in the morning gunfire was heard in the distance. Solders awoke instantly, combing the area. A search party went out to see where the gun shots had come from. Sleep was light and the night seemed endless as they waited for daylight.

The morning sky was full of cold and damp rain clouds with no promise of a better day. Heading out early as they promised, they heard *Destiny*'s name called over the radio.

"*Destiny* can you hear us?" asked one of the French soldiers.

"This is *Destiny*. What can I do for you?" Bob answered.

"We're wondering if you could tow us in. Our engine conked out and we're stuck at the mouth of the harbor."

Finding them was easy. Jim threw a rope and Bob towed the speedboat full of men to their dock.

"We are most grateful," said a smiling soldier. They waved

good-bye as *Destiny* sailed away.

Still beating and battling the elements, they arrived safely in Vanuatu the next day. It was Sunday and everything was closed on the island of Villa.

By three in the afternoon, Betty really felt sick. "I'm going to bed for a while."

"I hope you feel better after your nap," said Bob, very concerned. "We'll go over to the local restaurant for dinner if you're up to it."

Betty didn't feel much better when she woke up, but she managed to get dressed. The little restaurant at the end of the pier had a specialty—coconut crab. Remembering how delicious they were, she ordered one. The plate was covered with the huge red steaming crab. It was served in a tantalizing herb sauce. She took only a few bites and her stomach cramped as she broke out in a cold sweat.

Nauseated, she said, "It's no use, I can't eat. Each mouthful gives me horrible cramps."

"Don't eat, then. Don't worry, it won't go to waste," said Bob chomping away. Go back to the boat and rest."

Betty slept 'til early morning. When she woke up, she seemed to feel a little better. At least her stomach wasn't aching. Betty went out to the galley where Bob was sitting at the table, drinking orange juice.

"How would you like some pancakes for breakfast?" Betty asked.

"Wow! Do you feel up to it? I haven't had pancakes for a while."

She got out the pancake flour and mixed the batter. As she poured it on the grill, she noticed the pancakes didn't puff up. They laid on the grill like dead flat disks.

She put them on a plate and cut a small piece to taste. "These pancakes seem a little tough. Maybe I should make you something else?"

"No, that's all right. I'll eat them," said Bob, taking the plate from her.

"I don't think they're going to taste good. Let me fix you some eggs," said Betty.

"No way, I said I'd eat them," he said taking his first mouthful. His face twitched, and he snapped. "These are terrible."

"Give them to me. I'll make you something else," Betty said reaching for the plate.

"No, I said I'll eat them," Bob said in an irritated voice, then murmured "God, these taste like rubber."

Betty reached for them, and he blocked her hand, "I'm eating them."

Bob kept complaining, going on and on for about five minutes. Betty's stomach started to churn, and her head began to pound like the beat of a bongo drum.

Her temper blew, "Give me the goddamn things," and she reached for the plate. Bob blocked her hand. "You're bitching about eating them, but you won't let me take your plate. You don't want me to make you anything else, but you won't shut up." Before he could stop her, she grabbed the plate and she threw the pancakes on his head. The syrupy goo sat on top of Bob's head. His hair was matted with the pancakes as the syrup ran down the his face and dripped off his nose. He was shocked, but finally quiet. Running into the stateroom, Betty slammed the door and laid on the bed crying.

"I hate this boat. I hate this place. I want to go home," she screamed.

After a good cry, she calmed down. She drifted off to sleep and was awakened by gripping stomach cramps and a cold sweat covering her body. She knew she was really sick and needed a doctor. Where would she find one in Vanuatu?

When Betty went on deck where Bob was reading, he looked up and said, "How are you feeling? Come over here and let me hug you." She lay beside him as he kissed her hot forehead. "You feel like you have a fever. You really don't feel well, do you?"

"I feel like a zombie. I don't know what's wrong with me."

Bob was worried as he said, "Lets take a walk in town maybe we can find a doctor." Stores were scarce and they searched the town walking up and down each street.

"There's a doctor's office!" Betty said, pointing to a second floor office. "I hope he's in. I really need to find out why I'm so tired and have cramps all the time. I'd like to get rid of this bladder infection, too."

The doctor took her right away. His appearance looked like something out of Hemingway—shiny bald head; and a full face that looked like Mr. Potato Head. He had a bulbous red nose, lined with blue veins. His huge beer belly protruded out on his tall frame, and his hands were large and calloused. The way Betty felt, she didn't care what he looked like as long as he could help her.

After Betty explained her symptoms he checked her thoroughly. Then in what sounded like an Australian accent, he said, "I'd like to have a urine sample," he handed her a small cup. "We have a lab here, I'll check it right away."

Ten minutes later, he came back, "You have a severe staph infection, have you had any cuts or open sores?"

"Not that I know of," she said searching her arms and legs for sores.

He sat at the desk and asked, "Have you had any cuts, bruises or operations that have healed?"

"I had a root canal done in Fiji," Betty said thoughtfully.

The doctor was writing on a chart, "That's a good possibility, did he give you an antibiotic before and after he did the root canal?

"No," Betty answered. "I asked him about it but he didn't think it was necessary."

'It's a good thing you came in. The staph infection is traveling through your system. In another week you would have been in serious trouble. Here's three prescriptions. Two of them are strong forms of penicillin. The other one is to neutralize and ease the burning of the urinary infection. Your intestines, stomach and bladder are infected. It would have continued through the rest of your body. We see a lot of this in the mountain area of the gold coast of Australia."

Betty smiled, "Is that where your from? I thought I recognized the accent."

"Yes. I came here to visit friends. The regular doctor asked me to cover for him, while he left on a personal emergency. This is your lucky day. If I hadn't said yes, there wouldn't have been a doctor in town."

They went back to the boat and Betty rested, and after a week of medication, Betty's body started to respond. She was no longer nauseated and was able to eat. Color came back in her face and she started to have more energy.

"It's great to feel good again," said Betty, enjoying a martini at sunset.

"It's good to have you healthy again. I didn't realize how sick you were," he said as he hugged her close to him. "Now that you're feeling better I have a surprise for you," Bob smiled at her as they sat on the deck.

"What is it?" asked Betty, her voice raising in excitement.

"A special ceremony tomorrow—you'll see," said Bob. He was grinning from ear to ear.

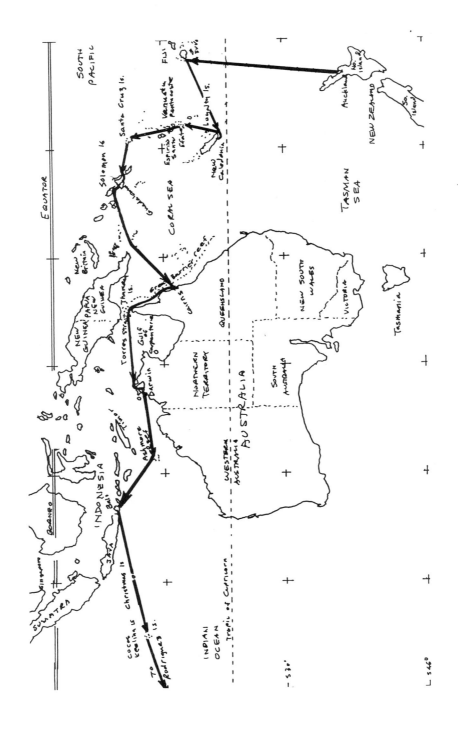

Thirty-one

The next morning, Bob told everyone, "I have a surprise for all of you. The main attraction in Vanuatu is the Yam Harvest at Pentecost. We're lucky to be able to attend the ceremony. Only fifty people are allowed to the sacred event and we've been invited. The men take weeks building a one-hundred-foot tower made from sticks and branches. They are tied together with twine. Twenty jumping platforms stick out at different heights on the tower."

"Come on, let's go," Betty said, climbing off the boat.

When they arrived at the village, men and boys were dressed in a ceremonial garments, called the penis wraps. A red cloth was wrapped around the penis, letting the testicles hang out. The rest of the red cloth was worn like a thong. The excess material was wrapped around their waist. Women were dressed topless in grass skirts and carried babies on their hips. They danced to the beat of the drums chanting spiritual songs.

Vines were carefully measured for the exact distance from the jumping platform, to just inches above the ground. When they stood on the platform, the vine was attached to their ankles and to the platform. After they jumped, their head was supposed to skim the top of the loose earth below. If they measured wrong or a vine broke they could break their necks.

The higher the standing of the man in the tribe, the higher off the ground he jumped. The chief of the tribe had the honor of going last. He leapt from the highest point, one hundred feet. As they watched, a few vines broke but no one was seriously hurt. It was a very unusual and thrilling event to see. That was the climax of their stay in Vanuatu.

Sailing around the islands of the Pacific was exciting, and the weather was more to Betty's liking—calm seas, light winds and beautiful sunny days. She was feeling much better, although she tired easily. They wanted to stop at Malikula Island. It was an important place in the history of the second World War. Army supplies were kept there and transported wherever the military needed them. The island was not a military base any longer, now the people kept themselves busy farming.

"I have a great idea," declared Bob. "The Coolidge transport was sunk here, it would be a sensational dive. Let's see if we can find a dive master to take us down."

It wasn't hard to find a dive master and he took them diving the very next day. They dove down eighty feet to the mighty ship. It was completely covered with various shades and shapes of coral. An amazing variety of sealife swam in and out of each port-hole. The Coolidge was no longer alive with soldiers but rather with many species of fish. They were greeted by a stupendous five hundred pound grouper named Boris. The grouper thank God was friendly.

Everything on the ship was still intact, including helmets, shells, guns. A long row of white spotless latrines glistened like monuments in the sunlight that filtered down through the open hatch. They swam in and out of the different areas of the ship, following barracudas, sharks and mighty Boris.

On their last day, the dive master took them to Million Dollar point, where army trucks, cars, tanks, planes and gear were dumped in the bay. Now divers could sit in the jeeps and planes, sixty feet below, and watch the curious fish. It was an exciting dive, and they took pictures of one another sitting in the jeeps and trucks.

It was a hot day in June, the temperature was always in the high nineties. They hoped to get a cool breeze as they headed out to sea. Betty and Bob were trying desperately to get along with Jim and Martha. At each port, they searched for new crew but there was none available. Martha spent so much time doting on Jim that she had little time for anything else. It was tough keeping things peaceful when Bob and Betty were seething inside. Martha and Jim knew they couldn't be replaced and were taking advantage of it.

"I keep getting the feeling that we're a pain in the ass to them," said Bob. "It's a hell of a way to feel on your own boat."

"I feel the same way," said Betty. "Their work is falling way behind again, and they're only sociable when they want something."

"We'll put up with them and as soon as we find new crew, out they go," said Bob.

It was just a sixty miles sail to Guadalcanal, and the South Pacific breeze pushed *Destiny* gently to their destination. Arriving at Guadalcanal, the were disappointed in the rundown condition of the area. The streets were wide concrete, built to hold the tanks and military vehicles that used to be there. Betty could picture how they rolled through the town during World War Two.

At one time, it was very prosperous—until the military left. After that, there was very little to support the area. Left over military Quonset huts were used as civilian homes and the place looked unkempt. There was a melancholy feeling to the place and stores that were open were dark and dingy with little to sell. It's easy to visualize the hustle bustle of the place when the military occupied the area. There were signs over closed places, JOE'S AMERICAN BAR or GOOD TIME CHARLIE'S. They could almost hear the laughter of the soldiers, and feel the heavy military vehicles rolling down the road.

Food was sparse in the supermarket with very little variety and the meat looked old and dry. Some cuts were tainted with an edge of green.

Betty looked disgusted, "I'm not buying meat here."

"We're leaving for home in a few days. It's time for me to go back to the doctor for my checkup," said Bob. "We can bring meat and supplies back."

When all the chores were finished on *Destiny*, Bob and Betty prepared to leave.

Bob called Jim aside and said, "You don't have to keep the boat here in the harbor. It really isn't a good holding spot. You handle *Destiny* as well as I can, so if you want to cruise around, you can. Just make sure you're here when we get back."

"You don't mind?" Jim said, surprised. "That's great, thanks. I'll take good care of her."

Leaving a list of repairs to be done and enough money for wages and food, they left for home.

Everyone was shocked at the amount of weight Betty had lost. She had gone from a size eight dress to a size four.

Betty went to her family physician for a complete checkup; he looked at her charts and said, "You've lost eighteen pounds since your last visit. Your cholesterol is still three hundred and forty-nine, your protein is extremely low."

"I told you about the staph infection and the medicine I took," said Betty. "It's just a matter of time before I put the weight back on."

Dr. Whitaker sat studying her for a moment then added, "I don't want you to leave the country again until your protein is normal. With it that low, you have no defense against infection." He was a very caring doctor and seemed concerned.

Then he looked at her like she was anorexic, "I want you to eat lots of meat, potatoes and milk."

Betty said in a hurt voice, "Aren't those things bad for my cholesterol?"

"I'm not going to worry about the cholesterol now. I want your protein and weight up where they should be." Then, seeing the expression on her face, his voice softened and said, "Well, do the best you can and come back next week. I want to keep a close watch on you."

The month went by quickly and Betty gained five pounds. Her protein was near normal, but the cholesterol was still high. When she went back to the doctor's for her final visit, he smiled and said, "I feel better about your condition, but I still don't think you should leave the states just yet."

"We have to leave, there are people waiting for us," said Betty in desperation. "We have a schedule to keep."

"I guess I can't stop you from going," said Dr. Whitaker. "I'll give you a couple of prescriptions. If you run into any problems, take them. Don't forget to eat and take your vitamins."

Betty met Bob at the airport. Bob had been in Boston getting his checkup, and received a good report. His doctor was still amazed at his recovery and that he was in such good shape.

With their medical problems taken care of, it was now time to shop for supplies for *Destiny*.

Two styrofoam boxes of frozen meat, chicken, and many other delicacies were packed, along with boxes and boxes of parts and supplies. Twenty movies had been taped for entertainment on board ship. Now it was time to say goodbye to family and friends. Knowing she had been sick was a worry to her children. They didn't want her to go back, but she was going. She loved them very much and would miss them terribly. Sailing had become a part of Betty's life, and they had grown accustomed to her being away. It was easier for her to leave this time. She laughed thinking, *Boy, I would have loved an excuse like this at the beginning of the trip.*

Thirty-two

Arriving back in Guadalcanal, they were met with confusion. The number of boxes they were bringing into the country was causing an uproar with customs. One corner of the styrofoam box had cracked open. Blood from a defrosted steak was leaking out. Bob was dragging the box across the floor, and blood oozed out in a steady streak.

"I hope they don't think we have a dead body in here," laughed Betty, pointing to the blood. "Are we going to have a problem?"

The customs officer looked down at the box, "Is that blood?"

"Yes it is and it's . . . ," before Betty could finish he yelled sternly, "Open that box."

Betty took the lid off and he demanded, "Why did you bring meat to our country? You should have bought it here."

Betty thought fast, "You don't have beef here, I looked before I left. I didn't bring chicken or pork. I'll buy that here." She hoped he wouldn't open the other styrofoam box. Another customs officer hustled over and asked, "What are all these boxes for? You will have to pay duty on all this."

"No duty," Bob said shaking his head. "These are parts and supplies for a boat in transit."

"Open this box, I want to see what you have," said the customs officer.

The box was full of video tapes and their eyes lit up. A big smile came across their faces, "You have blue movies? We have to keep them so we can inspect them."

Bob laughed and shook his head. "These aren't blue movies. They're just regular movies."

"What in the world are blue movies?" Betty asked curiously.

"He thinks they're porno films. You're not allowed to bring them into the country. They're hoping they're porno so they can keep them," laughed Bob.

Betty looked at the officers leering, and she said sternly, "Sir, we'll be leaving tomorrow, we must have the movies back by morning."

The officer smirked as he picked up the box of video's. He waved his hand toward the door. "You're free to go. I'm sending an officer with you to make sure everything goes to the boat. If the movies are not the wrong kind, we'll deliver them by noon tomorrow."

Destiny was in the harbor waiting for them. They received a half-hearted welcome from Martha and Jim. The crew didn't look too happy to have them back, and a feeling of intruding came over Betty and Bob.

"Did you take the boat out?" Bob asked.

"Yeah, we did, but we didn't go very far," said Jim. "Rather nice with just the two of us. We handled it great."

"Anyone stop by that we know?" Betty asked, thinking some of their friends might have come into port.

Martha got a funny look on her face and Jim turned a bit pink. "No—no one stopped by. We left right after you did."

Something was amiss and Betty wasn't sure what. *We'll find out later*, she thought.

The supplies were put away and the crew was overjoyed at the sight of the goodies they had brought back.

Jim licked his lips, "God, a good steak is going to taste great. My mouth is watering already."

"Blimmey, look at the variety of food, it's all scrumptious," Martha said, her cockney coming back.

Customs returned their movies just as they were ready to leave. "I must lock these up in your gun cabinet. You cannot see them until you leave the islands. We had no time to check them."

Bob thought a minute then said, "We haven't seen the tapes either. Suppose I give you six other tapes that we have seen. You can lock them up instead?"

Looking confused for a minute the officer stood thinking it over, "Okay, that will be fine." Before he could change his mind, Bob handed him six tapes and grabbed the others. The officer locked them away, sealing the gun locker with masking tape.

"Do not break this seal until you leave our area," he said sternly as he jumped off *Destiny*.

Betty stood laughing, "I don't believe you got away with that, you're a fast thinker."

Fueling and getting the rest of supplies on board was a demanding chore. Jim and Martha helped unpack and then the boxes were taken back to shore. So far they were lucky—no roaches.

When they left for the New Georgia Islands, they had pleasant weather with very light wind. A gentle breeze picked up around seven at night and they sailed a beam reach with friendly seas. Feeling tired from jet lag, Betty went below and slept until her watch at ten. As she came on deck, she could see lightening on the starboard side. The wind picked up to twenty knots and was behind them. She could feel *Destiny* skimming the water, glad to be set free.

When Bob went to bed, and she relaxed at the helm, with the wind blowing against her back. She felt comfortable being back on *Destiny*. Lightening was still flickering in the distance, lighting the night like a glowing ember. Alongside the boat was another sparkling scene of phosphorescence, dancing in *Destiny*'s wake. Almost hypnotized by the flashing lights, she never noticed the waves swelling up from the strong winds.

Thrashing against the hull, they turned *Destiny*'s smooth motion into an exaggerated rock. The boat heeled over so far it washed the toe rail in the water. Betty was thrown off her seat at the helm and on to the deck.

She had just gotten up when Martha came rushing up. "What's going on? You bloody knocked me out of me bed," she said in a snarl.

"It was just a change of wind. It's getting rough again," Betty answered, trying to hold her temper. "You better put up the lee cloth, or you'll get thrown out again." Martha went away grumbling.

Jim came up shortly to take his watch, and Betty went to her stateroom. Climbing in between the lee cloth, she tried to get comfortable and sleep, but she heard voices coming through the hatch.

"Hi, Jimmy-boy," said Martha. "I came up to keep you company. God, why'd they have to come back? Now we have to put up with them again. It was so nice by ourselves."

"Yeah, it was pretty nice. We could do what we wanted and go where we pleased. I wish they hadn't come back too, but hey, it's their boat," said Jim. "I wish it was mine. Someday I'll have one like this."

Betty was furious by what she heard. She laid there thinking how ungrateful the spoiled brats were as she drifted off to sleep.

By the next afternoon, they entered the harbor of Mavaro. They could see the natives rowing toward them in their dug-out canoes. The young men tried to climb aboard but Bob stopped them.

"Don't come aboard," ordered Bob. "Stay in your canoes and we'll look at what you have to sell."

They sat on the deck buying and trading for some exquisite carvings. Betty was handed a large beautiful trumpet shell. She was ready to buy it until two roaches crawled out.

Squealing, she shook the roaches overboard and handed the shell back, "Dip it in the salt water. I don't buy roaches."

"They won't hurt you lady," the natives said laughing at her.

Light rain filled the sky and the buying session ended. They went below to read while Betty baked a cherry pie and muffins. The natives peeked through the port holes and watched every move they made, until Bob chased them away.

While Betty was baking, she spotted a roach in one of the closets, "Oh no," she screamed, "I hate roaches." She grabbed a paper and killed it. "I don't want those damn things onboard."

Betty went frantic, pulling everything out of the closets. Soon, she was tearing every closet and drawer apart. She sprayed and dusted boric acid around everywhere, working for hours. When Betty was sure she had covered every spot, she gave up and rested.

Light rain turned to a drenching downpour, and the ominous clouds laid heavy overhead. A promise of gloomy weather for the next two days filled the sky. It was lunchtime and the smell of fried rice drifted through the boat.

"Martha, we can't eat rice again. I've reached a point where I'm sick of the smell," Betty said getting out the tuna fish for sandwiches.

Martha never answered. She continued preparing the rice mixed with eggs. Then she carried it up on deck, where Jim was waiting. They stayed by themselves and had very little to talk to Betty or Bob about.

Only bare necessities were being done now on *Destiny*, but Bob didn't feel like arguing about it. The respect between Bob and Jim was decreasing. They no longer acted like friends.

The rain continued, and wearing ponchos, they strolled through the village. They talked to the people and purchased more carvings. They natives were more interested in trading than getting money.

"I'll trade this wonderful carving for your VCR," said one of the natives who had peeked through the potholes.

"No way," said Betty. "That's a nice carving, but not *that* nice."

He kept pestering and another man chimed in. "I need a battery. What will you take for one of your big batteries?" He showed them several carvings, none worth a battery or VCR.

They were a beautiful, delightful race of people with high cheek bones and skin the color of honey. Their huge dark eyes shone with good health. The women's thick black hair flowed to their waists.

Later in the afternoon, a very distinguished looking man with a small child rowed over to *Destiny*. He was statuesque with picture-perfect white hair. Dressed in a flowered wrap tied at his waist, his bare broad shoulders and body was in perfect condition. Betty thought the man was in his forties and that was his son. They greeted him and asked him if he would like to come aboard. He was a delightful person, very well educated and seventy years old. The adorable boy was his grandson.

Bob was flabbergasted, "Whatever you're eating, I want some too."

It was still raining a light mist and Bob was lying on the bed reading. Betty laid beside him and said, "You know, all the islands are starting to look alike."

Bob looked up from his book and said, "Yeah, you're right. Huts and palm trees, and ninety-seven degrees everywhere we go."

Betty reached over and kissed him, then teasing she said, "Honey, this is your dream, and we have two and a half more years to go."

Bob rolled his eyes and said, "Don't remind me."

They both lay there in silence for awhile then Bob spoke hesitantly, "We could cut the trip short and head for home. It will take us almost a year to get there."

Betty felt a flood of hope run through her, she didn't want to seem overanxious. "It's up to you. I made a promise to stay as long as you wanted to."

Leaning over, he whispered in her ear, "I'm ready to head home."

"Yippee," Betty yelled, "I don't have to do another two and a half years of this. Maybe we'll be home in six to eight months."

They were motoring when they left the harbor. Beating against light wind; they would have to sail nine hundred miles before they reached Australia. The weather was hot and they were sweltering in the heat. Everyone prayed for strong winds to cool them and hasten the passage.

Feeling the wind change, they knew their prayers had been answered. Now they were close reaching with the winds ranging in the twenties. Charging ahead at eight knots was a reprieve from the doldrums. The heeling was bad, leaving only the portside for sitting or sleeping. Lee cloths were pulled out again and they were back to the dreadful motion and sleepless nights.

Coolness came upon them as they sailed closer to Australia. The wind continued high and the sea ranged up to twenty feet. Somber clouds layered the sky, like piles of dirty snow. Then a deluge of rain poured down saturating everything.

Making the best of it, they held on to keep from sliding from their seats. *Destiny* was thrown sideways as the waves thrashed against her. Water leaked into the salon again drenching the stereo and books. Betty could handle these situations better now. She didn't beat the mattress as often. But the motion still got to her and she felt seasick. They could put up with it knowing soon they would be in Cairns, Australia.

Cairns stood out against the horizon like a toy city. Immediately, Betty felt better at the sight of land, ready for civilization. They had made it in five days. When customs and the Health Department came aboard, they checked thoroughly in the galley taking eggs, fresh fruit, vegetables and any meat that was not cooked.

"Whoa, wait a minute. Don't take that meat," Betty said, she was aggravated. "I'll put it in the microwave and cook it in minutes."

"Just make sure you have it cooked by the time I'm ready to leave," the health officer said. "We don't have the diseases other countries have, and we don't want any new ones brought in. That's why we're so careful."

Cairns was a lovely seaside resort and the atmosphere was very laid back. Betty fell right into the swing of things. Martha and Jim took off for the rest of the day while Bob and Betty visited friends on a nearby boat.

"It was nice of you to let Martha's mother and father live aboard while you were gone," said Richard from the boat *Caloose*.

"You mean back in the Canary Islands?" Betty asked.

"No, when you were in Guadalcanal. Her parents came aboard right after you left. They went off sailing for the week. Didn't you know?"

"No we didn't," Bob said feeling betrayed by Jim. "I can't understand why they didn't tell us."

"We let her mother and father live aboard before. We didn't care as long as they let us know," Betty said bewildered.

"They're always talking about how tough they have it, and how hard you work them. Wish we had it that tough," said Marge laughing. "We really don't feel sorry for them."

Betty frowned, "You mean they come over to your boat and complain about us?"

"Sure, they tell everybody. We see what they do and how you treat them. They don't realize how good they have it. Hey, don't tell them we told you."

"We won't. Let's forget about them and go to dinner," Betty said half-heartedly, but she was steaming. Now she knew why they acted so funny when she asked if anyone stopped by.

The six of them went off to a Chinese restaurant and had the specialty, a huge four pound mud crab. It was very unusual but delicious. Betty tried to have a good time but felt uncomfortable. She wondered why Martha and Jim hadn't told them about her mother's visit.

The next day, Martha was sitting in the galley fooling with her shells, and Betty asked, "How's your mom and dad, have you heard from them lately?"

Martha never looked up from her shells. "Yes, just talked to me mum the other day, they're fine."

Betty stared at her and asked, "Are they planning on visiting soon?"

"No, dad's busy and mum doesn't want to come without him."

Betty could hardly keep from telling her what she knew. *That little liar*, she thought, *I'll never believe another word she says. I can't accuse her as she'll want to know who told me.*

Betty went over to Bob, who was reading. "Martha's letting on her parents weren't here. It's burning me up. We let her mother and dad stay onboard before. She even had her sister here one time."

Bob shrugged his shoulders, "I don't know what goes through their minds anymore. Guess I never did."

"Oh well, the heck with them. I'm going shopping. Want to come with me?" she asked as she nibbled his ear.

"Stop, you're tickling me," he said, trying not to laugh. "You know I hate shopping. I'm going to scan the marinas for new crew. See if anyone's available."

Betty hadn't been shopping by herself since Bermuda, and it felt wonderful. She loved Cairns, it felt like an upscale resort with unique boutiques. She spent the day going into all the shops, trying on clothes, and buying delicious Australian chocolates. The supermarkets were just like back home, with a large variety of everything. It was a fantastic day, she loved it when a place felt like home.

When she got back to *Destiny*, Bob looked gloomy, "I searched around, but no one knew of any available crew. We'll just have to keep looking, and put up with their shit till we find someone."

Saying goodbye to their friends, they sailed off to visit a few more areas in Australia. They would stop at Bathers Bay, seventy-two miles away. Once outside the harbor, the winds blew strong and the sea churned like a frothy washing machine. Betty was seasick again and the motion and wind was driving her nuts.

I guess this Cherry Hill girl will never make a good sailor, she thought. *I'm trying hard, I just wish I could feel the same sense of accomplishment and joy that Bob gets from sailing. This is an experience I will never be able to duplicate, or forget. Sometimes, I feel like such a pain in the ass with my moaning and groaning.*

They were moving at nine knots with forty-knot winds pushing *Destiny* through the rough waves. Gratefully, they arrived sooner than expected at Bathers Bay. Gusting winds whipped the sand on the beach, clouding the air. The bay was so rough and windy they couldn't go to shore. The forecast was for more of the same. Never setting foot on land, they sailed off in the morning to Pelican Island, an open reef in the ocean.

They dreaded the forty-seven mile trip, but to their surprise the wind died down and the sun came out. They made a short stop to take a break from the long haul to Darwin. Stretching their legs, they walked the barren island, watching large flocks of white pelicans and birds. The birds fluttered and squawked, making circles above them, alarmed at being disturbed. They stayed away from the nests that were hidden between the tall grass, spending most of the day enjoying as much of the island as they could. *Destiny* was leaving in the morning. Bob never stayed long in anyone place. He was a gypsy, ever wandering.

At five in the morning, he woke everyone by starting the motor. "Get up," he called. "If we want to dive the Great Barrier Reef, we have to get going. Have to make the best of this good weather."

Betty crawled out of bed grumbling, "I'm sure the great barrier could have waited a few more hours."

"Stop bitching wench, and fix me some breakfast," he chided.

It was smooth sailing on a bright, sunny day. They sailed till noontime then Bob anchored off of a small island. They relaxed and had lunch on the barren sandy shore, then took a ride in the dinghy. They wanted to find a good diving spot. Jim and Betty put their masks on and lowered their faces into the water, looking for some live coral. A lot of the reef was dead, but soon they came across an interesting spot. Putting on their diving gear they headed below, searching out the many wondrous, hidden, mysteries. When they surfaced after their dive, they found the current had picked up to a fast pace.

"Damn, are we lucky we came up right by the dinghy," said Jim. "Let's get back to the boat," he said as he climbed in the boat. When they returned, the gauge on *Destiny* showed the current was flowing at five knots of speed.

"We better stay here for the night," said Bob securing the anchor. "There's too many hidden reefs around. I don't want to take a chance of going aground."

As the tide rose, the island was completely covered. It looked like they were anchored in the middle of the vast ocean.

Everyone moaned at Bob's five A.M. wake-up call. They motored away on a seventy-five mile trip to Weymouth lagoon. It felt like the doldrums as they moved along slowly. Betty was relaxing on the stern reading, when she heard the engine cut back and Bob cussing.

Bob called out, "Betty go out on the bow and check for reefs. We're in shallow water."

Walking out to the bow she asked, "How did we get in such shallow water?"

"The damn gauge is not working, its reading seventy feet of water," said Bob. "You can see how shallow it is, can't be more than twelve feet."

Jagged underwater peaks could be sighted all around. Both Jim and Betty stayed alert, looking for darker waters.

Betty called out, "Head over more to the starboard side; it looks darker over there."

"We're in between two rough beds of coral," yelled Jim. "Go

369

slow until I signal, then bear to your starboard."

Bob made slow, careful maneuvers, gliding, as the crew guided him through the treacherous water. Several times, he reversed when the coral made a dead end. Two hours later, they were safely back to deeper water. They were alert for the rest of the trip watching the waters carefully.

They felt weary from the tension and stopped for a short break at Thursday Island. Their next leg was going to be a long one.

Bob checked his charts. "We have seven hundred and fifty miles to go before we get to Darwin. There's no more stops, so rest up."

"Bob, I'm giving you fair warning," Betty said in a determined voice. "When we get to Darwin, I'm going to hogtie you. I'm going to make you stay in one place for awhile. I need some stretch time."

"Okay, I'll give you some stretch time," laughed Bob. "What kind of a sea witch are you? You're supposed to enjoy the open seas, with the wind blowing in your hair."

"I'd enjoy a blow dryer blowing in my hair, and a haircut and I'm going to get one when I reach Darwin."

For the next three days, it was enchanting, sunny and calm with just enough wind for smooth sailing. Betty felt at peace with the world until she heard Bob say, "Damnit, the auto-pilot's broke. We'll have to steer manually from here on."

"I just hope this wind stays up. If we keep doing a hundred and fifty miles a day, we could be in Darwin, in five days," said Jim.

Conversation was sparse on *Destiny* as the five days crept along. The pungent smell of fried rice was served to Jimmy-boy every day. Betty cooked lunch for her and Bob. It was like they were strangers living on their own boat.

They were overjoyed at the sight of Darwin and anchored in Francia Bay. Bob found a mechanic and arranged for repairs to be done on *Destiny*. They found a travel agent to see what was interesting to do in Darwin.

"Going to Ayers Rock is impossible," the travel agent said.

"The planes are on strike."

"Could we rent a car and drive there?" asked Bob.

"The distance is too great to drive for just a few days," said the agent. "How would you like to go to Kakadu Park, in the outback? They have a four-day tour that's terrific."

They looked at the brochure, "If it's as good as it sounds we'll do it," said Betty.

Exploring the wonderful, Billybongs and seeing the huge salt water crocs'—up to twenty feet long, was mind boggling.

"This is the area where *Crocodile Dundee* was filmed," said their guide. "These are the caves you saw in the movies."

Strange, mystifying Aboriginal writings were on the wall. They were faint from years of wear but still very visible. Each day went quickly, and they collapsed each night at the Crocodile hotel.

When they returned to *Destiny*, Jim and Martha were sulking, waiting for their chance to get away. While they were gone, Betty shopped for provisions and Bob finished up the repairs.

"We need a cruising permit to stay in Indonesia. So far, we haven't been unable to get one," said Bob. "I hope we can get into the country."

"Several Yachties said they heard you can buy one there," answered Betty as she put the groceries away.

"We'll see when we get there. Lets get an early start tomorrow. We'll leave as soon as we refuel. The trip is nine hundred and fifty miles."

"It's amazing, the length of the trips don't bother me anymore," said Betty proudly.

Bob laughed and hugged her, "Yeah, you really are a sea witch now."

For days they motored on water that was as smooth as glass as they headed for Indonesia. The current was going in their direction, pulling them smoothly along. The passage was calm and tranquil, giving Betty the opportunity to paint. T-shirts were her latest creation. She decorated the front of the shirts with the fish designs. Then she sewed on shells they had found along the way. Betty also created earrings out of small shells to help fill the idle time.

The soothing breeze cooled their bodies and the birds entertained them in the cloud swirled sky. Soaring through the air on the wind current. Fish jumped high from the water escaping the predator below, but were scooped up by a bird scouting for his dinner. Swishing sounds caused by water brushed against the hull in rhythmic sounds, lulled them to sleep.

Meals were cooked with little effort. Martha and Betty still took turns cooking dinner. Jimmy-Boy still gets his rice at lunch. Martha's time was spent waiting on him while Bob and Betty made do for themselves.

After four days of sailing in the best of conditions, they spotted an island on the horizon.

Bob pointed ahead, "That's Ashmore reef. We'll stop for the night and take a break."

"I see boats that look like Chinese junks," Betty said as she looked through the binoculars. She could see the fishermen waving.

As they dropped the anchor three men came over in a skiff. They were from an Australian ship that was anchored there.

"Hi mates, welcome to our island," said one of the men. "Make yourselves at home, then come over to our boat with your Sheila's. We'll treat you to a Fosters®."

"Thanks, we'll be over as soon as we clean up. Say, are we allowed to go ashore?" asked Bob.

"Sure thing. That's the Australian National bird sanctuary," he said pointing to the flat sandy island, that was covered with saw grass. "Seventy variety of birds live over there."

Happy hour with the Australians was a treat. They sat on the big steel deck and watched the blaze of the orange sun drift slowly below the horizon. There were three men and a woman onboard the Australian survey ship. One man demonstrated their elaborate radio and computer systems.

"We spend nine months a year here keeping a check on the boats and the islands," said Milton, the radio man. "The Indonesian fishermen come in each night after fishing. They hang around this area for weeks, catching as many fish as possible before heading home. We have to check on them, and make sure the fish they catch aren't too small. We also have to watch they don't steal the bird eggs."

Betty thought the Australian people were interesting, she wanted to enjoy their company a little longer. After cocktail hour she invited them back to *Destiny* for dinner, a pot roast dinner was waiting simmering in the galley.

Morning came abruptly and at first light the Indonesians squabbled amongst themselves. Eight engines started all at one time, enough noise to wake the dead. Betty climbed sleepy-eyed out on deck, just in time to see the sun rising. Shadows passed overhead as a huge flock of birds flew by, searching for their breakfast. She dove into the translucent sapphire water and floated on her back, letting the temperate waves splash over her. She dove deep below and watched the fish in a feeding frenzy, chewing the green algae that had collected on *Destiny*'s bottom. Refreshed, she climbed aboard and rested on deck, while the morning sun dried her body.

Bob came up from below, "What are you doing up so early?"

They lounged in the morning sun sipping their coffee and enjoyed the view. The glistening white sand beckoned them and they both dove in and swam ashore. The birds squawked and hovered over them ready to attack if they ventured too close to their nests. Leaving the nests undisturbed, they looked for shells, enjoying the seclusion of the island.

Thirty-three

They said good-bye to their newfound friends before setting sail, heading for Bali, Indonesia. Moderate winds filled the main and mizzen while Jim raised the genoa. Peaceful and comfortable, they enjoyed the serenity and listened to Zanfir on the stereo— his music seemed to blend with the rhythm of the sea.

Bali appeared as the sun was setting, the harbor was speckled with many familiar boats. First to greet them was Roger from the boat *Winkler*. Tying his skiff to *Destiny*, he gave them the lowdown on their port of call.

"Did you get your permit?" asked Roger.

"No, still didn't receive it in the mail," answered Bob.

"Weying is the man that can help you get a permit, if it's at all possible," said Roger. "He comes around every morning at eight to help new boats."

"Did you get a permit yet?" asked Bob.

"No, I just got in myself. I'm claiming engine problems, so I can stay. Why don't you do the same?"

"Good idea. We'll include auto-pilot trouble too," said Jim.

Customs came aboard about noon the next day and Betty offered cold drinks—they requested lunch. After they ate several sandwiches apiece, they sealed the gun cabinet. "You have permission to go ashore and you can stay five days."

"Five days! We wanted to go see the Komodo dragons on Komodo island," said Bob.

"Do you have a cruising permit?" asked the customs officer.

"No," Bob answered sheepishly. "We would like to purchase one, or get permission to go to Komodo."

"Sorry, we don't issue them. The Navy is the one that gives the permits, or they could give you permission to stay longer," said the customs officers as they left the boat.

The *Destiny* group was disappointed and waited for Weying. He came by at two o'clock.

"We're hoping to get enough time to go to Komodo," said Bob. "What will it take to get the permit from the Navy men?"

"I don't know, but I will talk to them," said Weying with a wink. "Fifty dollars might do it. I'll go this afternoon and see what I can do."

"Okay, here's fifty dollars," Bob said with hope in his eyes. "Try hard. I really want to go to Komodo Island."

Early the next morning, Betty heard the murmur of people ashore as their voices carried into her stateroom. She woke Bob up, "Let's rent a car and drive around the countryside and really see Bali."

"There's no way I'll drive here. Did you see the traffic? Tell you what, Weying said you can hire a car and driver real cheap. We'll see Bali that way."

Their driver was gracious and showed them the many different sides of Bali. Touring the countryside, they were fascinated by the rice terraces that deck the mountainsides. The smell of incense permeated the air as they passed the many colorful sacred temples. Donning a shawl, they entered a temple making an offering of money, among the many gifts of food. Betty saw a crowd of people on their knees chanting in front of a cave. She wandered closer to see what they were praying to. Her nostrils flared from the rancid smell of bat guano. Looking up, she saw thousands of flying foxes clinging on the roof of the cave. Betty listened to the mystic chant with the background sound of the hideous shriek of the bats. It sent a chill up her spine. The overpowering blend of incense and bat guano caused her stomach to retch. With her hands on her nose, she went back to the driver.

The streets were crowded and traffic was maddening as the driver weaved his way through the narrow dusty roads. When they stopped to go into a restaurant, they were immediately surrounded by beggars and peddlers. As soon as they stepped from the car they were pulled, tugged, and chanting started, "please buy from me," or "money please."

When they returned to *Destiny*, they waited anxiously for Weying and he arrived late in the afternoon. Bob saw him coming and helped him onboard. "What did they say?"

Weying had a half-smile on his face, "The Navy men say

they will think about it."

"Think about it! What do they mean by that? We don't have too much time. I thought you said you could help us," said Bob a little frustrated.

"I do all I can, sir. Come with me tomorrow and offer them one hundred and fifty dollars. I'm sure they will give you permission," said Weying, almost pleading.

Bob was skeptical but he said, "It's worth the try if you think it will work."

Early the next day, they left to talk to the head officer to see if he could extend their time. When they got there they were kept waiting for an hour. Finally, the officer came over and smiled then took the money. "You can have three extra days, then you can renew again."

"We need a week to get to Komodo and back," said Bob discouraged.

"That's all we can give you," the officer said, as he walked out of the room.

Disgusted, Bob looked at Weying and said, "Goddamnit, I just threw one hundred and fifty dollars away. I'm going back to the boat."

Bob climbed on *Destiny* raving mad. "They got us again, Betty, they got us again. After all that money, they still won't give us the time."

The three of them sat in the cockpit very discouraged. Weying sat looking at Bob and shook his head in despair. "Give me two hundred more, I will convince them."

"No way, I already gave you two hundred dollars, and it's gotten us nowhere. I think they're just trying to bleed me. Let's pull up anchor and get the hell out of here. We've been here four days and I've seen enough."

Martha and Jim were in the salon listening. Martha said to him, "Listen to Bob. He always treats people horrible and loses his temper. If he paid another two hundred, we probably could go see the dragons. I don't want to leave yet. Tell him we don't want to go. Tell him off, Jim . . . tell him how we feel."

Betty couldn't believe her ears. She looked down at Martha and was about to say something, when Jim came to the companionway.

As he walked up the steps, he started to holler, pointing his finger at Bob, "We're not ready to leave. Why do we have to do everything you want to do?" he said defiantly. His face was red with anger as he continued, "Do you have to holler and lose your temper and make us miserable? It's all your fault we can't stay. Why don't you just pay the money?"

Bob was taken aback by Jim's attitude. He stood up and yelled back, "Jesus Christ, I just paid them two hundred dollars. I went to see them and almost begged. What more can I do?"

"Give them the money, that's what you can do," screamed Jim.

Bob sat down feeling confused and frustrated. Now his crew was outwardly turning on him.

Betty looked at Bob, he looked so defeated. She couldn't take their attitude any longer, "Shut up, Jim. You have no right to talk to Bob that way. It's not your money being put out." She walked over and looked down the stairway at Martha. She was sitting in the salon with a smirk on her face. "And you," Betty said, pointing at Martha. "You stop being an instigator, and keep your big mouth shut. You have no say around here."

Martha tried to act innocent, "Blimey, what did I bloody do? I'm just sitting here."

"Sure, Miss Innocent. I heard what you told Jim. Now just keep your mouth shut and stop causing trouble."

Martha came stamping up the stairs, "Jim, let's get out of here. I'm not taking that," and the two spoiled brats took off.

Betty fixed them each a cool drink, she couldn't believe the whole scene. As she handed Bob his drink, he said sadly, "Jim has certainly changed. He's not the same considerate kid I once knew. Why does Martha want to cause trouble between Jim and me?"

The next day, everyone avoided each other; talking only when necessary. Bob was busy installing a part in the auto-pilot.

Betty had bought gifts for her grandchildren and wanted to ship them home. "I'm going to take a cab to the post office. I'll be back as soon as I can," she said to Bob, hopping off the boat with her arms loaded.

She walked up the pier to a waiting cab. "Take me to the post office," she said as she put the boxes in the back seat and climbed in the front. The driver was a short, wiry pleasant guy with a broad smile, his name was Rio.

Bubbling with conversation, he fired one question after another, never giving Betty a chance to answer. "Where are you from? How big is your boat? What is your name?" Then squeezing Betty's upper arm, he added, "Oh . . . you strong lady, you some strong lady."

"Don't touch me," Betty said, pushing his hand away.

"How you get so strong?" Rio asked, trying to squeeze her arm again. "How old are you?"

"Hey, that's not a nice thing to ask a lady," Betty said. Then seeing the questionable look on his face said, "Okay, I'll tell you. I'm fifty-three."

"No, No, can't be. My mother is forty-eight, and she's all wrinkled. She looks weak, ready to die," he said, eyeing Betty up and down. Then, he changed the subject. "We get lots of Australian men here, but you no like them, I know."

"Why wouldn't I like the Australian men?" asked Betty, laughing at Rio's apprehension.

Rio rolled his eyes, "They drink too much beer, and have big bellies."

Then he parked across from the post office and helped Betty out of the cab. Rio ran into the middle of the street. Waving his arms, he stopped traffic. "Come, I make sure nothing happens to you," he said as he took her boxes and they crossed the street.

The post office was packed with people standing around talking. Rio placed her boxes on the counter, and said "I'll be right outside."

She waited for someone to wait on her, "Pardon me," Betty said, trying to get the attention of the man behind the counter.

A short thin man looked over and waved at two men sitting on the floor. "You must have them wrapped first."

Betty looked at her boxes wrapped in brown shipping paper. "They are wrapped," Betty said, not understanding.

"No lady, you must have him wrap them, to make sure they're waterproof." He pointed again to the men. They were weaving plastic mats that they placed on the boxes. They sewed all the sides and edges of the mats together, enclosing each package in the plastic.

Stooping down to watch, Betty asked, "That's a lot of work and time, how much will you charge me to do my three boxes?"

Studying the sizes, one man said, "They're big boxes, I charge you four thousand rupiah's."

It seemed fair to Betty, so she said, "Okay, you can do it."

She sat on a bench next to a local man and woman. Like Rio, they were very inquisitive, "What do you have in your boxes? Where are you sending them?" they asked.

Betty tried to explain what was in the boxes, but they didn't seem to understand.

Two hours later, the boxes were firmly wrapped and water-proofed. The man stood up and said, "You give me four thousand five hundred rupiahs," he demanded.

"No," said Betty firmly. You said four, and that's what I'm giving you." Betty was mad that he had raised his price.

The man behind the counter seeing her problem yelled loudly. "You said four, I heard you."

"You no talk," The man shouted as he pointed his finger, "No help her, you help me, I family."

The two men screamed at each other, their faces red with anger, their hands were waving in every direction.

Betty wanted to get her packages mailed and get out of there. "Wait a minute," she called out. Trying to calm everybody down. "I'll give you the extra five hundred rupiahs." *Geez, I'm standing here arguing over fifty cents.*

Rio had gone for the cab and was waiting for her and they drove back to the boat.

Paying the fare, Betty said, "Thank you for helping me. You're a good driver. Here, buy your family something nice," and she handed him extra money.

His eyes sparkled with happiness, "Thank you, nice lady, come see us again."

Bob met her on the deck, "Where have you been? I was beginning to worry."

"I had so much fun, I'll tell you about it later," she said cheerfully. "Are we ready to go?"

"Yes. I just got the weather report and it looks good," he said as Betty climbed aboard. He signaled Jim and said, "Release the lines, we're casting off."

They were headed for the northeast part of the Indian ocean, five hundred and seventy miles to a place called Christmas Island. The evenings were enchanting with a full moon and bright glistening stars dotting the sky. Betty loved the night watch, it had a calmness about it that made her feel content. Cool winds kept the temperature in the cabins bearable, as *Destiny* ambled along on an even keel. It made it easy to sleep. The winds went below three knots, so they motored along in the smooth water making it a delightful trip. Martha and Jim kept to themselves whispering, giggling, and playing cards. The smell of fried rice each day was getting nauseating. The galley was beginning to smell like a Chinese kitchen. Their work was never touched and there was a feeling of tension throughout the boat.

Bob looked out at Jim and Martha lounging on the bow. "They think we couldn't get along without them."

"I think you're right," replied Betty. "I'm sure they feel they could get away with anything they want. That's why they act so cocky."

Feeling a slight change in the wind helped brighten his spirits, Bob called out to Jim, "The wind's picking up a little, let's get the spinnaker up. Maybe we'll make better time."

Jim hoisted the colorful sail in place. It's always a beautiful sight to see as the brilliant colored sail billows high in the air . . . pulling them forward like a mighty God.

There was a dead stillness in the air—not a sign of a fish or bird, and they caught nothing but seaweed on the fishing lines. Like the cliché "the calm before the storm" they knew this peacefulness would not last.

Unmanageable changes in the wind pattern forced them to take the spinnaker down in the middle of the night, and they were back to rough conditions.

"I knew this serenity was too good to last," Betty said, her nerves on edge.

Destiny was back to her disco dance, and they were being tossed about with the rhythm. Not for long though, as their journey was ending tomorrow.

Off in the distance, they could hear a haunting melody of a muslim priest chanting high in the tower. It was an intriguing sound that echoed throughout Christmas Island. Customs officers greeted them at the Australian Island and they quickly learned the history of the island.

"The population is maybe two thousand and made up of Chinese, Malay, Indian and European people," they were informed by the officer.

They scanned the many cliffs and plateaus and walked through the rainforest. The muslim and bird chants echoed through the trees. Hundreds of magnificent birds, many the same variety as the Galapagos were flying everywhere. Thousands of red crabs carpeted the floor of the forest. Their migration to the sea would not be for another two months. Except for the eyesore area of the phosphate mines, the island was a back to nature dream.

A forest ranger offered to give Bob and Betty a tour of the island. Out of politeness, they invited Jim and Martha to come along. They stopped and looked over the cliff, the view of the sands kissing the multi shades of blue water was magnificent. The forest ranger walked back to the jeep with Betty and Bob and stood talking.

Jim hustled over to the jeep looking hostile. "We're not ready to go yet. Why do you always have to be in such a big hurry? Can't you ever just relax and hang out, instead of rushing?" Martha stood quietly by with a smirk on her face.

"Whoa, wait a minute. We're not rushing you," said Bob getting red-faced, but holding his temper. "Take all the time you want."

"We're not coming with you anymore. You rush too much and we don't enjoy it," said Martha.

"Hey, that's fine with us. We can certainly do without your company—especially with an attitude like that," Betty said.

No one talked the rest of the outing. Their attitudes had ruined the day.

Prayers from the tower occurred six times a day. It was a mystical rhythm that mesmerized...filled the air...pulled them to join in with the people, as they get down on their knees and pray to Allah. The haunting sound was enjoyable...except at four-thirty in the morning.

Snorkeling, diving and hiking filled their days. In the

evenings, they met other yachties at the dockside restaurant.

Before they sailed off again, Betty wanted to pick up a few supplies. Walking toward the store, she heard footsteps behind her.

Martha and Jim were rushing to catch up to her. "Betty, wait up, we want to go with you."

Oh no, Betty said to herself. *Not this again.* "I'd rather you didn't go with me. We only need a couple of things, and I didn't bring very much money with me."

They tagged along anyhow. Betty pushed the cart down the aisles and they started to fill the basket. Ten-pound bag of rice, candies, and personal articles were put in the cart.

"We don't need these things, there's plenty onboard," Betty said, putting everything back.

"I want to get this," Jim said, putting a cake in the basket and covering it up. "It's Martha's birthday tomorrow. I want to surprise her."

"We don't want to run out of this," said Martha, placing the huge bag of rice back in the cart.

Betty's patience gave out and her temper surged. She pulled the bag of rice out of the basket and threw it on a shelf, "Go back to the boat now. I don't want you here. Go."

Martha looked startled, then in a huff, said, "All we were trying to do was help." They walked out of the store mumbling.

Betty emptied the basket of all the unnecessary things and finished the shopping. The store delivered the food to the boat.

When Betty got back to *Destiny*, Martha was busy fixing fried rice. "Is that Jim's lunch?" Betty asked.

"Yes, Jimmy-boy is hungry," she said in a syrupy voice.

Betty stared at her and asked, "Are you preparing something for Bob's lunch too?"

"No . . . I never thought to ask him," stammered Martha. "I just thought I'd fix our lunch."

Betty was incensed, "You mean you're making fried rice for Jim, and you're not making anything for Bob?"

"I didn't know if he was hungry," Martha said as she continued to stir the rice. "I'm just doing ours. Is there something the matter with that?"

Betty was almost growling, "If you don't know what's wrong with that, then we really have a problem."

Tossing her hair from her face, Martha asked indignantly, "Are you upset about something?"

"Yes I am. I've had it up to here with you," Betty said, pointing to her neck. "I think we better have a talk, just as soon as I get these groceries put away."

"I want to know now what's bothering you," demanded Martha.

Betty responded sharply, "I said I'd talk to you later. I'm putting these groceries away."

Martha placed her hands belligerently on her hips and demanded, "You tell me now. I know you hate me, don't you? You want me off this boat."

Betty boldly met Martha eye to eye, "At this point, I don't give a damn what you do or how you feel. You want to talk now? Okay, then tell me, when did you and Jim stop working for us? We pay you a salary, but you act like you own the damn boat. When were you going to tell us you had your parents onboard?"

Martha's face went white and she stammered, "Who told you?"

Betty leaned in Martha's face, "Never mind who told us, why didn't you tell us?"

"I . . . I thought you knew, so I didn't mention it," she answered, unsure of what to say. Then she snapped back with, "You're just using that as an excuse. You want me off the boat." Martha ran crying up to the cockpit. "Oh Bob, Betty wants me off the boat. I don't know what I've done to upset her. I'm not staying if I'm not wanted. Tell her you want me to stay."

Bob had been listening to the whole scene, "Well Martha, if Betty wants you off the boat, I guess you better get off."

She ran out on the bow to Jim, "Oh Jimmy, they're making me leave," she said crying on his shoulder.

Jim patted her head, "Don't cry."

Bob stood up and with a stern face he said, "Jim, get her off the boat now."

Betty walked up on deck and sat next to Bob. Sighing, she

said, "Things really blew, didn't they. I just couldn't hold it in any longer."

"Well, problems have been brewing for a while. It was just a matter of time before it happened," said Bob. "Looks like we are going sailing by ourselves." He tried to sound enthusiastic as he added, "I'm sure we can handle it until we find crew."

Betty sat there still furious, "I'd rather handle the boat ourselves than have to put up with their arrogance. It was getting to be too much pressure."

Jim came back on board an hour later. "Martha's really upset, she's crying. If she leaves, I'll have to go too." He waited for an answer. When no one spoke he added, "I can't let her be alone, she wouldn't know what to do by herself. She's helpless and frightened."

Betty laughed, "Helpless! Martha helpless, are you kidding? She's not frightened or helpless, she's afraid of losing you. She's got her hooks in you and doesn't want to let go."

Jim sat on the bench, his shoulders slumped over, a sad expression on his face. "I feel sorry for her. I'm going with her, unless you feel you can't make it without us. Then, we'll both stay."

Bob took a deep breath, he was sorry to lose Jim. But he had really lost him months ago. "I'm sorry you feel you that way. You always told me you weren't in love with her, but you must be. You're really leaving because you think she's afraid of being alone? God Jim, remember she backpacked around Europe by herself when she was seventeen."

"I know, but that was a couple of years ago," said Jim sheepishly.

"We don't need the aggravation of you two being onboard. Tomorrow, I'll arrange for plane tickets to get you both home," said Bob.

Jim sat for awhile then said, "I'd rather go to England with Martha."

"No way," said Bob. "I have to pay your fare off the island, and I'm sending you back home. I'm getting the cheapest rates I can. Get your things off as soon as possible."

As Jim left, he said, "I'll be back tomorrow for our things."

Betty was still upset and she fixed them a drink. "I'm handling the motion and weather conditions better. The only thing that's going to be tough is the night watches."

Bob took a sip of his drink and sat thinking. He knew it would be tough on Betty, but she was a trooper. "We'll just have to take four-hour shifts. Handling the sails won't be hard, as they're all hydraulic. I could do it myself if I have to."

Betty gave Bob a hug, "I'm not really worried. We'll manage until we find someone. Lets stay home and have dinner and enjoy the privacy. We'll cook a couple of steaks on the barbecue and make a romantic evening out of this."

"You have something in mind?" asked Bob as he rubbed her back and kissed her.

The next day was spent getting *Destiny* cleaned up and planning their next route.

Jim stopped by to pick up their things and Bob gave him the plane tickets.

Jim acted nervous as he said, "Sorry this happened, I was hoping to finish the trip with you." Bob walked out of the room. He was so disappointed with him.

Betty looked sadly at Jim, "Things haven't been right for awhile. You both have become so selfish and self-centered. You really hurt Bob. He loved you like a son and you treated him badly. He would have done anything for you."

"Well, I hope there's no hard feelings," said Jim grabbing his last bag. "Oh, by the way, that cake you bought yesterday—can I have it? Today is Martha's birthday."

"What? You really have guts. I don't want to give her anything. I'm sorry we gave her the snorkel, mask and flippers before her birthday. She doesn't deserve a gift from us. Pay me for the cake, then you can have it. That way it's not from us."

Jim took the cake and threw down three dollars and said, "See ya. Sorry you have to sail alone," he said with a smirk.

Bob was lying on his bed when Jim left. He came out to the salon and said sadly, "He sure disappointed me. His mother and father are good friends of mine, too."

Betty walked over and pulled him to his feet, "Let's go have dinner on shore."

They joined Nester, Florence, and their crewman Norm, from the boat *Silver Cloud*. "Heard your crew left?" said Florence.

"News travels fast. How did you find out?" asked Bob.

"Saw her sitting at the bar bawling like a baby, and him gushing over her. I overheard them talking. Had a bit of problem?" asked Nestor.

Betty rolled her eyes as she said, "You could definitely say that."

Florence's face brightened, "Would ye be needing new crew?"

Bob's face broke out in a hopeful smile as he said, "Matter of fact, we do."

"We're letting Norm go. We have to be home by the twenty-sixth of September, that's three days from now. We can make it on our own from here."

Norm was tall, slender and about twenty-three with thick curly prematurely gray hair. He spoke the Queen's English perfectly and his gentle manner showed in his every movement.

Norm got up to get a drink from the bar as Nestor asked him, "How about it Norm, would you be interested in crewing for *Destiny?*"

"I am looking for another boat," said Norm all smiles. "I'll be right back."

Betty was so excited. Could they possibly be lucky enough to find crew on this tiny island? "Is he honest and a good worker? Is he easy to get along with?"

"Oh my, yes," said Florence. "He was like my own son, so well-mannered and always ready to help. He's not very experienced but he learns fast."

"Hot damn, looks like we have one crewman anyway," Bob said, hugging Betty.

Nestor and Florence stood up and said, "We have an early start tomorrow so we're heading for bed. Hope everything works out for you."

When Norm came back, Bob shook his hand, "If you want to come aboard, we'd like to give you a try. We can't pay you as you really aren't experienced. But . . . "

"Pay me!" Norm interrupted. "Why I paid *Silver Cloud,* one hundred dollars a month for room and board. The food was usually soup and cold biscuits."

"You're kidding! You paid them?" Betty said in surprise.

"There's only one stateroom on their thirty-eight footer. I had to sleep in the salon."

Bob gave Norm a pat on the back and said, "Well you don't have to pay us as long as you work and you'll have your own room. Once you're experienced we'll talk about salary."

"*Destiny* is a beautiful ship, I'll be proud to sail on her," said Norm. "When do you want me to come aboard?"

"Tomorrow will do. I have to sign my old crew off the boat with customs and immigration. Then, we'll sign you on." Bob thought for a minute and added, "We'll probably leave day after tomorrow."

"We really could use another person," said Betty. "Do you know of anyone?"

Norm scratched his head, "There's another guy on the island who might be interested. He's an electrician and since the mine shut down, he's been out of work. He's waiting to catch a plane home."

Betty sipped her beer and said, "Could you ask him if he's interested?"

"If he is, tell him to come over for an interview," added Bob feeling pleased. "Hell, we can always use an electrician on *Destiny*."

"Let us know as soon as you can," Betty said as they left to walk back to the boat.

Bob said gleefully, "Hot dog, we have one person, and he comes recommended. Things are looking up."

"I'm sure Martha and Jim think we'll be sorry we let them go. Yahoo, we have crew," cheered Betty, "let's hope the other guy is as nice as Norm. It's tough hiring crew. You never know what they're like until you're out to sea with them. You hear so many weird stories, and there are so many drug addicts around. I think we lucked out."

Doug showed up the next day all excited. "Hi mates," he said in a heavy brogue. "Hear you're looking for crew?"

"We sure are," said Bob, "come aboard, and let's talk about it."

Doug was Australian too, but just the opposite of Norm. Short, slightly bald with light brown hair. Unlike Norm, he murdered the English language. Doug had a very likeable way about him. A warm glow flowed from his small blue eyes that half shut when he smiled. They were happy with both men. Instincts told them both Doug and Norm would do fine.

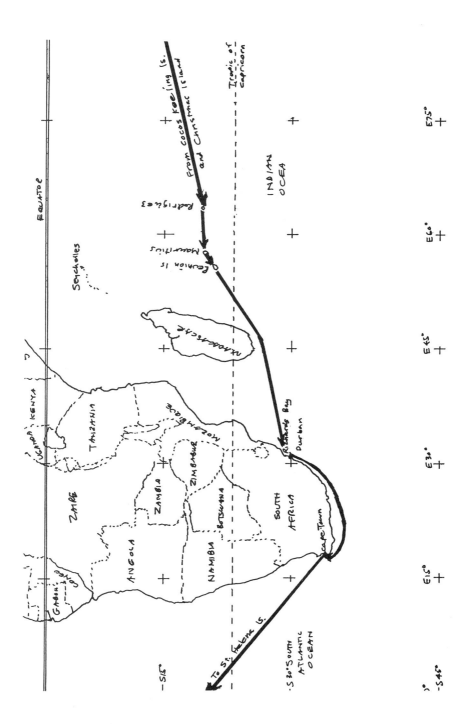

Thirty-four

When the new crew came aboard, a look of astonishment came across their faces. "We each have our own sleeping quarters?" asked Norm.

"Better than the Holiday Inn," said Doug. "Oh, where can I stash my scuba gear?"

"Scuba gear! You're a diver?" asked Bob.

"I'm a diving instructor," said Doug. "I hope I can get some diving in on this trip."

Betty saw two guitars propped up against the wall. "Who plays the guitar?" she asked, picking one up and strumming it.

"We both play," said Norm. "Doug's a little better than I am."

Betty went into the galley to fix dinner. When the young men saw the food that was served, they went out of their minds, eating second helpings of everything.

"You mean we get to crew on this beautiful boat and eat great food too?" asked Doug, grabbing a blueberry muffin.

"We'll do the dishes at night," said Norm. "After all you're cooking all this delicious grub. We want to keep the cook happy."

That night, everyone sat on deck as the crew strummed their guitars and sang.

"What part of Australia are you from, Norm?" asked Betty.

"I live in Esperance, in western Australia. My folks have a sheep farm there," said Norm. "There's about a thousand sheep in the herd. My brother has a sheep farm too."

"How come you're not home working the sheep?" asked Bob laughing.

Norm put his feet up on the helm, yawned and said, "Dad wants me to take it over, but I'm not ready for farming. When I graduated from college with a degree in agriculture, he expected me to work the farm with him. Guess he wasn't happy when I hopped a boat in Australia. I needed to see the world before I settle down."

Betty studied Norm, he certainly didn't look like the farmer type. Then she asked, "Think you'll go back home and farm someday?"

Norm didn't answer right away, he gazed out at the sea. Then he said, "Yes, I suppose so. I miss my sisters and family. My one sister's married, and since I've been gone she's had a baby. I'd love to see the little tike."

Bob looked over at Doug, "How about you, Doug, do you live near Norm."

Doug strummed his guitar as he answered, "I hail from Melbourne, me dad's a bartender there. I got offered the job at Christmas Island right after I got out of school. They paid good money and the diving was terrific. I wasn't too happy when the mine shut down."

"What about brothers and sisters," asked Betty.

Doug started to sing his answer as he played the guitar. "Two of each and they're scattered all over Australia, doing one thing or another."

Norm picked up his instrument and played along. Harmonizing together they sang their native songs, as *Destiny* sailed into the night.

"Do you men feel ready to stand watch tonight?" asked Bob. "They'll be three-hour watches if you're up to it. I'll take the seven to ten. Betty will take the ten to one and you two can decide on your hours."

"Sure, I took watch on *Silver Cloud*," said Norm. "I'll take the ten to four."

"No sweat matey, I can do the four to seven," said Doug.

They played their guitars a little longer then went down to their cabins to sleep.

"They are such gentlemen," said Betty. Then she laughed, "Unlike you, they haven't said a cuss word since they've been aboard."

"That's because they're not true sailors," said Bob, trying to hide his smile.

Steady winds of fifteen knots stayed on their beam for five days. Every night the crew sang and played the guitars as flying fish danced along the water. Betty was back to counting dead fish

391

in the morning. It was such a relief to have pleasant company onboard.

In the horizon they could see land. Cocas Keeling was where they were going to stop and rest. Their main goal was to reach South Africa.

After they docked, Bob said to the crew, "We're very happy with the two of you. We'd like you to sail with us for as long as you like."

"We were hoping you'd say that. We'd like to continue on," said Norm.

After they were at Cocas Keeling for two days, Bob said, "Okay, Norm and Doug, I'm going to see just how good you guys really are. This next leg to Rodrigus is two thousand miles."

"No sweat, matey," said Doug. "We can handle that."

When they left, the seas were calm and they thought the trip would be an easy one. They were wrong. The wind picked up to twenty knots and the seas were choppy again.

Betty started to feel seasick. "I haven't had to put a patch on for quite awhile. I thought for sure I had my sea legs."

"You get seasick?" asked Doug. "Here, I thought you were a tough chick."

"You'll see how tough I am," said Betty, heading down to the galley. "Watch me after I've cooked dinner."

Even with the patch, on the rocking and stifling galley made her feel seasick. She fought down the feeling of throwing up and went on with the cooking. Occasionally she went up to the cockpit to cool off. As soon as everything was ready, she rang the dinner bell. Without eating, she went to bed and slept until her watch. The crew devoured everything and then cleaned up the galley.

The wind stayed at twenty-five knots through the night and into the morning. Bob was reading a book, while Betty sat at the helm.

"I'm pleased with how well the men are working out," said Bob. "They're able to do almost everything on the ship without instructions."

"They're down at your desk now studying navigation," said Betty. "I wish the wind would die down a little. It would make

392

the sail more comfortable."

She no sooner spoke the words than the seas began to build to fifteen-foot swells. Forty knot winds ripped savagely at the sails.

"Let's reef the main and Yankee," yelled Bob, as *Destiny* battled against the winds.

"No sweat matey, we can handle that," said Doug, as the two of them grabbed the sheets. "Maybe we ought to throw Doug overboard. He's driving me nuts with that expression," laughed Betty.

Destiny bounced off the waves, causing a jarring motion, wrangling everyone's nerves.

When Betty took her eleven o'clock watch, the skies were dark with heavy rain clouds. The moon and stars hid behind the gloom of the night, making Betty's watch seem endless. She gazed through the haze looking for ships and hoping there were none close by.

Norm relieved her and she went below, ready to bury herself in the warmth and comfort of her bed. She drifted off for a few hours and then she woke up when she heard a panicked voice calling. Bob was out of bed immediately, realizing it was Doug on watch now. They both rushed to the deck to see what the emergency was. A huge freighter was bearing down on them too close for comfort.

Doug had the ship-to-shore radio in his hand, and he was still calling the ship. "I've been trying to get them on the radio since I spotted them an hour ago," Doug said trying to keep the panic from his voice. "They won't answer."

Grabbing the wheel, Bob steered away from the freighter. "Pull in the sails," yelled Bob, and Doug and Betty started to wench them in. The excitement woke Norman up and he came up to help.

"Why didn't you steer away from them?" demanded Bob.

Doug's voice cracked as he tried to explain, "I've been steering away from them. Can't you see we're way off course."

"For God's sake man call me sooner next time," Bob said grabbing the radio. "Ship on our port bow going north this is sailing vessel *Destiny*. Can you see us?" No one answered. "Ship on our port bow, this is *Destiny*, can you read me?"

Bob steered the boat as far to starboard as possible, then he put the strobe light on. It turned and flashed high above the mast. With the throttle full speed ahead, they continued to steer out of the way of the freighter. It was going at a faster speed than *Destiny*, and still heading for them. It looked bigger by the minute. The radar alarm was beeping a close contact signal. Relief came upon them when they heard, "Hello Captain, yes we see you. What's the problem?"

"What's the problem? What's the problem," shouted Bob. "You were about to run us down. Don't you keep someone in the radio room all the time? We have been trying to get you for an hour, and no one answered the radio," yelled Bob as he squeezed the hand control so hard it almost cracked.

The sarcastic voice came back, "We see you now, so there's no problem." Then the radio went dead.

"No problem. Why, you stupid idiots..." Bob called out venting his anger. "Those fools could have rammed us and never known it."

"That was extremely close, they could have killed us," said Doug as he lit his Camel® cigarette that was stuck in the side of his mouth. "They should have explained or apologized."

They sat quietly trying to get over the trepidation. Betty knew it was useless to go back to bed. They were all too keyed up and it was almost morning.

Sunrise never came as the sky was still filled with unfriendly clouds. A slow drizzle started, turning into a cloudburst. The winds increased to thirty knots and *Destiny* was bucking wildly against the waves.

Norm took over the helm, and Betty said, "I'm going below and make some coffee."

"Boy, I could sure use a cup," said Norm. "Would you bring up my raingear?"

Betty put a pot of coffee on and grabbed Norm's slicker. She stood at the foot of the companion way and yelled, "Here's your slicker," and she threw it up to him.

Norm reached for it, but the wind whisked it into the air. Doug was on deck smoking a cigarette when he saw the rain gear furling through the air. He made a lunge for it and slipped and fell. The decks were wet and he slid through the stanchions and went overboard. All that saved him was his one leg that had wrapped around the strut of the bottom railing. With strength from his pumping adrenaline rush, he managed to grab the top railing with one hand.

His cramped body ached in the bent position as he called out for help, "My hand's slipping. Help me, for God's sake."

The hard, biting rain whipped against him in the thirty-knot winds. He couldn't see and his fingers were growing numb.

Betty grabbed the helm as Bob and Norm rushed out to rescue him. The blinding rain slashed at their faces and they squinted to protect their eyes. They grabbed his leg and arm, as they tugged against the forces that were pulling him overboard. Norm slipped on the wet slick deck, almost falling. Bob tried to brace himself against the pilot house while they pulled and tugged Doug. *Destiny* heeled and rocked in the wild weather, making it hard for them to keep their balance.

Doug screamed, "Don't let go, matey. I can't hold on much longer, my hands are cramping."

"We got you, we won't let you fall," Norm shouted above the wind. "We're both going to pull at the same time. When we do, try to lift yourself." Looking at Bob he said, "Ready?"

They pulled with all their strength as Doug lifted his body. He wiggled between the railing and was back onboard. He laid there in the slapping rain, exhausted.

Then, a smile broke out on his face, "Darn near had me morning dunk. Don't believe I was quite ready for that," said Doug, taking a deep breath. "Look! I still have the slicker and me cig," he said, smiling. The drenched cigarette hung broken between his lips.

"What else can happen?" Betty said in pure frustration. "First, we're almost run over, then we almost lose a man."

"I think I'm glad they're almosts, and not happenings," said Norm. Then he looked at Doug and said, "Thanks chap, for saving my gear. I wasn't trying to save you, just didn't want to loose my slicks."

"After that heroic effort, how about some eggs, bacon and hot coffee?" asked Betty.

"Yeah," the men said licking their lips. "Make mine over lite," said Bob.

395

It was rough in the galley and the eggs slid around the pan. The yolks broke from the frenzied action of *Destiny*.

Betty called up, "It's rough down here, I'm scrambling the eggs. You're not getting bacon either, I'm afraid of the hot grease."

Still sailing with reefed sails, the wind hadn't eased. It was still a force six, but they were making good time. Waves thrashed across the bow pounding hard against the windshield.

With each exaggerated rock, the toerail dipped deep into the water. A flood gushed into the cockpit, filling it ankle deep. Gurgling sounds echoed in the air as the water was sucked out through the drain holes.

Bob stood at the helm, engrossed in keeping *Destiny* on course. He let out a scream and grabbed his neck, "Something hit me."

Startled, Betty jumped up from her seat, "What happened?" There was a large flying fish flapping in the water, at his feet. "Oh, for heaven sake, it's just a fish. It couldn't have hurt that bad."

"It hurt when it hit me," said Bob, rubbing his neck.

Betty examined his neck, "There is a little red mark there, that's all," she said as she kissed the spot.

"That's a maneating tiger fish. Look at those teeth marks," Bob pretended to whine.

Norm picked up the fish and waved it at him, "Watch out, he's still alive," he said as he threw it overboard.

"This trip seems to be taking forever, time's really dragging," Betty said feeling groggy.

"We've been sailing for five days and we still have five more to go."

"It seems like we're never going to get there," agreed Bob. "Let me see how the other boats are making out. I'll try to contact Winkler."

Bob had been keeping in touch with two other boats by radio. It helped pass the time. Hearing a friendly voice took the isolated feeling away. Their boats were smaller than *Destiny* and they were about five miles ahead.

With the exaggerated rock, it was too rough to read. Listening to Zamfir helped take Betty's mind off the ordeal they were going through. Two days later, there was a break in the weather. The wind cut back to fifteen knots and the ocean smoothed out. It was like a gift from heaven. Relief flowed over them as the tenseness in their muscles relaxed. Norm put the fishing lines out. Soon the reel sang out as they hooked into something big. Doug let out more line as the fish started to run. He could tell by the feel of the line that the fish was going deep. Bob tried hard to keep the speed down, as they fought to bring in the fish. Hearing a swishing noise, the water parted and a big marlin danced on his tail in full view. Light reflected on the rainbow colors of his magnificent blue body. They were captivated by this majestic creature's beauty and grace. Then, they were shocked back to reality as the marlin dove deep and broke the line.

Disappointed at first, Doug said, "I'd a set that beauty free anyhow. Well, at least he danced for us."

"Land Ahoy," called Norm, as he pointed ahead at a green spec in the distance. It was a sight they longed to see. They knew that Rodriques was a small French island, but it seemed like a green dot in the horizon. The land was surrounded by numerous peaks and mountains, with small dwellings placed sparsely around the island.

Destiny sailed into the harbor at Port Mathurin, in Rodriques, and Roger greeted them on the radio. "Hey *Destiny*, glad you made it. There's only one dock available."

"Then our only recourse is raft together," replied Bob.

"You're the biggest, so we'll put you in the middle. I'll go on one side, and Owen's boat *Winkler* can go on the other," said Roger.

"Fine," answered Bob. "One of you go along the dock and I'll pull in next to them."

Once they were rafted, together they went ashore to clear customs and make phone calls.

Betty called home and Loretta was relieved to hear her voice. "Everyone's been worried about you, Mom. It's been a long time since we heard from you."

"I call as often as I can," said Betty, apologizing. "Telephones are hard to come by in these small islands. Using the ship radio to call home is almost impossible."

"I understand," said Loretta lovingly. "It's just that we worry when we don't hear from you."

"The connection is bad. I can just about hear you," Betty shouted to be heard. "Tell everyone we're safe and we love them." Betty hung up the phone and leaned against it. She missed them and felt homesick.

As she climbed aboard, Roger stepped across to *Destiny*. "Have you heard the news?

Bob had been sleeping below and hearing the noise he came up. Seeing Roger's gleeful face he asked, "What's got you so excited?"

Roger was so exhilarated he could hardly get the words out. "Pope . . . John . . . Paul II is coming to visit this . . . little speck of an island. He's due here tomorrow."

Betty couldn't believe what she heard. "You're kidding! Are you sure?" Betty called to the customs officer standing on the dock. "Why is the Pope coming to such a small island? There are so few people here."

Speaking with a heavy French accent, he answered, "He was scheduled to go to Mauritius, then to Mount Helen." Then puffing his chest out, he continued, "He has never in history been here, but our people pleaded with him. His Holiness granted our wish and agreed to stop and bless our people."

"Do you have a place big enough where he can greet everyone?" asked Bob.

"Oh yes, indeed," smiled the customs officer. "We have built a stadium large enough for all the people to come, and pay homage to him. You can come too if you like."

"Thank you, we'd love to," said Bob. "Where is the stadium?"

"Just be outside tomorrow morning at nine. Hop on any bus or truck. There will be plenty of them to take everyone to the stadium," said the officer proudly.

While they were talking, a burly policeman walked over and hollered in French at the boats.

Bob couldn't understand him and asked the customs officer, "What's he trying to tell us?"

"He says you must move your boats at least three miles from the docks. They must have strict security for the Pope," said the customs officer.

"No way," said Bob and Roger together. "Not after all the trouble we had tying up here. Tell him we can't move, it's impossible."

It started out as a peaceful talk, but soon the two officers were into a full blown argument. The policeman walked away yelling with his fist in the air. "You can stay," said the officer. "Don't pay any mind to him. I will take the responsibility."

At nine sharp, in the morning, there were lines of old dented school buses and dilapidated trucks parked up and down the narrow streets. All the people were dressed in their best clothes. Women and little girls were decked out in bright, flowered dresses. Straw hats brimming with fresh flowers were worn on their heads. Their shiny new patent leather shoes glistened in the sun.

Men and young boys looked immaculate in dark trousers and clean starched shirts. They wore brightly colored ties and newly polished leather shoes. Proudly dressed to greet the Pope, they climbed aboard the buses and trucks. Norm and Doug managed a lift in a pickup truck. Bob and Betty grabbed a seat on a rickety old bus. It creaked and rattled as it stopped all along the roads picking up people until it was crammed full.

There were no seats at the crowded stadium. Everyone had to stand in the heat of the sun. Bright colored umbrellas could be seen here and there, shielding the ladies from the scorching rays.

"Yhoa, Betty and Bob, over here," they could hear Doug and Norm, but they couldn't see them. "Up here, Betty, look up."

They kept looking around for them. Then, Betty spotted their crew sitting on the roof of a wooden shed.

Waving down at her, they called out, "Come on up. There's plenty of room, and you get a great view."

Betty and Bob walked over to the shed. A makeshift ladder was tied together by ropes. It was attached to the shed by large rusty nails, some protruding out of the sides. They climbed up and sat alongside of Doug and Norm on the flat black tarred roof. They could see way above the heads of the crowd and onto the stage.

Two hours later, a line of black Mercedes appeared—the

Pope had arrived. He had an entourage of sixty people with him. At first, Betty was more interested in watching the awesome expressions on the people's faces. Then, the magnitude of the whole ceremony overtook her. Music began to play as the school band marched in. They carried flags of Mauritius and Rodrigues as the crowd cheered and sang. The Pope walked onto the stage and took a seat while speeches were given by the priest and several officials. Then, the Pope stood up and blessed his audience; speaking to them of the sins, beauty and rewards of life. The people wept with joy and happiness as they listened to the Pope. As the Pope walked off the stage, everyone seemed to be in a trance as he turned and bestowed his blessing again on them. He had given the people of Rodriques the biggest thrill of their lives.

Elated by the experience, the *Destiny* group returned back to their boat, riding high in a pickup truck. Not only did they revel in the experience of seeing the Pope, but of sharing the joy of the islanders.

Winkler, Owen and *Destiny* sailed out of the harbor together. It would be a short three days to get to Mauritius. They knew the winds were going to be rough, so each boat prepared for the onslaught. As they parted, they promised to keep in touch by radio.

The winds were blowing at thirty-five knots and *Destiny*'s motion was unbearable. Anticipating this, Betty made spaghetti sauce before they left the dock.

At dinner time, she went down to cook the pasta. The gimbaled stove swayed back and forth as the pasta boiled and hot water splashed out. She started to make a salad but the heat of the galley and the rolling motion was getting to her. She broke out in a cold sweat as her stomach twinged with nausea.

"Why didn't I cook the pasta before I left?" Betty stammered as she jumped out of the way of the scalding water.

Then, she grabbed the salad from the refrigerator, and placed it on a damp towel to keep it from sliding. Wearing padded gloves, she paced the sway of the stove. As the gimbaled stove swung out, she grabbed the pot. Aiming for the sink, she threw it upside down into the draining dish. Scalding steam bathed her arms and Betty bellowed with pain. She ran cold water on her arms to ease the pain.

Destiny heeled further, and her stomach wrenched. Bile flooded her throat as she ran for the railing. Breathing deeply she waited until she felt she could handle the galley again. Then, she returned to complete the deal. Betty rang the dinner bell and ran to her bed. The crew took pity on her, each taking an hour of her watch, leaving her to sleep the night away.

The Indian ocean was known for its vacillating weather. They had been getting a taste of it since they left Christmas Island. The next two days were calmer, down to fifteen knots and they made some headway.

"Sorry to give you bad news," Bob said to the crew. "We have to handsteer. The batteries are not charging and I'm afraid of loosing all our power."

"We don't have much further to go, do we?" asked Norm.

Bob checked his chart, "No, we should arrive in Port Louis tomorrow."

Port Louis Harbor was long and narrow, with very little room for yachts. *Destiny* was jammed against the wall with three other boats rafted against her. Isle de France, as Mauritius, was once known, had many faces. One look at the harbor and you could see a bustling commercial refuge for huge freighters, where they dropped off their wares, and reloaded. The city was large and dirty with small dark stores along the streets. A huge outdoor market was loaded with delicious fresh fruits and vegetables that put a glow in Betty's eyes. She hadn't seen this much variety since Australia. As she looked at the fresh meat hanging from hooks, she tried to identify the strange cuts. Flies swarmed over the meat and dirty hands cut the smelly carcasses. Betty decided she didn't need meat and walked away.

There was so much confusion in the harbor that Bob decided to motor over to Grande Bay, a lovely resort area.

After they finished their chores, Norm asked, "You don't mind if we take off for a couple of days, do you, Captain? We'd like to take a trek around the island."

"No problem, have a good time," said Bob. "See you when you get back."

As they walked away, Betty said, "I can't believe we're going to be alone. It's the first time in a long while."

It was December twenty-ninth, Bob's birthday. They dressed for the occasion and went out to celebrate. The nearby hotel had a gourmet restaurant and the food was served by waiters wearing white gloves. First, they drank a toast to Bob's birthday, then to their love and life together. After an evening of good food, fine French wine and dancing they staggered back to *Destiny* feeling exhilarated.

When Betty tried to climb onboard her foot slipped and she let out a yelp. She hung onto the railing as her body dangled over the water. She kept raising one leg after another trying to get on the boat. Bob stood there laughing at first, then reached out and grabbed her.

Giggling, she pleaded, "Please, don't let me fall in the water."

Bob laughed, "You look like you're riding a bicycle," he said as he pulled her safely back onto the dock. His hands explored the soft line of her back and hips. He hugged her close to him, giving her a long seductive kiss.

Whispering in her ear, he said, "That's no way to end an evening. I'll show you the proper way."

Bob lifted her in his arms and helped her onboard, then laid her gently on the cockpit lounge. Leaning over her he kissed her again. This time, the kiss was as tender and light as a summer breeze. His hand moved under her dress to skim her hips and thighs. The gentle massage sent currents of desire through her. His demanding lips caressed hers as his body imprisoned hers in a web of arousal. Burying her face in his neck, she breathed kisses, sending tingling feelings up his spine. Her body squirmed beneath him as the sexual pleasure rose through them, pure and explosive. Relaxed and content, they lay in each other's arms filled with an amazing sense of completeness.

They stared at the full moon beaming down on them, "Seems the last time you attacked me was when the moon was full," said Bob.

"I attacked you?" Betty said laughing. "Who kissed who first? Who pulled who down on the lounge?"

Bob tried not to laugh as he said, "You did, you ravished me. On my birthday, too."

Drifting off to sleep with the cool breeze fanning the warmth of their bodies, life seemed nearly perfect.

As usual, they were anxious to explore the island. They rented a small car and started on their trip. Trouble started within the first twenty miles. First the radiator steamed, then the engine started to knock, and then the car stalled out.

Bob got out of the car and put the hood up, "Goddamnit, something's always breaking down on us. They got us again, Betty," he said trying to find the trouble.

A small man on a bike stopped. He was dressed in a ragged dirty army coat. Cut-off rubber boots crusted with mud were on his feet. It looked like he hadn't washed in months. His tattered hair was covered with a moldy felt hat. Like a moronic cartoon character, he poked his head under the hood. Then jabbering away in French he rode off on his bike.

"What in the hell was he saying?" Bob asked, looking bewildered.

"I think he said he'll ride to town for a mechanic," said Betty.

"How do you know that's what he said? I couldn't understand one word," Bob said as he poked around the engine. "I don't know what's wrong with this damn car."

About a half-hour later a truck stopped, and four men got out. Looking under the hood they talked among themselves, then pulled a funny looking tool out of a box. Leaning over the engine, they used the tool in several places.

Bob watched them and said, "I hope they know what they're doing."

"Okay, try starting it now mister," said one of the men.

"What! You speak English?" Bob asked.

"*Oui*. Try starting the engine now."

The engine started on the first turn of the key. "Thank you," said Bob shaking their hands. "We're very grateful. How much do I owe you?"

"Twenty-five francs a piece," the Frenchman said, pointing to himself and two other men. "Our cousin saw you in trouble and sent us to help you."

"I'll bet that was that funny-looking man that stopped to talk to us," laughed Betty. "I told you I knew what he was saying."

"Franz, he is okay. Just a little loco sometimes," said the Frenchman.

Their troubles were not over. The car overheated every half-hour, and they had to keep adding water to the radiator. They were halfway around the island when the car stalled on top of a hill. There were three men standing in front of a store watching them. Bob tried several times to start it, but with no success. The men walked over and offered to help. "Get in the car," the men said to Bob. "We'll push the car downhill."

Betty and Bob jumped in and the three men pushed. It went swiftly down the slope and the engine kicked over. Bob shifted to second gear and the engine stalled again. It was slowly drifting and Betty quickly jumped out and pushed the car to keep it moving. The Frenchmen saw her pushing the car and their mouths gaped open. The engine started, and Bob drove off down the road. Betty was left standing there, as the car went around the curve and out of sight. The men were dumbfounded as they mumbled and pointed at her, they thought Bob had left her. It was only a matter of minutes and Bob was back. As she climbed in the car she heard the men cheering.

When they got back to the dock, a group cookout was being held at the marina. Everyone brought what they wanted to grill, plus something extra to share. While eating dinner, Betty watched the children playing tag. She was surprised at the number of children that traveled with their parents. She sipped her iced tea as she said to Bob, "What do you do with children under your feet twenty-four hours a day?"

Bob took a bite of chicken, and muttered, "You can tell them to go jump in the ocean, and play with the sharks."

"You would make a remark like that," she said laughing. Then she looked at some of the small boats the children were on. "It's got to be very trying at times for both the parents and children."

Their crew came up to the table, "Any more grub left?" asked Norman.

"Sure, help yourself," Betty said pointing. "It's over there on the table."

Doug, picked up his fork and dug into a piece of chicken. "Pretty good chook," he said. "Oh, we met some girls from Paris, they're real nice. Could we have them over to the boat tomorrow?"

"Sure," Betty said. "I'll fix lunch for them. Bring them over about twelve o'clock."

The next day, Norm and Doug brought the two girls for lunch. Monique was Norman's girl. She was tall, with the straight thin figure of a model. She emphasized her long attractive legs with an extremely short blue dress. Her long brown hair had reddish highlights and was pulled back in a pony tail which showed off her high cheekbones. Her complexion was the color of creamy peaches and brown penetrating eyes complemented her lovely face.

Doug's girl, Jazette, was short and slender with mousy light brown hair. Small freckles sprinkled her tiny nose like moon dust falling from the sky. Her round pleasant face was not pretty, but when she spoke, her lips curled up like a pixie doll and transformed her smile into a beautiful appealing sight. They spoke very little English. Their hand gestures and facial expressions helped them carry on a conversation. After lunch, Norm and Doug took the girls to the beach. They must have enjoyed each other's company, as the men never returned to the ship that night.

Mauritius had been fun, and they were very happy with Norm and Doug. They had taken to the sea like a duck to water, easy to get along with. Now it was time to continue their journey; next stop Réunion.

Their trip was short with calm weather and moderate winds. When they arrived, they found another long narrow harbor, and were told to tie up against the wall.

They had just docked when a man from the decks of a rusty old tub yelled over to them, *Destiny*, how about giving us a hand? Our motor's broke, and we need you to pull us in."

Norm looked up from his work and called back, "Okay, throw

us a couple of lines. Where are you docking?"

"We're rafting next to you," yelled the captain.

Betty took one look at the rusty steel boat and made a face, "Bob, I don't like the looks of that boat, it's filthy. Don't let him raft next to us." She looked sullenly at the ugly boat. "I'll bet that boat is full of roaches and I don't want roaches on our boat."

Bob laughed, "Betty you have a roach complex. What makes you think that boat has roaches?"

Betty's eyes were blazing, "I can tell, look how dirty it is."

"Can't you dock anywhere else?" Doug asked, tugging the line to pull the boat in.

"No," yelled the man on deck. "The dock master said this was the only place available."

After they had the rusty tub tied to *Destiny,* Bob said, "Boy, that was a tough job getting you in. What happened to your motor?" He never answered.

After his boat was tied on to *Destiny*, he looked across at Bob and asked, "Can I have permission to come aboard?" He stood there in pants and shirt that were so stiff and dirty they could have stood up by themselves. His sandal straps were broken and barely on his dirty feet.

"Sure, come aboard," said Bob, then he asked again. "What happened to your motor?"

"My name is Duke, thanks for pulling us in," he said as he sat down on the helm-seat. He picked some dirt out from between his toes and said, "Conked out a year ago. I don't have the money to get it fixed, so I have to make do." His greasy hair was stringy and long, badly in need of a wash and cut. It kept falling in his face.

Without prompting, he continued on, "I don't have any trouble with roaches aboard. I have geckos and they keep them away."

Betty looked over at Bob, and she thought to herself, *I knew he had them on his boat.*

"I can't stand roaches," said Betty. "Maybe you should give me one of your geckos." At that moment, a large cockroach flew over from his boat to *Destiny*.

She grabbed a magazine to kill it, as she yelled, "I didn't

know they could fly! Damn I hate them."

Duke's face turned red, "Well, guess I better get ashore and clear customs."

Betty was upset, "I knew it. I knew there would be roaches on his boat."

Bob patted Betty's shoulders, "Calm down, there's nothing we can do about it. Come on, lets go see what's going on around here."

Hitching a ride on an old pickup, they rode to the town of Denise. They were surprised how charming and cosmopolitan it was. Renting a Toyota, they drove around the island, encountering great mountains, magnificent waterfalls and fabulous restaurants. They found all the best parts of France had been placed right here on the little island.

Norman went off on a three day trip but Doug didn't feel well. He hung around and took day trips. A very attractive girl he met came for him in her car. There was a humongus German shepherd sitting next to her in the convertible.

Bob snickered, "Hey Doug, your date's here. She must have heard about your reputation. She brought protection with her."

Doug and his friend drove away laughing. He called out as they left. "I'll get even. Just wait."

Waking early from the noise on the pier, Betty went to prepare breakfast. As she was cooking eggs, she heard a door open and looked up.

Norman was coming out of his room, and he had an odd expression on his face. "You're up early," he said.

Doug's voice could be heard on deck along with a giggling female. She walked to the companionway to say something, but instead she saw Monique walking out of Norman's stateroom.

Sheepishly, Norm said, "We're going to take the girls to the bus, we'll be right back."

After they left, Betty laughed at their awkwardness. They obviously were not expecting her to be up. She turned the bacon over in the pan and thought about their experiences with Jim and Martha. *I better nip this in the bud*, she thought. *I don't want them bringing girls onboard as overnight guests.*

407

Norm came down the steps, he looked like a kid caught stealing cookies. He sat on the couch and softly said, "I hope you're not mad. She didn't have a place to sleep."

Doug walked down and stood next to Norm. His head was down and he swayed back and forth nervously. They looked like two little boys about to be spanked.

"What's wrong with a hotel," Betty asked straightfaced.

"Well, they were a little short on money, and so were we," said Norm.

"I'll let it go this time, but from now on, don't bring girls back to the boat to sleep," Betty said firmly.

Doug was annoyed and said, "Hey, my girl slept out in the cockpit. I slept in my bed alone."

"Yeah, sure," said Norm a little braver now. "That's because you two didn't hit it off. She wouldn't sleep with you. Besides, I don't see what's wrong with bringing them back here."

Betty stared sternly at Norm and said, "Would you have girls sleep with you at your house with your mother and dad there?"

Answering almost immediately, they both said, "No we wouldn't. We see your point."

"I'm glad you do, because this is our home. Now, enough of this. How about some breakfast?"

Their faces brightened, "Yeah, we're starved," they said, sitting down fast.

Betty handed them plates and said, "We have to go get our visas for South Africa today. So, don't go off anywhere."

After breakfast, Betty started to clean the galley. As she put the plates away she saw two roaches run for hiding. Betty pulled everything out of all the cabinets and sprayed the cubbyholes. Choking on the fumes, she went up to get some air.

Each night after that, she would do roach check. Putting the light on during the night, she would see the roaches. By the time she grabbed a paper or book to hit them, they had run back to their hiding places. In frustration and desperation she slapped them with her hand, killing three or four of them before they got away.

"Ugh, how can I do that? I'm getting grossed out," Betty said as she scrubbed her hand with Lysol® and hot water.

It was two in the morning but she didn't care. She grabbed the can of Black Flag®, and sprayed all the holes and cabinets that the bugs ran into. Then she crawled back in bed hoping she had killed them all this time.

Thirty-five

They were ready to sail for South Africa, and were well supplied for the ten-day trip. It was almost two thousand miles away, and that part of the Indian Ocean could be very treacherous—they had read about the ferocious storms that came up unexpectedly. Giant maverick waves could thrash across the decks, easily sinking a boat. For piece of mind, Betty stacked life jackets next to the helm. Then, Bob attached the safety lines to different areas of the deck. They were taking no chances.

On the day of departure the sun was shining brightly and a light breeze made them feel at ease. For six days, they had the best of weather conditions. Broad reaching, they were pushed gently through the immense body of water. Fifteen knot winds were blowing and there was not a cloud in sight. The sky seemed to meet the horizon and become one, surrounding them with a mass of multicolor blues.

Betty was tranquilized into a sense of security with those pleasant conditions. Going to the galley, she decided to make cream puffs. Beating the eggs and ingredients together, she worked away while enjoying the smooth conditions in the galley. The calm breeze started to build to twenty-five knots. *Destiny* had the wind at the stern as it heeled over and the wind lifted her bow as she surfed through the water.

Betty checked the cream puff shells. They had risen to a golden brown. She tried to get the filling made before the wind got any stronger.

Staying in rhythm with the gimbaled stove, Betty stirred the mixture. "I wonder why it isn't thickening?" she said. Looking around, she saw that the galley fan had blown out the flame. Fighting the sway of the stove she relit the burner. As Betty added more cornstarch, the boat swerved sideways. Half the contents of the box went in the filling.

"Darn, now I'll have to add more milk." The boat swerved

again and the milk gushed out. It overflowed the pan and ran over the stove onto the floor. Betty was in a horrible mess. In a fit of frustration, she threw the whole mess in the sink. Sliding around on the slippery goo under her feet, she slipped and fell on her knees. Sitting there in deep humiliation, she fought back the angry tears. She was caught in the rhythm of the waves that were thrashing against *Destiny*. Involuntarily, she slid back and forth in the mess.

Bob could hear the banging and hollering and he called down, "Betty, don't do too much when it's lumpy like this."

Crying, she yelled back, "But it wasn't rough when I started."

When she went to bed that night, she was exhausted, "I'm not doing roach check tonight," she vowed.

About three in the morning she woke up to go to the bathroom, and decided to do a quick check. There were no roaches in sight and Betty was happy, "I think I killed them all."

In the morning, the first thing she said to Bob was, "I didn't find any roaches last night. I hope their gone for good."

"I'm glad you got them before you killed us all," said Bob, smiling.

The fishing rods were still out from when the weather was calm. One of the lines went zinging and Doug picked up the rod.

He tried to reel the fish in, but it was difficult. "Slow the boat down, Bob" yelled Doug. "We have a big one."

All the sails were up and the wind was blowing twenty-five knots. "Betty, help me reef down the sails, it'll slow the boat down," called Bob. Working together, they pulled the sails in. The wind still had *Destiny* skimming fast across the water.

After twenty minutes, Bob called out, "What's taking you so long to get that fish in?"

Doug and Norm took turns on the rod, "The reel's slipping, and it's beginning to overheat," yelled Doug above the wind.

"For God's sake get that thing in or cut it loose. I can't hold *Destiny* down much longer," shouted Bob.

The men were tired and frustrated, but determined not to lose the fish. Doug fought for an hour, finally reeling the fish within sight of the boat.

"Look at the size of this monster," said Doug, ready with the gaff.

Norm brought the gigantic tuna to the side of the boat. "My God, he's immense. Cut him loose, he's too big to keep," said Betty.

"I think he's dead. He drowned from being pulled through the water," said Doug. They gaffed the tuna and the two of them tried to lift him, but to no avail.

Bob put the boat on auto-pilot and came back to help, "He's the biggest tuna I ever saw. You'll never be able to lift him aboard. Let's swing the halyard over, and tie a rope to the two gaffs and wench it up."

Hanging from the halyard, the fish was taller than Bob, who was six foot one. Bob shook his head in amazement, "This fish has to be at least two hundred and fifty pounds. Now I know why it took you so long,"

Pictures were taken with Norm and Doug standing beside it. They wanted proof they had caught such a fish. The men filleted the tuna, cutting it into big chunks. Then, they filled the freezer and Betty cooked some for dinner. Later, they would share it with the other yachtsmen and local people.

It was morning and Betty went up for her watch. "Bob, how far did we go last night?"

"We did one hundred and fifty miles. We still have five hundred to go. We're lucky so far, we've had twenty-five knot winds and rain but no big storms."

Conditions stayed that way as everyone lounged around the decks reading. Two days later, late in the afternoon, the wind grew to thirty-five knots.

Bob called out, "The wind's picking up and it's torn the sail loose from the halyard."

They could see the mainsail being ripped to shreds. "We're going to have to pull the sail down by hand. All the stays are busted," said Bob. Looking at the shredded sail. "We'll have to put the spare main up by hand."

Betty took the helm and the three men went out to change the sail. "Don't go out there without safety lines," Betty yelled.

Norman climbed onto the boom and started to work the sail down the mast.

"Get down and put these on," Betty called, waving the safety belts at the men.

Barely able to hear above the wind, they called back, "No time, we'll be all right."

Bob climbed on the cabin top and grabbed the loose sheet. Doug climbed up the steps of the mast and grabbed the boom. He wanted to keep it from swinging out until Bob could tie it down.

Winds thrashed the men while the ripped sail lashed their faces. A strong gust of wind whipped the sheet from Bob's hand, unleashing the boom. *Destiny* heeled to portside, causing the boom to swing out over the water. Norman was thrown off balance and he fell forward almost falling off. He wrapped his legs around the boom and held on. The winds had increased to forty knots and rain came teeming down as he hung over the water.

The sheet was flaring in the air like a wild snake, as Bob tried to grab it. "Goddamnit, I can't get it." He made another lunge and missed, almost slipping off the cabin. He grabbed the antenna and leaned out over the water, trying to reach the sheet as it whipped by his face. Finally, as it backlashed, he grabbed it.

Norman called out in a frightened voice, "Hurry and tie the boom down before I'm thrown off."

Betty let out a scream when she saw Norman hanging out over the water, "Oh my God! Hold on! Don't fall in."

She worked the helm with the waves, trying to keep *Destiny* under control. She was afraid any moment Norm would be thrown into the unruly sea. Bob held on to the sheet, pulling and straining against the tug of war with the wind.

"My feet are sliding," Bob yelled in panic as he grabbed the edge of the cabin to balance himself. Then *Destiny* heeled to starboard, and Norm was swung back over the boat, with a jarring thud. Bob jumped down from the cabin and tied the sheet securely. The men worked diligently for two hours as they replaced the mainsail. They battled the ferocious weather until everything was lashed down.

Coming back to the shelter of the cockpit, Bob said, "It seems like all hell broke loose. We're paying for those gentle days at sea."

They waited to see how *Destiny* handled the savage conditions.

"It's not going so good. We've got to reef all the sails," Norm called out, trying to be heard above the wind.

Doug looked out at the sails, "Reefing the mizzen and genie will be easy, but how are we going to reef the mainsail? Remember the stays are busted."

"We'll have to reef it down again by hand," said Bob. After they reefed the mizzen and genie, the men, reluctantly, went forward. Norman climbed up the mast and started to wiggle the sail down. Doug straddled one foot on the deck, then braced the other foot against the cabin top. Then he wrapped his arms around the boom, trying to control it. Norman and Bob inched the main down by hand.

They held canvas strips in their mouths to tie the sail once it was down. They worked with the wind beating against them. Rain thrashed their eyes, making it hard for them to see. "Keep the boat steady," yelled Bob.

Betty's stomach was in knots as she controlled the helm, trying to keep *Destiny* steady. She shook with fright at the thought of losing anyone overboard.

The wind showed no mercy, as it slashed at the half-reefed sail. Doug, using all his strength, held the sail down as they reefed it, and then fighting the wind, Norman and Bob tied the sail to the boom.

Working diligently in the worsening conditions, they finally secured the mainsail.

They sat in the cockpit, drenched to the skin, "That's the last time we're fooling with that thing," said Bob exhausted. "We can't make Durban, the weather's too rough. The barometer has dropped and the weather reports are predicting seventy-knot winds. I'll pull into Richard's Bay. We should be there late this afternoon."

Doug took off his shirt and wrung it out. "I'll be one happy duck to get out of this mess."

Betty shook her head in frustration, "Nine days at sea is a long time under these conditions. I'll never get use to it."

They were extremely happy to see land when they arrived at

four in the afternoon. Clearing customs, they went up to the yacht club, and were greeted warmly.

"Free champagne for you as a welcoming gift," said the bartender. "Anyone that can get here safely deserves it."

Betty looked tired and worn out as she said, "We're glad to be here."

Three days later, they were on their way to Durban, only eighty-six miles away. The weather was clear but the winds were still forceful. The crew was hoping there were no problems on this trip. They'd be content just to relax as *Destiny* sailed along.

Roach check at night had shown the bugs were gone. *Destiny* was rid of those horrible things. Everyone had told Betty that once you get them you couldn't get rid of them. Well, she did get rid of them. She'd sleep better from then on without roach check.

Thirty-five knot winds continued to blow on the stern as the boat rose high on a plane. She raced across the waves on a smooth sail, arriving in Durban in half the time.

Hellacious winds were still blowing at thirty-five knots as they pulled into the harbor, looking for a place to dock.

"When I pull up to the gas dock, jump off and tie us up," he said to Norman and Doug. "If the wind takes us we could ram anyone of the boats near by."

Bob had a troublesome time getting alongside the dock. The strong winds kept blowing against *Destiny*. On the fourth try, three men came to help. The crew threw lines to the men on the dock, and with their help, they were able to tie up.

Bob went to see the harbor master, "I want to get some diesel, then I need a slip."

"With this wind, the safest place for you is to anchor out in the harbor," said the dockmaster. "We're in for some pretty foul weather. Winds get up to seventy knots. If you don't anchor down tight, your boat will break loose, and go crashing around the harbor."

Bob took the harbormaster's word for it and cast out four anchors; one on each side, stern and bow. Once they were sure *Destiny* was secure they headed for happy hour. At the Point Yacht Club they listened to the bartender's stories about boats anchored in the harbor. They shuddered at his stories.

"When the wind gets around sixty knots, you'll see five or six boats break loose. They crash against anything in their way," said the bartender as he served another round of beer.

"Not a pleasant thought," said Bob ready to go back and recheck the anchors. "I think I'll sleep out in the salon tonight, just in case we have a problem."

Durban was a large active place with department stores and banks lining the streets. Everyone was friendly and helpful. They bought gifts to take home, as they were leaving for home tomorrow. Bob needed a checkup, and they wanted to spend Christmas with their families. They briefed Norm and Doug on what was expected while they were away.

Lists and arrangements were made for repairs. Then, they gave Doug and Norm enough money for wages, food and expenses. "You've been so helpful, I'm going to start paying you a salary," Bob said.

"We'll be back in three weeks, make sure the work's done by then," and as he handed them each an envelope. "Plus a little Christmas bonus. Hope it will help you enjoy your holidays."

Betty gave them a hug and gave them their Christmas presents, "Don't open them until Christmas."

"We didn't expect this!" said Doug. "Have a good time and Merry Christmas."

"Don't worry about anything, we'll take care of *Destiny*," said Norm. "Just have a good time."

Betty went to Boston with Bob for his checkup this time and they waited for the results. After his doctor finished the physical he said, "You amaze me. You're the only patient I have that recovered so completely from your virus and enlarged heart. I'm glad I didn't hold you back from going on your trip."

Bob was elated and after he filled his prescriptions, they headed for New Jersey.

Betty's grandchildren remembered them and stuck to them like glue. Santa was good to everyone on Christmas day, and before they knew it, it was time to fly back. Betty had adjusted to saying goodbye to her family, but not to going back to sea. She

416

was looking forward to the final end of the trip.

The crew was happy to see them when they returned to Durban. "The winds have been relentless. A few unlucky boats broke loose and crashed into the bulkheads," said Norman.

"*Destiny* didn't give us any trouble, she held fast. Guess we anchored her pretty tight," said Doug. "All the jobs are completed and we found a few extra repairs to do."

Bob was pleased as he inspected their work.

Betty went to provision the boat and was delighted to find fresh fruits and vegetables, and the prime meat looked superb. She stocked up on everything.

As she was unpacking the groceries, Bob said, "We can't leave until the wind dies down. When we get a good weather report, we'll take off for Cape Town.

Bob checked the weather fax each day and a week later he said, "Looks like we're in for lighter winds for the next few days. The scale reads ten to fifteen knots. We might as well make a break for it."

He called Norm and Doug on deck and said, "Lets get the anchors up. Pull the portside up first."

Norm started to wench it in. "Can't budge it, Captain. They don't seem to want to move." The three men worked for hours. Finally, the starboard anchors broke loose and they hoisted them up. The line was corroded with mud and sea growth.

"The port anchors are caught on something," said Doug, "I'll get my scuba gear and dive down. Maybe I can see what it's caught on."

The visibility below was so poor it was hard for Doug to see. Coming to the surface he said, "I can't see me own hand in front of me face." He tried again, this time feeling around for at least twenty minutes. Surfacing he give a victory yell, "I freed one. The suckers are caught on a cable line."

"Leave the other one down till we're ready to leave. Make sure it's not caught on anything," said Bob.

The three anchors and lines had to have the mud and sea growth scraped off. After they finished the job *Destiny* needed a wash down, and so did they. Tomorrow, they would leave for

Cape Town, eight hundred miles away.

They sailed away cautiously, as the winds were already at twenty knots. They were on a broad reach zooming through the water, making incredible speed.

Betty's night watch seemed lonesome. All she could see was the vast sea that surrounded her. She watched for ships while her mind wandered. She thought of Christmas with her family.

Lights from a ship could appear from a distance like stars in the sky, she thought. "Whoa wait a minute," she said outloud. "I think that star I'm gazing at is a freighter, and it's moving right for us." Betty checked the radar, "Damn it's on a collision course." Quickly, she changed course to starboard and lifted the radio speaker. "Ship on my portside traveling north, this is sailing vessel *Destiny*, do you read me?"

There was no answer. Seconds seemed like hours as she waited for a reply. The freighter seemed bigger than ever as it bore down on *Destiny*.

"I feel like a little bug about to be crushed," said Betty as she steered to starboard. Her heart was in her mouth as she called again, "Ship on my portside, this is sailing vessel *Destiny*, can you see me?"

The ship continued to barrel toward them. Betty snapped on the strobe light.

She started down to get Bob, but stopped when she heard, "Sailing vessel, *Destiny*. We see you. We are bearing to our starboard side and should clear you with no problems. Have a good night."

"What a relief," Betty shouted. "I'm not going to be shark meat tonight."

Another ship appeared on the radar, but this one was behind them. "Where's all this traffic coming from?" she said, still talking to herself.

Betty was sure the ship could see them and was not going to run them down. She picked up the speaker anyhow. "This is sailing vessel *Destiny* directly in front of you. Do you see us?"

"Yes, *Destiny* we see you. I thought you were a star at first, but then realized you were a sailing vessel. Where are you headed?"

"Heading for Cape Town. Is that where you're going? If it is, I have a feeling you'll get there before us."

"Right you are. We'll be passing on your starboard side, see you when you arrive."

In the morning, Bob was going over his charts," We should be getting close to the Cape of Good Hope."

"I'm dreading that passage," said Norman. "I've heard so many horrifying stories."

"We'll prepare for the worst and see what happens," said Bob.

Betty was nervous, "I'm stacking up the life jackets and safety belts. I hope we don't need them."

"We have the sails reefed and *Destiny*'s still moving full speed ahead. We'll get there sooner than we expected," said Bob.

They sailed on waiting for conditions to worsen, but were pleasantly surprised. The weather remained the same, and the forty-knot winds stayed on their stern. Once they were around the Cape of Good Hope, they were almost there. Soon they saw the welcoming entrance to Cape Town. Letting out a cheer, they knew they had made it.

They could see the colorful flags flying above the white stucco yacht club. Arriving just as the blazing Africa sun slipped beneath the horizon.

Bob radioed the dockmaster, "Where's the best place to dock her?"

"I have a place for you right in front of the yacht club. It's the safest spot to be."

"Can you get a couple of men at the slip?" asked Bob "I'll need some help getting in."

Forty to sixty-knot winds blew continuously while they were there. *Destiny* was tied down with seven lines.

Royal Cape Town yacht club was full of their friends. Hanz from *Eva* was there with his wife. She had flown in to be with him while he was in Africa.

"Hey Bob, would you mind if Doug and I take off for a week?" asked Norman.

"Sure, go ahead. Have a good time but make sure you come back," laughed Bob.

"No sweat matey, we'll be back," said Doug.

Betty walked back into the club to join the crowd at the bar. Someone was on top of the bar dancing and singing.

"What's going on?" Betty asked as she watched a man stomping his feet. He was trying to do the Irish jig.

"Marvin just arrived in his thirty-four foot boat. He's just happy he made it," said Hanz.

Destiny was hauled out of the water to have her bottom scraped and painted. She also needed a few repairs done. Every trip created a few more problems.

"Before we get home, everything on *Destiny* will break at least once," said Bob.

"You said that before and I believe you," said Betty. "Every time you turn around something's breaking."

"As soon as *Destiny* has her facelift, we'll sail off," said Bob.

"I'm not looking forward to going back out there, especially in these winds," Betty said. "We have over seven hundred miles to sail."

"You'll love it, I know you will," said Bob trying to tease her.

"Seven hundred miles, we just did eight hundred. Can't we stop somewhere on the way?" Betty asked despondently.

"We'll make a stop at St. Helena, and then go on to Recife, Brazil," answered Bob.

"We're definitely getting closer to the end of our circumnavigation, and to the completion of your dream. Wow, what an accomplishment," she said happily.

"These damn winds just won't give up," Bob said frustrated. "For weeks, they've been blowing between forty and sixty knots. When's this weather pattern going to change?"

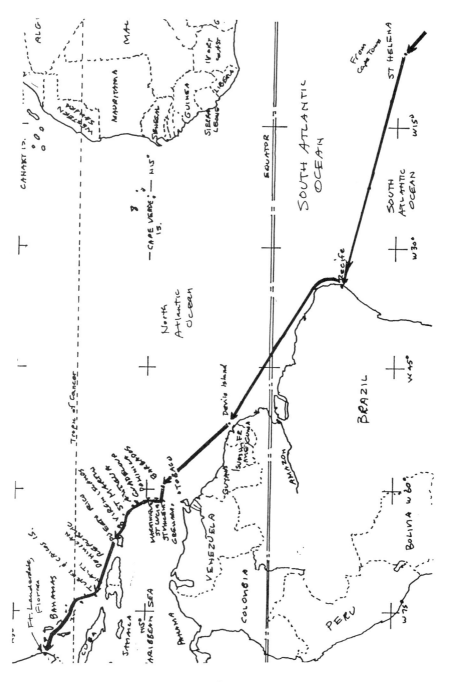

421

Thirty-six

For days, Bob studied the weather fax and finally his face brightened. "I think we should leave tomorrow."

"With these winds?" said Betty. "No way."

"No, wait . . . trust me. True, there's no sign of the wind letting up. But the winds will be at our back and they'll help us more than hinder us."

Betty trusted Bob's decision, "I have a feeling it'll be a rough trip. I'll cook lasagna now for tomorrow's dinner. All I'll have to do is heat it. Then, I won't have to spend much time in the galley."

"Like you said before, Bob. Might as well prepare for the worst, and hope we're wrong," said Norman.

Destiny moved along at a steady pace, with the wind on their stern. Betty's patch was on and the life jackets were close at hand. The wind was a steady force seven, sometimes edging up to force eight. Foamy waves splashed high above *Destiny*, showering the decks. The water rolled off leaving frothy bubbles, that glistened like tiny rainbows.

The smell of the briny sea brought back memories. Betty thought of the time she spent in Ocean City, New Jersey. The spray of salt water splashing onboard cooled her body. The wind's tremendous power pushed *Destiny* forward, moving and gliding her like she was on ice. Betty was amazed at the speed of a boat this heavy, as they bound ahead at nine knots. High winds of forty-five knots pushed them full force, making the days fly by.

On the third day the weather changed. During the night, the wind cut down to five knots, and they crept at a snail's pace. According to the charts, there would be constant high wind in this area. Instead they were in the doldrums. *Destiny* motored at three knots to conserve fuel. They were not sure if they could get diesel at St. Helena.

The unrelenting heat surrounded them, sapping their

strength and vitality. The unmerciful sun would make short work of their skin, but they sought shelter in the shade of the sails and bimini top. They quenched their thirst with ice water. Betty was so glad Bob installed the ice maker on gimbals. That allowed them to have ice all throughout the trip.

With the wind gone, *Destiny* started rolling. Betty could feel her body rebelling against the confused movement. Feeling nervous and about to have an anxiety attack, Betty headed for her stateroom. She hadn't beat the mattress for a long time, but she was about to make up for it.

After relieving her frustrations with a good cry, Betty came back on deck. Bob was at the helm and she said, "I seem to have lost all the stamina I had on the last few trips. I guess I've spent too much time on land. I definitely lost my sea legs."

Bored, she looked for things to do, "I'm going to do some wash, is there enough water?" "Should be plenty," answered Norman as he checked the gauges. "We made water late yesterday."

When the wash was done, she threw the clothes in the dryer. When she turned it on, it wouldn't work. Betty called out, "What's wrong with the dryer? It's not working."

"Here, let me check it out," said Doug, pulling the dryer away from the wall. "The dryer has a short in it somewhere. I'll try and fix it."

"What am I going to do with all these wet clothes?" asked Betty. Norman tied a line to the mast and cabin and she hung the clothes out to dry. "I hope heavy winds don't come up suddenly," she laughed. "If they do, our undies are going to be spread all over the Indian Ocean," she said laughing.

They had been at sea for nine days. Everyone was weary and wanted the trip over with. They were tired of the eternal blue and the vast lonely surroundings. Feeling a surge of nervous energy, Betty went to the galley to make a cherry pie. Successful at getting the crust made, she opened three cans of tart cherry. Placing them in a mixing bowl she stirred in the sugar and cornstarch. Her spoon hit something hard, "Oh no, they have pits in them." Betty started to take the pits out of each cherry. *Destiny* swerved and thrashed, and the dish slid back and forth under her fingers. She grabbed for a wet towel to place under the dish, but was too late. *Destiny* rode high on a steep wave when it slammed down the bowl fell over. The bright red cherries rolled all around the counter.

"Damn!" she yelled, trying to scoop them together. The heeling of the boat made them roll faster than she could grab. Holding a handful of cherries, she stood there helplessly as she watched the rest of the cherries plop in groups to the floor. Red blood-like juice ran down the side of the counter, oozing into all the grooves and drawers. When she stepped over to the sink to get a wet dish cloth she slipped. Landing in the middle of all the cherries, her white shorts soaked with cherry juice. Betty sat there in total frustration as the pie plate came tumbling down, landing on her lap. In a trancelike state she picked up the cherries one by one, putting them in the pie plate.

Norman came down to see what all the commotion was. He gasped, "Dear God, you're bleeding. Bob, Bob, Betty's hurt bad."

Betty talked like she was in a daze, "I'm not bleeding, this is cherry juice. The cherries got thrown all over.

Norman broke into a roar of laughter. Doug and Bob came down. When they saw Betty sitting on the floor with cherry juice all over her, they joined in laughing.

"Okay, so I'm the joke of the day," she said still half-dazed. Doug and Norman helped her clean up after which she threw the mess overboard.

They arrived at St. Helena's in the stillness of the night, glad for the safety and tranquillity of the harbor. They had been to sea for ten and a half days. When they dropped anchor, they were more than ready for bed.

In the morning they were well rested and took the dinghy to shore. They checked through customs and did the routine shore duties. St. Helena's was a quaint old island, and the town was completely surrounded by tall, thick concrete walls. There was an ancient castle that created a feeling of medieval times. Napoleon had been exiled there and they visited his house and burial spot.

Weather conditions in the harbor had changed to the worse while they were ashore. Winds were stronger and blowing from a different direction. When they got back to *Destiny,* she was rocking and swaying from side to side. Water poured in through the open portholes, and everything was wet. The bilge pumps were flushing out the seawater, keeping the boat afloat. They closed the portholes and mopped up the water, hoping the weather would change.

Drowsy from the wine from dinner, they crawled in bed and snuggled under the covers. They longed for a good deep sleep, but the rough rocking kept them awake most of the night.

Bob got up the next morning feeling like a grouch from lack of sleep. He went to town and returned in a better mood. "Diesel is available," he said, "they are going to deliver it in large barrels."

Doug scratched his head, and looked inquisitive as he asked, "How are they getting the diesel out to us?"

Bob laughed, "Wait until you see the old wooden boat they are bringing it out on. It's ready to fall apart."

Later that morning a twenty-foot rickety, wooden boat tied up alongside of *Destiny*. Two men attached a long rubber hose to the barrels and ran it up to *Destiny*. Both boats swayed in different directions, as a small motor squeaked loudly as it pumped the diesel into the tanks.

"They'll never be able to do it," Betty said watching in astonishment. "The boats are rocking too hard."

Both crafts rocked back and forth. As the wind seemed to pick up more momentum.

"I'm taking the dinghy over and do the grocery shopping," said Betty. "I can't stand to watch this."

"I'll take you over," said Norm. "You might need some help getting the things back."

When they returned two hours later, the men were just finishing. Diesel fumes permeated the air and fuel spilt on the decks and was running down the side of *Destiny*.

Betty climbed aboard and asked, "How'd it go, any problems?"

"As you can see, they spilled a lot of the diesel, and the motor conked out a couple of times," Bob laughed. "But they finally managed to get most of it in."

"Are we still leaving today?" asked Norm as he brought the groceries onboard.

"Definitely. If everyone's onboard lets cast off," said Bob.

At the start of the journey to Brazil, the winds were intense. Once past the island, the winds dissipated and Bob let out the sails. Steady fifteen knot winds kept the waters calm, and they enjoyed the peaceful sail. Clouds lifted and a cool breeze presented outdoor air conditioning, giving them a chill now and then.

"The days are going rather fast," said Norm. "I don't mind this leg at all."

"Yeah, I feel pretty good too. My spirits are up and my money's down. There's no place to go, we're out of bounds," said Doug looking cross-eyed as he spoke.

"What's that supposed to mean?" asked Norm, looking at Doug like he was nuts. "You been drinking or something. Have you had too many Fosters®?"

"Betty, what are you doing down there?" asked Bob. "Come on up and calm these two wallabies down. I think the sea got to them."

Betty called back, "I'm busy, I'm trying to make an apple strudel."

"Apple strudel! Never mind, stay down there. I'll handle the children," said Bob drooling. "How soon will it be finished?"

The strudel was baked with surprising ease and with no mishap. It was devoured immediately.

The spinnaker was up and it looked majestic by the way it ballooned out in the sky. It pulled *Destiny* along like a powerful kite. Force three winds caressed them, taking them gently to Brazil.

Doug and Norm tried to teach Betty to play the guitar, but she couldn't get the hang of it.

"I'll never learn. Forget me and play the blackbird song," she said. "I love to hear you sing it. It sure helps me keep my sanity."

Doug put down his guitar and said, "Think I'll pull out the dryer again. I'm going to fix it this time for sure." Fumbling for twenty minutes, he announced, "I found the problem. The dang blasted thing is wired wrong. You were darn lucky. You could have been electrocuted. Especially with all the water that has been poured on this thing."

After Doug fixed the dryer, he sat next to Norm. He had his fishing lines in the water and was strumming his guitar.

"What are you doing, matey, serenading the fish?" asked Doug. "Think they'll get on your line if you sing to them?"

"Don't be so smart, Doug, it doesn't become you," answered Norm.

"The bilge alarm's going off," called Bob. "Can one of you men climb down into the bilge and see what's going on?"

"You're busy fishing," teased Doug. "I'll go down and check it. I think it needs a new pump."

The bilge was such a small hot area to work in. Betty could hear him cussing quietly, the first profanity he had spoken the whole trip.

When he climbed out for a break, his shirt was drenched with sweat, "It's ungodly hot down there. I've never been seasick, but I think I'm gonna be." Downing two glasses of icewater, he climbed back down to complete the job.

The weather was still calm and Betty felt lazy. She wasn't planning on doing much today, but when she went to make sandwiches, the last loaf of bread was moldy.

Getting out the ingredients she called to the men, "I'm going to make cinnamon buns and bread, but I need help."

"Cinnamon buns! What can I do?" asked Norm.

"Here," she said, handing him the bowl of dough. "Knead this for awhile, but wash your hands first."

Norm looked at the dough and made a face, "How long do I have to play with this mess."

"Until I come up for it," Betty replied.

The smell of the buns baking in the oven drove the men crazy. As soon as Betty took them out of the oven, she heard a stampede and half the buns were gone.

"This is our payment for helping you," said Doug.

Bob could feel a change in the wind, "Let's get the spinnaker down, the wind's picking up," said Bob, walking out to the bow with a mouth full of bun. "I don't want any problems."

Doug and Norm followed, still stuffing their mouths. They took the pole down and brought in the sail.

"What do you want up, Captain?" Norm asked.

Bob was back at the helm, and said, "Put up the genie and Yankee wing to wing. It won't be as comfortable, but it's a lot safer."

Two days later, Betty started to make an apple pie. When she opened the closet to get the cinnamon, a roach fell out. It almost landed in the pie crust. "Oh shit," she said. "I thought I was rid of those nasty things."

Betty pulled everything out of the cabinets and sprayed. *It would be hard keeping everything on the counters*, she thought. *But she had to get rid of those crawly things*. Both the oven and dryer were on at the same time, and the galley was unbearably hot. As she sprayed, Betty tried to keep everything on the counters from flying around the kitchen. She was succeeding at doing two things at one time, but the fumes were making her irritable and dizzy.

"Don't know where these damn bugs are coming from," she grumbled. "I think they're going to drive me insane. I'll be dammed if I'm going to let them take over the boat."

By late afternoon, she was tired, hot, miserable and half-brain dead from the spray. Spending the rest of the day in her stateroom, she turned on the only air conditioner that worked, and cooled herself.

Lying there, she heard Norm let out a yell, "Yahoo, I caught a twenty-pound Bonito, we'll have it for dinner tonight."

Betty went on deck, "I don't mind cooking it, but I don't want anything to do with cleaning it."

"You won't have to clean it, I'll do it. I'll cook it, too," said Doug. "I'll still help with the dishes."

"What a break," Betty said as she headed back to her stateroom. "This is my night off."

In the morning, Betty was determined not to do much. She said that every day and ended up hot and worn out. She wanted to rest, because the next day they would arrive in Recife.

"Why are you taking down all the sails?" asked Norm, as he watched Bob reef the main and pull in the others.

"We've got to slow the boat down, or we'll arrive in Recife in

428

the middle of the night. I don't want to enter the harbor in the dark."

With very little sail up, *Destiny* started her exaggerated rocking. That made everyone uncomfortable. Sleeping was impossible as they rolled back and forth, in unending motion.

"Thank God the trip is almost over," Betty murmured.

They docked in the harbor the next morning.. The only place available was where the freighters docked, and it was in a rough area. They went over to customs, and presented their visas.

The officer looked them over, and with a scowl on his face said, "These are no good, they've expired."

"They can't be," said Bob. We haven't had them that long."

The officer was very nasty as he shouted, "They expired three days ago."

"Can we renew them?" Bob asked politely. "We've been at sea for fourteen days and we need supplies and fuel."

A young officer behind him smiled and started to say yes, but was cut off by the arrogant one, "No you can't. You can stay three days for supplies, then you have to leave."

"Only three days!" exclaimed Betty. "We've been out to sea a long time, we need a rest."

Sneering at them, he added, "There's also a three hundred dollar fine because your visa's expired."

"Three hundred dollars! I never heard of such a thing," said Bob angrily.

"You pay it or go to jail for a few days," said Mr. Nasty.

Upset about having to leave so soon and by the officer's rudeness, they went to the American Embassy for help.

"There's a new President in Brazil and he has changed the rules," said the man at the Embassy sadly. "He has even closed the banks and froze everyone's money,"

"You mean we can't even exchange our money?" Betty asked astounded.

"That's right." Shaking his head in despair he said, "There's nothing I can do to help you at the moment. If you want to stay longer, you can appeal the fine. Then, they have to give you five days."

"Well, five days is better than three. We'll tell them we're appealing the fine," said Bob.

"Maybe it's less trouble just to pay the fine," said Betty impatiently. "By the looks of the place, and the circumstances, five days may be too much."

They took a cab to town and were astonished at how poor Recife was. They were approached by people who warned, "Take your chains off and don't wear your watch."

A man walked by them and looked at Betty, "Hold your pocketbook close to your body or thugs will grab it from you," he whispered.

Norm and Doug were walking briskly down the street when Doug felt a tug on his arm. Two young boys about fifteen were next to him and tried to grab the watch off his arm.

"Whoa, no way," said Doug grabbing his watch, as the boys ran away.

"Come back here you little scoundrels," yelled Doug in close chase.

Doug was closing in on the kids when two rough looking men stepped out from an alley. They had thick two-by-fours in their hands, "Got a problem with those kids? Want to settle it with us?"

"No matey, none at all," said Doug, walking away.

"Mighty rough place here," said Norm when he finally caught up to him.

They took a cab to Colongo yacht club, it looked like a safer place to be. Before they had lunch at the club, Bob arranged for a slip for the boat. While they were having lunch they became friendly with a young Brazilian couple who offered to drive them back to *Destiny* in their speed boat.

"The tide is low and it is difficult to get through the shallow channel leading to the yacht club," said the young man as he pulled up alongside *Destiny*. "I'll have the yacht club send a small boat to help guide you through the channel and into a well protected slip."

Bob thanked him and promised to have dinner with them later.

When *Destiny* was safely in the slip at the yacht club, Betty and the crew cleaned the boat, while Bob went to see customs. He wanted to try and talk them out of the fine. When the work was finished, they sat waiting for him to return. He had been gone all day. Visions of him being mugged or killed went through Betty's mind. Then, she saw him ambling down the dock.

She ran to meet him, "What took you so long? We were really worried."

"They are still making us leave in three days, and the fine still holds," said Bob looking tired. "I went back to the American Embassy again. They said there's still nothing they can do. We have to pay the fine. Only good news is we have five days to fight it."

"We're not going to fight it, are we?" asked Norm.

"No, but it's a way to get a few extra days," said Bob. "I'm ready to leave tomorrow, but we need supplies. We'll take our five days if we need them."

The crew took off by themselves for a couple of days while Bob and Betty took a walk around town. They stopped to look at the things the vendors had to sell. Each time they stopped, Betty noticed the same two scroungey kids standing nearby. They were about fifteen years old. One had a dirty purple shirt on, and worn ragged jeans. His long black greasy hair hung in his face, and his teeth were rotten with decay. The other kid was dressed in a black shirt, dirty, beige pants, both torn with huge holes. His black hair was short and stringy and was stuck to his head from perspiration.

Betty nudged Bob, "See those kids over by the store window? I think they're following us. They're always right behind us and get closer each time we stop," she said, trying not to be afraid.

Bob glanced over his shoulder and saw them pretending to look in a store window. Bob whispered, "Let's turn around and stare at them, see what they do."

They stared directly at the boys, giving them their evil eye. The two boys became nervous and jumped in a line, pretending to wait for a bus. When the bus doors opened the boys shoved people in front of them. Bob and Betty continued to stare, intimidating the boys until they ran up the street.

"We're lucky you noticed them," said Bob with a sigh of relief. "They say they either slash your pocket to get your wallet or cut your bag straps."

Betty sighed, "It's definitely not like home. Let's go to the supermarket and see what they have."

When she got to the store, she was glad there was still plenty of food aboard. They got what few vegetables and fruit they could find, and took a cab back to the boat.

The cab driver pulled up to the marina, "You're fare is nine dollars."

"Nine dollars! That's too much. You charge by the zone, where is your fare chart?" asked Bob.

"No chart, no chart," yelled the driver.

Bob reached under the seat and pulled out the zone chart, "See, it says three dollars for this zone. You just lost your tip buddy," Bob slapped three dollars down on the seat.

They went everywhere in cabs, trying to see as much of Recife as possible, and constantly battling over the fares.

"I've had it with this place," said Bob feeling depressed. "Let's pay the fine and move on."

He entered the customs office and asked in a cordial tone, "Where do I pay the fine?"

All the officers ignored him at first, then the man sitting at the desk looked up and said, "Your fine must be paid at the bank in town."

Bob was infuriated and started to holler, "We just came from there. Why didn't you tell us that yesterday?"

Betty took Bob's arm and said, "Come on, we'll get a cab and pay the fine."

Back in town, they found a bank and walked up to the teller and asked, "Where do we pay a fine for customs?" She didn't speak English.

They searched around, but it was hard to find anyone in the bank that spoke English. They asked everyone and all they got in reply was, *"De sescribir et libra."*

Finally the manager came out, he spoke English. "You go to the stationary store, eight blocks from here. Buy a book of receipts and bring them back here. You'll pay us the money and we will fill out three receipts for you. Then you take the receipts back to customs for their signature. After customs sign the receipts, you bring them back to the bank. We will stamp them and keep one. You will take one back to customs and you keep one."

Shaking his head in disbelief, Bob said, "Good lord, what a mess to go through. Thanks for your help."

It took them an hour to find the stationery store. They bought the book of receipts and three hours later, the ordeal was over.

The same miserable officer was at the customs office. When Bob gave him the receipt, the officer growled, "They have given you the wrong one. Take this back and get us the right one."

"The hell I will," said Bob walking toward the door. "You want it, you get it. We're leaving right now."

As soon as they were back on the boat, Betty laid down in the cockpit, a cool breeze was blowing. She sighed as she said, "After six trips back and forth in this heat, I'm wiped out. I don't want to go out to sea, but I'm definitely ready to leave Brazil."

With an expired visa, they could not stop in any South American countries. That meant they could not stop anywhere for fifteen hundred miles. French Guyana would be the next port of call. Mild weather was in the forecast and twenty-knot winds were at their backs. They had the spinnaker flying high and *Destiny* sailed at eight knots. Four days out to sea the clouds covered the sun and the rain gave off a cooling bath.

"Hey Norm, start the generator. We need to make some water," said Bob as he sat at the helm on watch.

Bob could hear the generator grinding away, then Norm called out, "Looks like we have a bit of trouble. It won't start."

"They got us again, Betty, the gremlins are after us," Bob said with a bitterness in his voice.

"Calm down Captain, let your magic man have a look," said Doug, pulling up the floorboards. "I'll make short work of the problem."

While Doug was fixing the generator, the wind changed to a beam reach. Bob and Norm switched the sails, wing to wing to keep *Destiny* riding smooth. Doug was true to his word, the generator was fixed in twenty minutes.

Bob was pleased at the way Doug could repair things, "I'm so glad you came along on the trip, Doug. You're a big help and you're always in a good mood."

They arrived in French Guyana in eight and a half days. Bob dropped the anchor in Iles Du Salut harbor, at Devil's Island.

"Look at the waves in the harbor. It's not going to be good sleeping here," said Norm.

"Maybe the wind will calm down. We're only planning on staying a few days, just enough time to see a little of the country and restock," said Bob.

Guyana was a clean pleasant town, with a lot of sad history connected to it. A large military and space center was there. It was a big tourist spot with plenty of shops and hotels.

The next day they took a trip to Devil's Island, a very foreboding place. They walked past the collapsed prison walls. A few prison cells were still standing, but were worn from time and weather.

"You have to read this book I bought, Betty," said Norm. "It tells the history of Devil's Island. When I look at the prison cells and the dungeons, I shudder. I can visualize the horrible conditions the people lived under."

Betty walked through the grounds and said, "I'm getting goosebumps. I wonder if the ghosts of the prisoners are still walking around here?"

Norm crept up behind her and grabbed her, "One's got you now," and he let out a hideous laugh.

Betty jumped and squealed, "Don't do that."

They wandered through the cemetery, and looked at the names craved in stone. Hundreds of prisoners, officers and their families perished there. They died from malaria, dysentery and other diseases.

Betty walked inside a solitary prison cell to read the writing on the wall. Doug shut the door on her, "Let me out," Betty shouted. "It's pitch black in here."

"You're my prisoner until you promise to make cinnamon buns again," said Doug.

"I'll make them, I promise. Just let me out of this dank place," pleaded Betty. Then, she laughed. "Come on let me out, I'm ready to go back to the boat."

They had forgot again to close the portholes, and the floors and counters were soaked.

"Why don't we remember to shut these damn things," yelled Betty. "We all see how rough the harbor is when we leave. Look at this mess."

"I'll help clean up," said Doug, as he grabbed a mop.

"Betty, soon all this will be just a memory," said Bob.

Thirty-seven

The next leg would take them to Barbados and they left with perfect conditions. The trip went quickly with no mishaps and when they arrived, they had completed their circumnavigation.

Bob grabbed Betty in exuberant joy, "We made it, baby. We went completely around the world. Thank you for helping me make my dream come true," and he covered her face with kisses.

Betty was happy she was able to go through with the whole ordeal and proud she hadn't given in to her emotions. "I can't believe I made the whole trip. I was tempted to leave so many times," she said hugging him.

Their love for each other had strengthened with all the problems and adventures. If they could endure this, they could handle any crisis a relationship might encounter.

They celebrated with friends that had arrived in Barbados before them. Some were still on their adventure. Others had made the conquest like they had. Now it was a matter of getting *Destiny* back to Ft. Lauderdale.

Anxious to get home, they sailed straight through to St. Martin where they rested for a few days. Norm and Doug took off by themselves to see the island.

When they came back, Doug said, "I met an old friend from Australia who lives here. He's a builder and needs an electrician. He's offered me the job."

"Are you going to take it?" asked Bob.

"I'd sure like to," said Doug. "If it won't be putting you out?"

"Go ahead and take the job if you want to," said Bob putting his arm around Doug's shoulder. "We're sorry to lose you. I don't know what I would have done without you. When do you plan on going?"

Doug looked almost sad, "He's stuck for an electrician, so I'd like to leave in the morning."

"In the morning! That soon? We've been through so much together. I feel like I'm losing a son," said Betty, almost in tears.

"Guess we better take you out for a farewell dinner," Bob said, patting Doug on the back. "You've been a great help to me. We're going to miss you."

"Will you be able to handle things with just one crew member?" asked Doug.

"My son, Scott, is flying into St. Thomas," said Bob. "He'll sail with us and help out."

With sad farewells, Doug packed his clothes the next morning. "Thanks for all you did for me. I enjoyed every minute of the trip."

When he left, Bob said sadly, "Well, another crewman, from the chapters of *Destiny*, hits the dust. Let's prepare the boat and sail on."

It was a short sail to St. Thomas. They had no desire to stop anywhere else. They had been to all the islands before, and wanted to get home.

Scott was waiting for them when they arrived at St. Thomas. "Welcome back on board, son. Good to see you," said Bob.

"Hey, Betty, you're still hanging in there," laughed Scott as he gave her a hug.

She kissed his cheek and said, "God, it's good to see you. You're as handsome as ever."

With his arm around Betty he asked, "Hey Dad, where are we headed?"

"We're not making many stops, this is a fast trip home," answered Bob. "We're on our way to Turks and Caicos. Maybe we'll do a little diving there."

They had sailed all day and it was late in the afternoon. The sun and clouds made shadows on the water, and it was hard for Bob to see the coral beds. Motoring slowly, they tried to find a good anchoring spot in the open water.

Scott and Norm were on the bow talking and Bob called out, "Keep a good eye out for shallow reefs, they're hard to see this time of day."

The two men on the bow were engrossed in conversation,

and didn't see the huge coral beds ahead.

When they looked up, Scott yelled frantically, "Reverse engines. We're heading for an enormous coral bed."

Bob reversed the engine but it was too late. *Destiny* was completely entrenched in a bed of gigantic elkhorn coral.

"Goddamnit, why didn't you tell me sooner. Look at the mess were in," screamed Bob. "We traveled forty thousand miles around the world without a mishap. Look at us now."

Every turn he made got *Destiny* more entangled. The coral tore at the hull and the wing keel. Each movement broke off the tops of the seven foot antlers that stuck slightly above the water.

Betty looked down into the clear pristine water and watched the destruction. The big horns were thrashed in all directions.

Sadly, she said, "Look what we're doing to the superb elkhorn coral!"

Bob was turning right then left, with the motor in reverse. In pure frustration, he yelled, "The hell with the coral, look what it's doing to our boat. We could sink in this mess."

There was not an island in sight. They were in the middle of the ocean, somewhere between the Caribbean and the Bahamas.

After trying unsuccessfully to free *Destiny* from the brier patch, he hollered in desperation. "Lower the dinghy, and push against the hull. See if she moves."

Scott helped lower the dinghy and Norm jumped in. Putting the nose of the dinghy against *Destiny*'s bow, he throttled full-speed. Bob kept the gear in reverse, gunning the engine, pushing the controls full power. But *Destiny* was still trapped in a web of horns.

"Okay, Norm, try pushing on the stern on the starboard side. I'll gun the motor and steer to port. Maybe we can crash through."

Destiny still wouldn't budge, they were wedged in tightly. The wing keel below was getting sawed apart by the jagged coral. There was a small leak where water was seeping in. The bilge pumps were working hard. Bob knew it wouldn't take much before the coral made a bigger gash.

Two small outboard boats appeared in the horizon, coming directly towards them.

"Is this help or trouble coming?" asked Scott.

"Hope they're friendly. I'm not in the mood to be robbed or killed," said Norman.

They waited in anticipation as the boats got closer. "Betty, go down and get our guns. We may need them. We'll keep them out of sight until we see if they're friends or enemies."

Betty brought the guns up. She handed the Ruger to Scott, the shotgun to Bob and she kept the pistol.

Scott looked through the binoculars. "I don't see them smiling. There's two men in each boat. The boats are about twenty feet long and their engines look powerful."

As the small skiffs pulled alongside *Destiny* Bob said, "Seventy-five horsepower engines. That's enough power to help us; if they're friendly."

One man stood up and said, "Hum hum hum, you got plenty trouble, man."

"You can say that again," said Scott, trying to size up the men. They were big, powerful-looking men, and the *Destiny* group didn't feel safe yet.

They stared at the boat while they talked among themselves.

Betty looked over at Bob, "What's going to happen?" she whispered.

"I'm not sure. Just be ready if there's trouble," said Bob.

The boats moved to the bow where Norm and Scott were standing. "You trow us two lines, we gonna try to pull you off. If you push with your dinghy, my friend here will help push with his boat."

"Do you think it will work?" asked Bob.

"Don know til we try mon, but I tink it wil."

Scott tied the lines on the bow stanchions. "Here they come," he said as he threw the lines.

The boat throttled full speed as they attempted to pull *Destiny*. Bob opened his motor full power, and steered to portside. Norm had nosed the dinghy against the starboard hull, and the other boat came alongside him. They both revved their engines, pushing at the same time. Black smoke and gas fumes filled the air. The motors raced, trying to force *Destiny* out of captivity. Crunching sounds waved through the water as the coral was being demolished. They could hear the ripping, scratching sounds on the hull and wing keel, but she didn't budge.

Everything stopped as the native men viewed the situation again. "Hey bro, bring your boat out here wid us. Yhoa mon, trow us two more lines. We gonna use two boats to pull you."

The two boats pulled as Norm pushed with the dinghy, but still nothing happened. Then in a coordinated effort, they tried again. The small boats in front strained as they were given full power. The lines were taut with pressure, ready to snap. Black smoke filled the air, nearly covering *Destiny*. Just as they were ready to give up, they heard a loud crunch. *Destiny* broke through the coral and was free. Everyone let out a cheer.

Breathing a sigh of relief, Bob said, "We're so grateful to you. You went out of your way to help us. How can we pay you for all your help?"

"No worry mon, we want noting," said the four men.

"No, we want to show our appreciation, that was so kind of you. I don't know what we would have done if you hadn't come along," said Bob.

"Okay mon, give us beers," said two of the men.

"Give them a whole case," said Bob.

Scott handed down a case of beer and each man took a six pack, except one, who shook his head. "No tanks, mon. It's against my religion. I don drink beer."

"How about some coke?" asked Scott.

A big smile came on his face, "Fine mon fine."

They limped on to Turks and Caicos, with the bilge pumps going. When they got there, *Destiny* was hauled. The shipyard patched the hull and keel with boards and bolts. They hoped the wing keel and rudder would hold together until they reached Ft. Lauderdale.

In two weeks, they were sailing into the harbor of Ft. Lauderdale. The trip ended on the Fourth of July, a month shy of three years. Bob had fulfilled his dream. No matter what their future held, they had completed the ultimate journey. Circumnavigating the world, what more exciting thing could they do?

Well, both of their little black dating books were out of date, so they decided they might as well get married. After all, if they could live with each other for three years, twenty-four hours a

440

day and not fight—well, at least not too much—they must be compatible.

Yes, that's just what the gypsy and sea witch did. They got married in September and yes, they're living happily ever after in the town of Jupiter, Florida. Norman was an usher at their wedding and lived with Betty and Bob for a year before returning to his family in Australia.

Betty and Bob on Prison Island.